PERSIAN MOONS

Enhanced Edition

Author's Books
(As of June 20, 2020)[*]

Non-fiction

The Nature of Love and Relationships 2011, **2016**
Doubts and Decisions for Living:
   Volume I: The Foundation of Human Thoughts **2014**
   Volume II: The Sanctity of Human Spirit **2014**
   Volume III: The Structure of Human Life **2014**
Relationship Facts, Trends, and Choices **2016**
The Mysteries of Life, Love, and Happiness **2016**
Marriage and Divorce Hardships **2016**
Gender Qualities, Quirks, and Quarrels **2016**
Relationship Needs, Framework, and Models **2016**
Being Better Beings **2020**

Fiction

Persian Moons 2007, **2016**
Midnight Gate-opener 2011, **2016**
My Lousy Life Stories **2014**
Persian Suns **2020**

---

[*] 12 older books are Enhanced Editions and printed in 2020. They were resubmitted to the Library and Archives Canada Cataloguing as well. If a book's 'print date' on the copyright page is older, the newest version is available at Amazon and bookstores.

PERSIAN MOONS

A Novel

Enhanced Edition

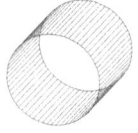

This is a book of fiction. Names, characters, and events are the creation of the author. Any resemblance to persons, living or dead, business establishments, events or places is totally coincidental. Names of the streets, cities, places and shops, when real, are used in line with the general public use of these entities.

First Edition Copyright © 2007 by Tom Omidi
Second Edition Copyright © 2016 by Tom Omidi
Enhanced Edition Copyright © 2020 by Tom Omidi

Omidi, Tom, 1945—, author
Persian moons / Tom Omidi—Second Edition

ISBN: 978-1-988351-14-8 (paperback)

I. Title.

Old edition at
Library and Archives Canada Cataloguing in Publication
PS8629.M53P47 2016   C813'.6   C2016-902403-2

Published by Eros Books,
Vancouver, British Columbia
erosbooks2020@gmail.com

Front Cover: From a Painting by Tom Omidi

Enhanced and Printed in 2020

This book is dedicated to the memory of over two million Iranian and Iraqi soldiers who killed one another in vain during the 1980s for the benefit of international bullies. Just another great example of human folly and vanity.

Table of Contents

Author's Note

Besides the format adjustments for easier reading, merely some modifications in the wording and dialogues highlight this new edition of *Persian Moons*. However, the story feels livelier with simpler words, too. I would like to thank some kind readers of the first edition for their invaluable encouragement and input. My own growth in taste and style helped the reediting as well. I hope the outcome warrants even a second read, while your input is always appreciated.

Obviously, the story novelty and realism have received the highest priority in *Persian Moons*. Deeply emotional episodes and suspense build up smoothly, while characters struggle with a variety of typical companionship issues in the new era. However, my strong secondary motive for writing novels has always been to portray social conundrums, especially family relationships, more vividly than is customary in popular fictions. All kinds of literature should, in fact, emphasize on personal and relationship dilemmas directly to stir the public's view of our deteriorating mentality and values. Especially, novels offer a great opportunity to highlight contentious social issues more effectively instead of pushing so much false sentiments and naive expectations.

Unfortunately, the mass of juvenile love stories propagated in modern societies has tainted our grasp of life and companionship needs. Our mushy romanticism, mixed with our misperceptions about individualism, has made it difficult for everybody to relate properly. More naïve is, of course, my hope that at least new generations might still have a chance to improve the health of their relationships and society.

New lifestyles are raising people's stress and depression, too, while personal and relationship conundrums are putting more pressure on society. Therefore, we are witnessing a global chaos in terms of world politics, public health, economy, environment, and family relationships. The situation will only worsen more rapidly, unless we appreciate the repercussions of our wasteful lifestyles soon and revamp our demented social values. We will face a horrific demise individually and globally if relationship conflicts keep ruining our spirits. In particular, future generations will pay dearly for our careless spread of such a confusing and corrupt culture.

Can we ever overcome our deepened illusions after decades of crooked social influence? Maybe it is too late already, yet we should reassess our true social needs in all respects now, even for a remote chance to sustain humanity. A fundamental overhaul in family relationships is necessary to curtail individuals' frustration and facilitate other facets of socioeconomic progress, too. More creative remedies and bitter sacrifices are required to refine our views about marriage, its traps, and its sources of agony. Even the reading materials propagated so recklessly merely for profit purposes must be gradually replaced with meaningful methods of expressing the reality of life and relationships in the 21st century. Authentic social values must fight off the mishmash of idiotic perceptions tainting our highly impressionable minds.

Many years of personal experience and research in the field of relationships only pinpoint the vast level of experimentation, learning, understanding, and selflessness required to effect our reorientation. Yet a worthwhile goal to undertake open-mindedly. Changes must start in our vision at a personal level, then in the family, before spreading them in communities and across the nations so mindlessly.

Anyway, while radical ideas are necessary at all social levels, incorporating some preliminary thoughts in a novel about the sources of relationship problems nowadays, and vast emotional challenges overwhelming us, can provide a steppingstone. Let us hope we succeed in building a better culture. Well… wishing and daydreaming about redemption is always easy and free! I hope you enjoy reading this new edition of *Persian Moons*.

Tom Omidi, Ph.D., Vancouver, 2016

PART I

The Masters' Boat

Prologue
Dying Moments
(October 1988)

Another gloomy fall afternoon in Vancouver, but at least the pesky rain has stopped. One exceptionally spirited, stunning Ms. Swanson parks her turquoise BMW M5 near Creekside Place and walks fast toward the building. In the elevator riding to the tenth floor, she rehearses her elaborate plan to seduce Darren for good this afternoon if that is the last thing she must do in her life. She giggles with triumph as Darren's unprecedented kind words on the phone this morning ring in her head.

"Come again?" she had asked him, not believing her ears.

"You can have the painting," he had said. "It'll be delivered this afternoon. Come and get it around four o'clock. It's yours."

After three years of wrangling and resistance, as recently as last night, about the ownership of the damn painting, winning tastes incredible. Still, she has wondered all day about Darren's intention with niggling, mixed feelings. On the one hand, his sudden generosity has felt fishy. So she is anxious to reach his apartment and pick up the *Woman in the White Dress* before he changes his mind again. On the other hand, his sudden change of heart has amused her all day, along with a fundamental, thrilling thought: *Maybe he's finally softening and willing now to love me again, like the good old times!* This delicious possibility has elated her all along with great hopes and images of Darren's eternal love and devotion, and she never letting him out of her sight.

She takes out a tiny mirror out of her purse, checks all corners of her face diligently for the last minute affirmation and grins with satisfaction before returning the mirror to her purse. Swiftly, however, the scene of those two chaps rushing out of the building ten seconds earlier agitates her. She charges toward Darren's apartment as soon as the elevator's door opens.

The loud music inside Darren's apartment smothers her knocking on the door. She turns the doorknob and it gives. Shouting "Darren" over the noise a couple of times from the crack of the door, she enters with caution. There is no response or a sign of him.

She moves fretfully amidst the spooky shadows covering the living room in the dying daylight. Next to the sofa, the sight of Darren knocked out on the floor startles her. She yowls and kneels to help him, but her hand feels sticky when she touches his neck. Peering at her bloody palm, her heart topples, imagining what might have happened. She cringes, gasps and curses herself. Ironically, this horrific ending could be of her own making. Her crooked plot has apparently backfired horribly just as her fortune had mysteriously begun to look bright today. All her hopes for finally owning the elusive painting and maybe Darren himself have vanished swiftly. All that fussing over her makeup, dress, and tender words to woo him has been in vain.

She runs to the balcony and yells at the people in the street for help. But they also look lifeless with their curious stares— bemused by her frantic words while pointing to something from the tenth floor. She climbs onto the lower bar of the railing and leans to scream louder at them. Still no reaction, as if they are all deaf and dumb. The scene of those dopes down there, wandering nimbly or watching her numbly, aggravates her further. She leans even more and yells harder. Still nobody seems to understand her words. Such a grim, hopeless situation! Yet a swift, appalling sensation shatters her brain beyond hopelessness...

In midair with disbelief, a rush of adrenaline dazes her. *Why airborne? Why in jeopardy? What happened?* How could her daylong glory of winning end so sadly? *Did somebody push me? Oh, God, please help...*

Futile prayer... Only the sight of the looming asphalt crushes her heart as her fall accelerates. Breathless, with bulging eyes and flailing arms, she begs the frozen pedestrians for help. But the dumb audience seems totally numb now, awestruck by the grisly scene they could be watching only in a horror movie.

Oh, please... help... somebody! Pointless pleading... Only the vagrant she had noticed from the balcony is approaching her trajectory unwittingly. His serious search for empty cans, steady walk, and tight clasp of the bursting bag had appeared annoyingly naive to her when she had been shaken by the dreadful sight of Darren's bleeding neck and seeming demise. His calm and focus, ignoring her screams on the balcony, had felt so bizarre.

But now he and his big sack look like a great landing target— a godsend—though he is half a second off the mark. She tries to grab him but she is paralyzed... In the end, it has been an unlucky day, after all..., although her very last thought is a splendid one: *If Darren is dead or dying upstairs, we'll join in heaven soon..., much sooner than it could've happened on this loveless planet...*

SPLASH!

She flattens in front of the vagrant after slapping him to the ground. Spectators retreat in awe, except for a guy who drags the vagrant away from the smashed body lying in blood and brain bits. The tramp is shaken for a moment—not much by the scene of the accident, though, as if still lost in his own wacky world. He leaps back on his feet, wipes the sprayed blood from his face and clothes casually, clutches his heavy sack, and scurries away without even minding or thanking the guy who had helped him.

The sergeant glances at the remains and recoils quickly before nauseating. His partner fetches a black plastic roll from the police car's trunk to cover the sight of the horrific abstract art plastering the pavement. They add their own artistry, though, by drawing the outline of the body on the sidewalk with a piece of chalk and stretching a yellow ribbon around a lamppost and trees.

"Anybody knows her?" the sergeant asks the crowd. Nobody peeps as he peers around. "What happened? Anybody?"

"She was yelling about something on the tenth-floor balcony and then fell," a man says, pointing to Creekside Place.

"Was she fighting with someone?" the sergeant asks.

"No, but she punched this guy before hitting the asphalt!"

The sergeant glares at him. "She did what?"

"She punched this guy's face in the last moment."

The sergeant observes others nodding. "Which guy?"

"He scrammed with his sack; turned into Pacific Street."

The sergeant calls his partner, "Wayne, call the dispatch to send a squad around Pacific Street and Granville to find a guy with a big bag. Then find the building caretaker and bring him here after checking this woman's apartment on the tenth floor."

Stretched stiff beside the sofa, Darren is losing consciousness while the phone rings faintly, as if echoing from a cave. At last, the answering machine turns on and he barely hears his father's rickety voice whining about his wicked young neighbour—'the piglet,' according to him. "Darren, this filthy piglet is driving me nuts! Yesterday a dozen cockroaches crept out of my mashed potatoes. I had spent all afternoon shopping and making those potatoes and steak! I freaked out, smacked the plate off the table, and stuck to the kitchen wall, trembling. I thought I was dying. The cockroaches crawled all over the broken plate and my food before vanishing into the narrow air this damn piglet blows with his torturing machines to control everything in my apartment. Call me right away… Right away, I mean it!"

Oh Dad…! Darren gasps. *How can I help a senile, stubborn old man deranged by seclusion?* Witnessing his father's agony has been a real torture, especially when imagining that similar genes could be haunting his own destiny going by the random symptoms alarming him now and then. Yet, *right now,* he gives not a damn about his feeble genes or destiny. *What was the point of all those efforts to grasp life and find peace? What peace!* The highlights of his life and then recent incidents roll in his head in daunting details in slow motion…

Yes… the painting… The story of the *Woman in the White Dress* began three years back, in 1985, right after he painted it at the shores of the Caspian Sea. The bad omen has followed it all along, but the sequence of ominous events started only four months ago.

Chapter One
The 200ᵗʰ Sin

**Four months earlier
June 1988**

1

D̶arren Durant imagines the walls closing in on him, like the times he had hidden in the dark basement of his dwelling in Tehran during Iraq's missile attacks—most nights for three years. Today, luckily, he can run to the balcony of his apartment in Vancouver, stretch his arms, and breathe some fresh air to boost his spirit. Beyond the calm, blue waters of False Creek, people and cars are mixing and moving on Granville Island, tempting him to join the cheery crowd.

His jittery mood nowadays is more puzzling than irritating. All those laborious lessons in meditation suddenly feel futile when he cannot even pinpoint the reason for his stress now that his life is finally flourishing. With the two hundred grand saved in Iran, he has bought a two-bedroom apartment in Creekside

Place. It overlooks Granville Island and Vancouver downtown to Georgia Strait and the Pacific Ocean. He enjoys the view of stunning sunsets and scintillating sailboats on False Creek from his living room while listening to his favourite music and drinking wine, sometimes with his female companions around. His recent contract with a major art gallery, the Elixir, provides the chance to present his art nationally. Ironically, the rising demand for his paintings in recent months is only raising his frustration about his enigmatic lethargy.

He reaches for the large paintbrush misplaced on the coffee table, glares at it with suspicion, and caresses its smooth, long hair. This habit usually calms his nerves by stirring his mixed passion for painting and pretty women. It also helps him focus on the incomplete paintings hanging on the walls and ponder the next steps.

The living room décor is awkward. The furniture is crammed near the kitchen and the sliding glass door that connects the airy room to a large, semicircular balcony. The idea is to keep the east corner of the room clear, to walk and paint leisurely near the big wall, which holds in-progress paintings on adjustable frames. The setup is cleverly designed for him to fit canvases of various sizes at desired heights. A few of his favourite works embellish the bedrooms and den, although he is considering giving them to Elixir to stop their nagging for more paintings.

Caressing the bristle brush feels futile, too, today. In fact, it is only heightening his sense of loneliness instead of improving his mood for painting. He drops the brush on the table, looks around with confusion, grabs his cotton blazer, and leaves the apartment.

Cuddling her white cocker spaniel, Mrs. Stanley appears in the middle of the elevator when its door opens. The dog peeps at Darren timidly, unlike its owner's prying stare.

He pets it. "How're you, Fluffy?"

"Going jogging?" Mrs. Stanley asks.

"In this long pants?" he replies with a smirk.

"Somebody's grouchy this afternoon!"

"Sorry... I'm just feeling a bit lousy today."

"You need a wife, Darren..."

"Yes ma'am! As soon as I find a nice one," he replies and winks playfully.

"How about me?" she blurts half-teasingly as the elevator door opens. "You think I'm old?"

"Nevcr...," he replies as he exits and rushes away.

"Never what?"

He only waves his hand, leaving Mrs. Stanley baffled in the lobby. He hurries toward the 'gondola' platform at False Creek and gets on just in time. The Aquabus traveling across the Creek to Granville Island does not look anything like a gondola, but that is what he prefers calling it to imagine living in Venice. The Granville Island stretches along the south side of the Creek, where shops and restaurants attract tourists and Vancouverites in throngs every day.

Once off the gondola, he peers long at his apartment on the opposite bank, as if to find his sneaky spirit gauging him amidst the grand view from his regular spot on the balcony instead of following him. He both enjoys and abhors playing this silly game that is turning into a weird obsession. He has always resisted the temptation of waving to his imaginary self teasing him from up there, except for once last month, when he could no longer deny his playful impulse. He waved earnestly and watched bystanders' reaction to his foolishness. Their tense curiosity to find the subject of his attention—as he had slyly anticipated—thrilled him. Yet, he also worries that these odd urges are perhaps the early signs of his mental slump. *Did my dad's condition escalate from similar silly urges and games? How much of his crooked genes I've inherited?*

As his second routine on the Island, he strolls to Opus and surveys the art supplies aimlessly. Today he buys a sable number 14, though. Then he meanders toward his favourite pub for a beer and burger. He checks his reflection in the windows along the way furtively, not really admiring himself, but mostly wondering who the heck that image is. After all these years, he still cannot imagine they are related, or even properly acquainted. At least, it still looks all right physically, he ponders with some satisfaction. His cyan eyes, shaded by bushy eyebrows sliding at a sharp angle near his temples, complement his robust, bony face. The petty bump on his nose, from a boyhood hockey accident, nonetheless enhances his masculine charisma. His full lips are well defined by pronounced outlines and a bright reddish colour in a rather pale face. Toned muscles swathe his slim, tall body, clad in line with his artistic knack for colours, contrasts, and contours. And the cologne he meticulously matches to his skin scent provides passers-by a last clue, just in case they have accidentally missed his pleasant looks, attire, or demeanour.

2

Only a few feet away from his window seat in the pub, the boats bobbing musically at the dock keep Darren in a trance. Minutes stretch as he lingers pensively, unable to make a plan. Suddenly, Mrs. Stanley's comment in the elevator about 'finding a wife' makes him chuckle, but also wonder whether his stress relates to his unsettling affair with Nora, the Elixir's manager. She seems edgy and looking for excuses to bug him too often these days. He pulls the sable brush out of the bag, caresses its hair, and re-bags it swiftly as the waitress approaches him with a grin.

"Hey, Cindy....," Darren says to her.

Besides his frequent visits and generous tips, the waitresses enjoy watching him play with his bristly blonde hair, like a perpetual tussle to tame it. It slithers defiantly over his forehead, which he ironically compares with the obstinacy of some women he had known, especially Erica, his ex-wife. Sometimes, it blurs his vision sneakily, too, as if enjoying his soft touch and subtle frustration. Short hair would reveal his long face, and no other style can be managed on such an unruly head. He is stuck.

"Do you need anything else?" Cindy asks with concern and a flirtatious grin. "Are you okay?"

He nods while checking the woman behind her. She is also measuring him merrily, waiting for Cindy to scram. Despite the tired hairstyle, tinted hazelnut, and a thinner face, she still looks gorgeous.

"Darren?" Elizabeth Conner exclaims, as if seeing a ghost.

"Hi, Elizabeth…" He rises with a wide grin, excited about a sudden link to Erica era. They hug as Cindy smirks with envy.

"Come, come; sit. It's good to see you after so long," he blurts, holding her hand. "Like a beer or something?"

"Beer's fine…," she says to Cindy and turns to Darren. "I didn't know you were back in Vancouver."

"But you knew I'd gone to Iran?"

"Erica said you were exploring the world!"

"I went to Tehran to work and forget Erica."

"How were those exotic Persian girls?"

"They helped… I was a complete mess when I ran to Iran."

"You guys couldn't really work things out, ha?"

"No… It'd become a torture living under the same roof with her." Darren pauses. "Is she still your best friend?"

"I guess… But she's changed a lot…"

"I'm glad you've noticed it too," Darren says.

"What happened between you?"

Past memories perturb Darren, gazing at her mutely, rather confused, wondering whether his old wounds have healed.

Noticing his tribulation, Elizabeth continues, "Let's discuss something more exciting."

"No. An old affair shouldn't depress me… But what can I tell you?"

"Everything… if you like… You guys have ruined our lives too…"

"We have?"

"Yes…"

"How?"

"Jeff and I are now too paranoid about getting married after watching you two."

"Are you guys still in love?"

"God knows!"

"And you don't?" he asks.

"Not really… All I know is that we get on each other's nerves regularly and then makeup a few midnights later with tension."

"I'm familiar with that killer routine."

"So you know what I mean."

"It's tough, especially for such a fun-loving, easygoing person like you," Darren says.

"He seems so different nowadays."

"Our personalities change, of course, but we feel differently about a person after a while, anyway."

"Yes… That's also true."

"Jeff's more like Erica if you ask me," he says.

"In what way?"

"Uptightness and high ambitions."

"You're right…"

"Destiny is cruel, always putting mismatches in love."

"You think so?" she asks wittily.

"Take our cases, for example. Erica and Jeff seem to have similar personalities, and the same is true about you and me."

"Yeah…?" She delivers a flirty smile.

"I think God makes us pay for the joy of love. We're always punished for our idiotic imaginations about love."

"Don't you believe in love anymore?"

"Well… Real love is not something to look for so obsessively or expect to find so easily."

"Oh…?"

"I'm serious."

"But without love we feel empty."

"I know… We've become this way recently." He pauses with hesitation, looking pensive, as Elizabeth observes him curiously.

He drinks the last of his beer. "You wanna go walk a little?"

She nods.

They stroll around the market and make casual chitchat.

What's he thinking about me and about Erica, right now and in general? Elizabeth wonders with caution.

What to do with Elizabeth? Darren ponders while gauging the bemused crowd.

People, pigeons, and seagulls mingle, though the birds are more focused. They fly in fast and snatch breadcrumbs or food leftovers while eluding the naughty kids. But people seem so aimless, just wandering sluggishly and peeping around stealthily —as if lost, spying, or only killing time before returning to their homes or jobs to repeat the same stressful routines.

Why aren't we as decisive and agile as these birds, despite our wiser brains, to avoid the hectic traps of life? Darren muses, then chuckles while checking out a cuddling teenage couple near the 'gondola' platform.

"What's funny?" Elizabeth asks, but the sound of a splash, screams, and laughter distracts them.

A few heroes rush to help the teenage couple out of the water, while the slippery edge of the creek makes the rescue harder and funnier. Finally out, they stand idle, peep around with blank eyes and embarrassment, water dripping off them. Shivering, the girl is about to cry, but the boy maintains a flimsy grin, peers around with a cheeky smirk, then grabs his girlfriend's hands, hugs and kisses her cheek passionately. Bystanders exclaim a wholesome "Ahhh…"

"Nice gesture," says Darren with a chuckle. "But they needed that cold water."

"What happened?" Elizabeth asks.

"Didn't you see?"

"No… Did he do it on purpose?"

"I don't think so. I guess he lost his balance when they were making out frantically at the edge of the platform."

"But you were chuckling before this mayhem began."

"I was watching them and thinking, 'Cool it, guys,' when they slipped into the creek. Maybe I jinxed them or made them jittery with my stare."

"Are you against love now?"

"No. But we must be more sensible about it."

"Sensible? How?"

"For one thing, we should admit that love isn't a reliable measure for building a good relationship."

"What's a good measure then?"

"We need a better culture and some new principles to relate realistically."

"New principles…? A better Culture…?!"

"Yeah… like before…"

"Before?"

"Before all these mushy movies and novels confused people."

"Darren, your experience with Erica has obviously scarred you…"

"Listen, what're your plans? Are you seeing Jeff tonight?"

"No, he's in Toronto… Why?"

"I thought maybe we could *jump* over the creek and go to my place. I live in that building."

She surveys the building he is pointing to and wonders how Erica would react if she finds out. Even worse, what if Jeff finds out?

"Hmm… I like to hear your ideas about love and marriage, but Erica and Jeff might not like it…"

"They won't have to know. Is it a sin for two friends to share their thoughts?"

"Depends on their thoughts…!" *He must insist more.*

"We'll come back here later for supper."

"Hmm…" *Still more.*

"My place has a nice view of the ocean. We can watch the sunset and have a glass of wine." Darren grins with charm.

"Well… Okay… But I can't jump over the creek."

"Let's take the gondola then."

"Gondola?" Elizabeth asks and Darren smiles.

The wet lovers board ahead of them.

3

Elizabeth peers through the sliding glass door toward the Island and the ocean beyond it. With a cluster of stratus amassing near the horizon, a magnificent sunset will probably erupt soon. The blinking green light of the answering machine lures Darren, though.

He listens to the messages and asks Elizabeth giddily, "You mind if I make two quick calls?" She nodes and he continues, "Find a CD."

He calls T.J. and discovers he has returned from Europe one week early, equally anxious to see him. They agree to meet the next evening.

"I hadn't spoken with T.J. for more than two months," he says with thrill.

"T.J.…?" she asks.

"Oh, yes… He is a good friend of mine and I missed him," he replies while calling Nora.

"Your message sounded urgent!" he says to Nora.

"Marcus wants to discuss a commission for a municipal hall. When's good for you?"

"Thursday?"

"Let's see…" She pauses. "Ten-thirty?"

"Okay. So how are you, Nora?" he asks. "You sound tired."

"Maybe… Can we meet tonight?"

"I'd love to, but I'm with an old friend after so long, trying to catch up," he says to Nora, while smiling at Elizabeth.

Elizabeth gestures that she can leave soon, but he waves and shakes his head.

"Maybe Thursday night?" he continues.

"We'll talk about it later." Nora hangs up abruptly.

"Sorry, Elizabeth…"

"Did you upset your girlfriend?" she asks with probing eyes, trying to conceal her blazing curiosity about his new friends.

"Maybe… But I'm not sure about my relationship with her, anyway," he says.

"Why?"

"It's getting complicated…"

"Yeah?"

"Yeah… When I returned from Iran, I looked for a gallery to represent me. In fact, I was a bit paranoid about my luck in this city with so much bad memories. I was thinking about moving to Toronto if I didn't get established here quickly, and to be near my father, too," he says, while opening a bottle of chardonnay and filling their glasses.

"How is he?" she asks.

"Not so good, I'm afraid… I'll explain later."

"Why'd he go to Toronto?"

"He was raised there. He has four sisters and brothers and other relatives there. After divorcing my mom, he decided to be around them, but soon drove them away, too… Living alone for many years has pushed him to the edge."

"That's a pity. Maybe you should go help him."

"Anyway, I showed my portfolio to several galleries, with no luck. One day I went to Elixir and met Nora, the gallery manager. After some chitchat, she looked convinced and asked me to leave my portfolio to show to the owner." He refills their glasses and leans back on the soft leather sofa. "You look bored. I should let you talk for a change."

"No, go ahead, tell me about your new friends," she says shyly, now quite curious about Nora. Her initial tension for being in his apartment has vanished due to the wine and his charm. She is glad actually, yet imagines a fuming Erica suddenly storming into the room and making a scene. However, Darren's ingenuous enthusiasm is convincing her to relax. "So your charm worked on her?"

"I worried about the same thing!" Darren replies.

"I was only kidding. You're a good painter *too*."

"Thanks, I guess," he says while gazing at the colourful horizon through the glass door. "Wow... Let's go out watch the sunset," he suggests and she nods. They take their wineglasses, step onto the balcony, and lean against the railing.

Mesmerized by the colour spectrum, green to violet and red to yellow, they linger silently, swept by the amazing Nature and their own private sensations, their souls swimming in separate soothing spheres. He has suddenly lost his urge to speak, rather odd and intimidating to Elizabeth after all the energy he had shown to entertain her. She is reluctant to interrupt his trance, but soon loses her patience. "So what happened with Nora?"

Startled, Darren stares at her a long while.

"Well... Marcus Elias, the owner, had asked her to view my paintings and choose a few for him to judge personally," Darren explains. "So she came over one day after work and picked three paintings to show Marcus, then promised me to convince him to take me on. I helped her put the paintings in her van and then asked her to dinner as a gesture of my appreciation. Eagerly she agreed. We strolled to Tony Roma's and had good conversation along with ribs and wine. I liked her manners and elegance, so I kissed her on the cheek when saying goodbye. She blushed, grinned, and drove away."

"So far so good!" Elizabeth says with a chuckle.

"Yes... Anyway, I met her and Marcus the following week and signed a contract. Marcus stressed that all decisions would go through Nora, and I should take her words as his. Maybe it was his way of flattering her. But his comment felt rather insensitive and worrisome."

"Why?"

"Well, it sounded like he was doing it only for Nora."

"It hurt your pride?"

"Yes, somewhat. More annoying was the idea of answering to her, though. And the big question was, *To court or not to court* her, because both options were risky now."

"So…?"

"The answer came in her keen eyes and I felt obliged to ask her out—against my better judgment. Later, her staff took fifteen of my paintings and she sold them in two months. Long story short, we've been dating with some type of tension. Especially, a secret she shared with me later made the matter too complex and touchy."

"Juicy secret?" Elizabeth exclaims with rising giddiness.

Darren wonders why he is sharing so much about his private life with Elizabeth so quickly, but then decides it might help him relieve his recent anxiety a bit. He sips his wine and continues, "She confessed to being Marcus's mistress. They'd been in love for five years after meeting one evening at a gallery opening. She'd become the gallery manager, while waiting for Marcus to make the final move about leaving his wife of twenty-five years and marrying her. But he never did it and their passion perished gradually. They've been trapped in a lousy relationship for the last two years."

"How about *your* relationship with her?"

"It's shaky too. We have fun when she isn't depressed about not owning a man. It shows in her eyes but she never complains. Tonight she got upset again, since I can't see her until Thursday."

"Are you worried about hurting her feelings or your career?"

"Both. But most of all, I don't like to be in the middle of this situation or compete with Marcus."

"She's got nerve, I tell you," Elizabeth blurts.

"I hate the idea of my career being in my lover's hand, again."

"Like the time you worked for Erica's company, eh?"

"Exactly… It's just too damn humiliating." He pauses to measure her mood. "How about a joint?"

"Okay," she replies, following him inside.

He fetches a small bag from the bedroom, empties some marijuana onto a newspaper, pours a few pinches onto a cigarette paper, and rolls it perfectly. He lights it up, drags a deep puff, and passes it on to her.

"I'm losing my mind," he murmurs in a muffled voice, still holding the smoke, shaking his head with distress.

"Why?"

"I believe I bought two bags of pot six months ago and hid one of them somewhere I can't recall, or maybe I'm mistaken, I don't know..."

"Maybe you smoke too much pot?"

"No, but my mind is dwindling fast," he replies with pain.

"Well, you've put a lot of pressure on it over the years, too."

"Yeah, I'm getting old!"

"You're only thirty, silly! Why do you try to sound like a sixty-year-old grouch?" she shrieks unconsciously.

"Are you scared of getting old and feeling lonely, too?"

"Don't be silly…," Elizabeth replies. "So who's T.J.?"

"He's an Iranian author Reza knew. You remember Reza?" She looks perplexed and he continues. "He visited us often when Erica and I lived together. He's a software engineer like Erica and has a consulting business in Iran."

Elizabeth grimaces with agitation, but collects her composure quickly. "Yes, I remember him now, vaguely…"

"He gave me T.J.'s number to contact him if I needed to clear my mind. We talk about life, happiness, and similar stuff. He's an interesting guy and challenges my mind. I like him."

"I hope you're not converting?" she asks with a giggle, the effect of the pot showing in her eyes.

"It's weird you say this…" He bursts into laughter.

"Why? You've had the same thought or urge?"

"No, I just remembered a recent dream," he says.

"What about?"

Darren rises and paces the room, stops and gazes at her now and then. "I don't know if I should tell you."

"Yes, you should… Tell me…"

"Well… Two bulky men were strolling along the Seawalk, chatting and enjoying the fresh air. Suddenly they stopped and began exchanging angry looks and words, which soon turned into screaming and swearing. Wildly agitated, they came together to intimidate each other, like two pissed baseball players. They banged their puffed-up bellies, pressed their foreheads, and yelled with fury. In the heat of the scuffle, as you'd imagine both their skulls might explode any second, they suddenly began kissing passionately. Such a horrible sight, I woke up with sweat and disgust, yet its absurdity also felt funny. We always try to be open-minded, but certain ideas take time to get used to, I guess."

"How do you interpret it?" Elizabeth asks teasingly.

"I guess it says sexual experimentation has no boundary."

"What do you mean?"

"I mean, we're all susceptible to pitiful perversions under right circumstances."

"Such as?"

"Just imagine two young men or women trapped on an island. Don't you think they'd eventually decide to help each other in all respects, including sexually, to make the best of their hopeless situation?"

"So when're you going to *the island*?" she asks, laughing heartily.

"I go to the island almost every day—Granville Island, where we met today."

"Maybe your dream has other interpretations, too."

"Such as?"

"I don't know…!" she replies wittily.

"Your frisky eyes show your dirty mind," he says.

"So now you can read my mind? What am I thinking?"

"That these two men were T.J. and I… Right…?"

Now they are ridiculously jovial, beyond this world's realms. The dream and the pot are making them feel silly and giddy as Darren saunters buoyantly and ruffles his hair playfully.

"Maybe T.J. is signalling you through your dreams," she says teasingly.

"Impossible! He's married and has three teenage daughters."

"So what's his interest in you now?" She laughs loudly again. "Doesn't he know someone smarter, closer to his age to talk to?"

"For one thing, he uses me for his new hobby—painting. He asks about techniques and tools while experimenting and reading books. So indulging me has some fringe benefits for him at least. We discuss many other issues, too, of course. Besides, he enjoys fooling with me or challenging my beliefs and principles."

"Is he against love, too, like you?" Elizabeth asks.

"Not at all… On the one hand, he likes to talk about attractive women and stares at them like a hungry wolf. On the other hand, he believes love between a man and a woman is a spiritual affair, somewhat different from the way it is abused in Western culture. In fact, 'love' is a main topic of our debates."

"So you still like girls…!" she says slyly again.

"Very much, in fact. That's the problem."

"What's the problem?"

"Being at the mercy of attractive women like you, but cynical about their love expressions."

4

Darren uncorks another bottle of wine and begins refilling her glass.

"That's enough," Elizabeth says with a guilty gesture. "I must go home soon!"

"Why…? The night's still young…" He pauses and stares at her before continuing, "We could go to a restaurant or call for pizza…"

"It's up to you, but I'm comfortable right now."

After ordering pizza, he gazes into her eyes, sombrely, despite his funny mood. "I'd forgotten what a fun person you are. I'm glad we met today."

"Me too…"

"Before you appeared, I was trying to analyze my muddy mood these days. You believe in destiny?"

"You still have your habit of analyzing everything to death? Don't you get tired?"

"I bet you quarrel with the same issues your entire life without realizing it."

"That's probably true," she says.

"Analyzing my problems or mood through meditation helps me build my beliefs and move on. For instance, not even T.J. can change my mind about my new impression of love."

"…which seems to be too negative now…," she completes his sentence.

"No, I think it's more realistic and practical," Darren replies.

"What's love, anyway, professor?" she asks with a smirk.

"That's a good question!"

"That's why I asked," she says and they burst into idiotic laughter again for a long time.

"Do you really still care to discuss this stuff now and ruin our moods?" he asks with surprise.

"Well, that's what you promised to explain tonight! Maybe your cute cynicism converts me, too."

"You see, nobody can truly say what 'love' really is—a joyful feeling, a divine experience, a fancy way of communicating, a psychological reaction, or any mix of these things?"

"Love is just a deep feeling. That's all," Elizabeth blurts.

"But this corny definition ignores too many psychological issues behind love."

"So what's your view?"

"My view is simple; but mostly I think love is just another myth," he says matter-of-factly.

"A myth? Are you gone nuts now?"

"No, we like to exaggerate our feelings to soothe our pains, pamper our lust, or even justify our melancholy."

The intercom blares from downstairs. Darren answers it, lets the pizza deliveryman in, and chats with him at the half-open apartment door. Waiting patiently, Elizabeth notices Darren handing him a few large bills while whispering about his lost bag of marijuana. Finally, Darren closes the door and pours more wine to sip with their cheesy pizza in a rather awkward silence. Then he rolls another joint.

"So you're serious about your views?" Elizabeth asks at last.

"What were we talking about?" Darren asks in a serious tone, conscious enough to know that the pot has jumbled his mind. After another deadly, long silence his mind jumpstarts abruptly. "Oh, yeah… Real love needs selflessness, which is similar to breathlessness. We can hold our breath a while to love someone, but not permanently."

"So, you think people are lying about being in love then?"

"Not necessarily, but often we don't know what we're talking about or feeling," he replies.

"We don't?" she asks with angst.

"No, the main problem is that we expect love to last forever, or else it hadn't been true. So we wash or tarnish our memories of love if our lovers leave us; we may even retaliate and attempt to kill them."

"They deserve to die if they cheat or lie," she interjects irately.

Darren giggles again from Elizabeth's rough reaction, which shows the effect of wine and pot, as well as her state of mind. She joins him in their long, baseless laughter again.

"So what're you saying, Darren?" she asks when they finally stop horsing around.

"All I'm saying is that a relationship lasts better if it's not bogged down by a corny 'love' impression. And we may enjoy more *amore* if we realize how flimsy love is, except for the love of our children, of course." He pauses and sips his wine.

She interjects tensely, "Which shows parents can still breathe normally and live long."

"No, parents suffer the most actually... 'Breathlessness' is only a metaphor, anyway. Don't use it literally just to contradict me…"

"Your life with Erica has really messed you up, Darren."

"And you're afraid of losing Jeff and ending up living alone."

"Oh, really…?"

"Yeah… Really…"

"You're an idiot! You know? I'd better go," she snarls, leaps out of the sofa with her forefinger pointing at him, while looking around for her purse.

Calmly, Darren rises too, laughs, and approaches her with wide-open arms, as if ready to embrace her. "I wonder if I should take your comment as a compliment."

"For calling you an idiot?"

"Yes… T.J. says we become wiser and happier the sooner we realize our idiocy."

"Good for you; as long as you remember you're a big idiot," she says playfully, cooling down a bit, but missing or ignoring his meaning.

"Thanks. You're quite an idiot yourself; stubborn too," he yells, extending his head forward, giggling, and horsing around.

"You've become too paranoid and weird," she says, imitating his motions and smirk.

"Silly."

"Imbecile."

"Stubborn."

"Crazy."

Bombarding each other with childish mockery, they realize they are mimicking Darren's dream. Enticed to playact it most professionally, they rant louder, ram their foreheads, then lower their jaws and begin kissing with great vigour. After ten seconds, they separate, look into each other's eyes and burst into rowdy laughter before hugging again and kissing passionately this time.

Darren hauls her toward the bedroom, lounges her gently on the bed, and resumes kissing her face, neck, earlobes, and hair in rotation. She joins in ardently, as though they had both craved this moment forever. Stripping her smoothly, he inspects every bit of her skin closely with all kinds of caressing, smelling, and smooching, both suffocating from pleasure, but desiring no relief. They gasp to survive and soar, but loathe any rescue or pause for serious breaths or thoughts. The inspection continues, Darren immersed in some tranquilizing ritual over her body, making love to her tenderized body finally with a placid rhythm and patience. After an enchanting flight to the never-lands, as serenely as their bodies reach climax, they descend the summit smoothly, back to the reality of two independent fleshes filled with sad, confusing emotions, rather like two suspicious strangers who had not spent the whole evening fooling around and laughing like kids.

They lie sprawled on their backs breathlessly while holding hands tentatively with scepticism. Darren turns toward her and caresses her hair. Two lumps of tears leak and lake outside her eyes, which baffle him for a second. He lurches to the living room, fetches their wineglasses, and gives Elizabeth hers.

"You have quite a technique!" she says wittily.

"I'm glad you approve…"

"I wonder how Erica let you go if you treated her this way every night. Or is this an introductory special for your new lovers only?"

"It all depends on my mood."

"Should I stay tonight so that you can explain more?"

"Absolutely, I love to explain 'love' to you all night!" He kisses her cocked nipples, sips his wine. "Of course, beyond lust and selfishness, 'love' also has a spiritual nature…" He notices her dozing off and stops blabbering. He caresses her soft buttocks curving under the sheet and pulls the blanket over her, Elizabeth peeping with half-closed eyes. He turns off the lights and falls asleep instantly. He is exhausted too.

5

Darren is standing bemused in the middle of a large compound resembling a huge supermarket with hundreds of counters and unending line-ups of desolate souls. At the far end, two counters are idle, attendants peeping around hopelessly for someone to approach them. He notices the sign: "120 Sins or Less." Quickly, he recognizes his whereabouts, as if somebody had whispered it swiftly in his ear; now he wonders: *How do I know how many sins I have?* Peering around, he sees another flashing sign that reads "Sinners' Service."

He hurries to the attractive attendant. "May I go to an express lane?"

She checks the floating monitor and cries, "No express lane for you! You have 200 forbidden loves alone!"

"200 forbidden loves?" Darren screams and wakes up.

His blurry eyes reveal Elizabeth, half-nude next to the dresser, brushing her hair. He blinks in disbelief. As she peeps at him in the mirror, he grins while admiring her gorgeous body.

"You think our love was forbidden?" he asks abruptly.

"I don't know what to think about last night. I'm in shock," Elizabeth replies, contemplating, not brushing her hair anymore. "I hadn't been so wasted and vulgar for a very very long time!"

"Then we must do it again soon."

"You're a bad influence, Darren."

"Thanks. Glad to be of assistance."

"I must be careful with you. I don't want to be spoiled."

He changes the subject to avoid embarrassing everybody. "You didn't tell me last night whether you believe in destiny."

"Sometimes I do, although I don't know what the heck it is," she replies timidly.

"Coincidence is the key to all the miracles of destiny, like you finding me at a particular place, time, and mood yesterday."

"Right…! What now?"

"We must meet soon, of course," Darren replies. Elizabeth surveys him sceptically and he continues. "We must figure out what last night meant."

"I don't know… I'm concerned about Jeff and Erica."

"True…" He smiles, recalling his dream about the 200th sin.

"Jeff's going to Los Angeles next week. I may call you," she says and starts to leave.

Chapter Two
Passion Rejuvenation

1

Darren's recent crabby mood is replaced with a jolly urge to paint this morning, thanks to the promising fresh affair with Elizabeth and T.J.'s return from Europe. Carefree and gallant, he tackles the first canvas with swift, spontaneous brushstrokes, not worried about ruining the painting if things got out of hand. But his strokes remain bubbly, landing softly at the right spots, lengths, and intensities. Accidents lead to nice surprises and nifty notions, which bolster bolder experiments and more exhilaration.

A sense of fulfilment completes his jovial mood at the end of the day when he witnesses the superb outcome and progress after weeks of lethargy and stress. Only the task of cleaning the brushes and palettes feels tedious. He has always fantasized about hiring a beautiful assistant to help with the pre- and post-painting chores, mixing paints, posing nude for him, and massaging him whenever he takes a break. *Perhaps someday soon! Painting a couple of nudes could be a good distraction, anyway, to boost my mood maybe! Would Elizabeth pose for me, maybe even in nude?*

What a day! Starting with such a weird dream, he giggles. *200 forbidden loves…! I bet the devil had somehow hacked those computers and fudged the stats.* Then opening his eyes to the charm of a naked beauty brushing her hair so elegantly. The prospect of inspecting her sexy body invigorates him. He has done a great job with the paintings. And, of course, meeting T.J. tonight would be fun, too. He plummets onto the sofa, gasps with joy, and jots down some delivery dates to give Nora the next day.

At 7:40 p.m., Darren sets off for Edgemont Village, a delightful neighbourhood in North Vancouver with six-dozen retail stores, two cozy coffee shops, a library, and an art gallery, all together surrounding a wide, treed boulevard. T.J. lives a fifteen-minute walking distance from it and Darren likes its serenity.

Waiting at a table outside the café, T.J. rises and they show their genuine delight with a firm handshake and hug. They buy espressos and pastries and return to the sidewalk table.

"Why did you return early?" Darren asks.

"I was bored. Too much vacationing haunted me, perhaps for not enough privacy and free time."

"I haven't been to Europe yet. Let's go together sometime."

"Maybe... It'll take me a long time to recover from this trip, though."

"So did you have fun at all?"

"Yeah. I enjoyed going to museums the most. But I got tired of strolling in the busy streets of Paris and eating in restaurants every day. I was at the mercy of relatives and friends, all trying hard to please me, which somehow agitated me despite the joy of seeing them."

"You know something, T.J."

"What?"

"Sometimes you're really weird and grouchy," Darren blurts abruptly, although he tries to spice up his point with humour.

"Why?"

"Well, traveling even to Paris bores you, you don't have a particularly exciting relationship with your wife or anybody else, and you have to follow a strict diet. What's life then? What's the point of writing so much, especially when only a few understand or care about what you're saying, anyway?" Darren asserts with a chuckle half-teasingly.

"That's a good question, my friend. But I enjoy writing and doing creative things; they keep me active and alive for now."

"Sorry for snapping at you." Darren pauses. "But sometimes you're really grumpy. Don't you think?"

"Yes, maybe…What do you expect from an old man?"

"You're not that old yet… So you didn't do any writing for two months?"

"No," T.J. replies. "I couldn't even take notes."

"Why?"

"Recently I'm often trapped without a pad or pencil when an idea comes to me. I'm getting sloppy. I—"

"Maybe we're catching the same disease…," Darren says. "I'm getting edgy and forgetful these days, too."

"But honestly, I'm not regretting it."

"How come?"

"I have too many notes. I cannot imagine using them in any kind of writing. I was flipping through my scrapbook yesterday. Either I haven't explained some ideas enough to recall their exact meaning, or millions of scattered ideas seem all over the place."

"Yeah?"

"I just found something common between us," T.J. says with triumph and a giggle.

"What?"

"We both have too much of something we can't handle!"

"What's that?"

"You have too many women hunting you, and I have too many notes haunting me."

"That's rue… But my women are haunting me, too," Darren replies. "We're both in big trouble, my friend!"

"Yeah… We're in big shit…"

"It wouldn't be so bad if we weren't so finicky or trying to justify our actions, too," Darren says with stress.

"Still, you're much luckier," T.J. says with a sigh.

"Why?" Darren asks.

"How can anybody even compare some lousy notes with the gorgeous women around you? I'd give all my notes for just one of them."

"Are you sure? You can't even handle your wife, Monsieur T.J."

"I can dream at least, if you don't mind."

"So what should we do, you think?" Darren asks.

"You probably have a better chance of salvaging your soul."

"I agree… All I need truly is only one loyal, smart mate."

"Here we go… You need to accomplish only one thing to redeem yourself, but I'm sure I can never write at least 500 books if I wish to use even my existing notes," T.J. says with despair.

"Still my job is tougher than yours, I promise."

"Well, enough about our dreams; how're you feeling?"

"Lousy, but I'm better since yesterday after hearing from you and meeting a gorgeous friend by accident all in the same day."

"Another potential lover?"

"Absolutely, we had exciting conversations and then some," Darren says with a giggle. "But nothing matches our hot debates. I missed your wisdom…"

T.J. blurts irately, "What wisdom, my friend…?! My only wisdom is to admit that I'm just another imbecile with my own weird views of this world."

"At least you know that and accept it," Darren replies.

"Yeah… My highest aspiration is to trust my thoughts and actions one day without always doubting or justifying them recklessly. That's the best I can hope for."

"That's exactly the kind of wisdom I was talking about. We mustn't start arguing about every word again already, must we?" Darren replies politely, recalling his dream about the two men arguing and kissing at the end. But he decides not to mention it to T.J., nor argue with him, just to be on the safe side!

"Why were you feeling lousy, anyway?" T.J. asks.

"Two reasons, I guess: Your absence and Mahroo's arrival."

"I believe you'd lost the opportunity of pouring your heart out to someone you trust. I've seen this need in you, but who's Mahroo?"

"Mahroo is Reza's sister. She's coming from Iran with her parents on Saturday."

"For a visit?"

"I don't know. They're disturbed by the war and her father has a heart condition needing a check-up. Reza's asked me to help them settle here and find a good heart specialist."

"I understand the hassle but what's your real concern?"

"I don't know."

"You don't know anything today, ha?" T.J. asks teasingly.

"Well… for one thing, expressing my sympathy to Mahroo might be an awkward task."

"Sympathy?"

"Oh yeah, her young husband died in a car accident just recently. He was a good pal."

"Anything else you're not telling me?"

T.J.'s tone and bluntness shake Darren, dipping him into deep thoughts.

They sip their espressos in awkward silence. T.J. considers raising another topic to relieve Darren's apparent sombre struggle with some memories. But then decides to let Darren deal with his daunting secrets personally. A tactful silence lingers as they keep watching people and traffic while exchanging subtle glances.

"I have no secrets, but a few odd events happened in Iran."

"Like what?" T.J. asks. "If you care to share with me…"

"You must hear the entire story if you're really interested."

"Let's go to my house then. Nobody's home to bother us. We'll drink wine and smoke while you become Shahrazad."

2

T.J. brings four bottles of wine, three of them in a bag. "This bag's for you; fine Bordeaux."

He then uncorks the fourth bottle and fills their glasses.

"I'll give you the highlight of my long story in Iran, if you like," Darren says after taking a sip of his wine.

"Yes, just the highlights are enough," T.J. replies with a grin.

"The whole thing began when Erica and I separated and Reza offered me a job in Iran, mostly for training staff for his growing company. I'd been working for Erica's company for a while after failing to live off painting. Her company marketed a popular piece of software internationally. Reza was the sole supplier in Iran, so came to Vancouver regularly and we met often. His job offer sounded silly, but the salary was quite tempting, even if I could find a new job in Vancouver. The only drawback was the war between Iran and Iraq. Still leaving Vancouver felt like a good break, as far away from Erica on this planet as possible. So I went to Iran in 1985."

****

(February 1985)

At Frankfurt Airport, Darren awaits the last leg of his travel to Tehran. A sudden realization jolts him like a thunderbolt: This is his last chance to smarten up and abort his travel plan. Although leaving Vancouver seems like a sensible idea to forget Erica, traveling to Iran feels silly at this horrible time. The news about the war escalating every day is disturbing, both sides becoming more reckless, threatening to use weapons of mass destruction. Iraq has evidently procured chemical weapons and factories from the United States, ready to deploy them on Iran. And the rumours hint that Iran is building nuclear weapons. Under this condition, Darren believes, only a fool would march into such a hellhole voluntarily, regardless of the rewards or his peculiar reasons for a refuge away from Vancouver and Erica.

Almost resolved to return to Canada, the call for Lufthansa passengers to embark startles Darren. Like a dope, he staggers toward Gate 8, presents his pass, and enters the boarding tunnel. *How selfishly I'm neglecting my lonely, loony father in Toronto for a silly adventure!* Every step is an agonizing foot closer to the no-return zone, yet he takes the next, until he is seated by the hostess. *I'm gonna die in Iran.* He wishes the pilot would order, "Kick this fool out of the plane." *I'm gonna die in a country fighting a major war, whose language and culture are weird, whose people are goaded by the fanatic revolutionary mullahs and mayhem, and whose government is mauling the U.S.—the "Big Satan," according to fanatic Khomeini.* The anti-American sentiments have escalated fast, as people blame the Big Satan for supporting Saddam Hussein to kill Iranians and their economy. *What if some hooligans take me for an American spy and simply slaughter me before I can prove I'm an innocent Canadian? I am a Canadian... What a relief!*

Darren's angst magnifies as the pilot announces that the plane cannot enter Tehran's perimeter due to an ongoing missile attack. The plane, twirling fast toward Tabriz, skews some passengers off their seats and they yowl. The swerving and passengers' commotion aggravates Darren's nausea from over-thinking. A ghastly silence prevails soon, however, and parents hush their restless children with tension, as though any sound could entice an Iraqi missile.

The plane lands in Tabriz at last and the passengers get free accommodation for the night. The stress and exhaustion prevent Darren from getting a sound sleep. At first daylight, he freshens up impatiently and takes a cab to the airport to explore the flight situation. "The plane will leave in two hours," the clerk says.

Reza's friendly face outside the customs gate and the animated commotion in Tehran's transit hall subdue Darren's anxiety about the war and life in an exotic new environment. All around him, the situation is hectic with rushing passengers and porters, emptied suitcases on counters, or half-open, hefty ones being dragged out of the terminal after an inspection. Bold and proud in Reza's company, Darren marches toward the parking lot, a porter straggling along awkwardly with his heavy luggage.

Within a week, Darren leases an apartment on the twelfth floor of a high-rise and decorates it with the modest furniture he buys or Reza brings. Both his work and life soon prove exciting despite the Islamic restrictions, curfews, and bombardments. The situation is not too bad, after all, except for the ordeal and hassles of nightly air raids, including the exhausting descents on foot to the basement and waiting for hours.

Gradually, Darren too accepts the war as a routine, while wondering about his luck to survive the next Iraqi missile night after night. On the other hand, the new lifestyle and challenges mollify his trifling sorrows and anxiety about abandoning Erica and Vancouver. His past petty problems feel childish in the scope of the catastrophes around him.

Learning to drive in Tehran seems to be the toughest task of his life, even more taxing than learning computer technology for joining Erica's company. Although traffic signs and lights stand on every corner and colourful lines set the boundaries, hardly drivers bother themselves with these formalities! They speed, manoeuvre recklessly, make abrupt halts, swerve to the edge of sidewalks, and challenge the changing stoplights. Traffic officers seem to be nonexistent or simply given up after years of struggling to stop and penalize the big volume of violators everywhere every single second. In fact, if they stopped this specialized mode of driving, the whole traffic would come to a stand still in this crowded city. Due to this seemingly natural phenomenon, nobody can drive civilly without facing severe abuse by the testy drivers wanting him out of the way. One must learn to drive accordingly, or leave driving privileges to the experts. Taxi services are rather reliable and cheap. Still, as a passenger, one goes dizzy even witnessing the drivers' skilful manoeuvres through the maze of cars at high speeds. Darren wonders with great admiration if any car-racing videogame could truly simulate the agility and intensity of the real-time driving in Tehran!

Darren makes Iranian friends, including beautiful girls who visit him furtively. Despite their conservative Islamic appearance, Iranian women are quite sexy and thrill seeking. With so many young boys in combat, dead, or crippled, men are scarce. Even worse, women's response to the fanatic Islamic rules and strict dress code has transpired in their exaggerated liberalism. The staggering inflation and unemployment also goads women to seek financially secure men. With such a shortage of eligible men, the social life in Iran is booming. Especially, for a rich, handsome Canadian, Darren's opportunities are endless. Soon, he is busy enjoying himself thoroughly, without succumbing to the devil completely.

3

With the workload stabilized, Reza invites Darren to his villa on the shores of the Caspian Sea. Early one Friday morning, Zia Taymori, Reza's brother-in-law, arrives at Darren's place to travel together.

"I'll be your chauffeur, butler, and entertainer," Zia greets Darren with his trademark theatrics—an embellished show of modesty and humour.

Darren tries to play along. "Should I sit in the back then?"

"No, no; I can't see your pretty face there."

They wiggle and giggle, while Zia insists on carrying and loading Darren's bag into the trunk, holding the door for him, and then closing it after a short bow. Driving from Tehran to Chalus, the main city before Reza's villa, takes six to ten hours depending on the driver and road condition.

"So tell me, is Tehran exciting enough for you?" Zia asks.

"Quite, actually," Darren replies teasingly.

"I hadn't heard about Vancouver before I met you. Are girls prettier or weirder over there?"

"They're just about the same," Darren replies.

"So, this means you've already learned a lot about Persian girls, ha, you devil?"

"Enough, I guess…"

"Be careful... You could get into trouble!"

"Yeah?"

"Really big troubles."

Zia stops frequently at roadside inns to eat or drink tea before lighting a joint and sharing it with Darren. They arrive at the villa late in the afternoon. Reza and four friends are sunbathing on the deck, drinking beer, and enjoying the sight and sound of the crashing waves.

"Come on, Darren. Hurry up. Come get naked," Zia yells from inside the villa repeatedly, interrupting the gang's mingling with Darren.

When Darren returns in his trunks, Zia propels him toward the sea. The deep floury sand slithers deep between their toes with an oozing sensation, but hinders walking. Zia's horse-playing makes Darren even woozier. The sea is windy and wild but still warm. They splash water or push each other under the big waves. The salty surf keeps them afloat slightly while they struggle to swim or stand in shallow waters. Sometimes, the rolling surf turns them upside-down, like ice cubes in a gigantic mixer—the pounding waves rolling and pushing from the top and the sinking sands hauling them into underwater tornados. All these turns and twists revive the effects of beers and marijuana consumed on the road and they feel inebriated all over again. Clowning and giggling, they scuffle to evade the fierce surf and get out of the sea. Their eyes red and itchy, at last they plummet onto the beach breathless before staggering back to the villa. The guys are putting charcoals in the barbecue to prepare shish kabob.

After dinner, the fiesta continues with more pot and poker. Reminiscing the school years in Los Angeles and beautiful girls, the guys blabber in Persian despite Reza's repeated reminder to include Darren. But, under the influence of alcohol and pot, they humour Darren with just a few words sporadically. Nonetheless, Darren prefers sitting on the side, drinking beer, and enjoying the atmosphere. Living in Tehran for four months now, he has adapted himself to this kind of treatment. At parties and work, people try to indulge him by speaking English, but it is not easy. So he delves into his own world and ignores the Persian words bombarding his ears more fiercely than all the Iraqi bombs dropped on Tehran. In fact, he resents the sporadic interruption of his thoughts when people, like these guys tonight, tease him with a random, silly joke or comment.

The following day, they drive along the coast near Chalus. The long highway snakes through villages and towns all the way to Baku, a border city in Azerbaijan Republic on the west coast of the Caspian Sea. The gang stops at some spots to take pictures and have lunch. They return in the afternoon, swim in the sea, and repeat their evening fiesta.

The Caspian Sea entices Darren. He enjoys the soft breeze carrying the aroma of the sea, pine and plane trees, wild flowers, and tea plantations. The rhythmic roar of huge waves crashing onto the beach is blissful, too. Even the mugginess feels pleasant. The ambience calms his nerves away from the war and the horrific traffic of Tehran.

Sunday afternoon, they head for Tehran, Darren with Reza, a faster but more disciplined driver. They stop only once, briefly, for dinner at a small inn.

"How was the Caspian Sea?" Reza asks Darren.

"I couldn't imagine such splendour in this part of the world. I'm inspired by the atmosphere and wouldn't mind going back to do some sketches and paintings."

"You can borrow my Jeep and use my villa any time you like. Traffic outside of Tehran isn't too bad."

"If I find the courage to drive!"

"I'll teach you, don't worry."

"I never thought I'd find the urge and courage to paint again."

"We cannot ignore our real passions forever."

"But without some recognition, art becomes only an added source of frustration. It may even drive a man cut off his ears."

"Ha… At least you still have yours."

"I thought I was done with painting."

"Why did you feel that way?"

"I got tired of failing, but mostly because it ruined Erica's perception of me as a real, successful man."

"I'm glad you've now changed your mind," Reza says.

"Me, too. Coming to Iran had felt useful to rebuild my life, but now I feel painting only for myself can help me, too."

"It's amazing how fate makes us see life in a new light. I'm glad we met and I brought you here, too."

"So you've played a big role in my destiny, too, ha?" Darren asks with a mysterious tone that makes Reza feel both tense and thrilled for different reasons.

"I don't know, but it seems you had to come all the way to the Caspian Sea to regain your urge for painting! Isn't that weird?"

"Maybe… That's another role you've probably played in my fate then, ha?" Darren asks still more mysteriously, which makes Reza a bit edgy, somewhat realizing Darren's clever insinuation about Reza's possible role in Darren's divorce.

"At least you have a new perspective about life now," Reza says cautiously, hoping to avoid raising any touchy topic today.

"Right… Just imagine me being so lost and glum over Erica when children and youths are dying in millions in wars or from hunger. What an idiot I've been."

"At least you're learning...," Reza says. "Most people go through life fully hypnotized by their egos and obsessions."

"Then I must thank Erica for both leaving me and introducing you!" Darren blurts with a tense grin.

Reza feels still more hints of sarcasm in his comment, as if the Caspian Sea had also made Darren nostalgic about Erica on top of rejuvenating his passion for painting, not to mention his odd sudden urge to raise old issues just to start an argument with him.

"I'm flattered," Reza replies calmly, trying to ignore Darren's sarcasm and avoid any kind of tricky conversation that could ruin their moods or all the fun they had shared at the Caspian Sea. "But it was also my luck that you gave up art, learned computer stuff, and came here to help me with this crazy situation at work."

"You believe in destiny and spirituality?"

"I'm learning," Reza says shyly.

"Do you have a teacher?"

"Yes… Zia's uncle, but don't mention it to Zia."

"Why?"

"Zia's a gifted engineer with a flourishing career. But he's a cynical and eccentric guy; maybe even psychotic. At the age of six, his parents died in an earthquake in Kashan. So, his uncle raised him in Tehran. He never got over the loss of his parents and moving to a new environment. Maybe childhood traumas ruined his brain. His constant clowning is for hiding his deep hang-ups. I didn't know these facts until it was too late."

"Too late?"

"After he married Mahroo," replies Reza, sighs, contemplates a while before continuing: "When we returned to Iran, he visited me often at my parents' house and amused everybody, especially Mahroo. At last, he sent his family to get my parents' consent to marry her. That's how I met Zia's uncle, Dervish Ali. You know what *Dervish* means?"

"No."

"Dervish is a man of spiritual beliefs and power, like a guru. Anyway, as much as I'm pleased about knowing Dervish Ali, I've felt sorry for having Zia as my brother-in-law."

"Is he violent or something?"

"Not really. He's just screwed up, especially in the way he mocks spiritual beliefs. He doesn't even visit his uncle anymore. To make matters worse, the way mullahs took power and abused Islam and the misery of the war with Iraq have made him even more cynical and a pushy atheist. He's right about social issues, but some of us still have strong beliefs."

"Are his beliefs causing marital conflicts, too?"

"No. Mostly his pessimism, despite his outgoing personality and playfulness, is hurting Mahroo. It may affect their daughter, Nazi, too."

"Have you ever confronted him?"

"Yes… Our mutual friends and I have tried a few times to convince him to lighten up a little, but it's useless. Mahroo likes him, but I know she's suffering. She just doesn't want to burden us by complaining too much." Reza stops at the side of the road when they approach an inn. "You want to eat something or use the washroom?"

"No, I'm fine."

"We'll be at your apartment in two hours."

"Just in time for air raids! Why doesn't anybody, the United Nations or the superpowers, put a stop to this nonsense?"

"Oh, they're running the whole show," Reza replies with grief.

The rest of the way, they discuss the world affairs and politics. Darren enjoys Reza's analysis of the superpowers' meddling in the affairs of less fortunate nations and exploiting them. He is stunned particularly by the story of the CIA staging a military coup in Iran in 1953 that overthrew Mosaddeq, the Premier of Iran for several years and his National Front cabinet. This was an act of US foreign policy, conceived and approved at the highest levels of government to return the Shah to power at the request of oil companies after the Shah had fled subsequent to the people's revolution.

"And now they're supporting Saddam to destroy Iran. They just butt into everybody's affairs shamelessly, and make people's lives more miserable every day," Reza explains.

"I agree… I think America is getting more arrogant every year," Darren says.

"They just wanna push their materialistic values on the rest of the world so shamelessly."

"Thanks for showing me the Caspian Sea," Darren says as he gets out of the car at his home.

"Ask me for the keys to my car and villa anytime you wanna go back there."

"Maybe in a couple of weeks or so, if you don't mind."

"Fine with me."

"By the way, can I meet Dervish Ali too?" Darren asks.

"Hmm… I'll find out," Reza replies timidly.

4

Darren's next trip to the Caspian Sea is experimental, especially the driving chore. Luckily, a female colleague, Roya Kabuli, agrees to accompany him, albeit in a separate car with a couple of her friends. After practising during slow traffic at night, Darren gathers enough courage to follow Roya's car to the Caspian Sea in Reza's Jeep. Under Islamic rules, they would be whipped, jailed, and possibly forced to marry if caught in the same car. To his surprise, he learns to drive a bit aggressively, according to the Iranian style. Surely, it will take him a few years to be qualified in the Iranian drivers' eyes. But merely gathering the nerve to steer a car without killing himself is a major achievement and another sign of his enlightenment, he believes. Destiny is opening new venues for him to revive his spirit, even if it requires driving so recklessly like Iranians.

Roya's generosity to drive such a long distance mostly for helping him obliges Darren to spend more time on romance with her than he'd hoped. Still he makes a dozen sketches and takes notes about each scene, along with pictures, all in preparation for the first painting.

In Tehran, he spreads the sketches and pictures on a table and studies them with passion and patience. He's unable to envision an inspiring composition and the air-raid sirens send him to the basement. He returns too exhausted to think anymore and goes straight to bed.

While snoozing, an image begins forming in his head. He pursues the adventure keenly as the picture evolves, bit by bit, until he envisions all the details. Ecstatic about the experience, he imagines the image will dissolve if he opens his eyes. It is fragile, like most dreams that evaporate once one awakens and tries to recall them. Like a drunkard, he is satiated with joyous confusion. He assumes that staying with the image long enough will chain it to his brain cells, before he opens his eyes and sketches it. Yet, his next conscious moment arrives at daylight.

Still recalling his agony last night in the twilight zone, he cheers when the picture created so painstakingly reappears in his mind with all its details. Swiftly he draws three sketches and gasps a sigh of relief. This particular painting can be done in the apartment, as every bit of it is imaginary, including the subtle surf washing the shore. Yet he decides to return to the Caspian Sea, where his passion was rejuvenated, to do this particular painting amidst the fragrances of the exotic flowers and plants filling the muggy air, with the sound of high surf pounding the shore.

Late one evening, Darren arrives at the villa, luckily alone this time, and gets everything organized for serious work early next morning. The excitement of the challenge ahead and the advent of a new era in his artistic life keep him restless all night.

After a small, quick breakfast, Darren begins throwing paint on canvas. His rapid brushstrokes and the impasto remind him of Vincent Van Gogh's paintings and he chuckles light-heartedly. The bizarre idea of Vincent's presence makes him shudder with goose bumps. Chatting with Vincent, however, appears to help him focus, but also avoid loneliness in the big villa. He paints leisurely and speaks with Vincent along the way for two days without anybody interrupting him. He pauses now and then for a snack or studying the progress. The sea calms down when he begins to paint a solemn mood, which he considers another omen

—besides Vincent's presence. He promises himself to document the mood and gist of his inspirational conversations with Vincent during the following nights back in Tehran. Exhausted after two days of hard work and chattering with Vincent, he stands back with relief and stares at the painting with a grin.

A man in jeans only is leaning against a chair, peering through a window overlooking a colourful, exotic garden that leads to a beach, where a woman in a white dress and wide brim sunhat is watching a sailboat, which is gliding slowly on the blue horizon, but nearly disappearing beyond the man's right view. He is admiring the woman who is immersed in her daydream, while surveying the sailboat solemnly. Darren chooses a title for the painting: The *Woman in the White Dress.*

Its overall structure and values look perfect to him. Thus, he decides to leave it to dry until he returns in two weeks to resume working on it.

"Is this what I think it is?" he asks Vincent loudly, staring at the painting and contemplating. No hint comes from Vincent. Yet Darren nods ardently and approvingly, plummets onto the couch, and bursts into tears. He weeps for five minutes, but then a big load seems to have lifted off his shoulders. He carefully hides the painting in Reza's bedroom closet, as the idea of somebody seeing it agitates him. He will also tell Reza not to show it to anyone, because it is about Erica.

The following day, he paints a landscape and leaves it in the living room in open view without fuss. He departs joyfully in the afternoon and arrives in Tehran near midnight, hoping to have skipped the air raid.

✳✳✳✳✳✳✳

"Your story seems to be a long one, Darren, ha?" T.J. asks.

"Oh, yes, but if you're tired, I can tell you the rest of it another time," Darren replies.

"No, actually I'm now getting hooked. I want to know what kind of mess you made for yourself in Tehran."

"So you want me to continue?" Darren asks.

"Yes, but let's go to the kitchen and make something to eat first," T.J. says, gets up quickly, and staggers toward the kitchen with Darren following him.

Chapter Three
The Midnight Angel

1

"Okay, now you can tell me the rest of your story in Tehran," T.J. says after they return from the kitchen and feel good about the supper they had put together quickly.

"That was a nice dinner, thanks," Darren says. "I didn't know you are such a great cook."

"I know you're mocking my cooking, but that was the best I could do after all that weed we've smoked," T.J. replies with a chuckle. "Go ahead with your story…"

"For five months, I traveled to Reza's villa and painted until atrocious snowfalls inhibited driving. So, I started painting only in my apartment from my pictures or sketches," Darren begins.

****

Two-dozen paintings have been completed so far and stacked up in the closet or around Darren's suite in Tehran. Meanwhile, he obliges himself to focus on a painting about his father, whose letters are getting bleaker every time, showing his surging senility, but still disregarding Darren's advice to join a retirement home. He gets depressed anytime he imagines his dad's faltering state of mind and growing hallucinations while living alone in icy Toronto with little mortal contact and support.

The *Woman in the White Dress* hangs in Darren's bedroom majestically now with a special aura that soothes his soul when he delves into it with a heightened passion for painting after years of abandoning the art world. Oddly, the idea of showing a man and a woman had also felt necessary for this particular painting against his normal inclination and strict philosophy. Well, since humans are so adamant to destroy Nature, he had sensed no point including them in his regular landscape paintings. How can water and fire be combined in a picture other than for showing the war between them? So his sudden impulse to include humans must have been goaded by a mysterious power, which seems to have possessed him throughout this particular painting, from inception to the last brushstroke! All this is his wild imagination, of course, Darren muses.

Reza arranges with a gallery to exhibit Darren's paintings, while planning secretly to buy the *Woman in the White Dress* himself.

"The gallery needs a price list," Reza says.

"Here…" Darren pulls out a list.

Reza reviews it. "Is this all your paintings?"

"No… Some of them aren't for sale."

"Oh? One painting in particular I wish to buy myself."

"Which one?"

"The one in your bedroom…"

Darren grins tensely. "I'm flattered you like my own favourite painting. But I'd like to keep it."

"I know. It was your first painting after so long."

"I also have other reasons," Darren replies with tension.

"Private reasons, I'm sure. But it has fascinated me too."

"Yeah…? It's funny it has *fascinated* both of us! I wonder why? What could be the demon in the painting *still* haunting both of us—perhaps that mysterious woman watching the boat?"

"Maybe… But I have an unselfish motive for buying it."

"Oh…? What's that?"

"I wanna buy it for Mahroo."

"For Mahroo?"

"Yes. The woman's melancholy moved me when I saw the painting in the villa. She reminds me of Mahroo. I really love her and feel guilty for bringing Zia into her life and causing her so much grief. She's suffering, but continues to tolerate the situation, mostly for Nazi's sake. She's sad and desperate. She's unaware of the gravity of her mental condition as we see it."

"Have you discussed your concern with her?"

"No I can't. It's not right. But my heart tore into pieces when I overheard her a couple of times confiding in our mother. I felt terrible. Her despair just drove me nuts."

"I'm sorry to hear that," Darren says.

"When I saw your painting, I felt I was the man watching Mahroo in her cherished white dress. He is concerned about the woman, but cannot raise the subject because it might hurt her feelings and aggravate her agony."

"Are you telling me Mahroo has a white dress like the one in the painting?" Darren asks with surprise.

"Yes … Maybe not exactly like the one in the painting, but very similar…"

"That's interesting…," Darren says. "So, you want to give the painting to her?"

"Yes… By giving Mahroo this painting as a gift, I hope she'll realize our worry about her stress and suffering. I can achieve this without saying a word or being too obvious. It might even give her a chance to open up to me a bit."

"Well, I hadn't imagined this painting could find therapeutic uses," Darren says with a hint of sarcasm. "But it has a special meaning and value for me, as you know."

"Yes, you told me it's about Erica…"

"Maybe I could paint another one with a similar composition for you?"

"Maybe… But there's something special about this particular painting. She appears alive as though trying to reach us. Have you noticed it?"

"Yes. That's another reason I like to keep it."

"Anyway, think about it; positively. Remember, you and I are like family. You won't be selling it to a stranger. Maybe after a few years, I'll sell it back to you if Mahroo agrees then, though I can't say anything to her about my promise to you or my real intention for giving it to her at this point."

"That's a tough position you're putting me into…," Darren says with a sigh.

"I'm desperately hoping to save the dying spirit of my darling sister," Reza blurts. "Somehow I think this painting can achieve that…"

"Okay, I'll think about it."

After Reza leaves, Darren lurches to the bedroom, plunges onto the bed and stares at the *Woman in the White Dress*.

Why should I be attached to a painting, especially this one? Doesn't my enlightenment depend on relieving myself from even the desire of 'attachment,' let alone an actual one? True, this painting has a sentimental value for me because I've projected my feelings onto it, to certain lines and colours I've thrown on a blank canvas. But where's Erica? Where's the soul I adored for all those years, which I no longer crave, anyway? In fact, I'd better forget Erica now finally… and keeping this painting would make it harder and only confuse me.

Darren feels relieved at seeing the bigger picture. He had fallen in love with the painting the night he had perceived the image, all the time painting it with Vincent around, and now that it hangs on the wall before him with its mysterious aura. He closes his eyes, as if printing the image in the deepest part of his consciousness.

"Do you want to go for a vacation—not on the boat yet, but to a friend's house, for now, until Erica is out of my mind forever?" Darren asks the *pensive woman*.

She is still gazing dolefully at the boat disappearing slowly in the horizon. However, in his mind, she waves agreeably without turning or showing her full face. Giving her up would be his most spiritual decision ever as well, Darren imagines with glee. *That is exactly why I should do it then!*

Before second thoughts spoil his divine feeling, he calls Reza and leaves a message for him.

"Reza, the *Woman in the White Dress* has agreed to be yours —only for a while, I hope."

2

Darren's message pleases Reza. But it also embarrasses him for having ignored Darren's six-month-old request to meet Dervish Ali. He calls Dervish Ali immediately and discusses Darren's request. Dervish Ali listens patiently before responding, "Reza jan, you know the answer. So what—"

"Yes, yes… I'd guessed your answer. But I couldn't ignore a genuine request carelessly."

"All right. Now you have my blessing to give him a suitable answer. Maybe later I can see you two together. Maybe you can help him for now. Ali's hand upon you."

Reza collects his thoughts and visits Darren the next day. "I talked to Dervish Ali about you and your interest in spirituality. He's agreed to see you later, but at this time he's very busy with special commitments."

"Doesn't he have regular classes?"

"He does, but only selected people can attend those rituals."

"I understand…"

"He asked me to explain some of the teachings of Sufism meanwhile. I'm not a guru, but perhaps I can help somehow."

"I was just wondering if spirituality can help me deal with my depression and pessimism."

"I'll help you weigh your emotions. If you couldn't find the answers, make a note until we go see Dervish Ali."

"Okay. Let me get the painting." Darren leaves and returns with the *Woman in the White Dress*.

"Thanks, Darren. I appreciate your sacrifice."

"No problem…"

"How much do I owe you?"

"Nothing, it's my gift to you."

"No, no, I must pay for it. It's hard to put a price on this—something everybody loves, but please tell me a price."

"I'd like to think I'm only lending her to you. Besides, I'm trying to value my special possessions differently now. This painting is one of them."

"Your mind is already more advanced than mine."

Darren follows Reza to the elevator and parking lot while safeguarding the painting. His sad eyes praise it all along, as if serenading an adieu aria from a famous opera to a departing lover. Then he feels Erica sailing out of his life for good now—finally, thank God.

3

Two nights later, Darren receives a call.

"Mr. Durant? This is Mahroo."

"Oh, hi… How's everybody, your little daughter?"

"Zia and Nazi are fine, thanks. We haven't seen you lately."

"I've been busy, when not hiding in the basement."

"Hopefully we'll see you soon," she says gleefully, with a trace of coyness in her voice. "Anyway, I'm calling to thank you personally for your beautiful gift. It is very lovely…"

He is speechless. He almost confesses that it isn't his gift to her, but rather to Reza. But then he finds it untactful to dampen someone's gesture of gratitude. Besides, maybe Reza had either intended to show Darren's generosity or just preferred presenting the painting to her in this manner. He shouldn't confess before consulting Reza.

After a long pause, he finally controls his nerves and replies, "You're welcome. I'm glad you like it."

"Reza said it's your favourite painting."

"Yes, this painting has a sentimental value for me." He swiftly regrets having blurted his emotions.

"Reza also mentioned your exhibition opening next week. He asked me and Zia to attend, if you don't mind."

"It's always a pleasure to see you and Zia."

"Okay then. Thanks a lot again, Mr. Durant."

"Oh, please call me Darren," he says casually, and then again regrets sounding personal.

"Okay, Darren, see you at the opening. Goodnight."

Mulling over the incident, Darren considers calling Reza, but quickly changes his mind. Obviously, Reza must have had his reasons, his tongue might have slipped, or Mahroo might have misunderstood him. *It's surely a simple mix-up; not a big deal. I'd better let it go before embarrassing everybody.* He has seen Mahroo at parties and had short conversations with her. These parties are usually too crowded and incoherent to him, mostly because everybody speaks in Persian. Sometimes, he has noticed young women measuring him or gossiping about him, followed by giggling or clumsy laughter. But Mahroo is always elegantly calm, mingling graciously, with a stunning beauty and figure. Another bizarre thing about these parties is the way women get rid of their Islamic kerchief and gown right away as they enter the house, to parade their hairs and bodies in the most liberal fashions, very much like a rebellious crowd. Even odder, when an actual raid, or hints about one, materializes, women's noisy scramble to find their hijab out of a big pile and cover their hairs and bodies quickly looks quite funny and educational. Raids happen when the Komiteh is informed of loud music or some other kind of forbidden activity in a house.

4

Darren keeps busy with the books and a manuscript that Reza lends him. He particularly likes the long manuscript, *Doubts and Decisions for Living*, written by an author named T.J.—Reza's new friend in Vancouver. Darren thinks this guy, T.J., has some good ideas, although he sounds like another lost soul himself. All along, he dreams about the gallery opening and the public's reaction to his new inspirations. His novel vision and boldness have emerged during a mystical trance often with Vincent's presence. Humorously, he also regards their cooperation a blessing that he cherishes privately. Nonetheless, these paintings represent a significant period in his life in terms of artistic achievement, self-actualization, and spiritual evolvement. They have at least brought him out of his artistic slump. Most importantly, they have helped him put Erica out of his mind.

The opening night is exhilarating, as his paintings sell in one hour and Mahroo arrives without Zia.

"Congratulations, Darren," she says with a soft voice and firm handshake.

"Thanks... Where's Zia?"

"He apologized; he was unable to come to Tehran."

She looks gorgeous, although only her face eludes the Islamic kerchief and gown. She gazes at him buoyantly all night, her eyes fixing on his with passion for seconds at a time. Darren enjoys the attention from such a beautiful creature, yet suffers from his rowdy sentiments that, in some moments, feel sinful. He tries to smile back cordially, but then gazes away swiftly or flees fast to another corner, pretending to be mingling. Sometimes he takes a guest to the farthest corner of the gallery to avoid her eyes. Still he feels a piercing tingle from her stare. But turning his head to verify, she isn't looking; though in a second she gently meets his eyes, seemingly awaiting hers. Then he hides his face abruptly with shame, all along realizing his childish gestures with further embarrassment.

After an eerie erotic episode throughout the evening, Mahroo and Reza congratulate him once more and leave. She squeezes his hand, her feverish palm infusing a flare of ecstasy through his body, her eyes reciting poetic verses, before leaving him alone in delirium.

The success of the exhibition and the exhilaration of the hot, surprising attention from a pretty woman, however innocent it might have been, evoke his depressed romantic emotions. *So, how can a novice like me proceed on the path of wisdom if he's so easily tempted by the ecstasy of success and forbidden affection? Have I failed the first test?* He wonders about his inner conflicts and whether they're good questions to ask Dervish Ali, if he ever gets a chance to meet him.

The fervour of both events gradually fades away over a week, though. *So, maybe I'm finding the answers without bothering Dervish Ali.*

5

Six months later, Darren feels a deep sense of self-actualization and spirituality. He has been painting even more seriously after the exhibition, while reading books and studying 'self-awareness' with Reza. Air raids are the only hindrance: descending the stairs every night and waiting in the dark basement. Still he knows that this inconvenience is a fair price for the lessons that the special circumstances in Iran afford him. *Missiles and bombs are falling all around me and I'm still alive.*

He muses over the previous night's incident: Reza was in his apartment, discussing the possibility of defining happiness, when the sirens blared and anti-aircraft guns impinged the silence and darkness of the night. Reza and Darren descended the staircase, alongside others, in an orderly fashion that residents had finally adopted. The parking area in the basement, with a steep driveway up to the ground level, was considered the safest refuge in the absence of bomb shelters. On the seventh floor, a man emerged from the stairwell door and charged down the stairs carelessly. He bumped everybody out of his way recklessly while clasping a large leather briefcase to his chest with crisscrossed arms.

"What's the matter with him?" Reza asked.

"He's usually running down the stairs and pushing others," Darren replied. "Maybe he's really scared."

A neighbour interjected: "No, he's only worried about that briefcase."

"Why? What's in it?"

"People say it's full of jewellery. He's a Jewish jeweller who's afraid about bombs destroying his shop one night and all his jewels disappearing in the aftermath, so he brings a good bunch of them home every night to keep close to his heart." Hardly had he finished his remarks when uproar erupted in the basement. When they arrived, the jeweller was flat on the ground with a bloody face.

"What happened?" Reza asked a resident in Persian.

"Two young men jumped him for his briefcase. He resisted, so they punched him. One of them waved a big dagger toward people, so nobody dared to interfere. Then, they fled with the case," Reza translates for Darren.

The caretaker was trying hard to calm the jeweller and help him go call the police. Clutching the caretaker's arm, he cried and cursed openly, spat blood, fainted twice, seemingly convinced already that the chance of finding the prowlers and recovering his jewels was zero. Still, the caretaker tried to propel him pitifully toward the phone in the main lobby. Somebody in their building had most likely leaked out the information about the briefcase, but whom and how to prove anything? With no insurance for this kind of robbery in Iran, his wealth and health had just vanished instantly. Darren and Reza exchanged dry, meaningful glances while recalling their conversations earlier about the *possibility* of defining happiness.

"The guy has been stupid, too, for parading that briefcase every night and hoping nobody would suspect what's in it or talk about it freely, at least for fun perhaps, until someone got tempted to rob him," Reza says to Darren.

"Are you saying he was asking for trouble?" Darren asks.

"I do," Reza replies. "But mostly to say he was quite stupid, exactly contrary to what he'd been thinking about his cleverness and presumed precautions all along."

"That's exactly what he needs to hear now... Go tell him," Darren says and they giggle, though feel pity for the guy.

Tonight, the sirens instigate Darren again, like the Pavlov's dog, to go to the basement. At the sixth floor, the Jewish jeweller, still baffled, staggers slower than a turtle. This time he has no case to carry, nor a case for caring. Residents descending at the normal pace bump him out of their ways against the wall or banister back and forth, but he is numbly unruffled. "Without the briefcase, why hurry?" his eyes reveal. "Why go to the basement at all?" But Darren believes that after five years of reacting to the sirens, people merely follow the routine unconsciously—an army of Pavlov's dogs descending the stairs.

Tonight, too, loud noises and frantic screams erupt as Darren reaches the second landing above the basement exit, while the crowd is filling the stairwell. He learns that the basement door is locked for some reason and the residents are stuck. They are just bitching and screaming about the thoughtless, missing caretaker and the stupid thing he has apparently done.

Darren pushes his way down to survey the situation: A thick chain has been run through and around the two small, glassless windows in the double door leading to the parking area. It seems the previous night's incident had goaded the caretaker to take this temporary measure to stop intruders from accessing the staircase and apartments through the busted emergency exit. A heavy-duty padlock ties the ends of the chain. Everybody examines the chain and the padlock to find a solution. However, they all quit quickly with despair. Some return to the upper floors to find the caretaker, call somebody for help, or maybe use the elevators, which they already know shuts down automatically during the air raids. Some have resigned and rest on the stairs, hoping for a miracle; maybe the arrival of the idiot caretaker with the key. "He's probably stuck in the heavy traffic somewhere," a neighbour yells. Others scream and swear. Only the jeweller stands calm on the upper landing with a smirk and solemn satisfaction. Tonight he is the bravest of them all.

A loud explosion, followed by a violent trembling of the walls, startles the crowd and they flip, fall, or howl. Dust gushes through the chained windows and from the cracks opening up in the walls. The trapped residents are now more frantic, thinking that the building has been hit by a missile. Nobody is hurt, but they weep and swear louder than the jeweller last night. Darren decides to inspect the chain like everybody else, more as a ritual now perhaps. But his scrutiny assures him that a radical solution is needed. Maybe he can remove the door hinges, but they are of the security type and impossible to unhinge even if he had some tools. He examines the double doors, jostles the two door handles, one on each panel. The doors jolt and the chain jingles, still too tight around the glassless windows to let the door panels loosen up.

He continues thrusting one handle at a time and yanking both panels from inside the broken windows. The chain's pressure against the solid oak panels, two inches thick, puts a small dent inside the window frames. A good sign. He resumes pulling and banging the panels, and a bit more of the wooden frame dents. The windows are about fourteen inches from the edge of each panel. So a lot of denting and tearing is required before the chain is released from inside one of the windows. Darren is determined, however. After a dozen forceful tugs, a half-inch dent in the right window looks promising. It also grabs the attention of some men who had been monitoring him pitifully and cursing him privately for making all that extra noise—a futile show of initiative and courage. They all rush to help now that he has apparently crafted a likely solution and decided that breaking the door is necessary. Two men at a time pull the doors, in a rhythmic motion. Within a minute, the dent is four inches; almost one-third of the job done. A glimmer of hope returns to the residents' eyes, while the men continue working in rotation. Ten minutes later, the helping men stand aside to let Darren take over. He seems eager to finish what he had started. But more importantly, let him be responsible for breaking the door and paying for all that damage!

Proud of his triumph, his body satiated by spiritual sensation and Samsonian strength, Darren puts all his might into a last pull to break the door: The tiny window ruptures, the chain flies, the two double doors fling open, and he is thrown off-balance down the stairs where the storage lockers are. He screams in pain and remains flat in the shadows, while people howl and charge out toward the parking lot like the freed prisoners of the Bastille.

He stares at his aching left thumb in bewilderment. It is twisted completely, now pointing toward the middle of his palm. He tries to straighten it, but screams from the excruciating pain blasting out of his right shoulder. The stairwell is now empty. Everybody has rushed to the garage, leaving him buried in the dark, dusty lower stairs. A few men had initially run to help him, but he had motioned them away, since touching any part of his body had been painful. They had left at last, despising his apathy and reluctance to get help. Now he is alone, as he had desired.

Holding his body still, he shifts the twisted thumb slightly. The pain surges in his left thumb and right shoulder, urging him to get up and out of that place to seek medical attention. Finally, he rises and ascends the stairs awkwardly. At the entrance, the broken door ajar and the locked chain dangling in vain from the left window, a couple of guys are returning to check on him after satisfying their curiosity about the situation in the parking lot and the earlier blast. Darren reels forward, ignoring the men watching him with concern and frustration for his tenacity and silence.

The residents are scattered around the parking lot, chatting in small groups or sitting in their cars. A thick fog of dust hangs in midair and another wave pushes its way into the garage slowly. Nobody dares leaving the basement to check the situation out there. After ten minutes, the sirens echo and the bright basement lights come on. The dust settles partly as Darren lurches toward the building entrance. In the street, he discovers a large crowd, an ambulance, and a deep hole filled with burning building debris.

The fierce sound of another explosion pins him to the ground. Smoke and fire blast out of the garage in his building. Watching the new commotion, he considers going back to help. But he turns toward the ambulance, thinking that, with his thumb and shoulder out of commission, he is helpless himself. The chaotic sight in the rubble subdues his pain, though. Dead bodies are lined up in one corner and people are carrying the wounded out of the ruins and loading them into the ambulance. A few, badly injured, lie in the middle of it, but the paramedics manage to sit four more in the corners of the ambulance and put one elderly woman in the front seat. At the last moment, Darren approaches the ambulance driver. He peers at Darren's warped shoulder and thumb and motions him to get in. Darren squeezes himself next to the moaning elderly woman, closes the door awkwardly with his left hand, and the ambulance pulls away.

Suddenly, another commotion goads the driver to stop for a man chasing the ambulance with a young boy in his arms. The driver gets out, assesses the situation and then opens the door on Darren's side, grabs the tiny, unconscious boy from the man, and lounges him in Darren's lap casually with no words.

Somewhat relieved, the father still looks puzzled and objects to the driver. But the driver pushes him away, shuts the door, shouts some Persian words to the man, and scurries to his seat. The ambulance pulls away, while the poor father keeps chasing it and yelling desperately again. He collapses at the street corner, jumps up quickly, and resumes pursuing it with blood running from his forehead now. He disappears in the dust at last as the ambulance speeds away.

The boy is unconscious in Darren's lap, soft like a rack of lamb. Many of his bones are probably broken, Darren reckons. A fracture runs from his hairline to the tip of his eyebrow, blood seeping slowly, though the crack seems clogged with mud and clotted blood. Darren's right arm hangs uselessly, but he holds the boy's upper body with his left hand despite the pain in his broken thumb. He sits stiffly to avoid hurting the boy or dropping him off his lap. His pain soars whenever he moves his shoulder to maintain the lower part of the boy's body, which keeps sliding away with the jerky motions of the ambulance. He squeezes and heaves his thighs to keep the boy steady.

The boy's subtle chest movements make a wheezing noise. The lines of clean skin etched below his closed eyes and along his muddy face reveal the traces of dried tears. Darren wishes he knew his name to call him. Instead, he clutches the boy's body gently, tugs him closer to his own chest, and squeezes the boy's arm once more.

To his astonishment, the boy opens his eyes slowly and peers at Darren with a gentle grin. Darren smiles and stares into his eyes, which glisten with passion and pain. They gaze at each other for one minute before Darren notices the glow in the boy's eyes diminishing until it is dull, yet he keeps staring. His chest movements and faint smile evaporate soon after. Darren shakes him gently and pinches his arm again, but the boy does not react and his body gets looser.

"This boy's dead," Darren mumbles to the driver. The old woman, watching him and the boy, faints over the driver.

"We're... right there... quickly...," the driver mumbles with broken English, struggling to straighten the old woman and steer the car at the same time.

A volunteer takes the boy from Darren and points toward the emergency entrance. Inside, he is led to a corner to wait. Later, he discovers that only bleeding patients are directed to the main waiting area. *What if someone's bleeding internally, you idiots?*

After an hour, a nurse emerges to get the patients' names and assess their injuries. Two hours later, he is still waiting. The nurse appears occasionally and reads out someone's name to follow her to the main room. He is frustrated, dizzy, thirsty, and hungry, but cannot risk leaving the area to find a water fountain or food.

The next time the nurse shows up, he flings out his fine arm. She comes over reluctantly and he pleads politely, "I'm fainting and the pain is killing me."

The attractive nurse checks her list without asking his name. "There's no express lane for you. We have 200 patients here alone," she says impatiently and leaves before he can object. She returns for him after 45 minutes.

The main waiting area is also chaotic, patients moaning and screaming, nurses and doctors running around firmly. The nurse shows Darren a wheelchair and leaves. Another hour passes, all along Darren leaning his head against the wall to avoid fainting. Sometimes a patient is wheeled toward the operating rooms at the end of the corridor. At last, a homely nurse arrives, reviews his chart, examines his shoulder and thumb, and asks how he feels.

"Terrible. I need a painkiller and water, please."

"Okay, wait a minute. I'll bring the doctor. After he signs your chart, I'll give you a shot."

Twenty minutes later, she returns with a doctor who examines him fast, instructs the nurse, and leaves with another nurse. The nurse pushes his wheelchair to a big room with drapes separating a dozen gurneys. She helps him onto an empty one, connects an IV to his arm and gives him a shot of Demerol. Finally, he relaxes, barely noticing the gurney moving for x-ray and surgery.

6

Darren wakes up mid-morning amidst the hospital's commotion. A volunteer helps him feed himself clumsily and a doctor checks him and prescribes painkillers. The volunteer then helps him into a wheelchair and rolls it to the main lobby. "Go call someone to come and get you. The phones are beside the reception."

He rises slowly out of the wheelchair and reels forward to call Reza. The tip of his thumb shows outside the cast and his arm and shoulder are protected by plasters. The pain is gone but he feels weak.

Near the reception, he hears his name and turns awkwardly like Frankenstein. Mahroo is smiling shyly, as charming as she had looked in the gallery six months before.

"What're you doing here?" he asks.

"I've come to take you home," she replies.

"How'd you know?"

"Reza found out about the missile hitting your neighbourhood last night and your ordeal in the basement. The residents had told the story to the caretaker and he told it to Reza. Reza had to fly to Dubai this morning, and Zia is in Shiraz as usual. So Reza asked me to come and get you."

"Thanks. But I don't want to trouble you."

"It's no trouble. Reza said you saved many lives."

"I did? How…?" Darren asks, but then remembers the second explosion in the basement. "I heard an explosion in the street."

"A gas pipe had ruptured when the missile cracked the walls of your building. It blasted later when someone lit a cigarette."

"Wow… That's terrible… I'm glad people had at least got out of the staircase," he says, trying to imagine what could have happened behind the closed door ten minutes earlier.

Outside the hospital, Darren recognizes the man sitting on the steps, weeping over a body in his arms.

"I'm sorry about your son," Darren says.

The man stares at him in bewilderment. Darren sits beside him and surveys the flesh in his lap. No mistake; it is the boy he had carried in the ambulance, wrapped in a shroud, with his eyes closed now. He gazes into the man's curious eyes.

"I carried your son in the ambulance, but he died peacefully before we got here. He was a brave boy. I wish I'd given you my seat to be with him when he opened his eyes to say goodbye. I'm sorry."

The mystified man looks up toward Mahroo with agony. She kneels next to him and repeats Darren's comments in Persian.

He surveys Darren, sighs, and blurts, Mahroo translating, "I wish I hadn't been working late and had died with my family. How can I live now? I laboured like a donkey to feed them, but let them all die in vain."

Mahroo tries to console him. "Don't blame yourself. This is fate. Your family is now in heaven with Allah."

The man cries, "But why? Why isn't He nice to me? I'm a good Muslim, I swear."

"Our fates are fixed. Let's help you now," she says helplessly.

"Thanks. My brother will come to take us to the cemetery," he replies, tears flooding his face. As Mahroo and Darren rise to leave, he pulls the shroud over his son's head and continues, "Ask your husband whether my son said anything?"

Mahroo blushes while translating the question, excluding the reference to 'husband.' Darren shakes his head before they leave.

She is bawling quietly at first, but then her face flushes with fury as she sits behind the wheel. "Shame on all those criminals like Saddam who are killing our children ruthlessly. Shame on the United Nations, which is only a puppet in the hands of the superpowers. Shame on all those cowboys who treat the rest of the world like cattle. Shame on all those intellectuals who only bite their tongues in silence."

Intimidated, Darren waits for her to calm down. She finally quits when they get to a pharmacy. She fills his prescription, and drives toward her house.

"Where're we going?" Darren asks.

"To my house. You can't stay alone in this condition."

"No, I don't wanna bother you. I'll be all right."

"Do not be shy, Darren. Reza asked me to help you until he returns in three days, and I'm happy to do it. Besides, Martha, my maid, will be nursing you while you rest in the guestroom. Nazi and I will go about our business as usual, as if you weren't there. So let's not argue," she asserts and speeds up to show her resolve.

"But…"

"Just relax, Darren, and let us take care of you for a few days,' Mahroo says while looking in his eyes with a soft grin.

7

Darren feels better already, lying in a comfortable bed in a cozy guestroom with maid service and homemade food. He changes into Zia's clean pyjamas awkwardly and puts his dirty clothes in the basket Martha shows him. He stares at the ceiling and walls and falls asleep. After lunch, he watches a video stacked in the TV cabinet.

Passing by the guestroom, Mahroo notices him watching *Sophie's Choice*. Two hours later, she startles him with only half her face visible from the crack of the door. "Did you enjoy the movie?"

Darren turns his head jerkily and it hurts. "Yes, I did."

"May I come in?"

"Yes, please," he murmurs.

She strolls toward the bed and stares at him. "It's a sad movie."

"How much agony we humans must bear, even for love?" he asks, admiring her lustrous hair hanging over her bare shoulders.

"A lot apparently," she replies.

"Even when we're lucky enough to find a comfortable life or a lover, another setback ruins everything soon enough."

"Love is a lousy affair, right…? Not 'splendid' at all…!"

Darren only nods pensively.

"How do you feel, Darren?"

"I'm fine. You like this kind of movies?" he asks.

"Yes, I like dramas, especially with a love story angle."

"What kind of love did Nathan and Sophie share?"

"A weird one... don't you think?"

"It was love out of necessity and loyalty between Nathan and Sophie, I think. For Stingo, it was only a raw infatuation."

"I guess," Mahroo replies.

"We think love has the same meaning for everybody. But it changes based on lovers' life circumstances and personalities."

"That's very true...," she says and pauses for his reaction.

As he stares at her in silence, she continues, "For me, love has been only an exhausting dream. Although I really like to feel loved."

"Most people have become too needy for love nowadays."

"Are you in the mood to walk around the house? I'd like to show you something."

"Sure," he says eagerly, tired of lying in bed all day.

She leads Darren to the living room, where he is impressed with the ravishing elegance swiftly. The grand room is tastefully decorated with stylish furniture and a large open area at the end. There, on the big wall hangs the *Woman in the White Dress* in a gracious frame with three spotlights showing off its colourful details, especially a variety of violet and red flowers in the garden leading to the beach. He falls in love with it all over again, staring in awe, reminiscing the hours he had worked on each section and detail. Four minutes of silence keep Darren in a trance.

"I'm the woman in the white dress apparently!"

"What makes her so special for you?" he asks timidly with scepticism.

"Her mood; the way she stares solemnly at the horizon and the boat. I also like the way the man gazes at her so anxiously from inside the room. Obviously he wants to go out, embrace, and kiss her, but he's hesitant; worried about a taboo, perhaps."

"Hmm..." Darren sighs.

After a long pause and measuring Darren, hoping for some kind of reaction, she continues, "I believe you're the 'man'!"

Searching for a proper response, he remains speechless.

So she continues, "No doubt you've expressed your feelings beautifully. It's amazing how you've captured my mood without even showing my full face; especially since we'd spoken only sporadically and briefly."

Darren feels trapped again; how should he solve this delicate dilemma? Telling her the truth would only crush her aching heart, not a tactful act to inflict upon such an elegant, kind host. It would also reveal both Reza's secret and intention after all this time. But how long can he let this masquerade continue? He must confess that he did not know her then, and even now, let alone portraying her in a painting he had created merely based on his love story with Erica.

"When Zia discovered that the painting was your gift and how much I liked it, he got really angry. He punched the wall with a glass of wine in his hand. It shattered and ripped his palm, and the wine splashed all over the wall and the antique carpet. He then grabbed a knife and rushed to tear up the painting, but I stood before him and swore that if he ever did anything to it, he'd never see me again."

"Oh, gosh! I couldn't picture this side of him," Darren says.

"Oh, yes. He has a hot temper beneath that easygoing face and comic behaviour."

"We all get upset sometimes illogically."

"But the problem is that we keep hurting one another with our temper and other quirks."

"That's true. That's why people hardly find peace."

"You're so pessimistic, too, like me."

"Experience and sincere self-analysis show our natural flaws and naivety... How much do you think you know about yourself, for example?" he asks, hoping to create an opportunity to explain Mahroo's obvious misunderstanding about the painting.

"Enough, I guess," she replies, somewhat bewildered and intimidated.

"You'd be surprised how little we know about ourselves, while our wild perceptions confuse us, too," he says carefully as a prelude to point out her misunderstanding. But, a sudden panic attack overwhelms him swiftly. "When is Zia coming back? I'd better go home."

"Why? What's wrong?"

"I'm worried now, considering his reaction to the painting."

"Oh. Don't be. He's not coming back soon."

"Still I shouldn't be here…"

"Wait until Reza calls tonight at least."

"No, I think Zia will get upset… I'd better go."

"If Reza says to go on the phone, I'll take you right away."

"Well… Okay… But I'd better go to the guestroom at least. Being near this painting and hearing these stories are stressful."

"True… This painting has caused enough gloom," Mahroo says tenderly. "But we must also accept the reality, ha?"

Confused even more by Mahroo's last comment, he still hates asking for elaboration and instead rushes to the guestroom.

8

Darren refuses to go downstairs for dinner. Instead, Martha brings his meal upstairs, while Mahroo and Nazi dine together, amazed at his sudden ungracious attitude. He, too, wonders about his manners. Why is he so defensive and fussy about her words? They may all be innocent chitchat, but he is too uptight about the meaning of every word or gesture. He wonders if he is attracted to her subconsciously, afraid of his lustful urges despite the lessons of integrity and self-control he has been trying to learn.

Later that evening, Reza calls and orders him to stay put until he returns in two days. The next day is even longer and more unsettling. Mahroo checks on him briefly a few times, to announce her departure or arrival, or to ask whether he needs anything. At night, he feels more relaxed about the situation, after enough contemplation and convincing himself that he has not committed any crime and being there is somebody else's idea—actually against his will. So, to show his gratitude and courtesy, he informs Martha that he will join the family for dinner.

When summoned for supper, he is quite chirpy, convinced that 'discovering' Mahroo is not a taboo, but rather a gesture of etiquette. He has probably offended her with his attitude enough already. He apologizes for arriving in his robe because of his condition, and he behaves quite jovially, to everybody's surprise. He jokes with Nazi and Martha, and grins at Mahroo, who has particularly dressed up for the occasion. Her straight black hair, sprawling over her bare, long neck, contrasts her snowy, soft skin. How can he not smile tenderly at such a pretty creature?

They drink wine and engage in a nightlong duel of alluring smiles and flirtation, somewhat impudently. His drastic change of mood surprises her, but she believes her story about Zia must have intimidated him. So why fuss now that things look on the right track? His sudden interest to 'discover' her comes across as an attempt to win her soul. Her romantic desires make her blush and he imagines she is drunk.

9

Darren senses a soul nearby at midnight, opens his eyes abruptly, and shifts his head with pain. The shimmer of her satin robe in the subdued darkness manifests her like an angel. The loose robe reveals the soft skin of her neck and her black eyes shine in her pale face. He is speechless, not only from the absurdity of her presence, but also his shattered senses in a twilight zone. For a long while, he cannot even remember where he is. He must be running a high fever or sunk deep in a nightmare.

She whispers instead, "What is it, Darren? Do you need something?" He only keeps staring at her like a zombie. So, she continues, "You screamed. But when I came to help, you were asleep, then screamed again and opened your eyes. Do you have pain... or had a nightmare?"

Mute, he blinks in the darkness, speechless like a corpse, thinking, *Maybe a nightmare!* She sits at the edge of the bed, holds and presses his hand. She then touches his forehead, as if checking his temperature. Yet, her familiar palm's heat surpasses his body's warmth vastly and fills him with a soothing sensation. His tension vanishes mysteriously. Her bare chest shows partially underneath the satin robe, thumping tempestuously. He is dying to caress it, but his hands and mind are numb. Again, he is the defenceless Darren in his nightmares, totally at her mercy, yet he realizes angels are only capable of healing and cleansing. *So there's no need to panic or fear her.*

The angel whispers, "I feel your passion, Darren. Fighting our temptations for a touch is tough. Only a hair separates a sacred love from a scandal, and no one can cross this thin line without tumbling into the hellhole. I know how you feel, but it's always wiser to sacrifice our love for saving our souls. We don't want to hurt anybody or ourselves." Darren stares at her hypnotically with blank eyes almost certain he is only imagining those poetic words rather than coming out of that angel's mouth. He merely keeps staring at her.

"If you don't need anything, go back to sleep," Mahroo says.

She gazes into his eyes for a moment, and then leans over and kisses his cheek. He is filled with ecstasy despite the numbness of his mind and body. Slowly she rises and reels toward the door even slower. She will never reach the door, he believes. But eventually the hallway light shimmers through the crack of the door, the slender flesh blocks it briefly, and it fades away as the light narrows and dies.

In the dark room, he is perplexed: *Was it all a dream?*

****

"It's midnight," Darren says, checking his watch. "I talked too much."

"Nice story," T.J. utters with blank eyes, looking rather lost about the story he has heard.

"I'm still not sure whether the last part of the story was real or only a dream or hallucination…"

"You don't?"

"Not really… In fact, almost everything felt surreal during the three days I stayed in Mahroo's house."

"It might have also been the effect of the painkillers you were taking," T.J. says.

"Yes, I wondered about that too…"

"So what's the ending of your story?" T.J. asks.

"There's no special ending. After that night, I felt homesick and disoriented, not only because of the events in Mahroo's house, but about how my whole life, including companionship and career, was unsettled. Maybe the war had also affected me more than I'd imagined. I didn't meet Mahroo again, despite my strong urges and curiosity. Finally, after working in Tehran for over two and a half years, I felt fidgety again. All this time, I hadn't spoken to someone without a Persian accent. They were nice people, but the language barrier, their lifestyle and culture, got to me. My main joy was going to the Caspian Sea, painting, and sobbing in private for one thing or another or nothing at all. That had become my only refuge all along. Witnessing people's misery and distress from the war, traffic and smog, and my meaningless affairs became intolerable for me. Above all, I felt partly responsible for Zia's deteriorating state of mind."

"What happened to him?"

"When he learned I'd stayed in his house for three days, he went berserk. With his depression and the painting's background, my intrusion was the last straw. He reacted harshly and forbade Mahroo to talk to me again. I wasn't invited to the parties anymore. Mahroo became more frazzled, mostly because of the way Zia treated and threatened her. Reza mentioned many horror stories about both Mahroo's and Zia's conditions, which affected him, too. Reza didn't blame me directly, since he'd been in close contact with me all along and knew that my messed up mind was somewhere else totally—trying to find my own sanity perhaps. So, at last, Reza agreed to my request to return to Vancouver. In fact, he generously paid the full amount of the contract, plus a lot more as profit sharing. He preferred to get me out of Tehran, too, I guess, so that perhaps Zia relaxed a little and things improved between husband and wife."

"But you weren't sure whether Reza knew about Mahroo's infatuation for you?" T.J. asks.

"No… I could not guess or ask Reza whether he knew what issues were bothering Mahroo or Zia, especially in relation to me besides Zia's general jealousy," Darren replies.

"And you were in Vancouver when Zia died?"

"Yes. Reza mentioned the car accident, somewhat relieved that Mahroo may now find a more suitable husband and put her life back together. I got the impression from him that she'd just recently hinted—perhaps only casually—at my possible affection for her."

"Are you in love with her?"

"No… I can't even have a normal, long-term relationship with someone these days. But I admit Mahroo's beauty is hard to resist. She's quite vulnerable, coming out of her present mess of a marriage, and I mustn't agitate her even more by giving her a wrong impression. A misunderstanding has gone too far for so long, all thanks to Reza's bad communication with her about the painting."

"I see! Your work seems to have been cut out for you," T.J. says with a chuckle.

Chapter Four
Chilling Memories

1

Darren arrives at the Elixir at 10:34 a.m., an excellent record of punctuality for him, even in Nora's opinion if she had not been so testy today.

"You're late again," Nora mutters with a smirk.

"I'm only four minutes late!" Darren replies with a glare.

"Jerry's waiting for you. We'll talk later," Nora mumbles without looking straight at him.

Darren throws a nervous grin at her and walks toward Jerry's office. Her attitude, apparently the upshot of their niggling phone conversation two nights before, vexes Darren. Behind the closed door, he indulges Jerry, too, for thirty minutes, returns to Nora's desk, and waits impatiently. She is probably hiding in the stockroom to irritate him, knowing that he loathes waiting.

After ten minutes, she peeks from the hallway corner and blurts, "I'll be with you in a sec."

He peers at her and Peggy Armistead, her assistant, who peers at Darren with a flirtatious grin today as well, while Nora gives her meticulous instructions, cunningly testing Darren's patience. Finally, she strolls to her desk.

"So what you think about the commission?" she asks.

"It's a nice project. But I'd better prepare some sketches and get his feedback before starting the actual painting."

"That's a good idea. He's grumpy these days. Did you discuss money too?"

"Yes."

"Well?"

"Well, what?" He feels like horsing around a bit for revenge.

"How much? You know he'll tell me."

"Yes, I know. You don't have to brag about it all the time."

"I'm not... Are you starting with me again this early in the morning?"

"Fifteen grand, plus maybe another five as bonus, minus *your* fat commission, of course. He should've offered the entire twenty unconditionally. Can you convince him?"

"He probably has his reasons, but I'll try…"

"I'd assumed you guys are familiar with my work by now."

"But this is much larger than your average paintings and also a bit trickier perhaps. So he may have a point," Nora says.

"I always do my best on every painting, anyway."

"You sound a little testy this morning, Darren."

"I am testy?" Darren asks, wondering if she has a point.

"Yeah, you are…," Nora replies impatiently.

"Forget Jerry. But do you also think that a promise for bonus would affect my efforts and creativity even if I was greedy?"

"So what's a good incentive for you to paint a special piece?" she asks curtly.

"I can't think of anything this moment. Do you?"

"Maybe a pretty whore to paint, too, afterwards?"

Darren resents her bizarre bitterness and sarcasm today. Yet, he shrugs with a devilish smirk. "That sounds interesting! Talk to Jerry about it. Maybe a nude goddess could arouse my super creativity to paint a masterpiece and more, after all."

"All right… I will," Nora says.

"But who'd be the judge? Not Jerry, I hope."

"How about a jury, based on their arousal from your nude masterpiece?" Nora says, while feeling really tired of his tenacity to argue this morning.

"And I guess you'll be the one going around measuring their arousals, one by one?" Darren cannot resist blurting the vulgar remark, against his normal inclination. Her odd rebellion today is rather unexpected and depressing. She is a master of intimidation, but the way she has also raised the devil inside him today is most humiliating for a person striving to cleanse his soul.

"We're both foolish today," Nora says with angst.

"You're right… I'm sorry."

"I guess I'm also a bit pooped these days," she says softly.

"Why don't you let me paint you in nude, anyway?" he asks with a giggle.

"Darren, we must talk," Nora demands irately.

"Let's meet tomorrow night… T.J. and I talked until late last night and I had to come here so early just for you taunting me."

"Fine… How about the new paintings?" she asks slyly, as if still seeking another excuse to nag at him.

Darren hands her the list he had prepared the night before, quite satisfied about his own intuition for having anticipated this moment and making a fictitious list accordingly. He cannot stop his sense of adventure and horseplay despite his desire to be a serious, spiritual scholar as well.

She checks the list in shock. "You're sure about these dates?"

"Yes, I worked a lot yesterday after such a long time."

"You got energy and inspiration from the night before, ha?"

Recalling Elizabeth, Darren agrees privately.

"Yes. I'd better go work some more today," he says, standing up. "You'll see the new paintings I've started tomorrow night."

At his apartment, Darren feels uninspired to paint, thanks to Nora's outrageous attitude. He grabs a beer and flips through his picture album to get ideas for another group of paintings. Often he combines the ideas from several pictures and adds his spicy notions to create a dramatic composition. He then makes some notes and puts everything, including a title for each painting, into an envelope, ready for the actual work.

He sketches for a while, then goes to the Island for supper, flirts with the waitresses a bit, watches an opera video in the apartment, and goes to bed early.

2

The next evening, he takes Nora to Chez Michel and orders an expensive bottle of Bordeaux, hoping the ambience would return Nora to her normal classy self. Still, she seems quite preoccupied.

"Jerry's arranging a publicity interview with the *Vancouver Sun*," Nora says.

"What about?" Darren asks.

"About the commissioned painting and its destination. Also, it's time for the world to learn about you. We're planning to have an exhibition for you in London next year, if you can paint enough."

"London, England?"

"Yeah. You're becoming a famous painter now. You'd better remember how it all started just a few months ago."

"I'll never forget how good you've been to me, Nora!"

"I hope so!" she said with a giggle. "We'll print a booklet of your works, too. Bring some pictures of your favourite paintings. The story of the *Woman in the White Dress* might also be suitable for the interview and the booklet."

"Thanks, Nora," he says, raising his wineglass, clinking hers.

"I promise you'll become a renowned painter soon if you just manage your life better and…" She pauses abruptly.

"I'll try. But life distracts us sometimes. I can't help that."

"You need a more stable life and relationship."

"Everybody tells me that recently!" Darren says.

"Like who? How many girls are prodding you like me?"

"Oh, never mind."

"No, just tell me."

"My neighbour, Mrs. Stanley, said it a few days ago in the elevator."

"We are all right, however. You need a new wife."

"I'm not ready yet…"

"You should at least have a serious relationship," Nora says.

"But most relationships kill our spirits nowadays. They make me so depressed sometimes I can't draw a single line for weeks."

"You must learn to focus somehow…"

"Well, that's why I'm spending so much time on meditation, instead of looking for a wife. Still, I'm saving a lot of time and energy with much less hassle."

"I know you're just kidding around. But your cynicism is too harsh. You're isolating yourself from the rest of the world."

"Yeah, something is wrong with me these days."

"Nothing is wrong with you. You're just becoming too damn cynical and philosophical about everything. That'll ruin your life and jeopardize your art in the process, too."

"But what can I do about this rotten world?"

"Nothing!" Nora gives up edgily.

"Are you mad at me for something special these days?"

"Listen, Darren, prepare and bring some sketches of the commissioned painting for the interview, too, if you can."

At his apartment, Darren pours two shots of Grand Marnier, sits beside Nora, and steals a kiss from the corner of her lips.

"You wanna listen to music or watch a video?" He asks.

"Whatever…"

"Last night, I watched the video you gave me. It's a very good performance. I love those beautiful arias and duets."

"*Tosca…*? Why don't you play it while we talk?"

Darren rewinds and starts the tape in the VCR. He then sits next to Nora and embraces her tightly, like grasping a brash pussycat and hampering its escape, all in a passionate and witty manner. "Well, my dear, what's really bothering you?"

"I'd hoped you'd realize my concerns yourself, considering your analytical mind. I hate to explain the obvious," Nora replies.

"Nothing's obvious to me. Besides, I'd never liked to pry into your affairs."

"Exactly. You don't care about me and my problems."

"I've always believed your personal life is private and you'd share it with me as much as you feel comfortable."

"My affair with Jerry should end, but I cannot figure out my relationship with you, either. I've been in a stalemate for a long time and my affairs' ambiguity is driving me nuts, especially when I see how cool you are about everything. I've been trying to gather a clue about your feelings, even if it's progressing slowly. But, honestly, I see nothing."

"I like our friendship. What else can I offer?"

"I'll never beg for romance. But since you're asking, I'll tell you that every woman likes to feel loved."

"Do you love me?"

"I don't know!" Nora replies with hesitance, but realizes her blunder fast. "But I could love you in the right circumstance."

"Are you saying that you'll learn to love me if I tell you *I love you*?" he asks, testing and teasing her playfully.

"I don't like your way of playing with my words."

"You're the one confusing the meaning of 'love'! I was just explaining the same point to my friend two nights ago."

"You had a 'love' problem with *her* too?" she asks slyly.

"I have no love problem. We were merely discussing social issues, including love." he realizes his big mouth has divulged incriminating information. Or maybe he is subconsciously driven to inform her about his other affairs. He wonders what he really prefers to do.

"Of all the issues in the world, you always end up discussing love with all your friends?"

"Not always…"

"I think you're manipulating all your lovers," Nora blurts with fury. Now her suspicion about his so-called *friend* two nights ago, when they had talked on the phone, grows stronger. *How serious his affair with that woman is,* she wonders.

"No, you're overreacting," he says sheepishly to calm her.

Yet, Nora is unwilling to let him off the hook easily now. She needs more information urgently. Darren's friend must have been a woman, for sure, despite his deliberate ambiguity and her pride stopping her from asking him directly, then and now. She thinks that learning more about his discussions with the so-called 'old friend' may reveal his type of relationship with that woman.

"So, what were you telling *her*?"

"That love is not a major factor for building a good marriage," he mumbles.

"Did *she* agree?" Nora hits another blow to confirm her sad suspicions completely, if he dares to ignore her reference to 'she.'

"I don't remember." Darren realizes his defeat. The answer is correct in itself, because he only remembers the final round of arguments, Elizabeth calling him an idiot, leading to exhilarating adventures in the bedroom. However, this is not something to ruminate on when Nora is questioning his integrity. Her repeated sneaky references to 'she' and 'her' are quite annoying. Yet his cunning refusal to deny or admit the truth has only raised Nora's suspicions. A bizarre sensation is dampening his spirit, while his emotions for Nora are derailing fast as well. His insincerity is hurting him, too, perhaps more than it is bothering Nora.

"What else you told *her*?" Nora can play her game forever now.

"That we express love superficially, a thousand times to many people to boost our relationships, flatter our partners, or be loved in return," he feels obliged to blabber only in hopes of distracting Nora, but has lost force and conviction. "We want to feel alive and complete by loving someone. And now you claim you can *learn* to love me… Love isn't something to learn or mimic!"

"You're talking nonsense," Nora asserts angrily.

"You don't even understand my points, so how can we fall in love?" Darren keeps arguing merely in hopes of distracting Nora enough to stop interrogating him about his 'friend.'

"Everybody knows what love is."

"That's what we think. It's all only our imagination, though."

"Have you ever loved somebody, Darren?"

"Yes… at least I thought I did!" He is struggling to stay cool, but suddenly feels the communication channels with this woman called Nora shattering, like a desiccated tree branch snapping—a sudden, weird, disheartening experience.

"Who? Erica? I bet that one bad experience has ruined you."

"All I'm saying is that people are often dishonest about love."

"Not everybody can be so casual like you about their feelings and needs. Most people have to use all kinds of skills, tricks, lies, and flattery to keep a relationship," she says with tension.

"And still you consider all that phoniness and trickery love?" he asks with distress. Deep down, however, he both respects and amazes at her honesty and nerve to blurt out the truth about the reality of relationships nowadays.

"Whatever… You just refuse to get my points today…"

"If you like to know, I really loved Erica and she said she loved me, too… And I believed her like an imbecile."

"Actually, I'd really like to know what happened with Erica, if you don't mind sharing your experience."

"My love story with Erica is depressing for me at least."

"Well… Forget it if you rather not talk about it…"

"It is, but since you're so eager to know, I'll tell you the tale of my lousy love affair and marriage."

****

(1973–1984)

Darren's primary image of Erica remained intact as the cute, clever girl he had courted during their adolescence. In fact, this persistent, naive picture confused him further when anger and antagonism besieged their last years of marriage. Especially, as Erica's evilness became more evident every day, his memory of their romantic times and her lost innocence and sweetness incited only more sorrow and sour thoughts for Darren. Those stubborn images also raised a deep sense of self-pity regarding his past naivety about her and human nature.

They had both endured growing-up traumas, high school pains, and divorced parents who had badgered and badmouthed each other mainly to win the sympathy of their children. They felt each other's misfortunes of living with their estranged parents and soothed each other's suffering naturally through heartfelt communication and funny family stories. Darren's insensitive mother died of ovarian cancer when he was seventeen and he became even more susceptible to Erica's affection. They fell in love despite their personality disparities and erratic struggles for both independence and dependence. They shared their juvenile thoughts and raw perceptions about life, love, and their future together. Their minds joined, while their physical encounters proved pure gold for an erotic novel. Sex was a heavenly ritual they had invented all by themselves—a sacred secret they savoured to save their souls. So, unlike their classmates, who changed partners frequently, they endeared their physical union as a temple for spiritual growth—a dais for worship. They were true sweethearts.

Their juvenile relationship evolved into a vivacious romance after high school graduation. They worked part-time, pursued their education, and planned to marry eventually. Most people envied their affair as a symbol of sacred affection. Erica studied computer science at the University of British Columbia, while Darren started at Capilano College, and then transferred to the Emily Carr Institute of Art. The first taste of reality befell them during the last years of college while they lived together. School responsibilities, household chores, and Darren's night job at a restaurant hampered their chance for romance. Instead, new friends and experiences kindled their curiosity for independence, which had been ignored. They agreed that some autonomy would nurture their relationship and prepare them better for their marital life upon graduation. They trusted life and love innocently.

Finally, the occasion they had waited and planned for, for seven years, personally or jointly, explicitly or dreamily, arrived. Darren Durant and Erica Swanson wed in July 1981, and spent a romantic honeymoon in San Francisco and Carmel.

3

Soon, career planning took precedence. Erica accepted an offer from her classmate, Cameron, to start a computer-consulting firm, SDI. Cameron's father, Ricky Slingers, provided good ideas and subcontracts. Within fifteen months, SDI became a major firm with forty employees. Erica was ecstatic about business challenges and success. After long hours six days a week, she still brought home more work and phone conversations with staff, Cameron, or clients. She drew energy and ecstasy from work more than anything else. And Darren began sensing a bizarre aloofness behind her apparent calm and lethargic passion. Still he hoped for a less hectic future once SDI's business settled and Erica's need for success subsided.

Conversely, Darren had not achieved much as a novice artist, despite his strenuous efforts. His works were presented in local exhibitions and he had won a few prizes, but had gotten no break. The harder he worked, the less he attracted tangible interest or support from major galleries. Two galleries presented his works tentatively, but could not sell him to their clients as an emerging artist. After two years of struggling, his self-image was shattering at the time Erica's was boosting daily. To alleviate his stress, he resorted to drinking. He dined alone outside regularly, returned home desolate, and drank for hours while waiting anxiously for Erica. Occasionally he cooked to amuse himself and left some for Erica, who normally lacked appetite or energy for anything.

One year later, proud Erica bought the house of her dreams. It became a heftier cocoon for Darren to feel lonely and trapped. He considered finding some kind of job soon to rescue himself, though not a kind disgracing Erica. But what? With the horrible economy and high unemployment during those gloomy years, finding a job not too humiliating for Erica's husband proved insurmountable. Stressed out and desperate, eventually he welcomed artist friends and neighbours who stopped by more routinely to drink and smoke pot. His demise troubled Erica, too, watching his anguish, lack of a career, and pitiful friends—*the losers*. She decided to confront him, but after their housewarming party, which was planned for the following week.

Their friends, including Elizabeth and Jeff, as well as Erica's colleagues came with presents and pretentious compliments. The hoopla only humiliated Darren and aggravated his sense of inferiority in the shadow of Erica's rising success and so many pompous friends, whom he despised—for unknown reasons, he admitted to himself.

Holding a handsome man's hand, rather like dragging him, Erica interrupted Darren's conversation with his father: "Honey, this is Mr. Reza Azimi." Darren stepped forward cordially to greet Reza, while his father vanished toward the bar. "Reza is our new associate, representing SDI's software in Iran. He arrived yesterday from Tehran, so timely for our party."

"Nice to meet you," Darren said, shaking hands with Reza. "Is this your first visit to Vancouver?"

"No. But, before, I didn't have so many friends and support; Erica, especially, is very generous," Reza replied.

"Isn't she?!" Darren said with agitation while suppressing his jealousy, especially for Erica holding Reza's hand when bringing him over.

"Reza will be in Vancouver for a while and return now and then," Erica said.

"That's splendid. I'm glad you feel at home in Vancouver now," Darren said. "Come and visit us when you're in town."

Darren looked for his father, who seemed annoyed by Erica's smirk and flirting with another man. Hoping to continue their conversation, he reeled toward him at the bar with scepticism considering his father's pensive look. He refreshed his gin and tonic and squeezed a lemon into it. "You want another drink, Dad?"

"No thanks... Why do you drink so much?"

"I don't!" Darren murmured glumly. "Besides, I won't be driving anywhere or anything tonight!"

"What was that all about with the foreign guy?"

"Erica has a lot of new friends now," he replied with sarcasm, which sunk his father into an even deeper sense of pity for his son. His contemptuous glare surged a sudden revulsion in Darren toward him and himself. A simple gaze reignited his suppressed wounds and resentment. Still he felt even lonelier when his father left shortly after, with his last trenchant look now engraved in Darren's brain forever. This single event fractured the shaky mental bridge between father and son even deeper.

The rest of the evening, Darren mingled with confusion amidst the crowd, smiled superficially, participated in small talks, and fled each scene when an opportunity came up. Elizabeth and Jeff were the only faces he remembered from the good old times when his relationship with Erica had been simpler. *How time changes everything and everybody!* Even Elizabeth and Jeff looked incognizant of his confusion and suffering. Recounting their high school mischief, they fooled around, but Darren could no longer grasp the meaning of those jokes or their mischief. Yet he forced himself to appear alive. Thank God, the party finally ended and the caterers left, too.

"What was the matter with you all night?" Erica snarled. She had already planned for a serious talk soon after this party, but not right after it, in the same evening. Yet his behaviour tonight alone had expired her patience to wait a few more days.

"What do you mean?" Darren asked with caution.

"You were even more pitiful than your usual depressed self. Why the long face all the time? Why do you embarrass me in front of my friends and colleagues?"

"I haven't been rude to your snotty friends! But I don't have any common interests or business to babble about with them."

"Because you don't make any effort to know them."

"I'm not looking for new friends… You don't seem to grasp what I'm going through."

"What're you going through?"

"I feel lonely and confused. So I'm trying hard to find myself before bothering to know others."

"That's too philosophical. Just say what's really hurting you."

"Maybe the problem is that you're so busy all the time, I've lost track of our relationship. What happened to all the love we shared not so long ago? How quickly you've changed, and you don't even feel it or admit it!"

"I haven't changed, but I must think about the future, mostly in terms of money. Who else is gonna do it? You're so bogged down in your artistic world and philosophy you've lost touch with reality."

"So now you're an expert in family affairs and I'm only a lost philosopher? I'm a loser?"

"I didn't say that! You accuse me of everything all the time just for dealing with your artistic failure."

"Aha! You just said it: My failure. You don't respect or love me anymore, because I'm a failure. You treat me like dirt or an orphan when I love you more every day. I resent this feeling."

Erica ran toward him, embraced him, and cried, "That's not true, not true at all; you're losing your senses. Of course I love you, with all my heart. Why do you hurt yourself and me so much? You must trust me and understand that everything I do is for us. Kiss me and tell me you love me, you idiot."

"You know I do. Naively, I think you may still love me, too. I'm trapped, and we both know it. But you're getting more careless every day since you sense my desperation."

"That's not true, Darren," Erica murmurs.

"It is and I cannot do anything about it other than waiting and hoping that perhaps some kind of work can ignite my sluggish life, so that you like me better, too. All these thoughts also make me more confused about what is really happening between us."

"Darren, why don't you come work for SDI?"

"Are you kidding me? What can I do for you?"

"You'd be surprised how much anybody can learn about computers with a bit of training. We need technicians at all levels. Computer consulting, networking, and graphics are growing fast, and there's a lot of work we can't handle. We'll sponsor your training and start paying you after two months."

"Are you serious? Is this really possible?"

"Of course… See, my darling, solutions are always around if we put our heads together. All along I've kept silent, to avoid giving you the impression that I don't support your passion for painting. But I knew there's no money and future in art. Maybe now it's finally time to wake up and smell the roses."

"Tell me what to do," he said with excitement, but felt a twitch of unease about her last comment. "I realize that working to survive is a social norm. But I resent turning into a slave just to survive. I especially don't know how work and success can have any resemblance to 'smelling the roses.' Don't bother giving me an answer, though, even if you have one; I'm exhausted." He then grabbed and kissed Erica's hands passionately, feeling giddy about the prospect of employment, make-up sex, and the humour of his earlier hasty comment to his father about not driving anything tonight. He would, in fact, drive a cranky, roaring Rolls Royce! "Let's go to bed and forget all the nonsense tonight."

4

As a technician at SDI, Darren's quick grasp of computer jargon and his tasks, mostly in networking, surprised him, though he still abhorred this line of work. On the other hand, being part of a progressive team of specialists boosted his confidence. He adopted a brighter outlook on life and abandoned drinking and smoking. The main problem, Erica's workaholism, continued to strain their marriage, though, especially after he began to imagine her work addiction was not the only obstacle in their relationship. Her excessive pleasantry with some colleagues often came across to him as flirting. Yet without any concrete evidence of infidelity, her cordial behaviour could also be justified as another business requirement.

One night he decided to confront her about their future when she came home around nine. "How's your life besides work?"

"No complaints. I really love my job," she replied.

"I know that already…! But what about other passions you might have besides work?" he asked with sarcasm, hinting about both their relationship and her private life.

"Is this another wild goose chase to analyze me?"

"Just a simple question… I have a right to know where we stand, or whether we're gonna have a family."

"That isn't my priority now. You don't know how difficult my job is."

"But your ambition is destroying our life. Obviously, you don't see me as an important man in your life. I can see how you admire Cameron and Reza, but ignore me, because I'm only a technician."

"You're talking nonsense and wasting my time. Go see a shrink to fix your head."

"My head is fine...," he replied.

"It's not… What are you accusing me of now?" she yelled.

Her outburst showed he had hit a nerve and the futility of pursuing the matter. He could not stop the course of destiny or Erica's possible affair. "Just forget it. Can we go out for dinner?"

"Okay…," she said reluctantly while getting up the couch at leisure and looking around for her purse. "It's Friday night and we don't have anything to do."

He ambled toward his Honda Civic, cognizant of her agony to ride in that old, rusty car. She noticed his intention, too, but decided to stay cool and play along with his childish game. She strode toward his car, adoring her shining new BMW briefly from the corner of her eye.

"Do you wanna drive my car instead?"

"No," Darren replied fast with pride painted by spite.

Erica's last comment haunted Darren as he drove in silence awhile. "The reason we don't have plans for weekends is because you don't stick to a fixed work schedule. That's exactly the point I was making earlier and you got offended."

"No, that isn't the reason… It's only because you don't like to socialize with Cameron and other people at work."

"Because you become too arrogant around them. And I don't like their attitude, anyway."

"What's wrong with their attitude?"

"Gosh… Don't even ask!"

"Oh, by the way, I've decided to buy season tickets for the Vancouver Symphony for Saturday nights. We can listen to good music, and then go for a late dinner. Okay?"

"That's a great idea," he replied, turning into the main street.

"I'll buy three season tickets, in fact, to take Reza with us whenever he's here in Vancouver. Otherwise, I'll give the ticket to one of my hardworking staff as a reward," Erica suggested so casually and convincingly Darren could not see any reason to object. Well, Erica had reiterated enough in the past that Reza had become SDI's main associate. SDI valued his business and contributions in terms of software modifications and innovations. *Besides, he's here maybe only a few Saturdays a year. Why make another case out of nothing?* So he only nodded.

She continued, "Reza's buying an apartment in Vancouver."

"To live in Vancouver?"

"A bit more than before. We've signed a contract to develop a new software together. I'm excited about it. He's a great system designer with many great ideas. We must take good care of him while he's here."

I bet you do! But immediately he thought that maybe he was overreacting or misunderstanding all these facts again. He could be cynical and consider this much attention to another man—especially such a handsome one—insulting. Or he could be a tactful gentleman and accept the realities of civilization and deal with them internally with silence, even though the rest of the world might be laughing behind his back at his naïveté. *Business requirements nowadays are too complex to imagine, or restrict. I must stop coming across as a retard by objecting to every single plan Erica has for promoting her business.* So, he shut up and kept all his haunting questions to himself.

But Erica, taking his silence as a sign of consent, continued, "Actually he's asked me to help him furnish his place. He doesn't know Vancouver, and he's busy working on several projects. I've agreed to help him."

Darren could not hold his anger any longer, "I'm surprised you have so much time for a stranger when you keep telling me you're up to your ears in office work!"

"He's not a stranger... Besides, this is a part of my job. Don't you understand?" Erica shrieked.

"What? Choosing his furniture and decorating his suite is your job?"

"Yes, in a way, it is. He doesn't know anybody in Vancouver and he's too busy when he's here, plus the fact that he asked for my help after admiring our house decoration and confessing to his low taste and patience for this stuff."

"You know that's all bullshit that you keep feeding me so casually."

"Go back home, Darren."

"Why...?"

"I'm not in the mood to go to a restaurant."

"No, I wanna go eat, and you must be willing to understand my concerns. Why should we always do things your way?"

"Stop or I'll jump out of the car," shouted Erica hysterically.

Darren slowed down. *I wish my car had those fancy gadgets to lock the doors and take her anywhere I want. Her fancy car has everything, but not my rusty carriage.* He approached the curb, but did not stop, hoping to speed up again as Erica calmed down. Realizing his intention, she opened the door and jumped out with rage. He pressed the brakes swiftly, but Erica collapsed onto the sidewalk. She rose quickly, though, and lurched in the opposite direction of the traffic to elude Darren. She seemed fine except for the dirt on her skirt, which she scrubbed off lightly.

Backing up in the busy street, Darren opened the passenger window and began begging, "Okay, honey. We'll go home. Come in, please. Please…"

But the louder he cried, the less Erica cared. She finally turned into a dark alley and disappeared. With a traffic jam behind him already, he could not drive back any more or turn into the alley. No parking spot was in sight, either.

Two blocks later, he parked in a 'permit required' zone hastily and ran toward the street where Erica had vanished.

The narrow, dark alley was deadly quiet and empty. Worried for her safety, he cursed himself for upsetting her to flee in this spooky neighbourhood. He dashed along the alley frantically and inspected the ghastly side streets, too, each creepier than the other. He screamed and swore loudly like a lunatic. A few youngsters stood in a dark corner and smoked pot stealthily. He approached and asked them about his lost woman. They glared at him suspiciously and one of them finally said, "No," to get rid of him. He returned to his car three blocks away in the main street. He pondered his options desperately and decided to drive around the neighbourhood, hoping the car's beams would detect Erica amongst the heavy shadows.

After canvassing the streets nervously for twenty minutes, he was on the verge of hysteria and heart attack. He felt responsible for her eerie disappearance and possible misfortune. However, both his patience and options felt exhausted. Accepting defeat at last, he headed for home. Yet, his mind revolted again only three blocks later: He should continue his search. What could have happened to her? How could have she vanished so quickly into dark air? Was she okay? Had some pervert abducted her, or heaved her into his house as she ran by it, and she did not even realize what had hit her until it was too late? He kept imagining the worst scenarios and cursing himself.

The idea of the slightest harm coming to her tore his heart. Yet, he could not stop thinking that only one them dying right away could solve their growing complex marital arrangement. Even worse was a brief, ludicrous thought about the timeliness and the time for showing a personal initiative regarding this liberating option! Which way—she or he—and how?

Driving around aimlessly another thirty minutes, furious and exhausted, finally he floored the gas hysterically. The poor old Honda screeched on the dry asphalt and swerved into the main street as he drove the rest of the way home with rage. He wished a ten-wheel truck appeared around a corner and smashed him into a thousand pieces. But not even the luxury of death was in his fate. Instead, he arrived home in one fuming piece. No sign of her inside the house, either.

He poured himself a glass of cognac, lit a cigarette, and thought about calling the police, but what to tell them? Only three hours since Erica, a grown woman, had just gone berserk and missing. The police obviously did not care about, or have time for, this kind of game. He drank more cognac, and smoked two more cigarettes. Close to 1:30 a.m., he decided to go to bed. She had probably gone to a friend's house. He considered calling Elizabeth to find out if she had heard from her, but changed his mind about calling her so late. *The hell with Erica and her folly.*

He lay on the bed and stared at the ceiling. What kind of life is this? What about the guestroom? He leaped out of the bed, rushed to the end of the hall, and opened the guestroom door with caution. There she was, probably sleeping for the last four hours he had been going nuts. He felt like screaming and banging the door so loudly the whole neighbourhood woke up, but he knew he was incapable of such impertinence. So, he closed the door extra-cautiously and returned to bed relieved, but quite perplexed about his options, especially the nasty one crossing his mind in the streets earlier—to kill either her or himself! Where was this relationship going?

Monday morning, he went to work casually. Performing his regular duties barely brought him into contact with Erica in the office, anyway. He reported to a young senior analyst who scheduled his assignments and monitored his performance. Not surprising to him at all, yet depressing nonetheless, Erica cared very little about his duties, perhaps because of the organizational hierarchy. His supervisor's rigidity and aloofness felt as though Erica and other staff had forgotten to mention to this jerk that he was the boss's husband. Was this sad, cruel reality intentionally hidden or was it only an oversight? Nah! The jerk certainly knew, but merely pretended he did not know or give a damn about it. Maybe he was even instructed to drive this loser Darren nuts?

Only in two urgent situations had Darren ever gone to Erica's office. He knew she was always busy—mostly in meetings with Reza or other hot shots. More humiliating was, of course, the authority she masterfully portrayed around Darren to keep him at a proper distance at work. Yet she was quite cordial with others, especially Reza. Their loud conversation and laughter filled the whole floor and exasperated Darren, more so now that Reza had come to Vancouver for a long stay. Since his arrival five days earlier, Erica left the office and returned with him frequently every day, which Darren assumed had something to do with the promise of helping him furnish his apartment. Despite his rage and gloom, Darren believed his options were limited. Besides, he loved Erica too much to leave her, at least until the day he was absolutely convinced their marital problems were irreparable—a prospect very likely right around the corner.

Three weeks had passed without either of them making any gesture of reconciliation and she kept sleeping in the guestroom.

On Sunday, he went for a stroll at the Seawalk, sat on a bench overlooking the ocean, and tried to assess his options. Leaving Erica meant not only separation from his beloved, but also giving up SDI and wondering whether any computer jobs were out there for him, considering his limited knowledge and experience. However, a life dictated by Erica seemed too humiliating and impractical. Would she eventually realize the repercussions of her attitude and lifestyle? Would she possibly change her mind and behaviour? Would it help if he went away a while, to scare her into modifying her attitude? Would she care, considering how completely preoccupied she was with her job and Reza? He even contemplated suicide, including the least painful means of doing it—this time mostly for humour only, as he was in control of his emotions much better these days. He even laughed lightheartedly awhile about his obsession to analyze everything with such diligence, even leading to such ludicrous ideas about death or murder. Nonetheless, he believed he must prepare an exhaustive list of options for consideration.

At the end, he concluded that leaving Erica before finding a good job would be unwise. His best option was to stick it out for now, pretending nothing had happened. *As long as my pride isn't totally crushed, I'll tolerate the situation, and the best way to do this is to show no sign of vulnerability, while disregarding her affairs.* He felt calmer when his options and position seemed rather clarified. He actually admired his agility at thinking and acting rationally, instead of letting his emotions force him into a destructive reactionary resolution. Suddenly everything seemed somewhat manageable and he was full of confidence. Thus, he decided to eat at a café and go to the movies.

Erica was up, watching TV, when Darren got home late that night. She surveyed him with curiosity, as though surprised by his subtle smile showing his newfound confidence. That damn smile, Erica thought, made him irresistible and playful again; quite different from how he had looked lately. Maybe he was starting his own affair, coming home late with such a mysterious, cunning grin. *He is a very handsome man, after all, and an artist, too.* Their eyes met briefly, but they winced fast to avoid losing the duel that had persisted for the last three weeks. She leaped out of the couch with her book, turned off the TV, and rushed to the guestroom.

Darren turned on the TV, flipped through the channels for ten minutes, then decided to go to bed, too. On his way, he noticed the guestroom light ricocheting from the side of the door, which had been left open a crack tonight. Was this an invitation? His heart pounded at the possibility of embracing her tonight. Maybe she was even coming to her senses and willing to respect his needs, if not surrendering to him totally forever. But hardly had he basked in these soothing hopes than the guestroom light was extinguished, leaving him with an even higher sense of loneliness and confusion again. A good portion of his confidence gained that afternoon evaporated just as a light went out. *She's surely playing with my nerves and pride, while fooling around with that sleazy Reza,* he felt with angst.

Was she sending a signal, but too embarrassed to admit her guilt and desire to reconcile? Was she only playing a game to humiliate him, emitting subtle signs before pulling back in an even timelier, clever manner just to drive him nuts? *These women are really cunning.* His unrelenting interpretations of the incident sabotaged his attempt to sleep. Even more overwhelming than his logical thoughts about Erica's intentions was his urgent urge to have sex with her, however. He was suddenly aroused—so romantically indeed. It was in fact beyond all the animalistic lust of the last fortnight that had come from his rising rage and a deep need for revenge. Besides, he believed, he must restore his dented manhood with all the confidence required of a young man. He should not let his ego, boosted after such elaborate analyses this afternoon, be smashed again by her game or erratic behaviour. A second later, he fought another thought: That coaxing her for sex would be humiliating and a harsher blow to his confidence if she only snubbed him. *Let's forget about it and sleep.*

Fifteen minutes later, relentlessly restless, his urge for sex was out of control. He thought about rapists: "Is this how they feel, or is their erotic behaviour purely psychotic? Some of them may be innocent, in the way this maddening urge can drive any man nuts —a fleeting insanity maybe. A social facility must be established for the unfortunate bastards who neither are married nor can afford a prostitute— something like a food bank. *After all, sexual deprivation is much harsher than hunger, I'd say.* But if such a social service or facility existed, everybody, including deprived married men like me, would lie or forge their IDs to use this sex bank. *What crazy ideas can emerge from a crushing reality in such moments of a person's total despair?"*

He struggled to amuse himself with humour to curb his lust mixed with passion, pride, and rage and fall asleep. However, a huge urge to wake Erica to make love hampered his willpower. Soon, his logic and legs out of control, he stood before the guestroom, opened the door slowly. She lay peacefully under the blanket with the contour of her sexy body enticingly vivid. His heart raced like a runaway locomotive, thrusting his entire entity forward enigmatically with tension. Unable to resist anymore, unable to reason, unable to respire, and unable to regard his poor ego, he pulled the blanket and slid under it smoothly, embracing her slender body tightly and kissing her neck and cheek voluptuously. Her moaning in deep sleep pestered his conscience briefly, yet he persevered, Erica passive at first, eventually joining in, accommodating him, and relieving his mind to focus on the job at hand. She enjoyed the make-up sex more than he did, more than ever, but resisted showing it, all out of spite, still.

5

Nothing changed in the end anyway. They only wore each other out with harsher quarrels and excruciating reconciliations more frequently. Darren stopped probing Erica or expecting anything from her, while job-hunting privately. They learned to live civilly and went to symphony or opera on weekends when Reza was in Vancouver, followed by a late supper at an elegant restaurant. She paid for the concerts and Reza paid for fancy dinners. And Darren felt like a bum allowed to tag along with two aristocrats out of mercy. Yet, he enjoyed their special attention to him. He merely humoured their hypocritical efforts to amuse him while exchanging flirting grins and words between themselves in a masterfully orchestrated manner. They conducted the entire affair even better than the Maestro leading the Vancouver Symphony Orchestra.

Both Erica and Darren felt their marriage was going down the drain fast. They agreed to go to a few marriage-counselling sessions, but remained cynical about their future together. Darren believed he had tried enough. *Erica is a victim of circumstances herself, unaware of her irritating idiosyncrasies*—a novel notion he had adopted after reading many self-therapy and psychology books. To bear the pain of living with her, he tried to remember those books' words of wisdom: *We're trapped and helpless by not only our flaws, but also pervasive social norms that impair our minds and judgments about the sensible options of living with lesser desires. We must become better people individually before we can truly appreciate the complexity and requirements of relationships.* So he strived for such enlightenment to become a better person, mostly for withstanding imperfect situations for his own sake. He strived to console himself and forgive Erica. Yet, despite all the niceties of such utter resignation, the isolation along with Erica's apathy proved excruciating.

Six months later, he finally gathered enough courage to leave her, although his efforts to land another job had led to nothing. He reckoned being a waiter or a salesman more honourable than continuing the kind of life Erica was willing to share with him.

He rented a tiny apartment, collected his personal effects one day and disappeared from her life. A note explained the hurdles of building a future together despite his enormous love for her. Attached to it were his resignation letter and a telephone number in case a section of his assignment needed clarification. He never returned to work, since he had already cleaned up his desk.

On the third night in his new suite, Reza called and insisted on meeting him. Darren agreed to see him the following day. Numb from the shock of separation and his haunting affection for Erica, he was still optimistic and daydreaming about their relationship's prospect. Maybe Erica was sending Reza to mediate and lure him back to her and SDI? Thus, he planned to pose difficult, yet realistic, conditions for reconciliation. But the more he looked for such 'conditions' and the chance of improving their relationship, the more discouraged he got. People do not change, Darren now believed, even if they understood their flaws. Therefore, instead of making a long list of demands, he decided to listen to Reza and the message from Erica first. He would then tell Reza to wait a few days for him to think and prepare his conditions. *This way, I'll show them how serious I am and how high a price she must pay to have me back. She must provide proper guarantees about her promise to change as well.* With his magnified ego, eager to set the tone of the future negotiation, he arrived a few minutes late for his meeting with Reza intentionally.

Reza rose to greet Darren, who apologized for his tardiness.

"What happened between you two so suddenly?" Reza asked. "You're both dear to me and I hate seeing you guys depressed."

"Thanks. But—"

"It was only last weekend we went out and had such a good time together."

"People with different life priorities cannot live together."

"Oh, Darren—"

"We'll never change, especially people like Erica!" Darren said firmly, hoping to set the tone of the upcoming negotiations with a strong opening. Reza must be fully apprised of the price Erica must pay to win him back. "Even if we were sincere, we'd realize soon how hard it is to change our nature and give up being who we'd like to be."

"Yeah… Even when people promise to change, it's only for calming their partners or buying time to weigh their options," Reza added, which alarmed Darren a bit, but he let it go.

"Exactly…! So, I should tell you that I'm serious about my decision and not in the mood to reconcile with her."

"No, no, Darren, I don't intend to reconcile between you two! Both Erica and I agree with you. You're right, according to Erica, in all respects, about moving out and trying to rebuild your life. She'd felt the same way about your relationship, but couldn't bring herself to ask you to leave. She's sad about losing you, of course."

Darren could not believe his ears. His brain seethed with a gush of blistering blood, while his body shuddered like a nude on top of a melting glacier. Especially after all that planning to be an iceberg himself, cold and tough, against Erica's heartbreaking pleas to take her back, he felt like a total idiot. Desperation and rage covered his face despite his efforts to show off his cool.

"So you bought her conclusion, too?" Darren asked at last.

"I did, after she explained your situation. Shouldn't I have agreed with her and you?"

"That's your decision...," Darren said with angst and anger.

"I'm sorry, Darren. But you've lost me!"

Darren was numb and speechless, sensing his own confusion about this meeting and what he expected from Reza. At last, Reza continued after a long pause and sipping his coffee. "So Erica is now planning to have her lawyers prepare the necessary papers and she's willing to offer you a kind of severance pay, even though you quit your job. She'll also give you money for settlement, of course. She still loves you and wants to help you in any way she can."

"Her generosity is commendable by the way she's so eager to dump me! She sends you to win my sympathy and fast consent, while rushing her lawyers to prepare the paperwork for divorce."

"No, you're wrong, Darren. She hasn't sent me and she might get upset or at least surprised if she finds out about our meeting here today," Reza said.

"She probably knows that I'm entitled to half of her assets or something, including her shares in SDI. I don't want to be greedy or hurt her, but I can squeeze her if I want to."

"That's true, and between the two of you, and your lawyers. But despite its high volume of business, SDI is apparently not profitable yet, thus its current value is negligible. They're also facing a lawsuit that may cost them a bundle. So I wouldn't count on a major financial settlement. I'm saying this only since I want you to plan more realistically. Have you found another job?"

"No, no hurry. I'm too exhausted to look for a job."

"Good. I wanted to see you mostly as a friend, regardless of Erica's reaction. You're a true gentleman and friend. I'll never forget the times we went out or smoked pot and laughed. I'd like to be your friend, no matter how things go between you two."

"I value your friendship, too, despite my confusion about our triangular relationship." Darren paused to gauge Reza's reaction.

Reza remained silent, contemplating Darren's loaded allusion, and staring at the foot of the adjacent table. After fifteen seconds, he looked up at Darren. "There's another matter I'd like to ask."

"What?"

"I have a job offer for you, which you may find ridiculous at first, but hear me out and don't try to answer right away."

"Go ahead," said Darren with curiosity.

"Well, you know that my company is expanding fast in Iran and Dubai. I already have eighty-six employees, but still can't meet all the demands. I need someone to train new staff quickly in networking and imaging. This position is also responsible for some administrative issues, contract management, and perhaps project development, if time permits. Especially, I need a person to monitor things for me while I'm in Vancouver. Of course, I have a partner who looks after general administration and daily operation. Just think about it…"

Reza's comments, mostly his straightforward assessment of his marriage, had shocked Darren all along, but his job offer sounded most bizarre. What did he know about Iran, its culture, and language? How would his limited knowledge of computers help Reza with all those duties he expected from this position? How could he train people whose knowledge of English was surely limited? Though teaching technical stuff needed more practical demonstrations than language.

"Isn't there a vicious war going on in Iran?" Darren asked.

"Yes, but that's nothing to worry about. You'll be quite safe. Besides, I'll make the risk worth your while. Life in Iran is more interesting than people here realize. You must come and make a lot of money, and enjoy living in a lively culture for a few years. So, think about it, and we'll get together—let's say Thursday—to work out the details."

"Okay. We can get together anyway—the two of us," Darren says with sorrow, wishing it could be a meeting of the three of them again, like the good old times.

"Any message you want me to take back to Erica?"

"Not really. I agree with everything she's proposed. It's better to get this over with as quickly as possible."

"You're smart, overcoming your emotions, especially about Erica's assets. You're so practical."

The idea of leaving Vancouver intrigued Darren, especially considering the grim job market around here. The Iran-Iraq war was irrelevant, because at this point, big risks or even dying felt inconsequential to him. Loveless, without a job prospect, his life was worth very little, anyway. He had nothing to lose and no worthwhile ambitions to keep him going. He was also tired of the whole world the way destiny had unveiled itself so far. Suddenly he felt he would never fall in love again. *How can anybody find love in such a hectic world, where ego, ambitions, mistrust, and lust have so vastly tainted our minds?* Maybe a new culture—an eastern philosophy, perhaps—could teach him something worth living for. So, before going to bed, he had already decided to accept Reza's offer. However, he would wait until Thursday to inform Reza, to avoid appearing overanxious or too desperate.

****

"In two weeks, I made all the arrangements to travel to Tehran," says Darren to Nora. "Reza returned before me after we signed a three-year contract, but promised to pick me up at the airport."

"Did you settle your divorce with Erica smoothly?" Nora enquires.

"Yeah… Her lawyers explained the financial situation and I signed the papers. With my rush to leave Vancouver, I would've agreed to anything."

"Did you see her before leaving?"

"No. We had nothing to talk about. A clean break is a treasure if one is lucky enough to appreciate the opportunity and grab it."

"How was Iran?"

"A refreshing experience. The people were great, but the war had spoiled everything for everybody."

"Well, you've had a bad experience with love. I understand. But it's time for you to forget the past and share the rest of your life with someone."

"Maybe someday… But right now I'm sort of paranoid about marriage."

"You see, Darren, my intention for clarifying our affair isn't only for my benefit! It would be much easier for me to decide, if my decision didn't affect you. Jerry seems to be okay with my relationship with you—and sometimes even supportive—as long as he believes we're serious…"

"So, he knows about us and is okay with it?"

"Yes, you men are really weird in the way your egos operate."

"He's probably only trying to get himself off the hook about his promise to marry you. But tell me how you think men's brain operate."

"You believe it's okay for your mistress to keep, or look for, a husband, but not dating others just for fun."

He bursts into laughter. "Excellent point! This is true mostly because women are more jealous and want to settle things fast."

"No, my point was that you men are a bunch of egomaniacs."

"That's true too… They all are; except me."

"Don't flatter yourself. Anyway, I'm upset for five reasons."

"Five reasons?" cries Darren. "What reasons?"

"First, not knowing where our relationship is going; second, the fear of losing my job in this economy; third, the possibility of jeopardizing our relationship by my mood or something; fourth, my worry about your career if I leave Jerry and Elixir; and most of all, I can't keep fooling around with Jerry anymore. Any of these reasons is enough to depress a person. And indecision is a tremendous headache all by itself. But everything depends on what we, or I, plan to do now."

"But remember that dating someone else's mistress hasn't been a flattering position for me, either. This is the first time you're saying something about leaving Jerry—not for me, of course, albeit a good decision for your own sake."

"I'm glad you agree…"

"At least now I know the reasons for your recent testiness. But making any quick commitment is illogical for me. Besides—"

"I thought we were building a good relationship!" Nora said.

"I agree, and I hate losing you too. But we need more time…"

"How much time?"

"I don't know…," Darren replies.

"But sometimes a clue or a plan can do wonders."

"We'll just have to be patient. We must analyze and deal with your concerns. But our relationship must grow without all these interfering conflicts, like Jerry, your job, my career, etc. We must build our relationship away from all these pressures, for God's sake. Now is actually the worst time to decide, exactly because of the five reasons you mentioned and more."

"I can't handle two shoddy affairs anymore. I'll have to do something about my life soon," Nora blurts.

"Then decide why you're still dating Jerry. If it's because of your job or my career, then the decision is easy—just quit if he doesn't leave you alone. You can also mention our relationship as an excuse for dumping him, if it may help his ego to free you."

"But how can I do that?"

"Tell him we're serious and we may get engaged soon, but don't put this idea into your own head."

"And you keep seeing other women…?"

"I can't promise anything…" Darren pauses as Nora droops. "But I don't expect you keep a stressful job just to protect my career."

"It's good to know…!"

"My career has always been at the mercy of my lovers; first Erica, and now you—that's just too damn depressing."

"I'll think about everything. I'm glad we had this informative conversation. Perhaps I'll tell Jerry to go to hell. The rest will depend on his reaction, which, as you said, shouldn't be of our concern, because we'll deal with the consequences later."

"That's wise, I guess."

"I still hope you'd love me someday, though."

"I already do, in my own way. Anyhow, let's not argue about semantics if we like to be together. You're wearing me down," Darren exclaims with humour.

"I am? How?"

"Painting rigorously to make your tough deadlines. Spending many hours, regularly, sorting out your problems. But mainly, trying to know you better, considering your fast and frequent mood swings."

"My mood swings are all your fault!"

"Everything these days seem to be my fault…"

"It is… You've messed up my emotions… Then I must also keep pushing you to do your paintings and make your deadlines. What would you do without me?"

"Without you, I'll be lost. You're my joy and inspiration," he blabbers with humour while pulling Nora off the sofa to show her his new paintings. He turns on the spotlights over the paintings.

"You've done a lot," she says, examining the new paintings, "and they look wonderful."

"I had help," he blurts with a grin.

"Who helped you, silly?"

"Recently, when I paint and listen to music, the spirits of prominent composers and artists make me feel more creative and carefree. They seem to do all the work and make it so effortless for me. The images build up on the canvas in such magical way I'm bind to believe some high spirits are doing the job. I'm just an instrument in their hands."

"Maybe you're smoking too much weed?"

"Nah. I think the spirits enjoy partying with me and painting, too, as if they've been sitting idle in heaven all along, waiting for someone to summon them."

"It's nice making new friends," she says teasingly, wondering if the man she is trying to lure for a serious relationship is already a lunatic.

"I knew you wouldn't believe me…"

"Actually, I see signs of heavenly touches in your recent works. So, just keep doing whatever you've been doing, even if it means partying with Mozart and Van Gogh. Now let's watch this last scene from *Tosca* before going to bed."

In that case, I must keep seeing Elizabeth more often now, Darren ponders, while wishing he had the guts to say it out loud to Nora as well. Instead, he embraces her and caresses her hair.

Mario listens to Floria's promises that he will survive the fake execution and they will go away together.

Chapter Five
Trouble Arrives

1

Outside the customs at Vancouver Airport, Mahroo, her parents, and Nazi embrace Darren warmly like a rediscovered family member. So much affection, even from Mahroo, even considering their past confusing flirtations, astounds Darren. Her snugly hug and two cozy kisses, boldly stamped near the corners of his lips, feel excessive.

Still more startling, her eyes hopelessly remind him of Zia and the chance of being a little responsible for his demise. He recalls their juvenile horseplay amidst the Caspian Sea's crashing surf. How could such a noisy clown have been so outrageously jealous and angry the way Reza and Mahroo had often claimed? *Like Pagliacci, maybe…*He feels sorry for him. Yet, the sensational tingle from Mahroo's kisses close to his lips returns his focus back to her gorgeous presence. Some scenes from their last encounter—the last night in her guestroom while Zia was away —flash before him. Life after Zia has definitely agreed with her, judging by her pulsating appearance—free to embrace life anew. All alone, like him.

Against his earlier plan, he blurts hastily, "I'm sorry about Zia's accident. Anytime I tried to call you, I lost my courage to discuss his unexpected departure. I hope you're feeling better…"

"Thanks, Darren… Where's the luggage carousel?"

"This way…"

Exchanging casual conversation and glances, Darren helps the family collect their luggage before driving toward home. "I've rented a furnished apartment in my building for you," he says.

"Sorry for all the trouble," Mahroo asserts.

"No problem."

"Reza said his suite is too small for all of us when he comes in a couple of weeks. I guess he was worried about his privacy."

"He probably is…!" he replies with a tense giggles about her wise observation, wondering if he would ever dare or care telling her about Reza's likely old affair with Erica.

"My parents and I prefer a place of our own, anyway."

"Let's hope it's convenient for everybody."

"Hopefully we won't bother you too much."

They arrive at Mahroo's new place around six p.m. Nazi, who has been cooped up in airports, planes and cars for twenty-four hours, gallops around the apartment like a mustang just cut loose from captivity. She explores every corner of their new home and asks about Vancouver, the Creek visible from the balcony, and a nearby playground. Darren humours her like testing the pleasures of parenthood. The others plummet onto the sofa, with gratitude toward Darren showing on their faces.

Darren orders pizza and turns on the news channel on the television. The daily broadcast about the Iran-Iraq war portrays scenes of Iranian casualties due to the Iraqis' chemical warfare. Later some analysts present deep political commentary about the use of chemical weapons. Darren gauges the newcomers' faces fixated on the television with dejection and nostalgia.

"Reza and I," Mahroo says, "are glad for the opportunity to bring our parents here. They're frail after so much violence—first the Islamic revolution and then this never-ending war with Iraq."

"Hopefully they won't feel homesick in Vancouver."

"Reza's living mostly here these days, so this is the best place for them. They have some good friends here, too."

"How long are *you* staying?" Darren enquires.

"It depends... Maybe a month; or forever, who knows!"

"I'm sure you'll like it here. Vancouver somewhat resembles the Caspian Sea region."

"My stay also depends on the people I know!"

Darren eats a slice of pizza and sets out to leave. "My suite is on the tenth floor; 1006. If you need anything, just come up or call me. Tomorrow, we'll go for a tour of the city and grocery shopping."

"You don't have to leave; I'll just put Nazi in bed, but I'm not tired."

"Your parents are probably exhausted too…"

"So maybe I visit you in an hour if you're not tired or busy?"

"Sure," he says politely, with scepticism.

2

Darren tidies up the living room and the kitchen a bit. At nine o'clock, Mahroo arrives in her tight, sexy jeans. He thanks her for the bottle of cognac and Iranian art souvenirs.

"You want anything to drink?" he asks.

"Perhaps a cup of tea."

"Teabag okay?"

"Sure… How's life in Vancouver now?" she asks.

"It's all right… Painting keeps me busy."

"They're nice, as usual," she says and nods approvingly, as she peers at the paintings on the walls.

"Thanks. How're you feeling these days yourself?"

"Empty and aimless…!" she replies.

"I understand… It was a terrible thing that happened to Zia."

"Well, he's not around to torture me but I still feel soulless."

"You mean you feel depressed?"

"No, it's more than that. It is a weird feeling I can't explain—something like a suffocating baseless melancholy."

"I know that feeling. Sometimes we lose our spirit," he says.

"Yes, that's it, precisely. It feels like my soul has gone on holiday without me or maybe somebody has stolen it."

"I hope it returns soon. Meanwhile, enjoy your freedom."

"Well, I thought so too. I believed I had plenty of options and chances to live free, but freedom seems to be only a fantasy, too."

"True… We'll never feel free or independent, because we're so attached to others and society, not to mention our hang-ups and paranoia," he says.

"Wow… You understand my sentiments perfectly," she says.

"Do you ever share your thoughts with Reza?"

"Seldom. He'll never grasp the depth of my problems."

"But he seemed concerned about you when I was in Iran."

"I know. We both thought Zia caused my depression. Now the poor guy is dead and I'm still lost. Reza believes I will feel better soon, once I find a suitable man."

"He's probably right!"

"I hope so too!"

"Zia's accident has surely affected all of you."

"Mostly Nazi misses him and his clowning around the house —although he was quieter, and angrier, during the last months before the accident. His suspicions had spoiled our lives already."

"Did he mention me again?"

"Only when blaming me for ignoring or disobeying him. He accused me of having feelings for you, which in a way brought you into the picture as a guilty party, especially for giving me the *Woman in the White Dress*."

"So his mood was probably a factor for his accident?!"

"Well… Nobody knows why he decided to return to Shiraz before schedule or drove so recklessly.

"I've felt badly anytime I remembered your story about his anger or possibly blaming me for something."

"Another incident also drove him overboard."

"What?"

"An explosion shattered his younger brother's legs in combat. A surgeon friend of ours swore that leg amputations were like an assembly line process, with four surgeons in his army unit busy all day. Dervish Ali's family nursed him after he was discharged. But one evening, he hung himself. Many of us who knew his mental condition thought that suicide, in some situations, might not be so sinful. Apparently, several thousands crippled veterans of this war have committed suicide so far."

"That's horrible..."

"This incident affected Zia too. Some people think his car crash was intentional. The reasons are compelling, because the autopsy didn't show any sign of heart attack or alcohol. No other car was involved, and the way he'd smashed the car into a line of trees supports the theory of suicide."

"I'm sorry for Zia's misfortunes, but more so for agitating him unintentionally. If I knew better, I wouldn't have given you the painting or stayed at your house. We're always smarter in the hindsight, I guess."

"But you didn't do anything wrong! If we could foresee the future, the entire world order might collapse!" says Mahroo. She pauses before continuing. "But something I've meant to ask you for sometime. I've controlled myself long enough... Promise to tell me the truth now."

"I'll try."

"Are you the man in the painting?"

"Umm... Yes, I am."

"Oh! Thank God..."

"Why is it important 'who the man is'?" he asks.

"Why is it so important, you ask?" she asks with surprise.

"Yes...," Darren replies sheepishly.

"You and I in the same painting is quite romantic already, even if the man wasn't looking so passionately at the woman sunk in such melancholy. Don't you agree?"

"Yes, that had been my intention. You're right...," he replies.

"Well…?" she asks with an alluring grin.

Darren just keeps gazing at her with bewilderment, unable to decide how to continue this touchy conversation. At last, Mahroo feels embarrassed about the long pause and blurts, "I'm glad my hunch had been correct all along. I tried to get a confession out of you a few times, especially when you stayed at my house, but you refused to answer directly, despite your positive hints."

"I've been conflicted by this matter all along," he says, getting ready to straighten her out.

"Then I didn't insist because I realized your noble reluctance to hurt my marital life and cause any kind of disgrace," she says. "You've been a saint."

Her allusions irritate him. This mistake must be rectified once and for all. He condemns himself for letting this confusion linger so long. But under the circumstances—when Mahroo had been so depressed, according to Reza—keeping one's mouth shut had been wise. But not anymore. He should act before the situation gets completely out of hand and his integrity shatters altogether. He wonders why Reza has not revealed the truth all this time.

So, with great caution, fearful of screwing up Reza's intention or Mahroo's world, he begins to explain: "You see, Mahroo, it's true that the man in the picture is me, but the woman in the white dress wasn't drawn with you in my mind."

"What? What're you talking about?" she shrieks in disbelief.

"Perhaps I should explain?" he murmurs timidly.

"Yes, please explain," she cries with a sudden anxiety attack.

"When I was painting the *Woman in the White Dress*, I was preoccupied with Erica—my ex-wife. I was depressed and eager to grasp the meaning of the senseless events and emotions that had ruined our marriage," blurts Darren cautiously, noticing Mahroo's surging anxiety as words pour out of his mouth. "So that particular painting reflects my past life with Erica; it helped me overcome the pent-up emotions inside me after our gloomy separation. I had her in my mind when I was painting it."

"So why did you say the woman in the white dress was me?"

"I never said that. That was only Reza's idea. He insisted on buying the painting since the woman in the white dress reminded him of you."

"He said that?"

"Yes, he felt you'd relate to the woman closely due to your problems with Zia. He hoped you'd get his message about your dwindling state of mind and seek a way out of your marriage."

"So it wasn't even a gift from you?"

"Well, not directly. I gifted it to Reza. So he might've felt more comfortable to present it to you as a gift from me as well."

"Then why didn't you deny it when I called and thanked you for 'your gift'?"

"I was trying to avoid interfering in your affairs, or revealing Reza's secret. Maybe I made a mistake about holding on to some information I believed wasn't important."

"Not important?" Mahroo shrieks.

"Believe me, it was merely an honourable mistake with noble intentions," Darren says.

"Thank you, your majesty!" Mahroo exclaims.

"Anyway, I don't think I should be blamed for any of this," he says with anguish. "I don't know anything about Reza's logic or intention for saying things in certain ways. Maybe he said it was 'a gift from me' without finishing his sentence, and so you assumed 'to you' instead of 'to him.'"

"You men are so insensitive. You're both idiots to assume things and put me through so much agony. You say you didn't mean any harm by hiding the truth. You assumed the truth would crush me, Reza's intention, or your generosity. You actually demand an appreciation for keeping a secret, don't you?"

"No, I don't… I'm only stating the truth…"

"But you have no idea what I've gone through the last three years, assuming a noble man loves me to the point of painting a masterpiece and giving it to me to express his feelings, and then keeping his passion to himself to avoid harming other people. You've hurt me more than you can imagine, and I burn with rage when I recall all those moments I sat near the painting, cherished it, and adored you as passionately as I believed you cared for me. It was like carving a sacred commandment, a divine tableau of 'love,' in my heart beat by beat, day after day, until it became my only refuge. You admit painting the *Woman in the White Dress* was for relieving your suffering, but never imagined that all those agonies were transferred to me the minute your painting stole my soul. If you thought drawing this painting on a piece of canvas was too emotional and painful for you, believe me, your anguish comes to nothing compared with my pains for painting our love in my heart and keeping it a secret, as I thought it was your wish. You have no idea, no idea at all, what you've put me through…

"I made a white dress *exactly* like the one in the painting and wore it in the house when I was alone. I waved my hand, begging you to break your silence and come to me, but you never moved. Some days I cried my heart out for hours, and when Zia arrived and noticed my red, puffed-up eyes—and once even in my white dress and hat—he suspected the worst. He usually went to the living room, glared at the painting, and cursed it from the darkest part of his heart. He knew my grief came from the painting and for its painter, but never dared to protest or touch it, knowing that I'd kill him if he went near the painting. In my dreams, I was luckier, as you usually waved back at me when I flung my hand to you. In some dreams—and sometimes daydreams in front of the painting—you came down to the beach to hold me, or I came inside to embrace you, and sometimes we strolled in the garden hand in hand, cheek to cheek, for hours, and you picked colourful flowers for me, and I cried, cheered, and chanted with happiness. But then I woke up again and realized how helplessly I'd been dreaming of being near you.

"Dear Darren, you did not only hurt me, but caused so much anguish for a jealous husband, to the point he couldn't tolerate the situation anymore and ended his life. After six months of howling and pretending to mourn Zia, when my tears were all for you, I decided it was time to act. No need to mourn anymore, since I'd come to you with my whole heart, body, and soul—a prize for waiting for me for so long. Instead I face humiliation and deceit —what a prize! I even told my parents about the love I thought we'd been hiding from everybody all along. Confused about the true cause of my stress for so long, when they finally realized that all the troubles were behind now that I was coming to Vancouver to be with you, they cheered up and looked forward to meeting and embracing you. Even four-year-old Nazi was ecstatic about seeing you, as I'd told her many stories about you. So even my parents and daughter have become victims of your silly game. Now do you still believe keeping such a foolish secret has been innocent and noble? What kind of a man are you? How badly I'd misjudged you! As far as Reza is concerned, I'm going to call him right now and give him a piece of my mind."

Mahroo leaps out of the sofa, runs to the door, to the hallway, and toward the stairwell going downstairs.

Darren chases her and yells, "Mahroo, please come back. Let me explain!"

The scene triggers his memory of many years back, the night Erica had jumped out of his moving car after their fight about Erica helping Reza decorate his new suite in Vancouver. He had only questioned her logic about spending so much time on Reza and so little with her husband. Was it really too much to ask and expect? How dare she run after a handsome man like Reza and leave him with the agony of guessing about her affairs and plans? He only wanted an explanation. But she had jumped out of the car and fled in frenzy into a dark alley, forcing him to spend hours looking for her like a lunatic. Now another woman had deserted him in distress. Thank God, at least she had not run to the balcony and jumped over.

It feels bizarre that Mahroo's dramatic reaction at the end had rekindled Erica's memory more than anything else, especially considering Mahroo's long account and delicate expressions of her amazing infatuation for him! It may also reveal something even more troublesome than his guilt for Mahroo's long agony: that maybe he is still obsessed with Erica, despite his assumptions about being over her. Another irony was that both incidents have been Reza's fault as well, although, deep down, he has felt guilty a lot himself, especially now. *Maybe my personality agitates women; perhaps the way I talk or try to be tactful? What's wrong with me? Am I really guilty of driving women crazy, including Nora, the way she has claimed a few times?*

For the last time he yells in the hallway, "Mahroo…" But she disappears behind the exit door.

With hardly any time to calm his nerves, the telephone rings.

"How'd things go with your friends from Iran?" Nora asks.

"I don't know how everything is going to work out!"

"Is there a problem already?"

"Perhaps…! I just had a conversation with Mahroo; she's been under a wrong impression for a long time. We had a scene when I tried to explain her misunderstanding. I don't blame her, either, because her brother and I have made bad judgments all along, without realizing it until now. I don't know how I can help them here, if Mahroo feels so negatively about me now. She just rushed out of my apartment in fury."

"Is this a love-related matter too?" Nora enquires.

"I'm afraid it is. Actually, it's more bizarre than any kind of love I've seen. I didn't know people could be in love for so long —three years, in this case—at such intensity and allow its agony cripple their lives. This kind of love is weird for us Westerners at least. We fall in and out of love much easier, especially when our calculations don't add up quickly."

"And amazingly, all these situations always happen to you!"

"Poor me…! I don't think I've done anything wrong, not in this instance at least."

"You must've done something to stir such passion and rage."

"Not intentionally…"

"Anyway, I've promised myself not to pry into your affairs. Have you had dinner, or wanna do something?"

"I'm too depressed to go out. You wanna come over?"

3

The next morning, Darren and Nora are having breakfast in the nook when a short, subtle knock on the door startles them.

"Good morning," Mahroo says shyly as he opens the door.

"Come in," Darren says with hesitation.

Mahroo steps inside and notices Nora's head sticking out from the nook, seeking the newcomer. Their eyes meet nosily. Darren detects Mahroo's intense stare toward the nook. He turns and witnesses Nora's glare, equally grave, their feminine instincts gauging the situation.

He introduces them tensely before turning to Mahroo. "I was planning to come over soon."

"We're ready."

"Are you missing anything in the apartment?" he asks tensely.

"No. I just came to talk to you, but you have company," Mahroo blurts rather loudly in a tense teasing tone.

"Use the bedroom if you want!" Nora interjects wittily louder with more tension.

"That's all right," Mahroo says and turns to leave. "We'll talk later."

Darren follows Mahroo, who throws another glance at Nora, nods with a playful eloquence, and leaves.

"What was that all about?" Nora asks.

"Beats me! I'm quite lost. Women of all nationalities are too complex to grasp."

"True. Men can never figure out the secrets of feminine mind; we wanna keep you confused," says Nora fretfully.

"More than what we are already?"

"Oh, so much more…! We'll drive you nuts or die trying."

"We know your powers."

"I sense a lot of anxiety and passion far beyond what you'd mentioned."

"So you think she loves me more than you do?" he asks with a chuckle, while Nora only shakes her head playfully.

4

Darren drives the family around the streets of Vancouver, mostly the North Shore region, and treats them to a nice meal at Earls before taking them for a major grocery shopping. They return home exhausted, ready to retire, except for Mahroo, who has been anxious all day to find him alone. In the elevator, she is glad that he declines her mom's invitation for tea.

"Is it okay, then, if I visit you?" she asks Darren.

"Sure...," Darren replies with hesitance, almost asking her for a promise not to attack him if she wishes to see him alone again. Yet he feels so helpless and gutless!

Ten minutes later, Mahroo raps her knuckles on Darren's door rhythmically, firmer and louder than this morning. As soon as Darren opens the door, she starts. "I called Reza last night. He finally got my point… about causing me only more pain with his foolishness and intention to save me. So I forgive you, partially."

"Oh…?!" he says with curiosity.

"Sorry for losing my temper last night. I was humiliated and your excuses only added fuel to my fury," she blurts.

He gazes at her with surprise and a subtle chuckle about her fast report and forgiveness, as if she had detected his hesitance in the elevator earlier to meet with her alone unless she promised to behave herself.

She continues, "But I must ask you a simple question?"

"Sure… If you promise I don't get into more troubles again!" he says with humour in hopes of smoothing out their relationship.

"Well, we'll see…"

"Okay... What's your question?" Darren asks timidly.

"On occasions when the matter of who is who in that painting came up, and the matter of it being your gift to me, did you ever think I might've gotten a wrong impression about your feelings for me?" she asks diligently like a Supreme Court Judge.

"Yes. I was embarrassed and considered clarifying the matter, but then felt my explanation might ruin Reza's intention or upset you, or maybe I was misinterpreting your words. So I decided to shut up and let the matter go away by itself."

"How many times did you feel I might've been misled?"

"Three times, I guess," he replies with apprehension.

"So, you knew on at least three occasions that I might've been on the wrong course emotionally and you deliberately ignored it, either out of pity for me or your pride. You assumed this situation was, at most, a simple flattery that would be forgotten soon?"

"I guess."

"Then you were wrong... You ruined many innocent lives by misjudging the consequence of your silence. That's all I wanted to point out to you; that you aren't quite innocent, after all!"

"But you just said, when you came in, that I was forgiven?" he says playfully.

"It was only conditional until I could sort out your subsequent behaviour besides the initial crime," she says also playfully.

"Gosh, you're really tricky."

"But tell me something..." She gazes into his eyes firmly.

"What?"

"If Reza expected me to project myself onto the miserable woman in the painting, who did he propose to be the man then?"

"Himself... Watching you from a distance and worrying about your marriage and depression."

"So you also knew this fact and could've at least clarified my misunderstanding when I asked you who that man was. I recall asking you this question specifically when you were recuperating in my house. You could've simply said it was Reza and the story would've ended immediately; or I would've picked it up with

Reza. But when I said I had a hunch it was you, you kept your mysterious silence, which would give anybody—especially a lonely woman—a sign of consent. What do you say about this?"

"But I *am* the man in the painting… Besides, how could I have imagined all these confusions or explain Reza's rationality and intentions for projecting himself into the man?"

"You're still trying to avoid your responsibility. That really hurts after admiring your integrity for three long years."

"I can see all these fine points only now. I'm sorry for my mistakes. What kind of apology would satisfy you?"

"None! This situation is unfixable after all this humiliation and my misplaced feeling for you. Seeing how happy you are with your lovers is too embarrassing when I'd all along imagined you adored only me. Even if you'd ever had any feelings for me, now or before, it'll feel fake and childish after all this mayhem. I'd better go," Mahroo exclaims tensely, tears flooding down her pale, tired face. She charges abruptly out of the apartment again, leaving Darren alone to munch on her words.

5

Mahroo drops by occasionally only to borrow something, which gives her an excuse for another casual visit just for returning it. A civilized atmosphere prevails, allowing Darren to help the family when necessary, and to communicate with Mahroo cagily. Her parents sense the gravity of the atmosphere without knowing what to make of it. Meanwhile, Mahroo hesitates to reveal her recent arguments with Darren and the fall of their love empire.

Darren's three-week anxiety about Mahroo's arrival subsides gradually, which helps him paint and meditate in the quiet of his apartment. Obviously, the unexpected turn of events about the infamous painting and Mahroo's ordeal somewhat upset him, but overall he is glad that the peculiar misunderstanding is resolved. Nonetheless, his prediction and stress about some unpleasant situation with Mahroo had proven justified.

He feels flattered occasionally when he ponders the sheer size of her affection, which she had kept to herself like a divine secret, while he had somehow let this emotional mix-up linger, perhaps unconsciously. Most evil has been his subtle thrill from Mahroo's open infatuation that he had felt from the very start, three years back, and still done nothing to rectify her huge misunderstanding. She is absolutely right: He has been quite guilty, if not wicked, he admits now whole-heartedly.

He realizes that any kind of relationship with Mahroo might prove catastrophic. Yet, her kind of love may deserve a reward, after all, he ponders. Maybe they in fact belong together. Why should she disappear from his life? Why should he torture such a loyal lover? Why should he torture himself? But how could he get her mixed up in his chaotic life? He closes his eyes and imagines her cute face, tears, and exquisite body... holding her shapely hands, now embracing her tightly, and now kissing her face and lips. She hides her subtle howling behind his kind, caressing hands by pressing them tightly over her face.

Peering at his empty hands closely and rubbing them together, Darren returns to reality, now overwhelmed by a different kind of anxiety: His heart and mind quarrel like two spoiled kids, his spirit refereeing like a helpless mother desperately watching her kids' senseless attacks and accusations, yet unable to judge. He chuckles and imagines that, like the distraught mother, he should pinch each child by the ear, drag them away, and lock them both in a closet. "You stay there until you have something sensible to say to each other," the mother says. But all Darren's spirit can hear from his heart and mind is more moaning and excuses, which only aggravate his frustration and sense of helplessness.

While bringing another load of paint to the canvas and starting new lines and shadows, his mind drifts off to his meeting with Dervish Ali in Iran, one and a half year ago. Dervish's words of wisdom about love roll in his head. They feel so timely again now with a few women, especially Mahroo, crowding his life and causing him so much confusion and headache.

****

Reza had convinced Dervish Ali to see Darren one afternoon. His small house was in the southern part of Tehran in a less affluent neighbourhood. The seventy-year-old house looked in excellent shape despite the discoloured yellow bricks, random cracks and chips, and minute graffiti on some corners of the outside walls—the neighbourhood kids' artistic expressions apparently. Like a small replica of the medieval castle gates, the entrance was a dark green bulky wooden double door about four inches thick and it looked even older than the house itself.

A woman wearing chador heaved the hulking, screeching door open in a slow motion and greeted Reza. Her face turned halfway from the guests, she avoided eye contact while her hand tightly clasped the chador near her mouth. She asked them to wait in the living room for Dervish Ali. Descending two steps, they came to a small yard fully covered in patterned, grey cement blocks. In the middle, a little pond stood one foot above the ground with its green ceramic tiles highlighting the hue of the gleaming goldfish spinning in clear water. Potted flowers, mostly geraniums, and shrubs surrounded the pond and another group stretched against the walls. Then there was a two-story brick building, sturdy and well maintained both outside and inside. Up ten tall steps to the second floor, they entered the living room with a dark brown Tabriz covering the floor and ancient furniture scattered modestly throughout.

Dervish Ali's wife returned promptly with a tray and placed it on the windowsill near the room entrance. She mumbled some words to Reza, who then carried the tray of teas and sweets to the table before them. They drank the tea in silence amidst Reza's random whispers about the woman and the house. Dervish Ali emerged after twelve minutes and apologized for the delay due to the afternoon prayer. A bulky, charismatic man with a peculiarly long mustache covering his lips, he wore a long, loose, buttonless robe with broad half-sleeves revealing the white shirt underneath it. A dire curiosity distracted Darren suddenly: *How can he eat food with that bushy mustache? He must be a guru, for sure, just for sneaking spoonfuls under that long mustache!*

After a short conversation with Reza in Persian, he turned to Darren. "So what's your question, my son?"

"Actually, I feel so confused nowadays I don't know where to begin. The main question bothering me is, 'How can I find peace and happiness when I feel so lonely, but cannot trust people anymore, especially women?'"

"Let's see if I understand your question. You're trying to find peace and freedom by eluding objects and people. But then you can't tolerate loneliness. Is this your question?"

"Yes. Mainly I wonder if I can ever love someone again, and if not, how to be happy alone."

"I see your dilemma. Without love, we feel empty, but then loving someone is always risky even if we knew how to do it."

"So what's the solution?"

"A wise man finds love inside himself, instead of hoping to get it from others. Or at least, he learns to live alone without a lover. Then he won't feel empty or lonely."

"How do I find it inside myself?"

"By becoming a good human being. It's your choice and art to love another person, object, activity, or nature. But expecting another person to be mentally and physically ready to love you forever is doom. You must love many things and people, merely for their basic properties and friendships with you."

"Does romantic love has any value then?" Darren asks.

"Romantic love has been confused with our personal urges to possess and dominate others or expect them to fit our personal values and lifestyle. With our huge egos, we impose our crooked views of love on others, ask them to change, and measure their love by their level of obedience."

"So trusting love nowadays is foolish!?"

"Love should give us inner peace and pleasure. Any love that causes pain and pessimism is already contaminated and no longer true! And like all other joys, love is flimsy as well. You cannot expect it to last or be mutual. Enjoy loving but don't crave love. Find things to love in nature and yourself."

"Not in another person?"

"Love a person only when ready to pay the price and know how to go about it without hurting yourself or her too much."

"Then I'd better look only for a reliable companion."

"At least you're smart to separate love and companionship."

"We cannot have both, right?"

"Only seldom! I'd say, 'Love not for the sake of marrying; marry not for the sake of love.' Try to grasp the meaning of my motto without getting thrown by its initial harsh impression."

"I understand," Darren said.

"Tell me."

"Avoiding obsession and ownership is the only proof of love's authenticity. And for marriage, one must first find good reasons for it without stressing on love. Right?"

"Yes… That's the gist of it. Compassion is a good thing for relationships, too, but it's different from 'love.' Right?"

"Yes," Darren says.

"You'll find many other reasons to support my ideas."

"So, it's wise to look only for a loyal companion?"

"Absolutely… But ignoring 'love' is not wise or easy, either. This divine feeling brings us inner peace and self-awareness, for some people at least. You must find love in yourself and spread it among other humans and things."

"Why is loving another person so difficult?"

"Because you must concentrate on his or her qualities and strengths, rather than criticizing him or her constantly. When you find beauty in a thing or person, try to appreciate and enjoy it the way it is while it lasts, because it perishes soon regardless of your passion and efforts to make it permanent. It'll slip away, become irrelevant as one matures in life, or its meaning changes."

"But finding and keeping even a companion is so difficult nowadays."

"That's true...," Dervish Ali says.

"Why?"

"Since we don't know how to treat and tolerate each other."

"So, now you know why I'm confused."

"I do. Yet, you may still find someone to share your lives in peace and harmony, without forcing your demented demands on each other. You could be lucky and find a quiet relationship filled with unselfish love. Sometimes, two individuals are quite smart and lucky to share both love and a good relationship."

"I don't think I'll be that lucky."

"Most likely! But I hope you get the gist of what I'm telling you and find your inner peace at least with or without love."

"I hope so too."

"These are only guidelines for you to ponder. One day you may grasp the meanings of my words. I see you as a smart man who only needs a platform to build his own beliefs gradually."

"Thanks, Mr. Dervish Ali."

"Do you have any other question?"

"Yes. I'm also unhappy about my own hypocrisy when I try to fit in this idiotic society. How can I become honest with myself and relax when it's so hard to curb my selfish urges or thoughts?"

"Your conscience apparently hurts you when, for example, you feel jealous or lie for convenience or tactfulness! Right?"

"Yes."

"It's strange that you feel, and suffer from, your own flaws. Most people only justify or deny them, hoping to fool others and themselves."

"Often I wish I could be like others, and rather reckless, too."

"Don't fight your conscience too much. Don't be so hard on yourself and others, either. Instead, learn to forgive them and yourself; learn to accept the reality of living in such a chaotic world. We can't change it, so cope with it."

"Yet, our coping efforts cause so much confusion and stress."

"Of course… Anyway, the fact that you wish to control your tacky urges and thoughts would most likely help you eventually.

With awareness, you'll gain more self-control and won't need to lie or be a hypocrite to deal with society."

"I hope I gain the wisdom to learn all these gimmicks…"

"I think you know how to get there, but just need more time to raise your self-awareness, build your convictions, and overcome your crooked habits. Create a simple life for yourself and control your ego and ambitions."

"I really hope you're right and I can find my way and peace."

"Be brave and keep faith despite inevitable disappointments. Learn about your true needs and feelings and resist the artificial ones. You don't need to be a phony man to be happy or get other people's respect, but don't condemn others and their ways of life, either. Try to humour people, bear their values and flaws, and follow your passions quietly on the side for your own sake only."

For two hours, Dervish Ali listened and responded to Darren patiently, until he seemed to have grasped the gist of Dervish's wisdom. Dervish Ali promised all these points would sink into Darren's mind gradually, although they might have appeared odd during this brief session.

Darren pondered Dervish Ali's advice quietly as Reza drove the long distance back to Darren's home, careful not to interrupt Darren's pensive mood. Getting out of the car, Darren thanked Reza and asked, "When can I see Dervish Ali again? I'd like to find out more about Sufism, if possible."

"Honestly, the prospects aren't good. He's a busy and private man. I had to plead for tonight's meeting; I can't promise he'll see you again soon. But I'll try."

Chapter Six
The Meaning of Love

1

Darren stops painting as haunting memories of Erica and Iran keep distracting him. Staring idly at lacklustre brushstrokes, even Mozart's rigorous performance in the background feels dull and irritating. He imagines Mozart grimacing at him for ignoring him and his heavenly arias that have always raised Darren's spirit. He drops the paintbrush irately, turns off the CD player, and hurries downstairs to get some fresh air.

Mrs. Stanley and her spaniel are strolling toward Mahroo, who is sitting on a bench near the Creek. For a moment, Darren imagines a young Mrs. Stanley as lovely as Mahroo. Perhaps she is thinking the same thing, looking at Mahroo, recalling youth and pretending life is still beautiful. He scurries to save Mahroo from her, to no avail.

"Hi, dear. Are you new in our building?" She asks Mahroo.

"Yes. I arrived last Saturday from Iran," Mahroo replies.

"You mind if I sit here?" Mrs. Stanley asks.

"Please…"

"So, how's the war? It must be hard on you people."

"It is. People are depressed and fed up."

"I was a young girl when my father died in the big war."

"Hello, ladies," interjects Darren.

"Hello, Darren," replies Mahroo.

"You know her *already*?" Mrs. Stanley asks Darren with a grimace.

He grins at Mahroo. "She's my best friend's sister."

"What's there?" Mahroo asks, staring beyond the Creek at the seemingly busy crowd in the distance.

"There're shops, fruit and meat markets, and restaurants. It's called Granville Island. Wanna go there?" Darren asks.

"Yes," Mahroo replies and darts off the bench.

Mrs. Stanley watches them rush away without inviting her, too. *One ages a few years and she's treated like an alien wanted on no planet,* ponders Mrs. Stanley with despair.

On Granville Island, Darren buys coffee and muffins and they find a table on the pier near the snaky Creek extending toward the ocean. He surveys the water curiously and Mahroo watches his pensive face with pity, both unsure what kind of conversation would be safe and proper.

Finally he speaks. "Look at the creek. You cannot tell whether it's flowing in or out. It looks stationary, but there're definitely currents down there."

"Like my life: Stagnant and meaningless, yet all kinds of turmoil push my nerves deep down."

"Like everybody's life. We all feel this way often."

"Most people seem to know how not to fuss about it so much at least."

"How're you feeling, Mahroo? Today, I mean."

"I just told you… Just floating in midair like a lost balloon."

"Where're your parents and Nazi?"

"They went out with friends."

"Nazi goes with them usually, ha?"

"They and Martha have practically raised her. I haven't been a particularly patient mother, thanks to you."

"Thanks to me? Is that my fault too?"

"I'd rather not talk about it."

"Sorry…"

"That's alright…"

"So you have the whole day to enjoy the sun and relax!"

"Maybe, but mostly to sort out my life's sudden changes."

"In what way?" he asks.

"All those years of suffering, at least dreams and sometimes soothing daydreams kept me alive. But now suddenly all my hopes and fantasies have dried up. With all the recent blows, my mind is dull and I hate myself for just sitting idly and watching time's futile flow."

"You sound like a poet! Your English is also commendable!"

"I guess that's how one becomes a good poet—through love and agony," she replies with a giggle.

"Yeah, life just goes by aimlessly when no specific desire or dream drives us… At least we agree about life being a big drag."

"We do, ha?" she asks with a smirk.

"Yes, I have my own chronic cynicism about existence and our pathetic struggles to get something out of our lives."

"In that case, maybe we should marry, after all!" Mahroo says with a teasing grin. "We'll be the most cynical couple on earth."

Darren burst into laughter, "Yes, definitely… I wonder who would drive the other crazier faster."

"Just imagine the kind of children we can raise," she says with a giggle."

"But we can make each other laugh a bit sometimes, too."

"You know… I just realized a big existential secret."

"What's that?" he asks.

"Now I believe that even the suffering caused by melancholic dreams is better than the calmness of a dreamless life."

"That's a profound thought."

"It's also another mysterious reality of existence," she replies.

"And another big dilemma for humans," he adds.

"When I found out that my thoughts about our love had been only delusions, I went berserk—you recall very well, I bet. But later, I realized I didn't wish those years had been any different. Although I suffered badly, without all that hope to find true love someday, I would've perished in such a crazy environment. Zia and the war had shattered my spirit. I had serious doubts about the whole purpose of living, anyway. In its own crazy way, thinking about you at least kept me alive and focused."

"So, am I forgiven *again*?" Darren asks teasingly.

"Not at all! The refuge you caused accidentally doesn't wash your deliberate, or at least thoughtless, handling of a heart-related matter. Your insensitivity can't be justified or excused. That part is final."

"You're so cruel to me despite your alleged passion for me."

"You deserve it. Make no mistake about it."

"Oh, dear...," blurts Darren, staring over Mahroo's shoulder into a distance, smiling with delirium.

Mahroo turns to find the cause of Darren's fervent fascination. Approaching them with a grin dreamier than Darren's is a pretty woman. Mahroo sits back with disgust as Darren rises and hugs the woman.

"We should stop meeting this way." he says to her, pulling out a chair for her. "Have a seat."

"I often come to Granville Island on Tuesday afternoons to meet a client," Elizabeth explains. "Usually I don't return to the office afterward."

"That's wonderful," Darren replies and then introduces her to Mahroo. The two ladies nod courteously but curiously.

"How's Jeff?" he continues, mostly for Mahroo's benefit—to divulge the existence of an important man in Elizabeth's life.

"Okay; going away to L.A. *next week* for business instead of this week," Elizabeth emphasizes, winking at Darren privately.

Darren thinks that Elizabeth's cunning comment could have actually raised anybody's suspicion. So he changes the subject quickly: "Mahroo is Reza's sister. She arrived with her parents and pretty daughter last Saturday. They're living in my building."

"How wonderful! Are you planning to stay in Canada?"

"I'm not sure," Mahroo replies passively.

Elizabeth feels unwelcome. They seem to have been in the middle of hot or intimate chitchat. She gestures to rise and leave, but Darren stops her. "Let me get you a cup of coffee."

Still Elizabeth insists on leaving after quickly measuring the atmosphere and concluding that not all parties appreciated her presence. "I should do some shopping and go make dinner. We'll call you soon, Darren. It was nice meeting you, Mar…"

"Mah…roo!" he interjects.

"See you, Darren," Elizabeth says, sauntering away, but then turning and waving to him sluggishly from afar, while his eyes trace her with passion for a long while.

"Another lover?" Mahroo enquires after a long silence.

"What? Oh, her…? No…" He is speechless. Lying is safer for Elizabeth's sake and for protecting his image. He is becoming a true hypocrite, although his lies seem to backfire eventually, anyway. "Elizabeth is Erica's best friend. I know her boyfriend, Jeff, too. I hadn't seen her for four years and then suddenly I ran into her last Tuesday, and again today. What a coincidence, eh?"

"Yeah, what a coincidence!" she replies sarcastically, fully disbelieving his insinuation of innocence. It is more sensible to trust her feminine intuition than all the garbage he is trying hard to unload on her. *How silly these men are, really,* Mahroo thinks. *Elizabeth is definitely another mistress and I don't blame her.*

Darren peers into her eyes and reads her thoughts. *Well, she didn't buy my bullshit and I don't blame her.*

"Must you always introduce me as Reza's sister? I have my own identity, you know."

"Sorry, but since Elizabeth knows Reza, I thought maybe the information was interesting."

"Does Mrs. Stanley know Reza too?"

"No...," he replies with a burst of laughter. "You become a bit uptight sometimes."

"Do I?" she asks.

"Listen, I didn't mean to make you suffer for loving me, even though today you've changed your mind and think it had actually been a blessing," he blasts due to his lingering stress. "Maybe your logic and perceptions need a serious review."

"Are you saying I'm a psycho?"

"No, but maybe you should go see a specialist to stop hurting yourself and others. Too much pressure eventually drives any man crazy, maybe even Zia too, you never know!"

"So you think I caused his suicide?" she asks with stress.

"Even I feel guilty sometimes about my own tiny role."

"That's a good sign at least... You should feel guilty...!"

"But maybe you're guilty of something, too," he says.

"Maybe... Maybe I should see a shrink for something... But how about you? Are you happy even with all these lovers hovering around you?"

"Yes, I'm happy."

"Just be honest with yourself at least."

"Actually, I try to do that too often even though it hurts!"

"So what's the verdict?" she asks.

"Sometimes I feel lucky and happy, but often not so much. But at least I'm trying to learn about love and myself outside the box," he says. "Maybe I'll be free and happy someday and find a good mate, too, if I clean my soul and mind. At least I'm trying —the same way your brother is."

"Still, you hope to find someone to love, right?"

"I guess... with a simpler view of love, of course."

"Simpler...! That's original!"

"Yes... Although it usually sounds crooked to others."

"Explain it. Maybe I learn something from you today."

"I doubt it. It may actually offend you."

"It won't. Don't worry..."

"Just love someone while you feel it sincerely and it works smoothly without demanding it and then let it go…"

"Is this all love means to you?"

"It's simpler… Admit it...," he replies with a giggle.

"Are you fooling with me today?" she asks edgily.

"I knew my view is against your impression of love. Sorry," he states fretfully, trying to avoid another round of arguments.

"But you agree a couple might love each other forever, right?"

"Sometimes… More importantly, though, most people can learn to build lifetime relationships without fussing so much about love."

"So you think building good relationships is wiser and easier without fussing about love per se?" Mahroo asks.

"Yes, that's my point," he says. "Love is just a myth, anyway. Even if it plays a role in human life, only a few might learn how to make it work."

"Why?" she asks with cynicism.

Darren hesitates, despising recent recurring situations forcing him to explain love to others. *What do I know about these stuff? Am I now suddenly a 'love' guru because I spent a few minutes with Dervish Ali and read a few books?* At the end, he decides to offer a simple explanation:

"Well, love starts with a fanfare—an attraction—but evolves through trials and errors toward utter beauty and joy. Even then, lovers must keep discovering interesting things about each other forever to retain their sentiments and avoid boredom, something like a self-actualization process. Most people run out of steam or patience to learn about their lovers other than maybe more flaws. So their love fades away."

"So all love affairs perish soon, you think?"

"Yes, scientific studies show love dies within six months to two years. Only a small group can keep their love forever, if they know how to feed the love cycle intuitively, or die before the cycles become too rusty and painful. Smart people flee fast if the cycle slows down noticeably, before they face the agonies of sluggish cycles."

"Then love is not merely a myth, after all," Mahroo says.

"It's not quite real, either. We're attracted to someone, call it love, and get confused. It's difficult for most people to nurture love properly even when someone grasps its meaning."

"And it gets quite excruciating when people don't even know what love is, you say, ha?" she asks.

"Yes, I think so…"

"So looking for love is futile then, you think?"

"That's how I feel. Most of us would be lucky to find even a manageable relationship, never mind a lasting love."

Darren pauses a minute to gauge Mahroo, who is pensive and quiet. He then continues: "As far as your love is concerned, it's been totally fanciful and against everything I just said. You knew nothing about me other than my appearance and a little about my origins. This is naïve even for the first phase of love—to discover your lover. Ask yourself—after all these arguments—whether you still love me, and if yes, why?"

"All I've known all along is my desire to be near you."

"But that's not love or enough for a long relationship! I hope you see your desire's vanity. We haven't had a chance to interact properly. Your love for me is built only around a deep confusion about the content and purpose of the *Woman in the White Dress.* It is on an even shakier ground than my love for Erica was."

"Yet, you still seem to be in love with her, aren't you?"

"No, I don't think so," he replies with tension and confusion.

"I think you are… And it is amazing…"

"You know what is more amazing?"

"What?" she asks.

"Your belief to sense my lingering emotions for Erica better than I do."

"But I'm right, aren't I? Most women can feel these things…"

"So how did you make such a huge mistake about my love for you?" Darren asks triumphantly with some kind of satisfaction.

"Our intuition isn't foolproof, of course. But maybe I wasn't wrong at all, after all," Mahroo says with a chuckle and a sense of satisfaction of her own.

"Still, I think the way you'd felt and lived for three years had been just *too amazing*," he says, proud of himself for forcing his big tongue to utter *only* 'too amazing' instead of 'too stupid.'

"In what sense?" she asks with irritation, rather realizing what Darren is implying.

"The way your basic imaginations alone had created such a fantastical love impression in your head toward me!"

"You apparently did the same thing with Erica, didn't you?"

"What do you mean?" he asks with another revelation.

"At least you've confessed and still believe you loved Erica for many years, right?" Mahroo asks slyly like a Supreme Court Judge again. "You loved her even after you felt she didn't love you as much as you'd imagined and maybe betraying you, too."

"Yes, in a peculiar way. And that's probably why I think the way I think about love these days... Don't you get it?"

"So the question is what your love for Erica meant then!"

"That's a good question, I admit. I know I was naïve about love then myself, like most people, and maybe you these days."

"Not anymore, ha...?"

"I hope so... But a more relevant question is, 'Why can't we become more practical and honest about our ultimate intention and stop making love a scapegoat for justifying our affairs?' And the question is, 'Why can't we learn how to build a relationship that fits the reality of life and forget about love to a large extent?' You should be more familiar with this idea than I am."

"How's that?"

"I learned that a great majority of couples in Iran concentrate on relationships instead of fantasizing about love."

"They're changing fast too."

"That's a pity... Love wasn't such a delusional and lucrative industry in older cultures. And now we're ruining them, too!"

"I agree that a good relationship is always the ultimate goal," she says as if just hoping to reconcile with Darren and move on.

"Alas we lose our chances simply because our impressions of love are so unmanageable. Then, as our love fades, we lose sight of the relationships' needs and let it slip as well," he says, feeling exhausted, yet unable to portray a useful picture of love and relationships to Mahroo. Then again, she seems to have her own valid perceptions about both love and relationships, despite her three-year fanatical love saga, not to mention her capacity and tenacity to challenge his theories like a guru as well!

"I know what you're saying. But your points have a flaw," she says.

"What flaw?" Darren asks with stress regarding her simple views tainting his elaborate theories.

"You're analyzing love logically," Mahroo asserts, somewhat intimidated by Darren's cynicism about her love for him.

"Obviously attraction and chemistry are beyond logic. And that's exactly why they can't be trusted or taken as the main factors for *discovering* another person," he declares.

"Yet we cannot avoid these natural feelings."

"That is partly true. But the problem nowadays is that general social deprivations make us vulnerable to the smallest dose of attraction."

"You're right...," she says sincerely as if recalling the external causes of her own past vulnerability—due to the war and a lousy husband—tainting her emotions toward him and in general.

"Yeah… We often sink ourselves in the ocean of superficial sentiments suddenly in order to soothe our sufferings and bring hope and moments of relief into our lives. We also create love to fight our fear of loneliness or to build our identities in a family."

Still appearing not totally convinced, Mahroo remains quiet, pondering his explanations. More surprisingly, her points seem to have shaken his own conviction about love, too. Yet he does not feel like pushing his or her ideas any further. Instead, he studies the rhythm of ripples ridden by the boats trafficking in the Creek.

"We'd better head home. My parents are probably back, wondering about me," she says with gloom and rises. "They've probably knocked on your door and assumed we were cuddling when nobody answered. One of these days, I should tell them we're through, but I don't have the heart to crush their hopes for my happiness after so long."

"You haven't hinted anything yet?"

"No… By the way, they're going to Whistler with friends this weekend. They've invited me, too, but I'd rather stay here and perhaps see you some more. Maybe you'd like to take me for dinner and dancing on Friday or Saturday night, or both nights," Mahroo imposes with great charm.

"Perhaps Saturday night, but I'm busy on Friday with Nora," he lies, hoping to save his Friday night at least. Seeing her once, preferably closer to the return of her family from Whistler, might be proper. He feels obliged to make her feel better about herself somehow and perhaps forgive him and Reza, too.

2

Mahroo's mom, Reza, and T.J. have left messages on Darren's answering machine. Mahroo's return has taken care of the first message and he should grill Mahroo before answering Reza's suspicious call from Iran. So he dials T.J.'s number, surprised how fast this old man has turned into a wise confidant. Of course, Reza's friendship feels even more critical and precious these days due to Mahroo's mood causing havoc for both of them.

Darren gives T.J. a general report about his life before getting to the main issue he had meant to rob on his face, "Now, it seems that my concern about Mahroo's trip to Vancouver had been quite justified."

"Yeah?"

"Yes. It all goes to show how our mystical psyche always sends us all these subtle hunches."

"Right…! Is there a problem?"

"She's been under the impression that I've been in love with her all along because of my painting that Reza gave her. Do you remember the story of the *Woman in the White Dress*?"

"Yeah."

"We had a big argument about who is responsible for her and Zia's suffering. Someone has made some misjudgments, but who? She's not forgiving me but also claims to love me. I'm starting to think she's a little bit cuckoo…"

"Why? You think she must forgive you first if she's allowed to keep loving you?" T.J. teases him.

"Is that a tough condition to impose, you think?" Darren asks and they burst into laughter. "But, seriously, I really don't need any more headaches, especially with Reza over this matter."

"Didn't you say she's gorgeous?"

"So? Don't you always criticize my sloppy flings?"

"I'm only teasing and testing you now. But I always leave room for flexibility, too, when some sensual factors exist."

"Like what?"

"Well, if she's such a unique goddess, I'd think twice before passing up the opportunity of courting her. But your point about avoiding unnecessary headaches also makes sense."

"So you're just a typical man with no fixed principles, eh?"

"I guess so. I'm a deprived man too, after all," T.J. replies.

Darren burst into laughter.

"You have a tough choice to make, anyway, my friend," T.J. continues. "But I wish I were lucky enough, once in my life, to have an angel like the way you explain Mahroo love me truly— such wishful thinking!"

"I can introduce her to you, to try your luck," Darren says.

"If I had luck, my name would've been Darren—not T.J.— and I would've been twenty years younger with the kind of hair you have. So, what's your plan?"

"I'm not sure—not because I'm getting tempted, but because I don't want to cause more hassles for her, Reza, or myself. I wish she'd return to Iran tomorrow and let me deal with the rest of my problems."

"Love affairs, you mean!" T.J. blurts jokingly.

"Whatever! But seriously, do you have any suggestions?"

"You're doing fine on your own. Just follow your intuition. As you said, your psychic hunches have proved reliable. Be kind and honest with her and resist temptation. Let her see that you're not as good as your appearance suggests, but also be kind to her. She's gone through a bad marriage and needs help recovering."

"Okay. I'll try to cope with the situation as it develops."

"Just stick to your plan. You know very well how they can lure us."

"I will. Enough about my problems; how're you doing?"

"I don't know how we can even bother talking about my boring life when even your problems are so intriguing! But thanks for asking. I'm busy with my usual stuff. My family will stay in San Francisco for another week since the kids have no school. So, I called to see what your plans are. Perhaps we can get together."

"Good idea, but my painting deadlines are up and Nora will kill me if I renege again. I'll see how work progresses and call you before the weekend. I'm taking Nora out on Friday and Mahroo on Saturday though."

"She's already softening you?"

"She sort of imposed herself on me."

"Exactly... That's one of their million ways!"

"Well her parents are going out of town and she probably feels too lonely, alone for the whole weekend," Darren says.

"But she could always go with them, couldn't she?" T.J. asks.

"Yeah, I guess so... Are you interrogating me, too, the way she's been doing last few days?"

T.J. burst into laughter. "I guess I was challenging your logic and excuses... That's all."

"Then stop it...," Darren says with a giggle. "Shouldn't she leave with some exciting memories of Vancouver at least?"

"Whatever…"

"I don't mind showing her a couple of clubs, anyway."

"Okay, if you know what you're doing. Call me when you're free to meet. Sometime this year, I hope!"

3

Darren needs all the details to deal with Reza. This special case requires some diplomacy and calm. So, despite the possibility of more arguments wasting his precious time and creative energy, Darren calls Mahroo to enquire about her discussion with Reza.

"Your parents left a message on my answering machine, probably worried about you..." He pauses as she starts muttering with somebody around her.

"Come over for supper… I'm making spaghetti," she says.

"No, thanks. I must do some painting. I just wanna know—"

"Come just for dinner. My mother insists."

"Okay… But I'd like to ask you something."

"What?"

"I like to know what exactly you've told Reza before I return his call; I think that's why he's called me."

"I'll tell you everything after dinner. Just get over here."

Darren calls Nora and makes a date for Friday. He then changes, grabs a bottle of wine from the rack in the kitchen, and departs for Mahroo's apartment. The supper is ready and Mahroo begins serving it after putting the bottle of wine, a corkscrew, and two wineglasses before Darren. "My parents don't drink wine."

She shows a special craving for wine tonight, gulping down fast every refill Darren offers her. Maybe their long debate this afternoon at Granville Island about the meaning of love has made her so restless and reckless, he muses with amusement and some level of guilt for the possibility of messing up her head more than it had been already. Half an hour later, dinner finished, the bottle empty, she is fully jovial. *I must learn to keep my big mouth shut more often!* Darren ponders.

"How was the wine you brought?" Mahroo asks at the end with a chuckle.

"Well… The few drops I tasted were fine," Darren says. "But food was surely delicious and I ate more than usual."

"I'm glad you liked it as much as I liked your wine," she says.

"She's a great cook, finicky about the food she makes for her special guests in particular," Mahroo's mom interjects in broken English.

"You're right. I haven't had such tasty spaghetti anywhere. I remember all her delicious food in Iran, too," Darren confirms.

"All this talent and beauty…! I see many pretty girls here, but Mahroo is different, is she or not?" Mahroo's mom blabbers with great passion, but also possibly using the occasion to practise her English. Her remarks remind Darren of a recent Italian movie he had seen, where a pesky mother praises her homely daughter in front of a potential suitor.

"*Maman…* Stop it!" Mahroo shrieks. "Stop pestering him."

"It's okay, Mahroo. Your mother's right." He then turns to Mahroo's mom. "So, how do you like Vancouver so far?"

"It's a beautiful, cozy city with clean air," she replies.

After tea and cake, Mahroo motions Darren to follow her to the balcony and closes the glass door behind them. They lean against the railing and survey the street below and the Island, where automobiles and people mingle in the dusk's dim light. Mahroo staggers toward the far end of the balcony, where the view of mountains in the north complements the south-westerly ocean scenery.

Abruptly she stands on the lower bar of the railing, closes her eyes, inhales a big breath with a gasping noise, stretches her arms toward Heaven, and howls, "Oh, God… Why did You create love?"

Mahroo's words and acrobatics jolt Darren fifteen feet away from her. With a good portion of her body above the railing, she might trip over immediately if she leans or her feet slide over the top of the curvy bar. She is surely drunk. He knows that yelling or dashing to catch her might startle her, lose her balance, and maybe even drag him down with her. Any kind of hasty reaction is risky. *But I must think quickly.* Eight steps to reach her, Mahroo still mocking God and destiny, with her arms flung in the air.

He ascertains she must not be startled even slightly, while he takes the first step toward her very softly, then the second... and the fifth... approaching her cautiously. But what to do once near here? She is probably unaware of the danger, due to the wine or her general mood these days. Or maybe she is planning to jump right in front of him out of spite or mere lunacy?

An odd idea crosses his mind as he ponders his options. He lurches the last two steps warily but does not stop. Once next to her, he bends his knees and jams her firmly against the railing. The weight of his body now protects them while she is tightly sandwiched between him and the railing. He gasps a big sigh of relief. Softly, he slides his hands over the length of her flinging, bare arms, until she lowers her hands and grabs his. Gradually, he brings all four arms down, wondering whether her parents are observing their erotic dance and interpreting it a thousand ways. Thank God, nobody has come out to scream at her or him. Let's hope they have not seen anything?

Focused on the nerve-racking task of rescuing Mahroo, still ecstasy overwhelms him. The mesmerizing scent of her body and the softness of her skin have inebriated all his senses. Her hot, arousing body temperature has evoked an excruciatingly erotic sensation in him. Holding her hands tightly, he thrusts her down the ridge of the railing. She turns slowly and seductively, pressing her big breasts against his chest. He is about to faint, which is surely not a fair reward for preventing a possible catastrophe. Soon, however, he regains his composure, takes a deep breath, untangles himself from her, and releases her hands slowly. They gaze at each other with surprise and ecstasy.

"What was that...?" Mahroo whispers in a wheezing voice. Darren's embrace, so tight and surprising, after years of desperate anticipation, has revived her spirit—a revelation sweeter than all her daydreams about this moment. His panting and sudden urge to hold her in his strong arms reveal his indisputable attraction to her, she is now sure finally. But then as she had turned to kiss him, he had rejected her and retreated! This is humiliating! What kind of flirtation is this, anyway?

"I'm sorry if I offended you," he replies.

"Are you shy or only mocking me?"

"No, please don't misinterpret my action. I had to bring you down the railing without grabbing or startling you. So, using my knees seemed the safest idea."

"Is this another game you're playing with me?"

"Oh, no, believe me… Sorry…" Darren is confused himself.

"Why don't you admit you're attracted to me, too?"

"No, it was nothing like that at all. I was only trying to prevent an accident. You'd put yourself in danger without realizing it. Please don't do that again. Promise!"

"Why do you care?"

"I like your whole family. Promise you won't do that again."

"I promise only if you confess you care for me the most and deeply. You don't have to declare eternal love today, if you're shy," Mahroo says with a chuckle.

"Okay. I care about you deeply. And I'm also attracted to you sometimes." He knows he is not lying. "But I can't be in love." *Gosh, she's really softening me, as T.J. had warned!*

"Maybe love comes later," Mahroo blurts teasingly. "I won't stand on the railing again. I want you to be happy with me!"

"Thanks."

"So you like to know what I told Reza?" Mahroo changes the subject quickly, as if protecting the milestone she has reached with him today. It is a great foundation to build on later if he really has some feelings for her.

"Yes. I don't want to upset Reza over a misunderstanding."

"I told him exactly how I felt about him after I calmed down and pondered our first night's conversation. Your explanations made a little sense and proved your innocence that night. I told him you believed this whole incident had resulted from Reza's miscalculated presentation of the painting to me. I told him we both felt he's responsible for three years of my pain. Then I gave him a good piece of my mind. I didn't accept his explanations or apologies after he realized how mad I was with him. At the end, I told him I didn't want to talk to him—for a while, at least—because he's destroyed my life by meddling in my affairs, even if he'd had valid brotherly concerns. Of course, I felt differently about your share of the guilt the next morning. But when I called him, I thought you were innocent and had almost forgiven you. So he got all the blames and curses I could think of at the time."

"But that wasn't exactly what I said and meant about his role in this matter," Darren protests.

"Didn't you say only Reza was responsible for everything?"

"Yes, but the way you've said it to Reza leaves room about my intentions. Actually, I'd said nobody knew about the pain we'd caused you inadvertently. Only Reza was slightly at fault for the way he'd communicated with you about the painting and whose gift it'd been to whom, that's all."

"That still sounds the same to me. And now we know you're as guilty as he is, because you and I talked about the painting and whose gift it was to whom on a few occasions, and you didn't open your mouth to correct my mistake."

"Yes, I agree with you…"

"Actually, now that I think about it, you've been responsible for all my confusion," she says as if awakened from a dream.

"I have?" Darren asks with angst.

"Yes. You're guiltier than Reza because you knew a mistake had been made and a misperception created, but poor Reza knew nothing about the consequence of his words and the growing misunderstanding behind the scene."

"Yes, I knew about the possible misperception, but I couldn't imagine it'd cause so much grief and chaos."

"Well… I think I'll call Reza myself to say I've changed my mind about him being the only guilty person. I'll say I've now concluded you are as much, or probably more, guilty than he is. Anyway, I won't forgive either one of you for a long time."

"Fine, I admit my guilt now. But can we somehow get over all these terrible mix-ups? How can I make you forgive me?"

"Love is the only cure, of course. But that ship has probably sailed now."

"We're most likely not compatible, anyway…," Darren says.

"Yeah... We've both had our shares of disappointments with love, but still seek a special person in our own ways."

"Let's hope we'll succeed to do so someday," he says.

"It's a pity our minds and circumstances didn't cross in the right way at the right time. Otherwise, we might've been perfect for one another. We had our chances, but maybe we blew them."

"You're right. It's strange how destiny betrays us."

"We humans are all doomed, especially if we're romantic!" Mahroo concludes with a sigh. "Let's go back inside. I wonder what my parents are thinking about us."

"I hope they didn't see me grabbing you so seductively," he says with a sombre voice.

Mahroo steps inside with a shy grin at her parents.

"Why was he hugging you, Maman?" Nazi rushes and asks in Persian. Mahroo is startled and her parents frown with surprise before turning their heads toward Mahroo and Darren back and forth. Darren wonders what Nazi had said to cause all that glaring and grimaces, while Mahroo seems lost in a haze. But he decides not to ask any question.

"He wasn't, honey," Mahroo replies to Nazi in Persian at last.

"Yes he was… Did he kiss you too?"

4

Later in his apartment, Darren calls Reza, who sounds upset at the turn of events and for being blamed for everything by Darren and Mahroo. His cold tone of voice, short responses, and abrupt postponement of their discussion to the following week, when he will be in Vancouver, annoy Darren. He feels sad for being in the middle of this absurd situation and causing Reza's hurt feelings. Yet, he decides to disregard his rather rude reaction for the sake of their friendship and rectifying the matter faster.

He surveys the in-progress canvases on the walls to assess his mood for painting, which is always established by the level of inspiration he gets within ten minutes or so. Sometimes, he forces himself to paint, despite his poor mood, but then only seldom attains a desirable height of creativity. On the other hand, waiting for the right mood is not realistic, either. *What is the meaning of 'perseverance,' then*, Darren wonders, *if I must always wait for inspiration?* Many times, persevering has indeed worked well for reviving his dampened creativity. But tonight he does not feel like testing his luck and hoping for possible inspiration through perseverance. So, he watches TV and goes to bed early.

5

Anxious about the painting deadlines, Darren tries to persevere for three days without compromising his artistic integrity and ending up with just a bunch of lacklustre canvases. So, he mostly procrastinates and considers the paintings not dried enough for adding more paint, which may kill the vibrancy of the adjacent or underlying colours. Thus, very little is added to the paintings. Mahroo visits him frequently, usually stirring some type of heated debate that often messes up his mood even further. Still, he enjoys her presence, while struggling with the unsettling questions about her love and his feelings, for which he has no remedy. The way he feels about her is weird all by itself. On the one hand, he is almost certain she is a lunatic—perhaps a sophisticated type. On the other hand, he thinks she is quite cute and charming. *How can I find a lunatic charming too? Isn't this world, especially human characters, full of intriguing mysteries and dilemmas?*

6

His apparent frustration with the paintings and slow progress are evident to Nora when they return from dinner on Friday night. All kinds of smudges and colour muddiness show in the same paintings that had looked quite promising to her earlier.

"Are you stalled again?" she asks.

"I don't know why I can't concentrate."

"You're apparently too distracted. What's going on, Darren?"

"Nothing special. But I'm not motivated," he replies.

"What happened to the masters who were helping you?" Nora asks teasingly.

He smiles, pauses, and then replies half-seriously, "They're also behaving weird these days."

"They are? How?" she asks, surprised with his serious pursuit of this topic, which might be a clue about his hallucinations and possible lunacy? *How can I find a lunatic so charming?* She thinks as though she had heard Darren saying the same thing recently about a different woman himself!

"They're all here to party, but just chat and laugh amongst themselves and fool around with their mistresses, except when they mock me or my paintings and giggle," he says boldly and playfully, thinking that it is wiser and funnier to merely blame the Masters and appear foolish than telling, or even contemplating personally, the truth about Mahroo causing a havoc in his life.

"Maybe they resent being ignored while you daydream about your mistresses, so they bring their own mistresses to teach you a lesson," she says playfully as well. "You invite them to help you, then waste a lot of time on all sorts of trivia instead of painting."

"Maybe you're right, but daydreaming isn't controllable!"

"Control its causes before they turn into hallucination."

"I'll try…"

"Just stop your mind from wandering off. Forget about your mistresses and who said what to whom at least when you're painting. What're you trying to do to yourself?"

"I guess I need some time off to figure out my life."

"Maybe we should go away together somewhere?" Nora says and Darren nods pensively. "Meanwhile, make the music louder and follow the notes more closely to forget other stuff. Study the Masters' books and the details in their paintings."

"I'll take your advice and the Masters better behave nicer, too. Or else I'll have to steal their mistresses," he replies with a wink.

"Don't you have enough already?" Nora says tensely, which reminds Darren of his promise to Mahroo.

"By the way, I'm taking Mahroo out tomorrow night. I hope you're not jealous of her, too! She hates it when I introduce her to others as my friend's sister, but that's really all she is to me."

"Oh? I think she's too gorgeous to be only a friend's sister."

"Of course, but many issues prevent us from being anything but friends at best. Besides, I have you; equally attractive."

"But your daydreaming habit seems to have increased a lot since her arrival!"

Darren hates his hypocrisy, thinking that his secret about Elizabeth is painful enough all by itself—*oh, how much I miss Elizabeth right now*. However, if Elizabeth had not appeared in his life, he would have surely fallen into Mahroo's trap already for a serious love affair. Only the delight of courting *two* beautiful women—Elizabeth and Nora—has immunized him, relatively speaking, against Mahroo's sex appeal. Meeting Elizabeth on the Island had been a timely coincidence, and starting an affair with her before Mahroo's arrival had been an omen. Poor Nora cannot imagine Mahroo would have become more than a daydream if Elizabeth had not shown up. But all these facts and secrets are also more signs of his hypocrisy—the dire weakness he had even confessed to Dervish Ali in Tehran. *Perhaps I'm not even honest with myself! Especially about my definition of love as such an elaborate and meaningful process. Am I simply avoiding Mahroo just to prove the integrity of my convictions? Are all my love theories and affairs just to defuse the chance and idea of being still in love with Erica, even after all these years?*

7

The next day, Darren raises the music volume to discern the notes and the tune of each instrument. His concentration attracts the Masters and ingenuity pours over the canvas once again. It proves a productive day since Nora leaves early in the morning and Mahroo does not interrupt him. He completes two paintings and repairs the smudges in another four. His perseverance to stay focused all day pleases him and he makes a mental note of it for occasions when he is not motivated enough.

He picks Mahroo up at 6:30 with a set plan to wrap up their dinner and dancing quickly and maybe meet T.J. afterwards if he agrees to have another late evening chitchat. With some makeup for the special occasion, she sparkles. After two glasses of wine, she is evermore pulsating as her cheeks begin to blush from the rush of blood. *I could eat her whole, even though I'm so full from that large steak,* Darren thinks, while they speak cagily to avoid another round of conflicts and commotions. Ironically, even their arguments normally arouse them sexually, anyway!

At last, she breaks the awkward silence, "Did you call Reza?"

"Yes… He sounded angry with me," he blurts.

"Oh, don't worry... He's only a bit upset about the way you'd explained the matter to me," she says.

"What do you mean?" he asks.

"He said there must've been a better way to handle the issue instead of you being so abrupt about it."

"Are you two now accusing me of being tactless, too? For bringing you to your senses?"

"No, I'm just repeating his words. He said he expected you to be more diplomatic about it."

"Diplomatic? How?"

"He said you could've explained my misunderstanding more gently, instead of giving me the shock of my life. He's right!"

"How else could I've explained that you weren't the woman in the white dress after admitting to be the man in the painting?

Any delay might've caused you more daydreaming and planning. I bet you would've been more furious if I'd waited even five more minutes."

"Maybe, but you could've still handled everything gentler."

"I don't think so…"

"I do. I agree with Reza… You could've put me down more kindly; I wouldn't have thrown myself at you that night, I promise."

"Gosh, this matter isn't going away until someone is really hurt, is it?" Darren quickly realizes the absurdity of his comment, considering Mahroo's deep suffering already. "I'm sorry. My remark was silly!"

"Maybe he's less upset now that I told him you're equally guilty."

"When did you talk to him?"

"Last night, when I was left *alone* by myself! He was relieved for not being the only guilty person…"

"Well, let's hope he's less angry now…"

"Forget the whole thing, please. If you and Reza still wish to argue about it, it's your business. I'm feeling fabulous after so long and don't want to spoil our evening. Can we go dancing?"

Darren knows a classy club requiring membership, though the bouncer also admits generous gentle patrons like him. The place is jammed, young men scrambling, glancing neurotically over the crowd, like vultures, for a pretty prey. When Darren and Mahroo walk in, everybody steps aside and admires their elegance and beauty, sauntering like two mustangs. And soon the waiter directs them to a small table that two young men give up sooner, just for indulging Mahroo and the pleasure of meeting her close up and saying hello to her, hoping she would remember their generosity if they catch her alone next time perhaps. Mahroo's soft grin and nod to them is a convincing reward already.

Mahroo orders a margarita and Darren asks for cognac. After a sip, she grabs his hand and leads him toward the dance floor next to their table. They dance closely to two slow songs before rock-and-roll invites the boys to show off their smooth moves. He leads her back to their table and she obliges reluctantly under the nose of the vultures hovering around, waiting for the subtlest clue. She sips her margarita and feels even more effervescent and idyllic, tapping her feet and flinging her naked arms around his face, showing off her shining exuberance. All that charm is irresistible to the young scavengers hoping all night to see free-spirited females calling them to the dance of liberty. They get ready to jump and rescue her, though a handsome man is, luckily, the closest to their table, and bolder. Sensing the impending attack of other scavengers, he leaps over quickly and invites her to dance. She seeks Darren's consent and he simply shrugs.

After a fast sip of her margarita, she jumps on the dance floor. Darren must witness her charm and the swarm of bees gathering around her if she sends out just a little scent. Aware of her game, Darren detests her disregard for his pride despite her normally abundant etiquette. Finally, she returns to the table, but now an unobtrusive line-up forms around their table to jump in first the second the opportunity arises to dance with her. Agitated, Darren decides not to partake in her masquerade and simply refuse to dance altogether. The option of dedicating himself to her and dancing continuously to dissuade strangers is absurd. It will be a clear sign of submission to her evil manipulation. In turn, Mahroo takes his refusal to dance closely to heart and decides to retaliate even more openly. She emits subtle signals, and swiftly a dozen guys compete around their table—pushing and shoving each other—to win her favour. She dances seductively, takes a break, orders another margarita, and dances with the scavengers again and again.

Fed up with the provocative situation, Darren decides to end this travesty and go home. When she returns to the table quite exhausted, he orders her to stay put while he goes to make a call from the public phone near the washrooms before they leave. He calls T.J., who agrees to come to Darren's house in an hour. Back at his table, he finds a guy sitting in his chair and chatting with Mahroo. As Darren waits in front of him with a glare, he vacates his chair with a rough gesture, but still sticks near their table to chat with Mahroo. She asks for Darren's consent to dance once more with the guy before leaving. Darren shrugs, still trying to prove his indifference to her allure and game.

He notices the guy's pushy attitude, whispering in her ears, she shaking her head or ignoring him. Once the music pauses, she is hesitant to leave the dance floor while he holds her hands, now blabbering so openly that even Darren can hear him from a distance: "Why don't you stay? Let him go. I'll take you home, or anywhere else you want to go afterwards. Come on. Don't mind that jerk."

"No, I must go. Let go of my hands, please!" Mahroo says.

"No, don't go. It's too early to leave," the guy persists. Though, it also appears that Mahroo is not assertive enough. So, Darren rises, to put her on notice about leaving. She resents his gesture—as subtle as it had been—and intensifies her game by lingering around the dance floor and flirting with the guy, who in turn sees a better chance of winning her over. Darren watches her game for a minute and charges toward the exit.

Alarmed, Mahroo pushes the scavenger brusquely, grabs her purse, and runs after Darren, who is watching her from the corner of his eye. Suddenly a heavy bang on the back of his neck rattles Darren. He goes dizzy but someone grabs him in time before he collapses. A skirmish erupts and, when he turns, the man who had been trying to lure Mahroo on the dance floor is glaring at him. Patrons have subdued him after punching Darren. Enraged, Darren charges to punch him, but the crowd restrain him to avoid further uproar. Totally agitated and ashamed, Mahroo holds on to Darren's arm, thrusts him toward the exit, and pleads, "I'm sorry, please let's go… I'm so sorry."

They ride home in absolute silence. Every time he glances at her, she is peering out the window, contemplating. He parks his Honda Accord in the garage and helps Mahroo get out of the car.

She is a bit drunk and apparently shaken by the turn of events. He propels her to her apartment and makes sure she is conscious and safe. He waits until she locks the door before going upstairs to his apartment. He is glad the night out with Mahroo is over as he waits anxiously for T.J.'s arrival.

8

Ten minutes later, the buzzer blares and Darren lets T.J. in.

"I'm so glad to see you, T.J."

"Me too, but can't we meet at a more decent time anymore? Are you so busy you can't share a few prime hours with your humble friend?" says T.J. half-jokingly.

Darren giggles. "This is a special circumstance. But I'm really happy you could come. Can you stay here tonight?"

"Why? What's wrong?" T.J. asks.

"I can't trust things around Mahroo." He explains the recent developments and the episodes in the restaurant and the club.

"That's horrible. But all this may be symptoms of love, too, you know?"

"Or lunacy? You'd stay here tonight, right?"

"Yeah, okay."

"Thanks. Maybe she's crazy or not. I don't know. In many ways, she's behaving like all the other women I've known—too sensitive but also manipulative," Darren says.

"Yeah… We're completely at their mercy nowadays."

"They just like to charm us and watch us dance like a cobra."

"It's just too damn depressing, though…"

"It sure is… What is happening, T.J.?" Darren asks with a chuckle.

"We're losing more autonomy and authority every day, that's all. They control the sex pipeline, and we're just too submissive and needy. Even when we seem to be making a decision, it is just for keeping them happy or quiet," T.J. exclaims with tension.

"Wow… I guess I opened a can of worms!"

"It's the only way to stop their nagging," T.J. says with angst.

"More problems in paradise with your wife again?" Darren asks with loud laughter. "I forgot her name, although you said it meant angel in Persian."

"That's right. Her name is Feri, which is short for *Fereshteh.* What an angel!"

"Trying to hold your mouth from calling her name has been a big challenge for your psyche all these years, I bet," Darren says.

"There should be a law against naming your kids Angel or similar ironic names when we know all humans turn into such devils…," T.J. says with anguish.

"How many times you usually call her name every day?"

"I call her very little, unless really necessary. I say *Khanum* (Mrs.) or *Ayal* (wifey) depending on my mood. Sometimes, I might even call her darling just to avoid saying Feri."

Darren leaves the room and returns fast with the bag of marijuana. He rolls a joint and continues, "Reza's coming next week… And he's apparently angry with me."

"Maybe we can get together then," T.J. suggests

"I hope we don't get into an argument, though," Darren says.

"Hasn't your discretion caused enough pains for everybody already? Confront each other to resolve your old grudges finally. Unless you have some new emotional issues, too!?"

"What emotional issues?" Darren asks.

"Honestly, the type of sensitivity you show towards Mahroo is more than a mere sense of responsibility for a friend's sister."

"Really?!"

"Yes. It seems—if I may speak frankly—you're enjoying the attention and the mystery this painting has brought to your life."

"Hmm…" Darren sighs.

"Actually, I believe you're enjoying the situation, at least subconsciously, more than you're willing to admit."

"What situation I'm enjoying?" Darren asks with confusion.

"That a woman of such calibre has admitted to have suffered for you so long and that your painting has proven so powerful to cause all this mayhem. But most importantly, you seem rather unsure about your feelings for Mahroo," T.J. says.

Darren remains pensive. T.J. seems to have a good point, as usual. "You think so?"

"I remember from your story of the incidents in Tehran that even then you felt attracted to her, but stopped your mind from wandering off. So, your brain may be still resisting her although she is free now. I can't say what exactly your feeling is, if it is not love per se, but maybe you're still seeing her as a possible taboo, love trap, or something like that."

"You're right, I guess. Often I think the same way. But the bottom line is that getting close to her is risky."

"Why? What's the risk?"

"I can't get attached mentally to someone or be responsible for her attachment to me, especially Reza's sister. I can't repeat my mistake with Erica when she insisted she loved me so much."

"Stop comparing everyone with Erica," T.J. says sharply.

"I can't help myself."

"Then, what's your obsession with Mahroo?"

"I'm only hoping she doesn't get hurt any more, as ultimately I'm guilty for her past pains. I may not confess to the extent of my guilt totally in front of her or Reza, but I must be honest with you and myself. I must've handled the matter about my painting and her mix-up differently, now that I think about it. Then again, I can't love her, either, although I may someday regret letting her slip out of my life. Do you understand my points?"

"Yes. But I know her only from the stories you've told me."

"Of course, I'd like to help her, too, if I can."

"Staying out of her life is the best way. Choose the right thing for you without letting her situation affect your decision; or else you'd prove your own claim about women manipulating us."

"That's exactly what I'd like to avoid," Darren replies.

"I agree. Courting her would cause only more confusion and pain, especially for her. Just don't let your guilty conscience mix with lust to mislead you."

"Do you want a little cognac?" Darren asks, walking toward the kitchen, but the telephone rings and he answers it.

"Hi… Are you okay?" Darren whispers.

"I'm fine. Can you come over; I have a surprise for you?"

"What surprise?"

"Come and see!" Mahroo says with a giggle.

Darren hesitates pensively, sceptical about visiting her again tonight and abandoning T.J. after he has made a special effort to come over this late in the evening. On the other hand, it would be irresponsible to ignore her request, considering her loneliness and depression. She may do something crazy, like jumping off the balcony. *One never knows what she's capable of. My refusal might cause a major catastrophe that I'll be unable to explain to Reza and his parents, even if I could forgive myself.* A solution occurs to him at last: "Okay, I have a surprise for you too."

"Okay, come with your surprise."

"All right," Darren says, hangs up, and then turns to T.J. "Maybe your chance to meet Mahroo has come sooner than you'd expected." T.J. gazes in confusion and Darren continues. "She wants me downstairs for a surprise, and when I said I had a surprise for her too, she said, 'Bring it.' You're the surprise."

"Me?"

"Yes. Let's go meet Reza's dear sister. He is your friend too, after all. Maybe you'll understand her better than me, considering that you both come from the same culture. Besides, I shouldn't be alone with her this late in the evening."

"As you said, it's too late to go for a visit."

"That's why it's better to go together at least."

"Does she know me?"

"Yes. Let's see if you can make a judgment about her sanity. Talk with her and ask her the right questions."

"I'm not sure it is a good idea…"

"It is. I've already promised her a surprise. It's a good idea to check on her because her parents are away and she is vulnerable alone," Darren pleads. Finally, T.J. feels obliged to comply.

Her apartment door is a crack open and a dim light flows through it. Darren knocks and calls Mahroo from the doorjamb.

"Come in, Darren, and close the door," Mahroo shouts.

Darren follows her order while letting T.J. slide in behind him, too. Only a small lamp at the far end of the living room is on. The silence in the dim light feels spooky as they wait inertly and inquisitively. Darren can see through the hall leading to the bedrooms. T.J. is concealed in the entry corridor, but can see the sudden shock on Darren's face, as if he was electrocuted, with his mouth wide open and eyes pinned toward the end of the hall. Intrigued by Darren's frozen face, T.J. leans to survey inside the hall. Mahroo is reeling forward in her tiny negligee. The contour of her exquisite body, perked up by two glamorous breasts, is highlighted by the glimmers glittering through bedroom doors. Smiling and measuring Darren seductively, she notices T.J.'s head, swiftly folds her arms over her chest, and screams, "Who'd you bring with you?"

T.J. withdraws with embarrassment as Darren keeps staring, everybody frozen now in his or her spot speechless. After ten seconds, Darren regains his composure and explains, "I brought T.J. to introduce to you. He's the surprise I mentioned and you said okay. I didn't know… I didn't know…" He cannot finish his sentence because he does not know what it is that 'he does not know.' So he turns to flee, but Mahroo summons him.

"I didn't mean to startle you," she says. "I just wanted to apologize for my behaviour this evening, especially at the club, before going to bed. You mind coming here and kissing me goodnight so I know you've forgiven me, please?"

Darren feels helpless. He peers at T.J., who nods calmly, then marches forward and kisses Mahroo's cheek. She reciprocates and he reels backward with his eyes hypnotically on the floor, as if leaving the presence of a sacred goddess to whom one should never show one's back, out of respect. Close to T.J., he glances at her once more and mumbles, "I didn't mean to startle you, either. Sorry for bringing T.J. without notice."

"That's all right," she says in a composed tone before raising her voice to address T.J. "Sorry we couldn't meet tonight, T.J. I'm terribly tired. Perhaps some other time—soon, I hope."

"Goodnight, Ms. Mahroo," says T.J. politely, turns toward the door, opens it quickly, and jumps out. Darren follows him and closes the door behind them—like two guilty kids just dismissed from the principle's office. A few seconds later, standing still and astonished outside her apartment, they hear the click of the lock. At last, they return to Darren's apartment without talking, but only mulling privately over the incident.

"Now you can't say you haven't seen Mahroo!" Darren says at last jokingly.

"No, I can't!"

"Was that revealing enough for you to establish an opinion of her and advise me accordingly?" Darren is ecstatic due to the effect of the marijuana and the image of Mahroo's beautiful body.

"She's surely nuttier than I'd thought, if not psychotic," says T.J. "But I'm no expert to judge her. Only a thin line separates sanity from lunacy when people have harsh experiences outside the norm, or when they develop complex personalities."

"Now we have another secret amongst us. I don't know whether we should bring tonight's incident up with Reza or not. What if she tells him everything herself? Maybe I should consult her about the right course of action?" Darren says with a mix of sarcasm and agitation while giggling.

"It's funny how somebody else's lunacy unnerves us."

"It's crazy, alright. I bet she's sound sleep already, not making anything of the incident five minutes ago," Darren suggests.

Chapter Seven
The Statue of Absurdity

1

On Sunday afternoon, Darren completes two more paintings, prepares a sketch for the commissioned work, and organizes his portfolio to show to the Sun reporter at the Elixir on Tuesday. The delivery schedule has been met, thanks to perseverance goading his inspiration. He calls Nora with the good news and a censored report of the previous night's big events with Mahroo; upsetting Nora with the disturbing truth is imprudent. Still, she brushes off Darren's fishy tale and hangs up hastily after stressing to be on time for the interview.

The interview at the Elixir goes well, judging by the reporter's fascination with Darren's bizarre confession about the Masters. He insists they inspire him, as though fusing with his body and mind during the painting process. The risk of readers finding his assertions absurd or delusional does not bother him a bit. The reporter chooses four pictures from his portfolio for her article, including the *Woman in the White Dress*—his presumed masterpiece. Her curiosity obliges Darren to reveal a bit of its story, too, while concealing the quandary surrounding it.

He rushes home, tidies the apartment, and hurries to the Island around the time Elizabeth had shown up the last two weeks. In his favourite pub, he orders a beer and a sandwich. Sipping the beer, he suddenly imagines Elizabeth on the pier near the market, staring at his apartment. He charges toward the pier. Exactly as he had envisaged, she is at a table, facing his apartment, drinking coffee. He walks behind her and covers her eyes.

"Guess who?"

"Jack the Ripper," she blurts.

"Uh uh…"

"Dr. Jekyll."

"Uh uh…"

"Count Dracula."

"Uh uh…"

"I give up. Kiss me—maybe I'll recognize you by a taste."

Still covering her eyes, he smooches the corner of her lips.

"A total stranger, thank God!" cries Elizabeth and rises, hugs him, and kisses him on the mouth very casually.

"This time, I found you!" he proclaims triumphantly.

"But I made it easy for you, hoping you'd remember today is Tuesday."

"A divine intervention happened too."

"Wow, a divine intervention!?"

"Yes, I'd gone to the pub and ordered my food, thinking that you'd show up there like the first time we met. Then, suddenly, I pictured you sitting here instead."

"But we met here last week, at this very table where you were luring your friend's sister!"

"Oh, you're right… But let's go to the pub now," he says, holding her arm and leading her. "Has Jeff gone?"

"Until Saturday…"

"I was wondering why you hadn't called me as promised," he says.

"I was sitting there and wondering if I should…"

"Why were you hesitant?"

"Isn't it obvious to you?"

"Forget everything… Let's go away too. I've finished the workload and feel like going somewhere to celebrate and forget everything here."

"I see what you mean… How is she?"

"You women! Nothing goes undetected around you, does it?"

"Nope. You must always be on your toes, fearful of our fury."

"I know. God's mastery in creating women is amazing."

"But we can't go away together. What would people say?"

"To hell with people… We'll just go hide somewhere."

"Not a good idea! Besides, what is our relationship, anyway?"

"We're in love—sweet love, my darling!" he says playfully.

"Stop fooling around, Darren!"

The waitress serves their food and beers while smirking at Darren's horseplay.

"I'm serious! In my book, we're in love," he says.

"But I've never said anything about loving you at all."

"You don't have to say it in words. I believe you."

Elizabeth bursts into laughter. "You're funny, you know?"

"Going away can help my spirit, too, which you know hasn't been great lately."

"Where can we go; how long? I have a job, you know?"

"Somewhere nearby, perhaps Harrison Hot Springs."

"I'll think about it. What's your plan for tonight?"

"Let's go to my apartment first," he replies.

After a long pause, she exclaims, "I'm serious, Darren…"

"What about?"

"What're we doing?"

"How's your relationship with Jeff, if I may ask?"

"I don't know…"

"You don't?"

"Sometimes we plan to get married. But often we clash!"

"Marriage won't help then. You must—"

"The irony is," Elizabeth interjects, "we fight mainly to save our relationship by changing each other's attitude."

"You cannot help each other or build a relationship this way."

"I know… You're probably right…"

"You see, the problem is people's obsession for both love and practicality to avoid the chance of getting hurt in relationships."

"That's right too. We want love but can't trust it," she replies.

"So, we remain confused and anxious forever."

"What's the solution then?"

"There's none, until couples recognize and handle the main hurdle," he replies.

"Which is?"

"Absence of guidelines or role models to help couples relate," he says matter-of-factly.

"True, no culture exists anymore to provide social discipline."

"Of course, marriage counsellors offer many general theories, but no agreeable principles exist, especially with women now adopting a more liberal role. We're facing a major crisis."

"You sound so certain and serious about your theories!"

"What's Jeff giving you in your relationship?"

"Stress. Our needs and personalities are so different."

"Then…?"

"We don't have the guts to split, either… Most relationships suffer from similar problems, I believe. At least we know each other to some extent."

"That's a lame excuse… What you're telling me is actually a typical case of modern relationships' impasses."

"So you agree most relationships get shitty these days?"

"Yeah, and that's why we should try not to get trapped again and again."

"But this is ridiculous...," she says helplessly. "Why can't we agree on some general principles to build our relationships?"

"Because we should first understand and accept the frailty of love and relationships nowadays."

"And then?"

"We must study and choose a suitable relationship model and a mate in line with our personalities and progressive lifestyles."

"Then again, we can't change our mentalities overnight," she adds. "It's tough to do it after a lifetime of bad training and building high expectations from life and marriage."

"Thus, couples wouldn't stop blaming one another for endless relationship conflicts or hoping to force one another to change," Darren reiterates. "We must learn these basic facts and grow lots of tolerance to improve our relationships."

"That requires lots of self-sacrifice and wisdom, too," she says.

"That's true… But this awareness and the energy we save can be spent on improving ourselves, which would then help prolong our relationships as well," he replies.

"These ideas sound too idealistic for the time being, though."

"I know… But eventually people, at least next generations, must somehow do it and change social norms. The sooner we accept, and handle, the sad truth about relationships, the sooner we might learn to live in some harmony."

"Again you've confused me about my life with Jeff, although you opened that can of worms two weeks ago when you made love to me so passionately. What were you thinking?"

"The fun part of it was that we weren't thinking. Didn't you like the sweet elixir we drank together?"

"I did! But I mustn't be drunken and deserted in darkness to find my way home!" Elizabeth recites poetically.

"Then give me your hand to lead you to my home," Darren replies, stretching his hand toward her.

She grabs and squeezes his hand. "I'll let you be my guide and guru, if you can rip my gloom and sorrow!"

"I'll do my best, my dear beloved, to bestow everything you desired." He chuckles while signalling the server for the bill.

"I didn't know you were a poet, too!" she says.

"You're not so bad yourself… Let's go," he says, wondering who is a better poet, Elizabeth or Mahroo!

They stroll toward his place in a jovial mood after they get off the gondola. Near the building, Mahroo is sitting on a bench with Mrs. Stanley, who turns to explore the cause of Mahroo's sudden start. Forcing a grin, pretending to be chatting with Mrs. Stanley, she watches Darren and Elizabeth staggering and giggling like two drunk lovers. Finally, they reach the building and disappear inside after they all wave at one another briefly.

"I think Mrs. Stanley is trying to make an assistant out of Mahroo for her spying business," says Darren jokingly.

"She seems like a great student to me, too," Elizabeth says.

"I don't think so... She's too classy to be dragged into Mrs. Stanley's world of espionage."

"You love her too, huh?" Elizabeth asks with jealousy.

"Don't be silly. Let's focus on us and the elixir we're gonna drink soon."

2

The sight of Darren and Elizabeth sauntering smugly toward his apartment hurts Mahroo more in terms of his hypocrisy than her jealousy. Naturally, she resents any woman luring him, even the ones merely checking him out in public places. But what pains Mahroo the most today is how those two jerks had pretended to be only old friends to cover up their affair when Elizabeth had showed up on the Island last Tuesday unexpectedly. She is mostly disappointed with Darren's integrity. He has not only lied about this particular affair, but also insulted her intelligence in front of another female competitor who knew at that instant last week that Mahroo had not believed their masquerade.

It is essential then, she decides, to verify her theory about his deception last week. She rationalizes that learning about Darren, especially his hypocrisy, can probably help her forget him for good. Besides, if proven capable of deceiving her now, he is proven capable of lying about the story of the *Woman in the White Dress,* too. Obviously, it will still be hard to interpret his intentions, or feelings for her, then or now. Anyway, the main point now is to test his capacity for deceiving Mahroo. *So how can I confirm whether they're having sex at this moment?* She invents an ingenious plan and convinces herself at last that her inquisition would not be disgraceful or tactless, because she must gauge his integrity once and for all. Maybe it is time to return to Tehran and forget all about him, after all.

She takes the elevator to the tenth floor and tiptoes toward his apartment. Her heart is racing in her chest from the fear of being caught. It will be too embarrassing to look into Darren's eyes ever again if she is discovered spying on him. She loses her nerve halfway before getting to the door. She stops, begins to retreat, but again her curiosity takes over and she proceeds, creeping forward cautiously. The hallway is dead quiet and no sound comes from his apartment, either. She listens from the doorjamb. Total silence. She presses her ear tighter while tilting her head and shoulder down slightly. Still she cannot hear a peep. Twenty seconds later, her ear aching, she raises her head to rest. She paces the hallway before returning to the eavesdropping position: Her ear pressed tightly to the doorjamb, her shoulder and head stooped, and her body twisted against the doorframe—like a snake twirling round a tree branch. From her awkward position, her eyes catch Mrs. Stanley standing at the end of the hallway, staring at her with suspicion and pity. Her pride shatters swiftly, but she recovers her nerve quickly and straightens her body up.

The two women gaze at, and gauge, each other suspiciously. As Mrs. Stanley steps forward, Mahroo soars out of her trance, shakes her head with agitation, rushes toward the exit at the far end of the hallway, and hides behind the door. Maybe Mrs. Stanley is just reporting her to Darren this very instant, she ponders with distress. She feels miserable and defeated but also curious. So she leans behind the exit door to peep through its small window. Carefully she raises her head close to the lower corner of the window. The hallway is empty. She breathes easier. Apparently, Mrs. Stanley has appreciated her sense of jealousy and aptitude for spying. Maybe she has decided to spare her from a major embarrassment. She wonders what Mrs. Stanley would demand in return to forget this incident. *I'll buy her a present, anyway, just to show my gratitude.* She runs downstairs to her apartment and closes the door behind her. Her parents and Nazi watch her with surprise, wondering why she looks so agitated, leaning against the closed door aimlessly with angst, as though preventing someone from getting in and slaughtering them.

Mahroo drinks a glass of water, plummets onto a chair in the balcony, and tries to envision the situation in Darren's apartment. Since she had not heard any voices from his living room, the chances are that they had been in bed already. However, she had eavesdropped for only one minute or so. What if Elizabeth or Darren had gone to the washroom or was contemplating on a question raised by the other? Although the chance of treason is higher than innocence, the evidence is not foolproof. Therefore, she must confirm her hunch somehow, maybe by dropping in on Darren with an excuse. It will be obvious and humiliating, but what other choice does she have?

Surely, spying behind his apartment door will be degrading, risky, and inconclusive again. But, realistically, he should be the one feeling humiliated if she discovers his two-facedness. He was the one insisting, on the Island, that Elizabeth was involved with another man called Jeff, both of them old friends of his; what kind of a friendship is this then? *I didn't ask them to explain themselves, did I? They were the ones insisting on clarifying their affair so fast idiotically.* She feels braver every minute and more convinced that her discovery should bring shame only to him, not her. It is in fact her duty—a matter of principle—to make those hypocrites realize this kind of attitude cannot be swept under the rug so casually without punishment!

Therefore, she decides to surprise Darren with a valid excuse. She collects her parents' immigration papers and hurries upstairs, determined to proceed naturally, in control of her nerves under all circumstances. She knocks on the door firmly, waits awhile, and knocks harder again more resolutely. Finally, the door opens and Darren's head and naked shoulder appear behind the door.

"Oh, sorry… I guess I've come at the wrong time."

"Hi, Mahroo—" Darren says with distress.

"Sorry for interrupting your… your conference… probably helping your friend with *her* relationship issues, too!" she states with stress on the last part of her sentence and gestures to leave.

"Ask me what you came here for," he says with impatience. "It must've been something important!"

"Just an immigration matter related to my parents. I wanted to consult with you before going there tomorrow," she says while shaking the papers in her hand. But that's all right now. Give me the address for the immigration office later tonight to take my parents there in the morning."

"I'll find it for you…"

"Just slip it under our door if you're busy until late tonight. I'll pick it up in the morning. You'd better go back on your friend now!" She says and disappears behind the exit door before he gets a chance to respond.

He ponders her last comment, 'Go back on your friend,' and wonders if it had been a slip of the tongue or language deficiency, but decides it had been neither. *Her English is better than mine, damn it!* Anxiously, he tries to gauge her rude intrusion, vulgar language, and abrupt departure. Instead of her, he is the one left with guilty feelings and shame; why? Maybe that had been her intention all along—to make him feel guilty. *She'd succeeded so cunningly,* he thinks as he walks toward the bedroom sluggishly with gloom.

Now Mahroo is certain of Darren's vast capacity for deceit, contrary to her feelings all along. Somehow, she had assumed that Canadians, especially such a handsome one, would never lie. *How did I come up with such a silly idea?* But what could his intentions have been for lying to her three years ago, or now? A few reasons occur to her. However, she is just too exhausted to pursue this line of thinking. She will never find an answer; only more puzzling questions and frustration may lead her to insanity. So, wisely, she drops the matter; suffice it to know that Darren is capable of lying and deceit, in addition to being a womanizer, even going by her observations in such a short period. Therefore, perhaps her feelings toward this man have been as irrational as coming to Vancouver altogether. Her parents could have easily come with Reza two weeks later. Still, not even this direct, incriminating information about Darren's character alters her feelings for him a bit. *Why do I still love this bastard?*

The ambience in Darren's bedroom is pathetic and quiet after Mahroo's intrusion disrupting his divine, diligent performance. Both Elizabeth and Darren have lost their edges and urges, lying pensively, waiting for the other to either ask a question or explain why Mahroo is allowed to be so spoiled and rude.

"I'm sorry for my friend's lack of consideration," he blurts eventually. "Of course she had no way of knowing what we were doing, especially with all the theatrics in front of her last week about no hanky panky going on between us."

"What was the urgent matter, anyway?" she asks.

"She needed advice and the address for immigration office. I'll give her the address later," he explains, unsure himself about the validity of Mahroo's excuse for intrusion.

"I guess I'd better go now. Suddenly I feel depressed."

"Let's smoke a joint. We'll get back in the mood."

"I'm no good under these conditions," she replies.

"I'm sorry…"

"But if you still wanna go away for a few days, I'll go. I'll tell Jeff when he calls that I'm going out of town with friends."

"That's just great. We both need a break now even more."

"Yeah, now suddenly I feel I need one right away, too," she says with a chuckle.

"Then let me call Mahroo right away and thank her for her timely intrusion," he says after his loud laughter.

"At least don't tell her where we're going…"

"Okay… Can we go tomorrow then?" he asks excitedly.

"After work, around five, I suppose."

3

Darren books a suite for three nights in the Executive Hotel in Harrison Hot Springs, but tells Nora and Mahroo that he is going away to Kelowna to visit a friend. Both ladies get curious and suspicious, but only Nora confronts him by stressing she may need to contact him for business at least.

"What business emergency?" he asks Nora irately.

"Just in case we need your permission to sell a painting below your listed price."

"Don't worry about it. I'll be back in three days," he replies with frustration and shame. "Actually, no more discounts from now on."

"That's a rather selfish attitude," Nora replies with stress.

Mahroo also enjoys hearing his lame story about his trip that confirms his lying habit, but also some sense of accountability toward her. Her chuckle on the phone had actually irritated him. Later, he regrets having called them. He must have just pretended to be busy, unable to return their calls. But it is too late, even if he dared leaving Mahroo and her family alone without a prior notice at least.

So, despite his enthusiasm, the trip feels doomed already. These ladies may soon challenge his lies, which could affect his relationship with Nora at least. She is definitely suspicious and angry, most likely assuming he is going away with Mahroo. And Mahroo has found more evidence of his duplicity. But he also hates his endless hypocrisy himself, in spite of his valid rationale to keep some personal matters private. *But why lie?* Nonetheless, he overcomes his gloom later in the afternoon after jogging six kilometres and letting the anticipation of courting Elizabeth kill his inner turmoil and nosy conscience.

On the way to pick up Elizabeth, however, a peculiar thought boggles Darren's mind: If jogging or pleasure could always curb our inner conflicts, the process of self-awareness breaks down drastically. We become men of low integrity—if not criminals—simply by learning to smother our sense of morality every time. But the truth is, he surmises, that suppressing inner turmoil would only lead to ultimate demise. Therefore, his mood improvement must be, at best, transitory. So what is the remedy now—while rushing for pleasure with Elizabeth? Why should he suddenly even fuss over these moral issues today, at this moment? These thoughts alone depress him again despite all that jogging. Then, he feels even gloomier and guiltier when he ponders and fails to fathom the reason behind his growing mood swings in recent months on top of his chronic cynicism.

He drives slowly with the aim of aborting the trip if he were inspired somehow to do so before reaching the rendezvous. *That's a deal,* the Devil agrees. However, he is not inspired in the least. Rather, his pleasure-seeking mind concentrates on a raw justification: He has not made any commitment to any of these ladies. In fact, he has always done the opposite without telling them the whole truth about his various affairs. And why should he care about Jeff? They have not been friends for a long time.

Finding Elizabeth so pretty near the bus stop, he decides his *deal* with the devil is off. Instead of being inspired vastly for higher integrity and self-awareness, he has found good excuses for being who he is! He must make the best of this trip, especially for making it up to Elizabeth for Mahroo's intrusion last night.

Elizabeth drops her small suitcase in the backseat and they set off for a romantic getaway. After forty-five minutes in the rush hour traffic along East Hastings and another forty-five minutes on Trans-Canada 1 East, they stop at Abbotsford for supper. There will be plenty of time to have supper and drive to Harrison Hot Springs in daylight, which extends well past nine o'clock in this part of the world during summertime.

A serene mood prevails as he drives leisurely, enjoying the view of the countryside in the fading daylight, with the soothing sound of the Dvorak cello concerto echoing in the background.

He blabbers with his regular charm about many topics, including his last visit to Harrison Hot Springs. Peering out the window, Elizabeth seems reserved, though, immersed in private thoughts, only nodding occasionally to acknowledge him.

"Do you enjoy the scenery?" he asks once to break her long silence.

"The countryside in this golden light is always relaxing."

"True. Vancouver is full of beautiful parks, creeks, and trails. Still, being totally surrounded by nature is something else— always refreshing."

"I feel like crying though," Elizabeth replies.

"Why?"

"I have a mixed feeling of joy and fear suddenly… Like I'm eloping."

"Fear?"

"I feel bad for cheating on Jeff. But mostly I'm fearful about having you in my life, or losing you; a new emotional dilemma! Why'd you have to come into my life?"

"Who knows what fate has in store for us! We must relax and focus on enjoying these fleeting moments."

"But it's not easy, nor wise."

"Actually I had second thoughts myself on my way to pick you up. Not in terms of why we're together, but for not being honest about it; I should tell Nora and Mahroo about us."

"Are you crazy? Don't you care about your honesty reaching Jeff's ears and causing me more trouble than I'm in already?"

"That's been my dilemma, too. I thought people deserve and appreciate honesty!"

"Thanks. But I'm not flattered by your alleged honesty."

"What's wrong with my honesty now!?"

"Do you want me to be honest as well?"

"Sure…"

"Well, how do you expect people take your demented sense of affection, which is shared amongst a bunch of women? What kind of game do you think you're playing by inventing a crooked meaning for love and pretending to be honest about it, too?"

"I've sort of come to a similar conclusion, albeit a bit more tenderly, about the difficulty of my approach. Many people have casual affairs regularly without commitment and emotion, don't care about being honest about it, actually lie about them, and don't face any consequences. But when I put a great of deal of thoughts and sentiments into my limited encounters with women, and despite my efforts to remain honest with people and myself, still I regularly annoy everybody and myself. Honesty doesn't pay anymore. So, tell me, what's the right thing for me to do?"

"Isn't that obvious to you?"

"No…!" he replies with surprise.

"Choose one companion and stay with her exclusively as long as you're happy together," Elizabeth suggests.

"Is this what you're doing yourself?" Darren asks cunningly.

"No… And that's why I'm feeling lousy. But you?"

"Why do you think I'm running away from Mahroo? You know the story with Nora, too. What do you expect me to do about us now?"

"I don't know either…," Elizabeth replies.

"Our relationship is one of those peculiar instances that no one can prepare for, or ignore when it happens. Our affair just happened. Now we need to be patient and see what it means. What other option do we have? You wanna leave Jeff for me?"

"I will, if you really want me to!"

"That shows how much you care about Jeff, and still stay with him out of habit or fear of loneliness."

"At least Jeff and I have an understanding and commitment."

"I can see your meaning of commitment!"

"Are you now questioning my integrity, too?"

"Well… I just don't understand the kind of commitment you and Jeff supposedly have. That's all."

"I don't like your tone and mocking Jeff and me."

"Sorry… All I'm saying is that I just don't know you enough or the kind of commitment you expect from me. Besides, I hate to cause a break-up between you and Jeff. You've got to decide on your own without my influence."

"Let's plan accordingly then. Let's focus on the next three days, as if we'll never meet again afterwards," she says tensely.

Darren is glad that at least Elizabeth has not yet jumped out of his car or asked him to return to Vancouver. *That damn incident with Erica ages ago doesn't seem to want to ever leave me alone,* he ponders with surprise. He feels good even about Elizabeth's offer to end their relationship after this trip. That might be a great idea for preventing a skirmish with Nora at least.

"What if we discover nice stuff about each other?" he asks teasingly to boost her self-esteem and saving the spirit of this trip.

"We'll see," she replies stiffly. "But we must have a general plan now; you're not the only one who detests dishonesty."

"Fine… That's just wonderful. We now have both a general and a special plan for the next three days! Aren't we efficient!?"

4

They reach Harrison Hot Springs at dusk. Despite the major changes, the main road to the lake near the Executive Hotel is recognizable to Darren. After checking in, he retrieves six bottles of Kootenay wines from a box in the trunk of his car, lays them carefully in a duffle bag, and returns to the suite. He pours two glasses of wine and makes a toast: "To a great relationship…"

"Or a good final trip," Elizabeth responds slyly.

"Or a good evening at least!" he enjoys playing her game.

They clink and sip their wines at last. He rolls a joint and soon they're carefree, ridiculing each other's quirks and their serious conversations and planning in the car. Elizabeth makes fun of Darren's constant struggle to manage the loose hair crowding his forehead. She clips a hairpin to secure it, then suggests shaving it off to see how popular his Yul Brynner impression would be.

Soon they embrace with great passion and immerse in a nude 'examination' of each other's bodies and souls. Thirty minutes of enthralling labour, they pass the exam with flying colours again and congratulate each other with soft kisses and caressing. Their dedication feels virtuously justified as they sense the inevitability of taking this exam over and over.

The effect of the pot and their playful moods intrigues Darren to play a more cunning joke on Elizabeth. As she escapes his tight embrace lethargically to visit the washroom, he sets up his plot and lights another joint when she returns. They seem to be in sync about the simple pleasures of life; another big credit for Elizabeth, in addition to her appealing looks, body, and character. She responds to his playfulness better than any woman he has known. Now he realizes even more how Erica's uptightness all those years had dampened his spirit. It seems he would never find all the qualities he admires in a mate in any one woman, *so I'm unfortunately forced into all these affairs and their conundrums*, he contemplates and giggles, while anticipating Elizabeth's return from the washroom.

As they enjoy the joint and giggle at dim-witted remarks, a knock at the door startles them. They only stare anxiously at each other. Eventually he leaps out of the bed and staggers toward the door with hesitation, turning every few steps to exchange glances with her. Her eyes popping out, her dry mouth wide open under the influence of the pot and his exaggerated panic, she picks up her wineglass and takes a sip nervously.

"Who can it be at this time?" he mutters with stress.

Elizabeth shrugs with equal distress and apprehension. At last, he reaches the door, peers through the peephole, leaps away fast, and leans against the wall in shock.

"Who is it?" she enquires, now totally flabbergasted.

"You won't believe it!"

"Oh, tell me," she whispers, bouncing out of the bed in alarm and pulling the sheet to cover herself.

"It's Mahroo," he murmurs with astonishment.

The knock on the door repeats a little harder.

"What does she want? What kind of a relationship do you have with this woman to chase us all the way here?"

"None… She's just crazy."

"Are you gonna open the door to see what's going on?"

"I'm afraid. She may kill us. She looks quite upset," he asserts after a quick gaze through the peephole and leaping aside again.

"Open the door; she may cause more problems if you don't. Are you afraid of a tiny woman?"

The next knock on the door comes along with a voice: "Room Service."

Elizabeth is baffled briefly before realizing Darren's juvenile sense of humour. She throws a pillow at him, rolls the sheet around her, and runs to the washroom. He opens the door and tips the guy for following his instructions to the tee. A glass of icy champagne is ready for her when she returns to drink with the delivered snack.

"When did you arrange this silly trick?" she enquires.

"The last time you went to the washroom. Cheers!"

"Cheers, my crazy lover," she smiles and drops the sheet. "Why are you making it more difficult for me to dump you?"

"Why do you pee so much?" he asks with a chuckle.

5

The next day is devoted to outdoor recreation, which feels both wearing and refreshing after all their recent bedroom fun and folly. They enjoy the mineral water spa, sunbathe a bit, and swim in Harrison Lake. Surrounded by layers of enchanting mountains in the far distance, and a large, woody island in the middle of it, the lake offers a tranquil atmosphere, exactly as portrayed in the postcards. They jog along a nearby trail before spending another hour around the lake, swimming occasionally in the cool waters, and resting in tree shadows.

At eight p.m., they are dressed up, ready to dazzle each other and the public with their elegance. Strangely, they have packed formal outfits for such a short, casual trip. Elizabeth's off-white sexy gown accentuates her tanned skin and lustrous hair, now clustered behind her head like a blossoming rose. They look strikingly handsome together, which rekindles Darren's memory of his arrival at the club last Saturday night with Mahroo. Swiftly he compares Mahroo and Elizabeth, like judging a Miss Universe pageant, his decision needed instantly. At last, he decides Mahroo is the winner, if only because of her large, dreamy, black eyes, seldom found in this part of the world. Elizabeth enquires about his sudden silence and daydreaming, looking so openly amused and joyous. Darren whispers, "Your beauty amazes me," while musing over the result of the contest he had just fathomed in his mind. Then he kisses her.

At the hotel's elegant restaurant, the Captain greets them warmly and asks whether they have a reservation. Darren shakes his head and yet the Captain obliges. "This way please," he says and starts fast toward a few empty tables at the east end of the restaurant. They follow him along the path in the big hall before Elizabeth stops halfway abruptly in her footsteps. Her face pales and her body quivers, as her eyes remain pinned toward a table at the far left side. Pushed by a strong urge to flee, yet she is frozen mostly by her shock and anger perhaps. Darren traces her gaze and recognizes Jeff at a table leaning toward a young woman, either kissing her ear or whispering into it. As Darren stares at him, Jeff jolts and looks up at them.

Suddenly a scene: Jeff and his companion at the table on the left side of the hall, and Elizabeth and Darren lingering in the centre, probing one another with bewildered stares, all frozen, along with many nearby patrons caught in the crossfire of laser beam, sharp communication of eyes and minds. The world has come to a standstill, except for the Captain, who has walked ten paces ahead of Elizabeth and Darren, unaware of the catastrophe behind him. At last, he stops, looks back, and loses his poise as he realizes the patrons' failure to follow his strict instruction. Fully flustered, he peers at the nearby diners with a timid smile to control his nerves, then raises his hand to beckon the disobedient party of two.

"This way, please," he says, trying to reinstate his challenged dignity without distracting the nice patrons around him too much.

To his amazement, however, a big mutiny is on hand. Darren and Elizabeth frozen, either gone totally deaf or ignoring his authority outright. Waiting like the Bounty's ousted captain, he considers abandoning ship to save his stature, but also hopes the mutineers come to their senses and reinstate his authority by realizing how necessary it is to follow him. What should he do? *They forgot to teach us the protocol for a situation like this, when fellow diners disobey a captain's orders and stop marching safely to their tables!*

For fifteen seconds, the awkward scene keeps many people hypnotized while their heads turn from left to the centre of the hall and back. The young woman with Jeff is merely puzzled by so many people, including Jeff, frozen in their spots and all the unflattering glares and exchanges of thoughts.

Eventually, the dramatic scene begins to unfold when Jeff rises in slow motion, still not believing his eyes, or unsure how to react under this circumstance. Darren shakes his head as though awakened from a dream, witnessing the collapse of towers of hopes and memories. He ponders the means of reacting in an odd situation like this. *What is the etiquette? It's a pity they didn't teach us at high school how to react when caught cheating with someone else's sweetheart.*

Elizabeth makes the decisive move at last. She turns tensely and storms out of the restaurant. Darren is still gauging Jeff, who is standing motionless, like a *statue of absurdity,* gazing at him. Then he charges after Elizabeth. The disgraced, patient Captain feels the final blow—abandoned and embarrassed before the crew he had successfully directed and seated at specific tables. Yet, he is somewhat relieved to see the mutineers disembark at last, letting him regain some of his honour and authority. So, he scurries in long strides back to his command in front of the hall.

Elizabeth dashes toward the hotel entrance and disappears. Darren charges after her and catches up with her in the parking lot. He grabs her arm and thrusts her toward his car, while hoping nobody can find them in that dark, secluded corner. He is sure Jeff has not noticed which way they had gone after leaving the restaurant. In his mind, actually, Jeff is still frozen at the table in the same position, *the statue of absurdity*.

"Do you know her?" Darren asks as soon as they hide in the backseat of the Honda and lock the doors.

"No. Do you think they're having an affair?"

"Are you kidding me? Didn't you see the look on his face?"

"You think he got the same impression about us?"

"Of course! Why are you so slow suddenly?" he says.

"I was just hoping for a little room for speculation."

"You wish!" He sighs, caresses her hand and kisses it.

"But I'd like to find a way to challenge his impression."

"To deny our affair?"

"Yes. Let's invent a story," she says, her mood changing fast.

"Tell him we came here to catch him cheating on you," he suggests teasingly, yet she starts pondering his odd idea giddily. Meanwhile, he wonders about the way she is more interested in saving her own face than worrying about Jeff's infidelity. That surely says a lot about her character, but also her feeling about her relationship with Jeff. *What happened to her feelings for me and willingness to drop Jeff only if I asked her to do so? These women are really hard to figure out or trust!*

"Yeah...," she says with a sly grin at last. "Why not?"

"Why not what?" he asks with disbelief.

"Why don't we claim we came here to catch him cheating."

"'Cause it's silly! Put yourself in his shoes. What do you see?"

"I don't know! Two idiots?"

"Exactly. Two idiots dressed up for dinner, following the Captain. If we'd come here to catch him, we'd be in jeans, tired, angry, and bypassing the Captain to confront Jeff quickly. My presence is another clue, as you could've not just found me and convinced me, out of the blue, to assist you with your detective work. That's too ridiculous."

"You're right…"

"Besides, right now Jeff is probably asking the concierge for my room number. When he finds out that I've been here with *a* Mrs. Durant—according to the hotel registration—he'll know we've been shaking it up here since last night, rather than arriving just now to catch him in action. So let's admit—we're caught!"

"You're right. We're caught! Maybe I should've fled before he noticed us," she reiterates.

"Why didn't you?"

"I was frozen from anger."

"But you handled yourself perfectly, fleeing the restaurant."

"It was a spontaneous reaction. I didn't know what to say, even if I dared making a scene. Also I needed fresh air before hyperventilating from a mix of anger and guilt."

"What should we do now?" he asks.

"I don't know! Return to Vancouver? But I can't go home."

"You think he'll go back tonight?" he asks with sarcasm.

"I don't think so. You're right."

"So you'll be safe lonely at home, but is it the right strategy? We must stay here for the same reason he is."

"You're right again. I have nothing more to lose now."

"The way you've been saying 'you're right' to me all night reminds me of my friend's story." She nods impatiently but he continues, "He claimed his girlfriend always said, 'You're right' about everything for six years. Then, the day after the wedding, the first comment he made, she said, 'You're wrong,' and he's been 'wrong' ever since about everything." In spite of his effort to cheer her up, she only frowns at him for his supposedly funny account of women's cleverness.

"You know what?" she states. "I actually wanna return to the restaurant with you as if nothing has happened. Let's have our juicy steaks and then go back to our suite and make love until morning."

"Jeff may still be there and confront us in front of everybody."

"I don't care… You think I kept saying, 'You were right,' for nothing? Let's go," she orders, her mood improving fast by the minute, now seemingly more vengeful than remorseful all of a sudden.

"Just wait a second. Get off your high horse! Let's cool down before we go in and punch Jeff in the face, instead of following the poor, confused Captain again. You've made that Captain lose all his dignity and confidence tonight! If we go back there and Jeff confronts us, I'll have to leave immediately, because I can't defend myself when deep down I know I'm guilty. That'll ruin our plans; you'll probably get furious unnecessarily again over something that's irreparable, instead of thinking straight to find a proper solution. But I like the second part of your suggestion, about going to our suite and making love until morning."

"No, I'm actually very hungry suddenly," she says.

"I'll order room service and we'll have a big fiesta."

"No, the restaurant. You know what? If he confronts us, I'll tell him something that will burn all his brain cells."

"Like what?" he asks.

"I'll say I've known about his affair and lured you in out of spite, and I'm here all dressed up and pretty to make him suffer in public," she replies, a little calmer and more devious instead.

"How're you going to explain our earlier silent confrontation and bursting out like the whole incident was unexpected? How can you deny the shock on your face, let alone the impression on the faces of the Captain and his crew after your reaction?"

"Don't worry about those details. He's been shocked himself and won't remember or analyze the situation as delicately as you are. Besides, if he asks, I'll tell him that although I knew about his disloyalty, I was shocked when I saw him so cosy with that bimbo with my own eyes. I reacted because of my hurt emotions. But now I've regained my senses and would like to continue with my plan to be with you. I want to show him he doesn't deserve me and I can get myself a better man as quickly as I desire. And I wanna show him and the Captain that I'm now ready for a big steak and two bottles of wine," she insists with absolute courage and conviction.

Her swift change of mood and attitude astounds Darren. Her agility to invent such a wicked story is even more amazing. He also admits privately that her deviously manufactured account of their affair is more decent for his image. The option of having an affair in secret will portray him as a cowardly and sneaky person. But the option of consoling a desperate woman victimized by her inconsiderate boyfriend will make him look like a saviour. He will be a hero for accepting the responsibility of comforting a dejected woman. "Okay, if that's what you really want, I'll go along with it."

With their heads held high, they return to the restaurant. The Captain trembles at their sight, though. He peers around timidly, contemplating his options: Could he refuse them for retribution when there are plenty of empty tables? What if they make a new scene, especially if he rejects them? The overly confident faces of the two ex-mutineers, plus the twenty-dollar bill Darren flashes before him, eventually persuade him to smile. "Are we ready for our seats now?"

"Yes." Darren says. "She needed some fresh air."

"I hope you feel better now, miss. This way, please, miss," the Captain states with sarcasm despite his haste to grab the twenty.

Jeff's gone. So they follow the Captain without a hitch. Once seated, the Captain bows with a sigh of relief and leaves. *Some silly people may think my job is ridiculous, just showing patrons a table and then go away, but they should've seen me tonight.*

"Where're those dirty bastards," Elizabeth growls.

"Don't get carried away. We're guiltier than they are."

"How do you figure?" she asks with annoyance.

"The young girl probably didn't know anything about you, but I knew the long history between Jeff and you."

"But the story we agreed on in the car stands. Promise to back me up completely on this matter."

He has already decided the option of being a *kind knight* is more appealing than being a *coward Casanova*. Still, he takes his time pretending slyly to be pondering before nodding.

"He'll tell Erica too!" she says.

"What? Oh, yeah!" He sighs, and then continues, "But I don't care. It may only ruin your reputation and relationship with her; mostly because she can't imagine you'd betray her."

"I wouldn't worry about that; I know certain things she did to you worse than this," she blurts but regrets rapidly.

"What things? What do you know?"

"Nothing. Forget what I said. I'm sorry."

"Not this time… I've noticed you hiding secrets from me, maybe to spare my feelings, but now you must come clean."

"Darren, please. What's the point of torturing yourself?"

"No way… Tell me…"

"Just let it go, please."

"If you want me to support your story about our affair, you must confess. Actually, I'd already guessed something before our separation, but maybe you can confirm it. It'll help me get some closure about what went wrong in my marriage."

"Something related to a man you knew?" she asks to test him.

"Exactly… Tell me what you know."

"No, you tell me what you think."

"I think Erica had an affair with Reza. Right?" he asks.

"Yes, you're right again, for the hundredth time tonight."

"Explain then… I don't care about Erica, but I must deal with Reza."

"All I know is that they began an affair a few months before you left Erica. But, from the beginning, Erica imagined you knew about it and it was only a matter of time before you left her, which she was obviously looking forward to."

Darren feels humiliated and sad, but regains his composure quickly. "So what happened to their hot affair?"

"They broke up after a year or so. I despised her for cheating on you but kept quiet. Now I'm glad she'll face justice while I'm finding comfort in the arms of the man she stupidly drove out of her life. I like fate bringing the right people together. I love you, Darren. Let's go make love till morning, like I promised." She feels giddy from the wine and the juicy tenderloin.

6

Elizabeth yanks her shoes off her feet quickly, jumps onto the bed, hides her face in the pillow, and blubbers with tension. The reality is finally kicking in after all that wine, Darren thinks with some guilt about his role in all these revelations. After all, she has seen ten years of her life go down the drain in one night. On the other hand, he is happy her monotonous relationship with Jeff has possibly ended, for her own sake. He caresses her hair and whispers soothing words in her ear to relieve her tension and perhaps salvage the evening for some sensual adventures. He achieves only his first objective: She falls asleep. He pulls the bedcover over her and murmurs, "Great…! What happened to your promise, my superwoman—all-night sex, eh?" He checks his watch and decides to go to the cocktail lounge for a drink to untangle his own nerves perhaps. *Oh, what a shitty evening,* he whispers.

As he exits the elevator in the lobby, he sees Jeff. He tries to retreat and hide inside the elevator, but their eyes meet. Jeff hoists his arm and runs toward the elevator.

"Wait a second, Darren." Darren exits the elevator again.

"What's going on?" Jeff asks nervously. "What're you and Elizabeth doing here?"

What an idiot! "Ask Elizabeth. She'll explain everything."

"Okay. That's why I was going to the information desk to call you and come up to your suite to talk to her."

"She's gone back to Vancouver."

"Tell me the truth; I've got to talk to her right away."

"As I said, she's not upstairs, and I'm going to the bar. You may join me if you wish."

"I like to go check for myself," Jeff insists.

Darren is hesitant. Refusing Jeff's request hints his deceit, but complying will cause chaos. Jeff might be able to get his suite number from the concierge, anyway. He resents losing Elizabeth to Jeff, especially if they reconcile and leave him here alone. So he takes a risk: "If you really wanna go check, I'm in suite 312."

"Can I borrow your key, then, or shall we go together?"

"No. I'm going to the bar and don't give my key to anybody."

"Okay, I'll join you in the bar if she isn't upstairs."

As soon as Jeff disappears inside the elevator, Darren hurries to the concierge to use the phone. He dials 321. It keeps ringing and nobody answers.

"Please pick up, Elizabeth…," he mutters with angst. Almost hanging up to rush to the bar before Jeff returns, she answers. "Listen, Elizabeth… Hang up now but wait for my call in a few minutes. Don't answer the door, anyway." He then charges to the bar and orders a drink.

Jeff returns in a fury. "A Chinese guy is in room 312."

"Why'd you go to room 312?" Darren says. "I said 321."

"Can I see your key tag?" Jeff asks.

Darren flashes the suite number on the key tag.

As Jeff dashes toward the elevators, Darren calls Elizabeth. "Listen carefully. Jeff's running around like a mad wolf. I had to give him the suite number and he's on his way upstairs. Don't answer the door or the phone until I come back upstairs."

After ten minutes, Jeff returns in distress. "Are you sure she left this late?"

"Yes."

"How long have you guys been…, doing whatever the heck you're doing?" Jeff asks.

"As I said, ask her all your questions, but it's not what you think."

"So how is it? Explain it to me."

"I can't. How about your affair?"

"That's what I must explain to her before she gets the wrong idea."

"Isn't it a little late for that? She was absolutely devastated and left the hotel with fury."

"It's all a misunderstanding. Tell me where she is."

"I don't know."

"You're lying!" cries Jeff, quite agitated and drunk.

Darren decides to leave, to avoid a confrontation. But Jeff chases him and grabs his arm. "Tell me what's going on. Tell me where she is."

"I don't know, I said," Darren replies, pulling his arm away.

As Darren turns to leave, Jeff clutches his arm tighter with rage. Darren yanks his arm free with a big thrust, maddening Jeff enough to land a fast punch on Darren's cheek. Enraged, Darren throws Jeff off balance onto the floor with one swift thrust. Jeff stays on the floor, embarrassed by yet another defeat. Darren rubs his aching cheek and walks away, glaring at Jeff with contempt. Outside the hotel, he meanders for fifteen minutes before going back to his suite when there is no sign of Jeff. Elizabeth is sitting anxiously at the edge of the bed. He tells her the story.

7

Early next morning, Darren opens his eyes to Elizabeth's gaze. His head and cheek still ache.

"What…? What's wrong?" he asks.

"What do you think Jeff meant about our misunderstanding?"

"Oh, gosh, you woke me up just to ask me that?"

"I'm worried about something…"

"About what?" he asks with surprise.

"I'll tell you in a second. But first tell me what he said."

"He said we misunderstood him! That's all…"

"Do you think he's trying to confuse me?"

"I think he's inventing a story to prove his innocence."

"But how can you be so sure it's not a misunderstanding?"

"His reaction in restaurant: Frozen and mute like a statue."

"He might've been shocked at seeing us."

"I doubt it," he says, feeling guilty about his ulterior motive for convincing her.

"I disagree. Maybe a true story exists to exonerate him, but I'm concerned about a more important issue."

"What's that?" he asks.

"If there's a misunderstanding, my version of our affair can't fly," she argues.

"What do you mean?"

"I mean, if he has a valid explanation, my claim would be a fat lie in addition to the original crime of having an affair with you. So I must invent a story to convince him equally that I'm innocent as well. I can't admit guilt if he has a story that proves his innocence. It'd be too humiliating."

Darren nods, amazed by women's gift for sorting out these complex dilemmas so diligently. "But how would you know he's not lying?"

"That's why I've lost my nerve. I don't know which story or option to choose, and whether to listen to his explanations."

"I see your dilemma."

"You must help me choose an option. You're involved, too."

"Let's have breakfast in our room and then go to a nearby park to discuss your options."

"No, let's go have breakfast somewhere else, too."

"Okay, I'll go downstairs first. You join me in fifteen minutes if I'm not back up here. Don't answer the door or the phone. I'll wait in my car after checking things downstairs and enquiring about Jeff at the reservation desk."

8

Darren finds out, and tells Elizabeth, that Jeff had checked out late last night, which means he had booked a suite for at least one night. The likelihood that he returns after going to Vancouver and not finding Elizabeth appears slim. Therefore, they decide to stay one more night in the hotel as planned and return the following day. After long deliberation, they agree she should stay in his apartment while sorting out her situation with Jeff. She will try to explain her affair with Darren and its circumstances only after assessing Jeff's story. Meanwhile, Darren would not respond to any questions until Elizabeth invents *the story*. They will also decide about their own relationship and how to handle Jeff within a week.

Their third night in Harrison Hot Springs proves almost as productive and pleasant as the first one, although they remain vigilant about confronting Jeff, who could return for Elizabeth after failing to find her in Vancouver. Still, they venture in and out of the hotel separately, Darren always scouting their routes first. Recounting the recent events and scenes, they also laugh heartily under the influence of pot. They believe their fates are fusing mysteriously through a bunch of bizarre coincidences, forcing Elizabeth to let go of her dismal relationship with Jeff. The more they smoke, the more last night's events appear funny, and the more logical their plans and commitments for a future together sound.

After a late lunch in Abbotsford and a short stop at Cultus Lake for a romantic stroll, they arrive at Darren's apartment on Saturday afternoon. Darren helps Elizabeth settle in the master bedroom before listening to many messages on the answering machine and scanning the mail. Everybody has called, some more than once. He calls Nora last with anxiety, while making up a bunch of lies about everything, especially Elizabeth's skirmish with her boyfriend and asking Darren to stay at his place for a while. Nora sounds testy, especially after Darren declares his plan to visit T.J. in the evening instead of seeing her, which would annoy Elizabeth, not to mention the need for more lies to Nora about his trip and Elizabeth's stay. Visiting T.J. would surely be less offensive to both ladies than spending his evening with either one of them. *Lucky T.J.! What a mess,* Darren ponders dolefully. T.J. would probably go dizzy listening to bizarre stories Darren would share with him about his growing headaches in messier relationships every day.

He peers around the apartment and outside the window. After only three days of absence, the place is soulless. He plays a CD to summon the Masters, surveys the incomplete paintings around the room, and feels depressed for wasting his life on worthless conversations and affairs. He needs a short nap.

In the master bedroom, he lies naked next to Elizabeth and embraces her snoozing body.

Chapter Eight
Vincent's Venture

1

Dreary Darren arrives at T.J.'s house before Reza.

"What's wrong?" T.J. asks.

"Getting punched by two men this week because of two women hasn't been fun."

"One must be prepared to pay a price periodically for all the pleasures one pursues persistently," T.J. says facetiously.

"Teasing me again with your Peter Piper talk?" Darren asks edgily. "I bet you'd prepared this corny phrase to use on me one of these days." *Anybody can predict the perils of my lifestyle!*

"Sort of... But mostly as a philosophical notion applicable to many people nowadays," T.J. replies with pride.

"So now you finally got your chance to use it on me, eh?"

"Just to cheer you up... You're getting edgier every day."

"But I'm stuck, T.J. Can't you see?" he shrieks, tempted to punch this foolish old man in the face. *T.J. seems oblivious to my turmoil, too. Maybe he's jealous or been jinxing me all along.* Luckily, he recalls his dream about the two men arguing and kissing, regains his composure, and apprises T.J. of recent events. "On top of all these hassles is my new discovery about Reza."

"What has he done now?"

"Just an old issue that has been bugging me for so long."

"What's that? If you don't mind telling me…"

"His hypocrisy. I never accused him of seducing Erica. But now the matter has been confirmed by a reliable source. He must understand that my suspicions all these years, while pretending friendship, have hurt me deeply."

"That's a tough one!" T.J. whispers while looking away.

"Yet, his betrayal makes me ashamed of myself, too."

"Why?"

"For seducing Elizabeth. How dare I criticize Reza when I'm equally weak around women?"

"Well… only you can help yourself in that respect."

"But I must confront Reza, too."

"You're all over the map today with your guilt versus anger."

"I know… Did you know about Reza and Erica?"

T.J. stalls deliberately, hoping his silence ends this topic.

"Well…?" Darren insists.

"I'd heard something through the grapevine leading to my wife and daughters. You see, many women look at Reza as an eligible bachelor. I'd say forgive Reza and forget everything."

"But h—"

"Let's value his friendship, despite his flaws," T.J. says while staggering to answer the doorbell. "Our friendship is special."

2

Reza looks excited as he steps inside, hugging T.J. and Darren. "Have you heard the news?"

"What news? We hear lots of news all the time," T.J. answers with a grin, winking at Darren inconspicuously.

"The war is finally over after eight years. Iran and Iraq have signed a UN resolution," explains Reza ecstatically.

"Hurrah," T.J. yells cheerfully, while Darren reflects on his own memories of the damn war… about the agony of human folly that manifests in all forms. Over one million Iranians— mostly teenage soldiers—and a similar number of Iraqis had to die in vain, not to mention the number of crippled veterans and the victimized families who lost their sons and husbands, all due to the egotism of naïve leaders and filthy international politics.

"What did anybody achieve after all these killings?" Darren asks pensively.

"Nothing at all. Only destruction and death. That's how our humanity is defined these days," Reza replies.

"You look great, Reza," T.J. blurts to change the subject.

"How are you, Reza?" Darren asks.

"I'm happy about my parents living in Vancouver now, but Mahroo worries me."

"Why?" enquires T.J.

"Has Darren mentioned anything about her depression?"

Noticing T.J.'s indecision about a response, Darren interjects. "Yes, I've mentioned my responsibility for giving her a wrong impression. Her marital life and the war had probably set off her condition already, though, before my painting created mayhem. She just used the painting as a refuge to relieve her tensions, but sadly it caused her a different type of melancholy."

"Great," Reza says. "Then T.J. can join our discussion about helping her. I don't think she needs serious therapy—although she'd refuse it, anyway. My parents only listen to her, too. So I can discuss my concerns only with you guys."

"What concerns?" asks Darren impishly while staring at T.J., hinting about the *naked* evidence they had recently witnessed themselves.

"Her anxiety attacks and melancholy. My parents have taken on the responsibility of raising Nazi. They've hoped to relieve Mahroo's burden, but mostly to save the child from her mood swings. They'd witnessed her apathy toward Nazi and spending many hours alone in her room or with the painting in the living room. She isn't violent, but I sense my parents' caution around her to protect both Nazi and Mahroo."

"Many of us suffer from odd eccentricities," Darren says.

"But she's too idealistic in a world that has lost its senses and morality. Most people realize the absurdity of the world and we all try to adapt somehow. But her anger with people and social systems is crippling her. She's oversensitive and withdrawn from people because they seem phony to her."

"But her problems," interjects T.J., "might lie beyond the simple symptoms of depression and fantasizing, or be nothing at all. Leave her alone as long as she doesn't hurt herself or others. Or convince her to go for a routine psychological test. She's smart enough to recognize her situation?"

"I agree," Darren says. "She either needs professional help or not. You must make that judgment. Afterwards, it's only a matter of convincing her to see a specialist. Our judgment is based only on limited contacts with her; we aren't specialists, either." Darren glances at T.J., with a subtle grin, hinting again how limited yet *exposed* their experience had been last Saturday night when they had visited her. "Personally, I can't be of any use, especially since you've already criticized my tactlessness."

"What criticism?" Reza asks.

"About the way I'd told her she wasn't the woman in my damn painting."

"I only said that although you'd explained the truth, the way you'd handled it, considering her situation, hadn't been quite smooth. I just wanted to calm her down and convince her that everything we've done has been for her own sake. That we've been truly worried about her."

"Mahroo was already mad at me," Darren says. "Then your comments made me look even more insensitive. Did you really have to put these new ideas into her agitated mind."

"I'm sorry. I didn't mean that either," Reza says.

"You know I wasn't a part of your scheme… I knew nothing about her infatuation with the painting, either. Maybe if you'd given me a heads-up, I would've prepared a *smoother* approach. But how'd you expect me to know she'd been projecting herself onto the woman in the white dress for so long? I just learned about it just a few days ago from her only after I told her the truth about the painting."

"I didn't know the real cause of her bizarre behaviour, either, until last week when she called me to explain her conversations with you in Vancouver," Reza says. "Then I realized why she'd behaved so strangely all the time we were blaming Zia for her depression. Zia had hinted a few times that he suspected Mahroo worshiping you through that painting, but I never listened to his nonsense…"

"You should have…," Darren interjects.

"Yes, I know now… But, then, I thought her attention to the painting was for the exact reason I'd hoped by giving it to her: To help her get my message, calm down, and decide about her future, so I was happy about it in fact. That's all!"

"Yeah, you're right," Darren says with a tone of compromise. "You learned the truth only now yourself."

"But you weren't right, apparently," Reza blasts. "You didn't act, although you must've sensed that something was wrong."

"But I didn't know exactly what to think or tell her without jeopardizing your intention…"

"You could've at least given me a hint, like what Zia did."

"Maybe I should have, now that you mention," Darren says.

"All along, she'd probably been living as the lover of the man whom she'd believed was you, apparently from your hints. I can't be responsible for that, too; you'd told her, or implied at least, that the man in the painting was you, without clarifying that the woman wasn't she. You only told her half of the truth." Reza pauses before continuing. "You left room for imagination, which then turned into the weirdest case of fantasy ever."

"I realized my mistakes only recently, like you," Darren says.

"Mahroo living as the woman in the white dress most likely drove Zia to suicide." Reza pauses, apparently gathering courage. "Admit that you're responsible for this chaos the most, even if it boils down to the simplest fact that you're the one who painted the *Woman in the White Dress* so lively in the first place."

"It's bizarre to be guilty of being a good painter as well, like I didn't have enough faults already!" Darren says with humour.

"Don't you think she's pretty enough? Don't you like her?"

Darren stares at T.J., who is equally stunned, then gazes at the corner of the ceiling, searching for a tactful response to Reza's outrageous questions. Fortunately, the telephone ring interrupts everybody's rumination. T.J. leaves the living room, answers the phone, and returns quickly, looking for Darren. "It's for you!"

Darren gasps a sigh of relief and reels toward the phone, still chewing on Reza's ridiculous questions. "Hello."

"Sorry to bother you, but I must talk to you right away."

"What's wrong, Elizabeth?"

"Jeff was here."

"What'd he want?"

"Nothing special… Other than my confession perhaps…"

"Was he angry?"

"Yes, but he got the impression I'm living here alone."

"Alone…? How…?"

"I told him you were staying at your friend's house."

"But he's going to find out."

"How?"

"What're you thinking, Elizabeth?" he asks with confusion and stress. "Are you asking me not to come home?"

"No, but I was intimidated when he showed up at the door. I wasn't ready to explain our affair. Your absence convinced him to leave after I let him check the apartment."

"How'd he find my address? You called him?"

"He got it from Erica after telling on us. I talked with her too."

"So Erica knows everything?"

"Yes. She sounded upset about us but tried to control herself."

"What'd you tell her?"

"Nothing. But I promised to explain my side of the story, too, later. Just be careful coming home tonight."

"What'd Jeff say about his affair?"

"He says the bimbo we saw is his boss's pregnant mistress, apparently unwilling to have an abortion. So, the boss had sent Jeff to somehow convince her to stop her foolishness."

"Lame story… Don't you think? Why had they ended up in Harrison Hot Springs?"

"I asked him the same question and he said she works there and some other stuff to convince me."

"So why had he told you he was going to Los Angeles?"

"Exactly… When I asked for proof, maybe by letting me talk to her or his boss, he said he must first get his boss's permission. So, I said I'll explain about us when he's given me proof of his innocence," she says with triumph. "He tried to drag something out of me, but I was adamant and he left quite upset. I had to give him your phone number, so if you don't mind, you should let me or the answering machine get all the calls for a while."

"Do you think I can come home tonight at least?"

"Absolutely. I'll keep the bed warm for you, my darling."

Back in the living room, Darren notices T.J. and Reza quiet, wondering about the caller and the nature of his conversation based on what they had overheard inadvertently.

"I'm losing the control of my life… I'm not sure how safe it is for me to go home, men hit me in public places, can't answer my own phone, my girlfriends want commitments from me and—"

T.J. interjects, "One must be prepared to pay a price perio—"

Darren interrupts T.J., "Shut up T.J." Then continues, "And now I must confess to my dear friend that I like his psychotic sister as well. All right, I confess. But I don't know what kind of a relationship she expects from me, or I can give her, especially with her melancholy that everybody seems so worried about."

"It's so sweet to acknowledge your feeling for Mahroo! But I agree this wouldn't solve any problem while you're up to your eyeballs with your girlfriends and their headaches," Reza says sincerely while T.J. nods agreeably. "I thank you for leaving Mahroo out of your hectic world. She has enough problems without becoming another victim of your adventures."

"This is a sign of Darren's true enlightenment," T.J. says.

"Absolutely," Reza concurs.

Darren interjects, "Did you give my address to Erica?"

"Yes... Long time ago...," Reza replies timidly.

"This is a good example of people's unintended acts causing trouble. I'm not listed in the phone directory for a reason... Your careless act has caused an additional headache for my girlfriend and me. I don't want to blame you, but use this example just to show how my innocent and supposedly tactful communication had been misunderstood by Mahroo."

"I'm sorry! I didn't know your address was confidential."

"Exactly. Often we can't predict the outcome of our actions."

"Let's forget the past and focus on the present," Reza says. "You don't seem to have any suggestions for Mahroo, other than seeking professional help, if necessary. But, sometimes friends can help better than a professional."

"That's true," T.J. says.

"I wish Mahroo had a wise friend to help her; something like my friendship with Erica and you when your life was in turmoil. You said not even marriage counsellors could help you, but my intervention helped you guys handle your depressions faster. I'm not bragging, but just comparing Mahroo's case to yours three years ago. That's all I hoped you could do for Mahroo. She won't listen to anybody, especially me. But you have a special influence over her that may come in handy for calming down her nerves."

"So you thought you were doing us a favour by sleeping with my wife?" Darren says with agitation, but forces himself to smile and sound witty, too. "I'm sorry for not thanking you much sooner for being such a considerate, horny friend."

"You and Erica should judge your cases and my involvement on your own," Reza says. "You don't know much about Erica's mental state when I met her. But, you may still remember your own condition. You were like a dormant volcano, burning like hell deep inside, despite your calm appearance. You were about to explode and destroy yourself and everything around you. Again, I'm not trying to brag or anything, but my suggestion to leave Erica and change your environment helped you a lot, to the point of becoming a famous painter now."

"But it was all for your own benefit, on top of causing our separation to begin with. You felt guilty and tried to make up for it by offering me a job. Or simply get me out of Vancouver altogether, to be alone with her?"

"No way… I'll be happy to explain everything in detail."

"It's not necessary."

"But I really like to get this big load off my chest," Reza says. "You must know the facts."

"What facts?"

"For one thing, I encouraged Erica to continue working on her relationship with you, otherwise she would've given up much sooner. Another proof of my goodwill is that I planted the idea of Erica employing you in her company. But you had no clue about her life aspirations, or ridiculed them. I don't blame you because you were preoccupied with your own career problems. You were bitter and she felt your unconscious hatred of her achievements simply due to your inability to compete with her professionally."

"I never wanted to compete with her," Darren shrieks.

"Perhaps you didn't believe in success and prestige. But you probably felt inadequate, witnessing her obsession for success and expecting you to be successful, too, to make her proud. So, she suffered not only for being blamed for her ambitions, but also watching you perish instead of becoming somebody—for her sake, if not for your own benefit. At the same time, she faced all sorts of business problems she couldn't discuss with anybody, especially you. She was inexperienced in the field of computers, but had plenty of innovative ideas. Her partner wasn't bright enough, although his father introduced many new clients—"

Darren interrupts him, "I really couldn't care about her work problems then, nor like to hear about them now."

"That's exactly the main issue Erica complained about so often, which also started her dependence on me... She said you didn't care about her and her growing headaches."

"She had created all that mess for herself...," Darren shrieks.

"No... She was stuck in that bad position," Reza says. "The company had to expand fast and learn management techniques and all the nitty-gritty of software development to compete with established companies. She worked over twelve hours a day without making a dent in her workload. Beyond the burdens of program development, delivery schedules, and client satisfaction, they had to deal with many inexperienced and demanding staff. Finding and keeping good employees was difficult: They worked a few weeks then left for a higher-paying job."

"Well, she loved her job, she always said so," Darren says.

"That's true, but besides her business hassles, she was worried about the effect of your career setback on your relationship. Instead of relying on you to share her problems and challenges, she had to listen to your stories about life miseries or watch you get drunk or stoned with no plan to rescue yourself. She needed someone to talk with about her work and home problems and I happened to be there to help her with work issues initially, and then home problems. Then she got addicted to me for relieving herself psychologically. And eventually she felt romance relieved her stress faster than talking alone. I tried to fight the temptation, but sadly, I wasn't as strong as you've been with Mahroo, especially when she claimed your separation felt imminent. She explained why and her reasons appeared well thought out and logical for both of you."

"At the end, these are all excuses. They can never justify what you two did to all of us," Darren says with angst.

"I'm sorry for not being a stronger person. But I never meant to entice her away or cause your separation. As you know, our relationship lasted only fourteen months. We weren't suitable for each other, either. I guess she saw some of your boring, unstylish life philosophies in me and realized how strongly I valued my friendship with you. For the sake of our business relationship, we ended our emotional one. We go to the Vancouver Symphony when I'm in town and perhaps dinner afterwards, but that's all."

"Thanks for trying to justify your affair with my wife…!" Darren exclaims with sarcasm, yet also feels a gratifying relief for grasping Reza's rather humanistic role in all these nasty affairs. *If I weren't such a spiteful person, I should go kiss his hand, too!*

"I'm only telling the truth, and I don't need to justify myself to anybody," Reza replies.

3

Silence rules in a bizarre, tense atmosphere, everybody pondering Reza's lengthy confession, consuming tea and Danish pastries, exchanging subtle glances, and surveying the furniture or pictures hanging on the walls. The pending issues between Darren and Reza appear largely clarified.

"I appreciate your confession, anyway," Darren says at last.

"And I'm really glad for unloading this big burden off my chest at last," Reza replies.

"We often blame others or circumstances for our mistakes. You and I aren't different."

"Yes, we're all weak humans that keep hurting one another every day," Reza replies.

"Our wild imaginations raise our suspicions and lead to hasty judgments, too," T.J. adds.

"Not to mention the effects of our wild urges, in spite of our efforts to stay good friends and ethical," Reza adds.

"I think some form of feminine seduction always ignites all love affairs," Darren says with a sigh. "Although women may get lured by men, too, usually they start an affair and let it proceed."

"I'm glad you say that," Reza says with a sigh. "In a way, I feel I became a victim myself in this affair—the one with Erica."

"Weirdly enough, I see your point, Reza," Darren replies. "In this special case, I find you only a little guilty and see Erica as the weak link without enough integrity; worse than I'd ever imagined possible. All the times we went to concert and dinner, I only blamed her for being deceptive and unappreciative of our life circumstances. Surely, our marriage condition wasn't ideal, but partners must be willing to face tough circumstances and tolerate each other better, while working on their relationship problems."

"Amen...!" T.J. blurts.

Darren continues, "Erica should have shown more patience and understanding despite my melancholy. Isn't this the point of partnership? Instead, she looked for a chance to abandon me and eliminate one source of her headaches. Why didn't she quit her job instead? Maybe I'm unrealistic, but if she loved me, the idea of growing compassion and showing it must've occurred to her eventually, if not naturally."

Reza and T.J. nod approvingly. After sipping more tea, Reza addresses Darren: "Thanks for forgiving me somewhat. We can't live and find peace without forgiving people. But maybe I don't deserve it. Betraying friends is against the basic principles of honour. I'm pissed at my own friends' hypocrisy and integrity."

"You too?" Darren enquires.

"A close friend of mine, who is a fanatic Muslim too, lured me into investing over two million dollars in a lousy venture," Reza continues. "Not only had he fudged the documents to prove the viability of the venture, but also lied right to my face before and after grabbing my money. In fact, he scammed a bunch of his close friends. Even worse, he now arrogantly denies or twists his previous claims and promises."

"Humans are becoming less trustworthy every day," T.J. says.

"That's true... Another friend, an alleged confidant, revealed my private feelings and secrets to others," Reza says. "So, some caution is always necessary in this crazy world. The difficulty is knowing whom to trust or suspect, and when. We waste energy to gauge our friends constantly on top of handling all the growing deceit in society. That's just too much struggles, disappointments, cynicism, and sufferings to deal with every day."

"You two just can't stop whining today, even when trying to forgive each other, ha?" T.J. says jokingly and they all laugh.

"We always whine," Darren says and they giggle tensely.

"But you guys are right. It's sad to feel my friends and family have disappointed me more often than strangers," T.J. says.

"Then we suffer more from our own dirty deeds," Reza adds.

"That's true," Darren says, pondering and suffering his own sense of betrayal toward Jeff, although he prefers to believe Elizabeth is probably more responsible for letting this happen.

"So let's not allow false imaginations, or a woman, destroy our special friendship," T.J. interjects. "And let's stop whining so much all the time as well."

"I agree," says Reza while Darren nods in agreement, too.

"Sharing opinions and compassion is our strength, so unlike common friendships nowadays, which are so shallow, just sitting around, chatting nonsense, boozing, and telling jokes," T.J. says. "We should also help each other when possible."

"That's true," Reza agrees wittily. "We mostly smoke pot...!"

"I say this in line with your request about Mahroo," T.J. continues. "We could put our heads together and make some judgments even though we aren't psychologists. The question is whether we, especially Darren, can help Mahroo?"

"Thanks, T.J., for caring about Mahroo!" says Reza.

Reza's tone sounds odd and insulting to Darren, as if only T.J. cared about Mahroo, while Darren was a callous jerk. Yet, he hates to start another row after all this preaching and forgiving.

"You sneaky rascal...," Darren says to T.J. nevertheless.

"What did I do now?" T.J. asks sheepishly.

"You made all these discussions just to raise Mahroo again?"

"Maybe...!" T.J. chuckles slyly.

"But what do you think we can do or talk about?" Darren asks, agitated by the idea of opening up this topic again. Despite all the friendship gestures and values pronounced this evening, he still resents being dragged into Mahroo's problems, especially after being blamed for her depression. Are these two silly men expecting him to befriend or court her for some unpredictable turn of events?

T.J. replies, "We must earn her trust somehow to test her mental condition beyond her sad obsession with Darren. But ironically, Darren is the only one capable of gaining her trust. My suggestion is to decide whether to interfere in her life or not first. Let's take a minute while I fetch you some drinks."

4

Darren and Reza ask for gin and whiskey respectively. They just exchange glances in silence while pondering T.J.'s suggestion. Agitated, Darren paces the room and then stops at the window. He surveys the passing cars and an elderly couple crossing the street with their Labrador—also old, judging by the way it limps with angst. Pooped yet dutiful to each other, the couple drag to finish the evening walk—their final means of physical activity. Darren imagines them as young lovers forty years earlier, with copious hopes and plans, now only counting the moments left or recounting the memories adrift, maybe looking forward to their grandchildren's visits to Vancouver during Christmas or summer. Communicating telepathically, the couple and their dog march in harmony until they are out of Darren's sight behind the trees where the street turns. *I'll be like that old man soon myself!*

T.J. returns with their drinks and peers at his flustered friends alternately for a sign of inspiration. None found, he tackles the matter directly: "Any thoughts?"

Disappointed by their silence, T.J. continues, "How about Darren giving Mahroo painting lessons? You," he nods to Reza, "can plant the idea in her head casually with a promise to get Darren to teach her."

A glimmer of hope sparks in Reza's eyes. Nodding to T.J. cordially, he notices Darren's anxiety and drooping with a sign of irritation. Darren's silence agitates T.J. and Reza and they feel embarrassed for having put Darren on the spot, while exchanging guilty glances. After all, he seems under stress these days, and adding to his concerns is rude. Darren drinks the last dose of his gin, extends the empty glass to T.J., and asks for a refill along with a couple of aspirins.

"You have a headache?" T.J. enquires.

"And dizzy too. My mind is exploding from your ideas. My nausea could also be from the recent punches to my head."

"You'd better see a doctor then. Let's go to the Emergency."

"I'll be fine. It's probably only stress," Darren replies to T.J., then addresses Reza as T.J. leaves the room, "You think T.J.'s idea has any merit?"

"I see some benefits in it."

Again silence lingers until T.J. returns with Darren's order.

"What kinds of benefits do you see?" Darren asks at last.

"A hobby may soothe her suffering if her tension turns into creative energy and perhaps lift her spirit. Second, during this experience she may find a friend in you to analyze her situation and life aspirations better than she could do privately through self-pity. You can teach her meditation too. And third, she'll get over you when she realizes you're not such a special creature after all," says Reza half-teasingly.

"I'm sceptical about your last two points. But a hobby or a hubby may do her good," Darren says. "I can find her a teacher. But maybe you could find her another husband. A more stable one this time, please!" They all laugh before sinking into deep thoughts again.

"The whole point is to encourage her to talk to somebody. It'll be easier to convince her if you're the teacher," Reza says at last. "Otherwise, she'll resist the idea, like all my other suggestions. Don't dismiss the second and third points lightly either. As an instructor, you'll have a chance to make her express her feelings on canvas and verbally, and then perhaps help her deal with her personal concerns. You can redirect her negative thoughts and self-pity into awareness exercises and creative ideas. She wouldn't allow any other teacher do that to her, even if she agreed to take lessons from a stranger."

T.J. nods in agreement throughout.

"But I'm not a psychologist," Darren exclaims.

"It's not required. Besides, you're good with this stuff," Reza says.

"Why we don't learn any lesson from our mistakes is beyond me!" Darren says. "We've been struggling for the last few weeks to correct the headache our meddling in her life has caused. We tried to guide her into doing some self-therapy by lending her the *Woman in the White Dress* and we failed miserably."

"I bet her first painting would be, *the Man in Blue Jeans Watching the Woman in the White Dress,*" T.J. says cunningly and they burst into laughter.

"Are you mocking my sister now?" Reza asks with a grin.

"Sorry… I was just trying to picture her sitting there behind the easel and thinking about her first subject to paint," T.J. replies with loud laughter. "Besides, she may like to take her revenge."

"You're funny too, sometimes," Reza says.

"What makes you think any kind of prying into her life again wouldn't be as catastrophic as the first attempt?" Darren asks. "Our naïve tactics backfired and everybody got hurt, especially the person we meant to help."

"We must be clearer this time perhaps...," Reza suggests.

"But we can't be clear at all. I'm concerned that any further involvement may cause more false imaginations or confusion, leading to still more frustrating and irreparable circumstances. Something could go wrong or Mahroo might misunderstand our intentions again, because we can't tell her directly what we're aiming to achieve, right?"

Reza doesn't respond, seemingly pondering Darren's points. Therefore, T.J. feels obliged to jump in. "Of course, there're risks in pursuing this plan or any plan, but we should weigh the merits and decide whether our prying is better than doing nothing. Reza is the person to decide, but also be ready to accept responsibility for the consequences."

Reza interjects, "You're both right. Let me think more and perhaps test Mahroo's reaction."

"But if you're counting on me in any way, I need more time to think, too."

"Without mentioning your name, perhaps it's useful to know how receptive she is to the idea of taking on a hobby or getting some meditation lessons, anyway. She's bored doing nothing all day alone here in Vancouver besides thinking about you."

"Maybe! But remember, I really believe that my involvement would be a bad idea, for her sake and mine. I don't know how to make her feel close to me without getting emotionally involved, and that's the last thing Mahroo and I need in our lives right now," Darren replies.

"Is romance the only way for you to be near a woman?" Reza says and they chuckle.

"You couldn't do it with Erica yourself, could you?" Darren asks with a smirk.

"No, I failed too… You're right," Reza replies in distress.

"Let's wait and see how we feel in a few days," T.J. says.

"How's your headache and nausea?" Reza asks.

"It's better but I must go home to sleep," Darren replies.

"If Elizabeth lets you!" murmurs T.J.

5

Everybody is quiet for ten minutes as though tired or worried about raising another argument.

"Are we square on all accounts now?" Reza asks Darren.

"I guess so," Darren replies, looking at T.J. to see if he has anything to add. T.J. appears pleased with the outcome of his mini-intervention to settle the matters of concern between friends. After a long pause, however, Darren turns to Reza and asks, "Now that the identity of the *Woman in the White Dress* is cleared and the painting has no value to Mahroo anymore, what's the chance of me getting it back?"

Swiftly agitated, Reza appears to be searching for the right words. T.J. notices the return of tension and maybe another big misunderstanding—this time about Reza's promise to return the painting to Darren eventually. Therefore, he tries to pacify the atmosphere. "Darren, please come to the kitchen to get some ice cubes from the freezer while I refresh our drinks."

When they return with the drinks, Reza still looks anxious, in deep thought. Now he is the one pacing the room. Darren realizes the gravity of his question.

"We don't need to discuss this tonight. It's not really urgent."

"Let's go over this matter tonight, too. I recall discussing the possibility of returning it to you under the right circumstances. Although you loathed selling it, you gifted it to me at last after I explained how it might help me get through to Mahroo tastefully. Although she knows its story now, some other issues still make it difficult to return the painting to you."

"Like what?"

"First of all, I don't know whether or when Mahroo is willing to detach her feelings from the painting, even if she convinces herself that she isn't the woman in the white dress."

"You think she might still believe she's actually the woman in the white dress despite my confession?" Darren asks in shock.

"It's possible… I can't really ask her to return it in her present state of mind. Second, she may think she owns it, anyway. It's been her property, and God knows when it may change hands, if ever. And third, if she returns it to me, don't I have the right to decide about all other circumstances. If the painting is released from all its legitimate obligations, then, by all means, I'll return it to you. I promise. But I simply can't guarantee the time or circumstances under which this will happen."

Darren is getting dizzier with all these ambiguous accounts of promises and obligations about the painting. He tries to keep his cool by taking a deep breath. "Here we go again! There's another mix-up here, since I remember exactly what we talked about!"

"I know. I'm sorry, but other complications have risen along the way," Reza replies.

"What complications?" Darren asks with frustration.

"I can't discuss them tonight...," Reza replies sheepishly.

"I thought the painting would've served its purpose once it was no longer of benefit to Mahroo. Now you sound like other obligations exist—which I know nothing about—in addition to Mahroo's possible senses of attachment and ownership."

"Yes, that's true...," Reza says mysteriously with desperation.

"Not to mention the big chance that she might always believe to be the *Woman in the White Dress!*" T.J. interjects jokingly.

"Well, maybe she is, after all!" Reza says mysteriously.

"I really don't want to make a big case out of this painting tonight. You know I'd really like the painting back and I'm sure you'll do your best to return it as soon as possible."

"I promise to bring it straight to you the minute it is released from all the ownership and sentimental attachments."

"Are there sentimental attachments to this painting other than Mahroo's?"

"Yes... But I can't elaborate now," Reza replies cagily.

"Not yours, I hope?"

"No, I have no personal attachment to this painting, I assure you," Reza says.

The telephone rings and T.J. leaves to answer it, then points to Reza, who goes to the phone and returns quickly with distress. He explains his father's agitation on the phone about Mahroo's long argument with him and her mother this afternoon and then going away. Since she has not returned yet, they are worried and want Reza to go and do something. So, Reza excuses himself and leaves after offering Darren a ride home considering his headache and dizziness. However, Darren declines his offer on the grounds he'd feel better soon or stay with T.J. overnight.

6

Darren stares at T.J. who seems equally disturbed by the news about Mahroo's sudden disappearance. They wonder what she might have done to herself now.

"Why didn't you let him drive you home?" T.J. asks.

"I would've felt obliged to help Reza look for Mahroo, which I'm hesitant to do. Also, I'd like to speak with you for a minute."

"Sure…"

"You knew how Mahroo's arrival has made me anxious."

"Yes."

"And still you make all those crazy suggestions and jokes!"

"I'm sorry… But I was hoping to help Reza and also do something for Mahroo. We know she might need help."

"I guess. But I'm not the right person for this job."

"Why not?"

"For one thing, her feelings for me. I'm attracted to her in a peculiar way, too, but logic dictates to stay away from her and this type of infatuation."

"That's true…"

"I've made a point to know a woman fully before getting too serious with her. But now Mahroo is challenging my pledge to stay practical. By avoiding her, I'm trying to control my urges and stick to my basic rules. The reason I didn't want to go look for her and my reluctance to teach her painting or meditation are all part of my dilemma about her. I'm avoiding her not because I'm careless, but because I should not give her another wrong impression about my feelings for her, especially considering her history of depression and lunacy, to put it mildly."

"We all have odd obsessions and quirks that make us look crazy to others when they get to know us better; just some people can hide it better than others," T.J. proposes. "I think it's a part of human nature to be wild and idiotic, but we try to appear civilized through ethics and etiquette. We try to tame our wild desires and imaginations, which then causes other types of abnormality."

"I know, but she seems to be in a special world."

"You shouldn't make a hasty judgment based on what others say or even her soft lunacy now and then. Most geniuses have benefited from their bizarre perceptions of the world and many of them gone totally cuckoo, too. "

"You may have a point," Darren says. "Maybe she's only a lonely genius!"

"You know that when someone expresses ideas against social norms and common beliefs, he's labelled odd and abnormal. But following our demented norms without even understanding their meanings and values will never give us wisdom. Aren't we all crazy in the way we waste most of our lives on collecting wealth and power that have no true value at the end?"

"Yes, we surely are…"

"Aren't we crazy when our greed and ego make us kill one another instead of adopting simpler lifestyles to make the best of our short lives?"

"Yes, we surely are…"

"So, who's to say whether Mahroo is crazy or not? She may be different or oversensitive."

"That's true, but sometimes people go completely nuts out of desperation, loneliness, or due to life pressures."

"Of course… I know that, but I doubt Mahroo is at that stage, or at least I hope so. You have a chance to stop that possibility!"

"Maybe. My father is an example of how things go wrong so quickly."

"What happened to your father?" T.J. enquires.

"He went into comma two years ago and doctors pronounced him terminal. But before I returned to Canada, he recovered. In one of his letters, he explained his near-death experience—NDE —during the comma. I could not believe his claims. So I read many books written on the subject by scientists with Ph.D.s and MDs. Did you know more than ten million verified NDEs have taken place in the U.S. alone?"

"No, I didn't"

"Scientists believe that NDE experiences are consistent, yet it's unclear if it is a spiritual experience or a scientific thing. At last, I believed my father, especially when his lifestyle changed. He had never been a religious or spiritual person, but became one overnight. Now he spends most of his life inside a two-bedroom apartment in Toronto to read and meditate, and has stopped answering the phone recently, too."

"Are you in contact with him at all?" T.J. asks.

"We've exchanged letters to maintain a minimal relationship. I believe my letters are his only source of contact with mortals' life. He gradually trusted me enough to explain the supernatural phenomena surrounding his life, the light and premonitions he receives through angels and saints in particular moments in the twilight zone, and now even during waking hours. He's gotten the habit of predicting the future now, too. And more recently he's been claiming to have become a saint himself."

"It's really sad...," T.J. says.

"Maybe loneliness has driven him to this sorry state, though his logic and perception of the world affairs seem intact. So, it's hard for me to judge him, though it's easier to assume he's lost his mind. A normal, outgoing person has suddenly turned around one hundred and eighty degrees and created a world for himself that's probably only hallucination. Even more worrisome are my own conditions."

"What conditions?" T.J. asks.

"Well… If my mind is genetically defective like his, I might fall into the same trap if I stay lonely too long. My loneliness and struggle to find a good companion may drive me mad, anyway. These chronic worries also complicate my opinion of love and relationships. It sounds crazy, but sometimes I feel, and even see, spirits around me, especially when I think about them and wish them to come around."

"Here we go… You doubt even you own sanity...," T.J. Says.

"Yes, I do."

"So how can you judge Mahroo so harshly?"

"You're right, I guess… What if I'm going insane already? Maybe my madness is even worse than Mahroo's. But honestly, I enjoy, and actually need, these spirits' help, mostly for painting. They inspire me, as if being connected to the universe and all the creativity I draw from it."

"Thanks for confessing! You're probably crazier than Mahroo then, and it's good you've noticed it yourself. Then again, many of us have wild fantasies sometimes, which aren't hallucination. 'Supernatural' sounds obscure but hard to deny. In terms of a companion, we'll never find a perfect match. Just hope for the best, take the risk, and then learn to tolerate the imperfect conditions of marital relationships."

"You sound like Dervish Ali now. Thanks for listening, T.J."

"If you don't want, or can't afford emotionally, to get closer to Mahroo, I understand it, too. I'll take back my proposal when I talk to Reza; or actually, let me call him right now and tell him why we should drop my suggestion," T.J. proposes.

"Don't worry! He has more immediate concerns right now, looking for Mahroo and all. Tomorrow, I'll be blunt and tell him that my commitments prevent me from taking on other tasks. Besides, these days I bring bad luck to myself and people around me, so why bother getting involved? Sometimes I consider going to live on an island alone, to free the world and myself from pain and troubles."

"Maybe I should go with you … My life is getting tough too."
Darren bursts into laughter. "Can you run away from Feri?"

"I'm actually looking for an excuse to elude my Angel wifey"

"It might be a good break for both of us!"

"I'll try, but maybe you're overreacting and stressing yourself out for nothing. You must meditate more to calm your nerves."

"Actually, meditation is making me even more sensitive and susceptible to graver pain instead of making me relax."

"Are you sure?" T.J. asks.

"That's how I feel. In fact, meditation may also make Mahroo more pensive and crazier," Darren replies. "Don't you agree?"

"No, I don't think so, but it might help her forget you at least."

"Now you're gone mad yourself, expecting such a big miracle from meditation!" Darren says seriously before they both burst into laughter.

"At least meditation has made you funny," T.J. says after his long laughter.

"What's happening, T.J.? Why is life so difficult and erratic, especially when we try to bring some minimal order and sense to it? Where have I gone wrong and how much sins and karma should I account for?"

"Well, now you're really starting to scare me...," T.J. says.

"Am I?" Darren asks.

"Yes, now you sound like the way you described your father. Maybe it was only his confusion that drove him to isolation and hallucinations as well. Are you now following the same path to your demise?"

"I hope not… But your point sounds likely."

"You should get hold of yourself, continue your meditation routines, anyway. Remember that these kinds of thoughts and setbacks happen to everybody. You're not alone in your journey of life and you're not the only one with all these doubts. Your problems will disappear soon and then you'll complain about boredom and monotony. Learn to ignore these short setbacks and take them as tests of awareness. You must prove yourself to reach higher levels of peace and spirituality," T.J. suggests.

"I'm trying, but sometimes I feel down and anxious about my beliefs. So, I need your wisdom as a friend. I hope you don't mind too much being in the middle of my conundrums." Darren pauses while standing up. "I'd better go."

"It's always a pleasure to collaborate on the issues boggling your head. Stay overnight if you're still dizzy."

"I'd better go check on Elizabeth. I feel responsible for her, too, now that I've stolen her from her crazy boyfriend. I didn't know he had such a temper, though I shouldn't blame him much under the circumstance."

Behind the wheel, Darren realizes he has lied again: He is not feeling better at all. He lingers while T.J. watches him from his living room window, wondering about Darren's condition. The full moon shines sneakily from beneath the masses of speeding dark clouds and a drizzle spatters the windshield. As T.J. steps outside to check on him, Darren starts the engine and pulls away slowly, hoping to drive home extra-cautiously for twenty minutes before the rain starts or his thumping headache and dizziness worsen. The clouds race eastward, masking the mooching moon sporadically, but luckily, no sign of heavy rain. Before turning into the garage, he imagines seeing the shadow of a figure behind a pillar monitoring the traffic around the building. When he parks the car and looks for the shadow, it has disappeared. Carefully, he lurches toward the elevators, turning his aching head left and right to ascertain nobody is approaching him.

Inside his apartment, he locates the bottle of aspirin at last and takes two tablets with a cold soda he grabs from the refrigerator. Quietly he then walks to the bedroom and enjoys the sight of Elizabeth's body, partly highlighted by the moonlight. He wishes he were feeling better, agile enough to slip under the blanket like a snake to examine her without a hiss until the very last second when she screams out of her sleep with ecstasy. Alas…

He sighs and returns to the living room, sinks onto the sofa with his head resting on its back, and closes his eyes to mitigate his dizziness. It helps, but the giddiness turns into a big tornado inside his head, which is a funny sensation amidst the pain. He repeats opening and closing his eyes for fun. Twirling in the heart of the tornado, he plans to rest awhile before moving to the bed.

7

The moon's gaudy glimmers flicker through the wide glass doors onto Darren's face. He opens his eyes slowly and discovers, to his amazement, everything around him still, with no sign of the revolving world. An urge to trace the eluding moon and the bubbly billows hovering around it besieges him. The hypnotic eastward-rushing clouds, the moon appears to be racing for the ocean in the west. Its reflections on the wobbly creek turn the sharp edges of the meandering ripples into millions of glistening stars. The tinier waves dance away sneakily across the cobalt waters to reach the bank and kiss the rich vegetations covering the bank. Further out to his right, a sailboat approaches smoothly through English Bay. Its white sails, drenched in the moonlight, contrast the dark waters of False Creek and brighten the boat's upper deck, where people are shuffling around giddily. Leisurely the boat sails forward—and sometimes, it appears, backward—to come straight across Darren's viewpoint, then inching into the inner part of the Creek on his left-hand vista. A few dozen men in old-fashioned attires mingle on the main deck, while another group traffics in and out of the stairwell leading to the lower compartments. Waves of laughter and cheers explode from one corner of the boat sporadically amidst the soulful music echoing from another side.

Darren's eyes are pinned on the scintillating sails, which swing rhythmically in the silky wind, and then the mast tilts slightly as the boat draws closer to the bank on Darren's side of the Creek and approaches the quay. It finally docks and soon the music stops abruptly. Instead, jolly roars and laughter enliven the atmosphere. The moonlight brightens the deck briefly to allow Darren take a glimpse of the loud fiesta. People are singing and dancing without music, but then the clouds kill the moon and sink the boat in darkness. Briefly, under the teasing moonlight, a white image glows amongst the dark-clad men. It reaches the edge of the boat, where some men lift it up and put it on the pier. Moving fast toward the lamppost, the white image emerges as a woman in a long white dress and a white, wide brim sunhat hiding her face. She waves elegantly to the cheering crowd on the boat before disappearing amidst the dark sidewalks and the surrounding buildings.

Stunned, swiftly Darren grasps the spirit of the moment and the people manifesting it. A river of tranquility washes over his bewildered mind and rejuvenates him to a cheery mood parallel to the men's on the boat. Unconsciously, he waves at them and strives to yell, but no sound escapes his dry tongue and clenched jaws. A chill wind is whizzing and the drizzle prickles his face; still he is reluctant to go back inside. Soon the sound of music reverberates from the boat again along with occasional claps and laughter. Then the boat sails gently on the reverse route it had traveled to drop off the woman in the white dress. As it finally approaches his viewpoint, he begins waving again buoyantly. Nobody responds from the boat, possibly unable to see him on the dark balcony. He turns on the lights and resumes flinging his arms. At last, some men on the boat react by flailing their lanterns in a beckoning motion. Waving more heartily, he howls with joy when the boat slows down and sails closer to the bank. No doubt, they are acknowledging him.

Darren hesitates, wondering about their intention, yet the men keep inviting him as if they have now recognized him and want him aboard. At last, he decides to oblige. With a blink of his eyes, he is reeling along the bank at the speed of the boat. The men, now appearing more familiar to him subconsciously, wave and howl, but no one offers a means of boarding, nor does the boat intend to dock. Flustered, he keeps chasing the evading boat. The rising uproar of the men inviting him aboard is more frustrating now, as if mocking him instead of honouring their invitation. Yet Darren is too involved with the idea of joining them, as though his spirit and pride depended on it. Maybe they are teasing him with their mock invitation while he chases the boat like a fool? *How far are they planning to drag me along the bank before speeding away and laughing at my exhausted flesh and shattered spirit? But I'll persevere, even if I shall die proving myself.*

To show his frustration, Darren begins yelling at the men louder than they are yowling on the ship. Surprisingly, his spirit is soaring with exhaustion. His resolve is acknowledged at last and the men suddenly become more serious to bring Darren aboard. As a natural phenomenon, they seem to agree, though, that the boat cannot dock. They tie a rugged rope to a ring on the high mast and precisely measure the length of its free end. A few knots are tied near the end of the rope, which holds a four-pound bar. They roll the end of the rope and throw it toward Darren, who nods desperately while attempting to grab it.

A dozen times the rope reaches Darren but slips away rapidly, the men hollering, rolling, and throwing it again. By luck only, he eventually catches the rope and bends his knees swiftly to take off. He flies fast toward the boat, almost into the arms of the men ready to catch him. But the length of the rope and his upright legs exceed the tip of the railing by five inches. He crashes against the bulwarks and falls into the Creek, while the rope skids coarsely out of his hand. The water is cold and the laughter on the boat colder in his ear, though the men rush to help again. Despite its slow speed, the boat is eluding Darren, who is still in shock; the men scream: swim, swim, swim faster. Slogging fervently for two minutes, he reaches the boat and struggles to stay at least within reach. The curvy freeboard is slippery, has no cracks or edges to hold on to, and the bulwarks are high. The men throw the rope for him, but he screams in pain as he grabs it. He raises his hands to show his bleeding palms, ripped by the rope's spiky strands when pulled swiftly out of his hands during the last swing.

The men seek a solution while he swims stubbornly alongside the boat. One of them brings a long, sturdy rod and extends it toward Darren. He manages to hold on to it with pain and the men try to pull him in, to no avail. Either he lets go of the rod or the men cannot reach him to clasp his hands. One of the men shouts to Darren to lean on the end of the rod on his belly while holding on to it tightly. Then, a couple of men put their weight on the other end of the rod and pull him out of the water, dangling in midair, like playing teeter-totter. Next, another group pulls the rod slowly until he is within their reach. They clutch his arms and bring him aboard at last. Both grateful and proud of his triumph, he shivers while surveying his surrounding, which appears blurry and blue.

A man helps him change into dry clothes, another offers him a glass of cognac, and the third one rubs some sacred balm on his bleeding palms. The pain and scars disappear instantly. Soon his eyesight normalizes, too, along with the colour of his face, which now glows near the warm lanterns. The boat is bigger than he had imagined from the distance of his balcony.

Darren glances at the men around him. Their distinguished, familiar faces suddenly trigger his mind to appreciate the majesty of the moment—the largest gathering of the Masters he has ever experienced, and within such an intimate environment. He can now touch them and also comprehend their unfamiliar languages. Yet, he remains sceptical about their intention for inviting him aboard. What can be their interest in him? He is hesitant to speak, fearing they may realize he is only a commoner, maybe mistaken for someone else. He loathes losing the opportunity to mingle with such an elite crowd of humans, so he just waits quietly in awe, thinking that the pain of getting there had been worthwhile in itself, regardless of the prospects.

8

"Do you know us?" one of the men asks Darren.

"I recognize most of you! You're our idols and inspirers. You're Socrates, I believe…" Darren pauses, while considering taking a risk. "But do you know me?"

"You've called upon our friends often for inspiration. And we always look for good candidates to join our club, too."

"Then I'll become an elite spirit like you?"

"It all depends on you. You have a chance, but opportunity, compassion, and perseverance are most crucial to get here."

"So you can't help me?"

"We only inspire people who call upon us to achieve their goals. But we know nothing about their chance of immortality.

That's all part of your ingenuity and wisdom to choose the right life path and philosophy," the philosopher explains.

"Hmm…" Darren sighs in bewilderment.

"One thing is clear, though: You would've not been allowed to board this ship if your chance wasn't good. On the other hand, getting you aboard wasn't easy, either. Some candidates embark smoothly without getting wet, falling in the Creek, or banging their heads against the boat. You had to struggle to get here, which shows you still have a distance to go to prove yourself, but it also shows your perseverance and commitment."

"How about the woman in the white dress?" Darren asks.

"She got on and off like an angel, which shows her great chance of joining our club, perhaps as a saint."

"Who is she?"

"We only see visitors' spirits. So I can't describe her by a worldly description."

"I understand! I'm in this fantasy world temporarily and you can't divulge its secrets to a wandering soul!"

"No, that's not what I just said. Besides, this isn't 'fantasy' in the way you're thinking. The only sense of 'fantasy' here is its eternal peace and plasticity. This is the real reality unlike your world of false and freaky perceptions. You're living in a world full of illusions and dreams without even the basic principles for a peaceful existence."

"We are?" Darren asks timidly.

"Of course… Your social order is fantasy; your political and economic systems are whimsical and built around selfish views of life and humanity. Your judicial systems and religions are funny. Worst of all, your relationships with friends and family are fanciful imaginations and unrealistic expectations, thus you suffer forever. Why do you think people have so much stress and live in constant insecurity and anxiety? From birth, you live in a fantasy world filled with artificial values and ideals, which you teach to your children as reality, too. Maybe someday you'll join us and learn the difference between reality and fantasy."

The philosopher is interrupted when a man returns Darren's dried clothes, helps him to change again, and then guides him to the lower deck to meet Vincent.

In a small cabin filled with paintings and sketches, Vincent is sitting on a bench in the far corner in front of an easel and canvas. Darren muses that if Vincent were paid for the paintings piled up around him according to the going rates, he would be the richest person in the world. Yet, he had to suffer a lifetime of misery and poverty before finally giving up living like a dog.

"Well, let this be a lesson to you," Vincent whispers. "You should be thankful for being somewhat fortunate. I'm especially surprised how quickly you've forgotten all the misery you saw in Iran. How soon you mortals forget the meaning of real suffering and return to your pitiful moaning and despair."

Vincent pauses awhile to gauge Darren's pensive expression before continuing. "Maybe artists suffer a bit more than common people, because they think and feel deeper. Still, you must count your blessings and court your fate. Haven't you received enough hints about a real world more serene and meaningful than the one you're perceiving and living as a mortal? Haven't the Masters' manifestations and inspirations still offered you a refined source of enlightenment? How else are you humans going to learn who you are and what your life missions are? Just tell me, what is the meaning of this crazy world you've built for yourselves?"

"What is this?" Darren exclaims with angst. "Did you bring me here just to listen to your whining about the world's problems and insanities and be blamed for them as well? Don't I deserve some relief at least in my dreams?"

"No. We're only hoping to help you as a possible candidate to join our club. But you seem incapable, like me, to make a life for yourself or learn from your mistakes. You're still too arrogant and stubborn."

"I'm trying, you know!" Darren says. "Perhaps you noticed my struggle tonight to embark this boat. I almost killed myself for the privilege of being around you for a moment. However, the wisdom to always do the right things doesn't come easily. Deep inner conflicts and people burden my spirit often, to the point of losing my sanity and stamina sometimes."

"All this pulling and pushing around you are part of your training and finding enlightenment if you face them selflessly and compassionately. Otherwise, you'll lose both your spirit to pursue your worldly passions and the chance of becoming an elite soul."

"So, you think I'll still have a chance to become an immortal spirit?" Darren implores.

"I don't know… But you almost missed the boat tonight and you may never get another chance to come aboard unless you learn the meaning and purpose of your life on your own."

"What am I supposed to do?" Darren asks.

"Rely on the mystical signs around you. It's only up to you where you go from here. This special moment is merely another learning opportunity for you. We don't know the future and can't show you how to control your inner conflicts and attend to your real work —your mission."

"Thanks for being my mentor, anyway" Darren says.

"Remember our advice: You're living in a perceived world that has no resemblance to, or value in, the real world. You must find the real world outside the norms and conditions that society imposes on you arbitrarily. You may become an immortal painter if you can see, and believe in, the world beyond your immature perceptions. Let your passion guide you beyond the notions of logic, including painting's rigid rules. Then let this awareness and energy direct you during your temporary life. We'll be around and help you as well. But first, you must learn to help yourself and those who look up to you for inspiration. Then whenever you call upon us, respect our presence by staying calm, attentive, and inspired. Losing your mind to trivia and mindless quarrels only obstructs your creativity and freedom."

"I feel a connection to this real world just as you appear, even before the brush touches the canvas. I respect not only who you are and how you inspire me, but also the signs you send me about this real world," Darren says.

"That's not enough. If you want us around you, you must find the wisdom to be around us, too."

"I'll try to be more focused to gain this mysterious wisdom. I'm also learning to trust destiny in the moments of doubt," says Darren, sensing the time has come for him to depart.

"Before you go, there's something I must tell you, which is more important than everything I blabbered about so far."

Darren turns and peers at Vincent who continues, "Remember I have a special interest in your favourite painting as well."

"You mean the *Woman in the White Dress*?"

"Yes. That's the only major work I've ever helped anybody create. When you called on me, I got somehow absorbed in that painting. The composition came from your emotions, although I helped there, too. The woman attracted me as she came to life, stood on the sandy beach desolately, and waved at the boat so elegantly. The more the painting advanced, the more I became involved in it, and then realized I had to give her something more than a life on canvas. So, I asked the angels to infuse a delicate soul into her, too. They found a broken soul awaiting its destiny and borrowed it for this painting to make her look so alive."

Vincent pauses a few seconds before continuing: "I realize the chaos this painting has created, all because of someone's broken soul trapped in the painting. I know the soul belongs to someone special, and it may be redeemed soon by its rightful owner. I'm sorry for the trouble the painting has caused you. But I'm glad for making the angelic soul on the canvas thrill certain individuals. I did it out of love, and now it is perhaps turning into someone's destiny. I'm happy indeed about my deed. And I want you to know that this particular painting is more divine and dear than you'd perceived. So cherish it and bring it into your destiny." Noticing Darren's confusion, Vincent stops to give him a chance to muse before continuing. "You don't believe me?"

"I do. I'm just amazed, unable to interpret your confession. I knew there was something odd about this painting, but I didn't know it was blessed by a broken soul that your angels had blown into the *woman*."

"Well, she's only holding a special person's soul for now…, until the owner puts her affairs in order and reclaims it later."

"Do you love the woman in the painting, too?"

"Only as a soulful creation until it lasts as such."

"Then you condemn our common meaning of 'love,' too?" asks Darren cautiously, as his usual topic of curiosity.

"I don't condemn it. It's just naïve! I know you're a romantic man in search of love; I admire your tenacity."

"Yes… I'm a doomed romantic despite my desire and efforts to be practical!"

"True!" Vincent murmurs, watching Darren's pale face. "Do you have any special wish?"

"Well, I'd still like to grasp 'love' eventually. And perhaps die as a passionate hero, like in Puccini's operas."

"Good luck!" Vincent says, turning his head around toward the canvas.

Darren turns to leave, but suddenly freezes in his footsteps. He pauses for ten seconds under Vincent's curious eyes before asking, "Are you still pessimistic about humanity and its future?"

"What do you think? Why do you ask me?"

"I just remembered how you felt about this matter, especially your last words on your deathbed, 'There'll never be an end to human misery.'"

"Do you think anything has improved? Is there any hope on the horizon that you know of?" Vincent enquires irately. Darren droops as if everything were his fault. He feels sorry for opening the can of worms and giving Vincent another chance to start whining all over again—like the Socrates on the deck before. *He seems to be blaming me now for all the world's troubles more than he's been cursing humans all along! This Vincent Van Gogh is really weird!*

Feeling Darren's sense of guilt and desperation, Vincent still continues, as if enjoying his only opportunity after so long to whine again about humanity, "What morality and social values! What progress! And the irony is that only humans cause human misery. You should be ashamed of the way your civilization has grown out of control by greed and lust, not to mention the way you inflict misery upon your beautiful and bountiful planet. Is it odd that you all suffer your entire lives, too, out of ignorance and ego? No… There's no hope, and I stick to my initial judgment— there'll never be an end to human misery. Period."

"Hmm… Sorry…" Darren sighs and leaves in melancholy.

9

Outside Vincent's cabin, Darren stares at a man waiting for him.

"You don't recognize me?" the man asks.

"Sorry! But your face is familiar," Darren replies ruefully.

"I'm Giacomo Puccini. You called my name a minute ago!"

"Oh, yes… I love your operas."

"I like your paintings too, especially the one Vincent likes."

"Thanks… I told Vincent how I wished to die *eventually* like one of your heroes with plenty of love in my heart."

"Everybody wants to live and leave like a passionate hero. But only seldom we find the courage to choose the path for it."

"I must prove myself somehow, I hope."

"I hope you succeed."

"There should be special things I could do," Darren says.

"There are plenty of things you can do. Maybe you can also do a painting about one of my operas. I'd like that."

"That's a great idea! Which one would you like me to paint?"

"You choose! Do you have a favourite yourself?"

"I like them all, but I favour *Tosca* a little more these days."

"Paint that one then. Remember, I'll be watching you all along!" Giacomo smiles and helps him go back to the main deck.

Darren wonders how far the boat has traveled and how he will disembark. He trembles at the thought of having to bear another torturous routine to get off, too. On the upper deck, he finds the boat already docked at the exact spot where the woman in the white dress had disembarked two hours earlier. A few men help him get off and everybody waves to him, albeit less vivaciously than they had for the woman in the white dress. He reciprocates and rushes home as the boat sails away toward the outer part of the Creek again.

In the apartment, exhausted and thirsty, Darren grabs the can of soda from the coffee table and drinks another sip. It is still cool, to his surprise, despite the heat and humidity. He lies on the sofa, shuts his eyes, ponders his conversations with the Masters, and soon he is unconscious again, back to his dreamland, hoping to visit the boat again perhaps!

The soft tingling of some fingers caressing his chest awakens Darren.

"Why don't you come to bed?" Elizabeth asks with concern. "It's so late."

"I will. I had a headache, but it's better now," replies Darren, but swiftly gets anxious about Mahroo's disappearance. He feels obliged to call someone and enquire about her. He checks his watch and decides to call Reza first.

Reza answers woozily and Darren asks about Mahroo. "Oh, yes, she showed up about—let's see… two hours ago, safe and sound. She refused to tell us where she'd been, though, as usual."

PART II
The House in Eternity

Chapter Nine
Rival Lovers

1

The enticing aroma of coffee awakens Darren in the warm cuddle of Elizabeth. But he is startled swiftly by a freaky vision of Jeff breaking in, charging into the bedroom, and catching them stuck together like a baloney sandwich. He opens his eyes wide fretfully and finds Elizabeth staring at him.

"You woke me up again?" he mumbles.

"No…!" she lies slyly. Letting him sleep longer is unwise, considering Jeff's imminent barging in any minute. "Coffee?"

Yawning, he nods. She brings two cups of coffee and jumps back onto the bed to blast off the rest of his lethargy.

"You're so perky this morning! What's up?" he asks.

"I'm just happy to be here with you. Did you sleep well?"

"Yeah…"

"You looked wasted last night, snoozing on the sofa."

"What a night!" he mutters, recalling his adventure. "I saw a shadow lurking in the garage when coming in. And this morning, I imagined Jeff breaking in and killing us in bed."

"That's why I woke you! I'm sure he'll show up soon."

"You wanted to be sure I was wide awake when he kills us?" he asks with a chuckle. "You hate to see me die in peace at least, in my sleep?"

"Yes, we must share even our last minutes of torture… But let's decide what I should do," Elizabeth replies.

"You should let me sleep…," Darren whispers while closing his eyes again.

"No more sleep… Can you get serious for a second?"

"No, I can never be serious about anything before noon…"

"Come on Darren… What should I do?"

"What about?"

"About us…"

"I cannot tell you what to do with Jeff. You must make that decision on your own."

"Do you want me to stay with you?"

"If you like…"

"What do you like?"

"I like you no matter where you live…"

"Oh, gosh, you're so generous…"

"I know, but still you'd better make these decisions yourself."

"I'd like to stay with you even if Jeff can prove his innocence. Is that okay?"

Another tough question for his weary brain this early in the morning. Accepting her offer creates a commitment, and refusing it is rude. These women are really tricky in conning us. "You're welcome to stay if you think that's the right decision for you…"

"Then I'll tell him the truth about us. Denying it would be silly now."

"I guess… Call him before he comes over, anyway…"

"Let's have breakfast first… I've made omelettes," she says, walking toward the ringing phone. After five minutes, she hangs up and stares at Darren, who is drinking his orange juice fretfully.

"It was Jeff. He's agitated… I guess he suspects my lie about you staying somewhere else…"

"Wow… He must be a genius then, making this incredible discovery all by himself…!"

"Stop kidding around, Darren…"

"Maybe he was the one lurking in the garage last night?"

"Maybe…"

"So what happened?" he asks.

"I promised to meet him in an hour to go for coffee."

"Good idea." The phone shrieks again. She answers and gives the receiver to Darren.

"What's wrong, Nora?" he asks.

"Must you ask…?" She pauses. "Does our relationship feel normal to you?"

"My goodness… We had a similar conversation just recently. Letting a friend stay here shouldn't disturb you or strain our *friendship*," he replies cautiously to avoid infuriating her or Elizabeth, who is eavesdropping. Meanwhile, listening to Nora's nagging and innuendoes, he suddenly feels an urgency to review all his relationships, especially since Elizabeth seems determined to stick around indefinitely.

"I know you're busy with women...," Nora says, "I'll decide about us soon! The reason I'm calling is to pass on a message."

"What message?" Darren asks.

"Marcus doesn't want to proceed with the commission work, after all. He'll pay you five hundred for the cost of the sketches."

Unnerving sensations avalanche through his arteries. He squeezes the receiver in his frozen hand, imagining the imminent course of ominous events unfolding because of Nora's mutiny.

"But why?" he asks.

"I guess he changed his mind," Nora replies.

"Did you have something to do with this?"

"No… Well, it may have something to do with my nasty mood last week, barking at everybody. When he accused me of ignoring the business, I felt guilty and cried on his shoulder. He got upset, cursed you, and left in agitation. This morning he called me at home with the message I gave you. I'm sorry."

"I never intended to annoy you," Darren whispers, "but I've been preoccupied recently. I resent my mood too."

"That's your problem! I wish I knew how to help."

"Convince Marcus to reconsider. I promise it'll be a great piece," he pleads so openly even Elizabeth feels sorry for him.

Nora remains quiet, waiting for a more tangible concession: At least dinner tonight. But Darren doesn't dare ask her out while Elizabeth is glaring at him from across the nook and munching her omelette nervously. "I'll make it up to you soon," he offers at last. "I'll call you and we'll go for a fiesta, I promise." But Nora, unimpressed by his empty gesture, hangs up after a long pause.

In anguish, he lingers with the receiver dangling in his hand. Losing the commission work is a bad omen. Behind a superficial grin to Elizabeth, he wishes to be left alone to mull over the new development. A familiar sense of defeat, recurring from the Erica era, engulfs him. Is his career in jeopardy again? *How fragile artistic life is! How many times should I go through this shit?*

"What're you doing today?" Elizabeth asks to engage him.

"Nothing special!" He pauses. "Probably paint."

"That's good."

"Come back soon."

"Sure… I'll get rid of Jeff quickly."

Darren starts Mozart's D minor concerto, rushes to the main closet, and chooses a 48 x 36 inch canvas. He draws the outlines quickly and stands back to judge the scales and the balance of the composition. Oddly, the first sketch looks perfect. He mixes some creamy paint on the palette and spreads the first layer on the canvas when the phone interrupts him. He places the loaded brush upside down in a glass jar, wipes off his hands, and picks up the receiver. Her voice twinges his heart.

"How're you, Erica?" he says.

"All right… Life goes on." She senses his quiet shock and continues, "I called to talk to Elizabeth. Is she there?"

"No, she's gone to see Jeff and discuss their problem."

"Can it be fixed?"

"I don't know…"

"I couldn't imagine you two making fire together."

"Life is full of surprises!" he replies slyly.

"But Jeff's losing his mind and I'm caught between them. Is she doing all this just for a flimsy fling? When will she return?"

"Hard to say."

"And you're waiting for her impatiently, eh?"

"I hope she makes the right decision if their relationship is worth saving. Has Jeff been seeing someone?"

"I don't know. But I must put some sense into her head."

Darren is glad to find an ally. Maybe Erica could convince Elizabeth how imprudent sacrificing her life for him would be. Especially, recalling Nora's spite this morning and considering Elizabeth's demand to decide about their relationship soon, he welcomes Erica's meddling. "Be my guest."

"She's been avoiding me recently," Erica says. "Maybe I should come over and wait for her instead of leaving another message?"

"You wanna come to my place?"

"If you don't mind. I'd like to see you too, if you're free."

"Sure… okay… I'll make fresh coffee then."

"I'll be there in thirty minutes."

A nostalgic memory of the old era overwhelms Darren like the way he got overanxious in his teenage years—a sadly bizarre phenomenon, considering his normal confidence around women nowadays. Erica is crushing his self-image due to the recurring emotions, yet he welcomes the childlike excitement of yesteryear rather carelessly. Reminiscing their ancient romantic moments, as well as his mood while painting the *Woman in the White Dress*, he sets the painting material aside and makes a pot of coffee.

2

Mahroo is dying to go upstairs to see Darren, but has no excuse to justify a casual visit. Despite his vile love affairs and duplicity, she is unable to abandon him. Beneath all the thick layers of scepticism, still a glimmer of hope keeps her optimistic about winning his heart eventually. She misses him, even his idiotic arguments, after only one week of distance. She weighs the two options of calling him or dropping by unexpectedly. Asking for an appointment with the man she believes will be hers someday feels absurd. She should tame him through assertion not etiquette, she reckons. Besides, she prefers monitoring him in his usual environment, with or without another woman amusing him. *I'd rather see a wild tiger roaming around in its natural habitat than a tamed one rotting in a cage,* she justifies.

Mahroo takes the stairs to avoid neighbours or Darren's lovers in the elevator. On the tenth-floor landing, she checks the hallway through the tiny window. It is empty. However, as she opens the hallway door, the elevator bell blares. Swiftly she retreats and peeps through the lower corner of the window in the stairwell door. An unfamiliar, pretty woman exits the elevator and checks the apartment numbers. She finally stops at Darren's apartment and knocks on the door. When it opens, she smiles affectionately before disappearing inside the apartment casually. Feeling totally humiliated and defeated, Mahroo flees to her apartment and throws herself on the sofa desperately. She is tired of witnessing all these women around her beloved and feeling helpless to do anything about it. Maybe it is finally time to forget him. *Darren doesn't seem to understand my love. I should know when to quit,* Mahroo thinks, wiping her tears. *I'm now tired of watching a wild tiger roaming around so much in its natural habitat already!*

3

Erica holds Darren's hands long, hugs him tight, then snatches a quick kiss from his mouth. He steers her toward the sofa while baffled by his erratic eroticism that is not even merely lustful. *How can I juggle so much romantic feelings for several women at once? Especially for a woman who's hurt me so deeply?*

"Nice apartment," Erica says as she walks toward the sofa and glances out the glass doors. "Such a great view…"

"Yes, the sky and ocean moods are splendid."

"Apparently they've been inspirational! I read the *Vancouver Sun* article about you. Congratulations!"

"Thanks."

"Your paintings' pictures and the article were interesting, in particular about the *Woman in the White Dress*," she says.

"That particular one has attracted a special attention and—"

Erica interrupts him. "Are you surprised?"

"Yes, somewhat…," Darren replies with confusion.

"Well, you shouldn't be…"

"Why's that?"

"Because I was told I'm the woman in the white dress."

"Oh…?"

"You've captured my mood so nicely."

"Gosh…, here we go again!" he sighs as he recalls Mahroo uttering similar words just recently.

"What do you mean?" Erica asks with surprise.

"Nothing…"

"I'd meant to thank you for painting me so elegantly and mysteriously," she blurts.

"You're welcome… If it shows how mysterious and sneaky you are, then I agree with you about being a good painter…"

"I've always appreciated your sentimentality, especially when I'd done you wrong. Then again, such inspiration might not have transpired any other way."

"Really…!?" Darren exclaims.

"Really… Don't you agree?"

"You're still so full of yourself, aren't you?" he blurts.

"And you still have a hard time facing facts, don't you?"

"What facts?"

"That only your rousing grief could at last stir your genius and deep feelings into such artistic works. And that I've in fact played a crucial role in creating a masterpiece, too. Don't you think?"

"So you think all the grief you caused me was rousing and now want even credit for it, too?"

"And all the love attached to that grief…," she replies boldly.

"I guess Reza has mentioned my state of mind and rage when I was painting the *Woman in the White Dress*?"

"Yes… And I'm looking forward to hanging it in my living room," she proclaims matter-of-factly.

"Oh…? You're planning to have it too?"

"Obviously…! It's about me and it's been promised to me."

"Who gave you such a ridiculous promise?"

"Reza, of course… He told me how you adored the painting and who the woman in it was. So I told him to buy it for me right away. The more he insisted you don't want to sell it, the more I pushed him to get it for me somehow. We both imagined, of course, that I'd be the last person you'd consider selling it to. You would've surely refused to part with it if you knew Reza was buying it for me. I—"

"That sleazy Reza! He never stops amazing me with his tricks."

"Don't blame Reza," Erica says. "I insisted until he finally agreed to use Mahroo's mental distress and his concern for her as an excuse. But he was also in love with me and eager to please me. So he basically did it out of love."

"It is interesting how you're willing to exonerate Reza just to brag about his obsession for you and the way you abused him."

"Well, I'd never tested another man's passion for me, since you stole and ruined my youth," she replies.

"So what happened to all that love?" he enquires, trying to confirm Reza's account of the affair and satisfy his own curiosity.

"Now you're keener about my love affair than the painting?"

"Not really. I just couldn't imagine Reza being such a weak person, too, like me, and fall for you and your tricks so easily."

"Actually, I believed my influence over Reza was endless. I also wanted to test his loyalty. So the more he insisted you'd never give up the painting, the more I pushed him for it. Clearly, the fact that it related to your feelings for me and our past history intrigued me, too. I've always cherished your love for me."

"But he never gave you the painting, anyway...," he says.

"Well... After he convinced you that the painting was for Mahroo, he gave it to her for the sake of appearance, with a promise to get it back from her soon. But she got attached to it and he lost his nerve to recover it from her. He kept promising to get it back, but got angry when I insisted."

"So you drove Reza crazy with your pushy attitude, too, ha?"

"I misjudged his level of tolerance. Neither of us could've imagined Mahroo's kind of attachment to the painting. She's a lunatic or something, I guess."

"So Reza simply didn't dare or care to get it back for you," he stresses with sarcasm.

"Yeah... Alas, this very painting ruined our love affair."

"I'm glad that Mahroo's infatuation with the painting at least served a great purpose," he says with another chuckle.

"The only purpose I can think of is that Reza lost my love."

"You stopped loving him since he refused to hurt his sister?"

"Well, his refusal to complete our plan, all out of pity for his troubled sister, bruised my ego. I assumed his love for me was so deep he could even kill you or Mahroo at the end if you guys wouldn't give up the painting voluntarily."

"Thank you for confessing that you don't even mind getting me or others killed for your selfish needs," he says with rage. So you and Reza also broke up just because of the painting?"

"Mostly... That's the big irony, isn't it?" she says with stress.

"Wow, this painting seems to have done a lot of damage in many ways...," Darren says with a tense giggle.

"I guess I pushed Reza a bit too much," she says with a sigh.

"So you're admitting to be the sleazy person, not Reza?"

"No. I'm only explaining that after all the hassle I've gone through, on top of losing Reza, the painting belongs to me. Now, I desire and deserve it more than anybody else."

"Is that right?" he asks with a smirk.

"Reza agrees that I deserve it, too, at least because it is about me. He's promised to bring it to me as soon as Mahroo is done with it. Now that she knows the truth, she might give it up soon."

"You two make me sick."

"I know you're expecting to get it back, too, based on Reza's stupid promise to return it to you someday. So I had to clarify the background. Reza owes it to me and I'm anxious to have my painting soon at last. If I get tired of it or find no sentimental value in it, I'll give it to you; but right now it belongs to me."

"You just want to win in this competition, too, as if it were another game or business, don't you?" Darren says.

Erica stares at him with a smirk. "No, I'm proud that your love created a masterpiece and Reza's love will bring it to me."

Listening to still another story and secrecy behind the painting is shocking and depressing for Darren. New surprises just keep popping up from various sources, but Erica's claim of ownership is the most infuriating revelation.

"You're getting more selfish everyday, aren't you?" he says. I can't imagine I was once in love with you—such a conceited, materialistic person. When you want something, you invent any despicable gimmick to get it, no matter who gets hurt."

"Again you're hasty in judging me. I assumed you'd be thrilled with my craving for a painting you've created based on our love. If I'm the main subject of this painting, and considering its sentimental story, who else deserves to have it more than me?"

"Now I know there was a divine purpose for my failure as a painter then. It at least showed me your true nature."

"You're overreacting like usual. You must be flattered in fact by my appreciation of your ingenuity in a likely masterpiece and showing your feelings for me so delicately and heartily. I want it because I still love you and I adore the work you've created out of sheer love and our memories together."

"You still love me?" Darren asks in shock.

"It sounds crazy, I know… But I do unfortunately."

"You do?" Darren cannot still believe his ears.

"Yes, and I'm also grateful to you for making me immortal, like Mona Lisa perhaps, in a painting that has received so much attention already and might become your best achievement."

"Leaving you has been my sole achievement in life—the only right thing I've ever done, not this painting," he says with despair.

"Perhaps I'm selfish and materialistic, in your opinion, but in this case you must agree that lots of sentimentality lies in both my desires for you and the painting."

"Sentimentality? Huh! Your conspiracy with Reza has been despicable. Besides, you crave this painting only because it has turned into a controversial object."

"No, I want it because it is about us… Besides, I can't think of any justification for anybody else keeping such a sentimental art about us. I don't want our love story in anybody else's house, at least as long as I'm alive."

"You're just too stubborn as usual. That's the only reason you are obsessed with this painting," he says with despair.

"You're wrong," she shrieks. "But let's not argue. It seems we'll both try to get this painting in any conceivable way due to our own obsessions, if not out of spite."

"Looks like it…"

"At last we have something to compete for against each other. If my goal to get this painting can stir your urges for competition and winning, I think I'll be doing you a favour. You may not get it in the end, anyway, but will learn how to fight for a purpose instead of wasting your life on philosophy and meditation."

Despite his rage, Darren decides to stop their futile argument, which shows their deep disparity in philosophy and outlook. He recalls similar useless struggles in the past. Her view of life has not changed a bit. Mortifying himself to explain her vile nature to her is futile. So he shuts his mouth and starts toward the kitchen. He returns with two cups of coffee, wondering about God mixing a pretty appearance like Erica's with such an appalling character.

4

After a long pause, Darren asks, "So, how's your business?"

"It's growing and more organized now. I wish all that work pressure hadn't shattered our love. I wish we hadn't been married then or could forget all the bad memories and start fresh now." Erica's rotating romanticism sounds weird to Darren, considering her antagonism just a minute before.

"You think you can handle a relationship better now?"

"Failing in two relationships has taught me a lot, I suppose."

"Maybe you've learned to set your priorities better. But still it doesn't mean you can build a good relationship."

"Why?"

"Because it needs lots of personal virtues and sacrifice. Only few know the meaning of integrity, let alone practising it."

"And you think I lack such qualities?" Erica asks fretfully.

"I don't think… I'm sure."

"Just because you say so?"

"No, since your ego and obsession with success have ruined you. Change is hard for most people, anyway. That's why I have no grudges against you, despite all the harms you've caused me."

"I thank you for your generosity on behalf of all the ignorant people on this planet, including myself… Have you ever thought you may be crazy?"

"Of course… A benefit of self-therapy is that we realize our idiocy and flaws more clearly. We learn how our mentalities and personalities have been screwed up from all the hassles of living. And we admit that our flaws make us hurt one another with our cruelty and irrationality. The bottom line is that we're all crazy in our unique ways."

"Then how so many people connect and make families, etc.," Erica objects. "Even bad people must somehow learn to live in some form of harmony with one another."

"Most families are in trouble nowadays, not to mention all these marital agonies and divorces."

"So you think we can't change even if we eventually feel the need for it?"

"Most often we cannot."

"Why?"

"It's just human nature, plus the rising social malice. We just can't change our mentality easily and survive in society as well."

"So, we're all doomed, ha?" she asks.

"Looks like it. Our personal needs and quirks are out of control and they clash constantly in relationships. We drive each other nuts with our endless needs and odd demands. Relationship conflicts have skyrocketed and no role models or family rules exist, either, to control couples' communication and egos."

"But we loved each other and lived together for many years even with our big differences."

"We got along while we weren't too eager to prove ourselves. When we began facing life challenges, our priorities changed and our relationship lost its innocence."

"Do you still love me, Darren?" Erica asks.

"No."

"Not even a little bit? Don't you miss me sometimes?"

"Well… our memories feel both nostalgic and romantic sometimes," Darren replies with stress.

"How about Elizabeth? You love her?"

"I like her. I have a more natural relationship with her than I can remember having with anybody."

"So it's possible that you two could get serious?"

"I don't know. Life is full of surprises. How about you? You have anybody special in your life?" he asks.

"No. I guess I'm married to my work and can't cheat with a human."

"But work didn't stop you from cheating on me!"

"Then, I was confused and faced many problems at work and home. Like a knight in shining armour, Reza came to my rescue at a good time to relieve both my work and emotional issues."

"I didn't see any sign of stress in you all those years…"

"I might've appeared calm. But I suffered a lot and am still paying the price for letting you go. As I had some hope in Reza, I seemed relaxed. But soon I realized what a mistake I'd made. You think nobody can change. But I've learned good lessons from my experiences. You must let me prove it to you."

"It's not necessary," he says.

"Why are you so cold? Is this the enlightened Darren you're boasting about?"

"All I'm saying is that your personality is your business. It cannot help us anymore."

"Still you could show compassion, if not passion. What's wrong with us having a civilized relationship?"

"We can't be friends after everything we've gone through! Although…!" he pauses abruptly, fully alarmed about the major leak in his supposedly refined theory of love. All his convictions about self-control seem in big jeopardy while a sudden erotic feeling toward her is besieging him so naively again.

"Although what?"

"Nothing…"

"Just tell me what you were going to say."

"I was just puzzled by my bizarre emotions again." He cannot even control his tongue. "To be honest, I could rip you apart sexually, despite the rage you've raised in me all afternoon."

"Why don't you then? Who's stopping you?" Erica asserts seductively.

"I have enough trouble and confusion already. I cannot add another puzzle to my long list of dilemmas."

"Why you lose your nerve when it comes to me, especially now, after seducing me with your words? Why stop now that I'm telling you that I'm attracted to you more than ever this instant," Erica whispers with a voice cracking from erotic sensations.

"Why are you playing this game?"

"I'm not playing any game…"

"We can't have any type of relationship. Period."

"Why not?"

"Because… Besides, Elizabeth will return any minute."

"I don't care about Elizabeth finding us necking. Besides, there's something you must know."

"What now?" he asks with exasperation.

"I'm legally still your wife."

He springs off the sofa like a rabbit and yowls like a bear. "What?"

"Well, the papers you signed gave my lawyers the power to act on your behalf when the divorce papers were ready. I refused to sign them and convinced my lawyers we were discussing reconciliation. With all the SDI's business I gave them, they cooperated fully," she says giddily. "So you're still mine legally."

"Why? Why didn't you sign the papers?"

"I couldn't forget you, especially after Reza and I separated."

Darren plummets onto the sofa in shock, stares at her blankly, puts his head on the armrest, and closes his eyes in dire despair. Showing even a bit of his fury would only gratify her. He blames himself for trusting her lawyers and not following up the matter. He murmurs without moving his head or opening his eyes, "You must sign the papers and get this matter over with right away."

Instead of a reply, Erica moves forward and sits next to him, touches his chest, and brings her face close to his. Her familiar, exhilarating scent numbs Darren's brain, all his cells tremble like a volcanic matter ready to explode, and saliva gathers in his mouth like a hungry panther. But how could he justify getting involved in yet another affair under the present circumstances, especially with the worst possible candidate? Definitely, no valid prospect exists for this affair, other than jeopardizing the chance of a promising relationship with Elizabeth.

"She knows we're still married," says Erica, as if she had read his mind.

Startled, Darren opens his eyes, "Elizabeth knows?"

"Yes. She encouraged me too; maybe she'd had a crush on you all along and hated seeing you disappear from our lives."

"But why didn't she mention anything to me about it?"

"Perhaps because she thought you already knew."

"Why would she assume that?"

"Because I told her so," Erica says.

"You told Elizabeth that I knew we're still married?"

"Yes."

"But didn't she suspect your story when we didn't get back together after I returned from Iran?"

"I told her you're still undecided and needed more time."

"So she thought we're in contact?" Darren asks.

"Yes, she also assumed I visited you sometimes."

"She did?"

"I guess so… I've been following your life through Reza, anyway, except I didn't know about the level of your success until I read the article in the newspaper yesterday."

"Why have you been so sneaky about this matter?"

"In my mind, you've never been out of my life."

"When did Elizabeth tell you about her affair with me?"

"Two weeks ago. She explained the circumstance leading to kissing you. Obviously, I was shocked, but knew I had no right to stop her, especially when we were practically divorced and the chances of us getting back together were slim. I couldn't confess suddenly that you didn't know these issues."

"Why? Why didn't you tell her the truth then at least?"

"I didn't know how to react after Elizabeth sort of hinted that your interest in her was a good indication that you don't want to come back to me, knowing that Elizabeth would tell me about your affair eventually," she says.

"Was she trying to discourage you about luring me?"

"Sort of… Your affair would've been a clue about your wish for the divorce to proceed. However, her success to flirt with you proved nothing, as I knew you didn't know we were still married. So, after some thinking, I just ignored her interest in you, hoping she wouldn't dare to steal you from me, cheat on Jeff, and throw away a ten-year affair so lightly, probably for nothing…"

"But your calculations proved wrong," he says with a giggle.

"She behaved totally foolish to come live with you so quickly. So I had to come and confess everything I've told you now."

"You should've actually told her the truth," Darren says. "It would've stopped the matter getting out of hand."

"Maybe you're right. I should've clarified the matter for her before… But at least I'm here now to take care of this mess."

To Darren, everything appears too ridiculous and surreal— both Erica's schemes and Elizabeth's behaviour. Even weirder, Elizabeth has not told Erica everything about their first romantic night together, except for a kiss, according to Erica. If only Erica knew what had happened between them the very first night, he ruminates! But he decides to keep his mouth shut, pondering the wiliness of both women and how two close friends have been fooling each other. Erica takes the prize, though, considering her conniving schemes, which might have forced Elizabeth to lie inadvertently. Yet, Elizabeth has been at fault, too, mainly for not asking him about his feelings for Erica and the chances of reconciling with her. Had she been caught off guard, or in fact hoping to sabotage the chance of Darren and Erica reconciling. Nevertheless, she should have asked him about Erica later or mentioned something at least—assuming, of course, Erica was not lying about Elizabeth's knowledge of his marital standing.

He attempts to sit straight and elude Erica, but she thrusts at his chest to pull herself over and closer to him. Their faces come two inches apart, gazing at each other, she seductively and he in disbelief. Finally, Erica pushes her lips on his, softly but firmly. He tastes the sweetness of her kiss after so long, the lips and scent he has always adored. He feels he has thought enough about the consequences of kissing her back and the possibility of irritating Elizabeth. Especially with all the developing information and Elizabeth's sly involvement, he is too outraged to be concerned for Elizabeth or his own tight principles about the kind of woman allowed in his love life. His philosophical integrity is, of course, badly compromised again. *But I should take the risk for the sake of Erica's cooperation in signing the divorce papers,* he justifies humorously, while cursing the devil having a party inside him. *My alleged love theories have been shattered fast in recent weeks one after another, so easily and deplorably, by one woman or another... Oh, my gosh!*

He pretends to play along with her advance, until it is too late to withdraw. He begins kissing her hard and undressing her with rage. She is suddenly turned into a piece of marinated meat—soft and wobbly, without willpower. Darren pulls her legs across the sofa and lifts the right one up, so that most of her body covers the length of the sofa. If Elizabeth arrives, she will get the shock of her life. *Good!* he ponders, happy about giving her her own keys. *She deserves it!* Examining Erica's long-forgotten sexy body, he realizes she does not have much time from the way she heaves and breathes. So he penetrates her gently and hopes for the best. His intuition is right, as she reaches orgasm in a matter of a few thrusts. In her sinking eyes, Darren sees her soul reaching out and observing his devotion blissfully. She closes them and mutters, "I'm sorry, Darren, I haven't had sex for ages. Please forgive me." *Wow, she's become so polite as well!* he muses amusingly. *That's a first! Who are these women with such erratic moods and personalities?*

5

They dress fast and Darren refills their coffees while ruminating. He regrets submitting to Erica's charm all over again and acting like a child against his basic courtship principles. Even worse, her spooky quiet over her triumphant face reveal a pre-storm force hovering furtively in midair. Then two tiny streams of tears sluice down her cheeks followed by a subtle howling. What has he done now? Perhaps she is also remorseful, like him.

He stares at her curiously, pondering his options. Without proper knowledge of the cause of her turmoil, it would be risky to ask her a question sounding insensitive or stupid to her—that he recalls very well from yesteryear. Conversely, if she is seeking attention to express her feelings, not interfering quickly enough will result in being labelled uncaring or ignorant. Still the main problem is that if he mistakenly interferes too early or late, she turns hostile and blames his idiocy. In the past, when attempting to explain his dilemma about her testiness, she had accused him of lacking foresight. So he had learned to wait awhile, to gather enough courage and clues about the safest course of action in such circumstances.

At last he dares. "What's wrong?"

"Nothing."

"What's bothering you then?" he asks softly, feeling guilty for having made love to her.

"I feel lonely. I need a sensitive man who understands me."

He feels obliged to embrace and console her, although he is dying to fool around with her like the way he often does with Elizabeth only for fun. "Oh, there, there." He pats her shoulder. "We all get that feeling."

"My life is empty too," she confesses, wiping her tears with a tissue.

"Anything else?" he asks with a giggle, feeling really forced, after all, to tease her a little just in hopes of restoring her mood.

"I see you're still a clown...," she mumbles with angst.

"Because the feelings you mention are epidemic nowadays; but having a companion is also a burden. Our lifelong struggle to be both free and in love is maddening."

"I prefer to have a companion."

"Your preference is also admirable, but again an epidemic as well," he says, undecided to keep fooling around with her, which he now suddenly feels so up to, or show merely more sympathy.

"Thanks... Don't you prefer to have a companion?" she asks.

"Of course, I do; everybody does. But finding the right one is difficult and living with an incompatible one horrific, as you recall. You know these facts, so why fuss over them?"

"Please come back to me, Darren. I need you. You'll see I can be your soul mate, after all. Now that my business is manageable and you're a famous artist, we can focus on what you always wanted…," Erica says with an air of mystery.

"What's that?"

"A big family and spending time together. We can have a baby right away, if you wish."

"Oh, please, Erica. Don't ask me such a difficult thing and expect me to crawl back to you on my hands and knees. Don't you remember how we argued over a painting only an hour ago. We're just different."

"Do you want me to pay you for that painting to prove I'm not greedy? How much do you want? Fifty thousands? Sixty?"

"No, Erica, I don't need your money. Besides, I can't think straight these days, even if we do have a chance. It's a mistake for me to make any fast decision, let alone one of such magnitude."

"I'm not asking for any commitment. I only want you to go pack your suitcase and come home with me before Elizabeth shows up. Without you around, she can think much better, come to her senses, and return to Jeff. You'll be doing everybody a big favour. My home is your home, the way it used to be. We'll live together and see how things work out. If we got along nicely, you move back in for good and we merely tear up the divorce papers. Nothing has to be done; we're already married. You'll have a big studio for painting instead of working in such a small place. I'll be around when you need me and you'll have your privacy when you like. I'll love you and will take care of you and our baby."

Not even Erica believes her vivid sentimentality. She stares seductively into his eyes, searching for any gleams of softening. He is moved by her unprecedented benevolence, imploring God, *Why are you testing or teasing me? What have I done to deserve so much affection these days? I'm sure the day will come when nobody will pay half the attention I'm getting from these beautiful creatures all at once. They may have their flaws, but maybe one of them is suitable for me, once I learn to deal with her quirks. Is this the sign of bad times ahead? Am I going to pay soon for all the boons you're granting me now? Is my punishment coming soon in the form of the wrong choice I'll end up making about these women?*

"Your offer is tempting," Darren blurts. "Going away with you may solve many problems, but quick decisions usually lead to disaster. Give me a rain check and let me handle my pressing problems before considering your offer seriously."

"Please make a decision now."

"That's impossible," he replies.

"Why? Why?"

"Because we're different at many levels. But I'll think more, I promise, especially about the fact that we're still married. Then I'll spend time with you to find out whether you've changed."

"So you believe I might've changed, after all?"

"That shows my naivety, doesn't it?"

"No… It shows you're perhaps less stubborn these days."

Darren burst into loud laughter for her unprecedented sense of humour. She has always been witty in her own right.

"Come home today on a trial basis while you straighten out your problems," Erica continues. "Imagine I'm not there and the whole house belongs to you. Come on, be brave."

"Please, Erica. Let's not be hasty. I owe it to Elizabeth to wait and see how her discussion with Jeff has gone."

"You don't owe her anything. I bet she's reconciling with Jeff already. She'll come back to break the bad news and your heart. Leave her before she gets a chance to dump you," Erica says, too jealous about leaving him with Elizabeth even one more night.

"You may be right, but I'd like to be here when she returns. Actually, you should stay and convince her to return to Jeff."

"Will you come home tonight with me if she returns with the news of leaving you, or if I convince her to go back to Jeff?"

He finds her proposal reasonable. If Elizabeth decides to leave him that very night, he will feel dejected by the sense of rejection. A break from Mahroo and Nora could help his mood, too. He can tell them he is going away for some time, or just the truth: That he wishes to explore the possibility of reconciling with his wife.

"Okay. That's a deal," he says.

"Go start packing then while we wait for her."

"See! You're already bossing me around."

"I just wanna take you home tonight. I'm really lonely in that big house, please come with me…"

"You talk about me like an object, like my painting."

"Sorry. I'll try to be more careful with your sensitive soul," she says, getting off the sofa and approaching him, who has been pacing the room impatiently. She puts her arms around his neck and hugs him; then kisses and touches him passionately.

"Not now! I'm not in the mood," he moans.

"Then prepare yourself for tonight in my king-size bed."

Darren only grins and detaches himself from her gently with a motion toward the kitchen to fetch a glass of water.

6

They wait anxiously for Elizabeth's arrival to settle their fortune and future. Erica's heart stampedes like a stallion on a long track approaching the finish line. She must win. Why is not Elizabeth arriving to announce her decision to return to Jeff? Every minute, now that a waiting game is on, lasts like eternity. They are dipped deeply in their thoughts, plans, and promises. Trying to interpret each other's occasional smiles and facial gestures, they envision the consequence of their reunion. The idea of Elizabeth's arrival opening a new chapter in their lives prevents any other thoughts and conversations. Therefore, a dreadful silence lingers. Darren makes sandwiches and they nibble on them quietly. Erica feels responsible for the tension in the room, so she attempts to find a topic for discussion to allay these excruciating moments.

"What were you painting?" she asks.

"I was experimenting with an idea. It'll be a painting about my father and me. I'll conceal our faces discreetly somewhere in the painting while also showing our feelings as the main theme. I'm waiting for an inspiration."

"What're the outlines on the canvas then?" she asks.

"An uphill path through a large, colourful field with fences on both sides. I'll paint an older man leaning against the wooden fence and looking up toward the horizon. He reflects the hardship we must bear to climb up this symbolic path of life that leads to heaven. But I'm still not sure how to include the other elements of the painting effectively."

"Have you named this one, too?" Erica asks.

"The *Path to Heaven*. I'm trying to demonstrate my hope of meeting and communicating with my father, at least in heaven."

"He never remarried, did he?"

"No. He dated some women, but never got serious or kept them happy. He'd become grouchy well before falling seriously ill and going into a coma for two months. In fact, if Alice, one of his lady friends, hadn't persuaded the caretaker to open his apartment door and found him unconscious in the bedroom, he would've died three years ago. After his miraculous recovery, however, his mental health worsened. He stopped his relationship with Alice for unknown reasons."

"Maybe he was angry with her for saving his life!" Erica says with a chuckle.

"Probably… I was happy when at least Alice courted him. He's now totally isolated from the rest of the world. His mind and body have deteriorated due to loneliness and hallucinations."

"Let this be a lesson to you. You need a good companion to keep your life busy and intact," she says jokingly. "Plus a baby."

"Sure. But first show me where to find a good companion..." He burst into laugher.

"The older you get, the more paranoid and fussier you'll get about a partner and the hassles of family life."

"I'll remember your advice! But where's Elizabeth?"

"That's a good sign!" she says. "She might not even bother returning here today. Right now, she's either having fun, or trying to find a good excuse for dumping you. Let's leave."

"Erica…!"

"At least start packing."

Darren pretends she is joking and smiles timidly, yet loathing her arrogance. He checks his watch anxiously; three hours since Elizabeth left. *What if Erica's right and Elizabeth doesn't show up soon? Then I must honour my promise and go home with my wife—how funny. Although I could renege on my idiotic promise to her without worrying about my stupid pride or integrity.*

7

The buzzer blares at last. He answers it and lets Elizabeth in, wondering why she has not used her key. He opens the apartment door, too, gazes into the hallway toward the elevators, then turns his eyes blankly back to Erica. She looks equally agitated. Five minutes elapse and no elevator bell blares as the two of them stand stiff silently. He returns to the sofa. Another five minutes pass without a sign of Elizabeth.

"Now that's a bad sign, if it was Elizabeth who rang the buzzer."

"What do you mean?"

"If she's down there, she's being held up by Jeff, which means he's still pleading his case unsuccessfully, otherwise he would've rushed her to come up here, get her things, say a fast goodbye, and leave."

"Right! Your feminine sense sorts out these points instantly."

"Are you sure it was Elizabeth?" asks Erica.

"You still have the habit of doubting my intelligence, even for the smallest point like whom I talked with on the intercom?"

"And you still have the habit of taking every comment I make literally? All I meant was that perhaps…" Erica does not know how to finish her sentence tactfully.

But Darren, noticing her hesitation, interjects and finishes it for her: "…that perhaps I goofed?"

"I only wanted to break the silence and that phrase turned up in my head."

"That's even worse, because the first thing that pops into your head is that perhaps I goofed. Besides, you asked this question twice. You still think I'm not as intelligent as you or your ideal man."

"Not true. You're the one criticizing my ambitions. You think you know more than I do, in addition to being a sensitive artist. And I didn't ask you the damn question twice!"

"There's a difference between criticizing someone's mentality and treating him like an idiot. I never said I'm better than you."

"Yes, you did!" Erica shrieks.

"It was a joke and it related to your personality, not stupidity."

Without grasping each other's points, they scream fiercer just to hold the upper hand. Elizabeth witnessing the scene at the door is amazed not only at Erica's presence, but how effectively they demonstrate their animosity. In bewilderment, she is assured that her affair with Darren is safe, although he is still Erica's husband. He will never go back to this bitch. She is indeed so sure she would have only laughed her heart out if they confessed to their immense intimacy earlier this afternoon and their plan to elope if Elizabeth stopped being a pest. At last, she decides to intervene, despite the loud entertaining performance, mostly to go rest on the sofa.

"Guys, guys!" Elizabeth yells. "Everybody can hear you in the street. What're you doing here, Erica?"

The estranged couple stop shouting at each other and stare at Elizabeth with curiosity about her delay and her verdict on Jeff's case. But only a veil of indifference covers Elizabeth's face as she saunters toward the sofa. Meanwhile, her last remark burns Erica's brain, as if she already owned the apartment with a right to demand a reason for Erica's visit.

"I came to see you. Darren told me you'd gone out to see Jeff and would return soon. How'd it go?" Erica asks, trying hard to control her nerves.

"I got rid of him for good. He's suddenly so possessive and passionate. But I can't forgive him; he's not giving up his plea of innocence. Besides, I think I love Darren already more than I ever loved Jeff."

"You do?" Erica shrieks, her agitation rising even further by Elizabeth's arrogance and blatant confession. *Is she saying these things just to infuriate me?*

"Yes, I do... Actually, I've lost my love and respect for Jeff. He's driven me crazy all afternoon, trying to convince me one way or another, by begging, threatening me and Darren, showing affection—you name it. I think he's the greatest actor on earth, or he's just gone berserk. He followed me into the lobby downstairs and still struggled for fifteen minutes to change my mind. The neighbours watched him cautiously, like facing a mad dog. Then came that friend of yours, Mahroo. She stopped and watched him plead, while I was trying to flee and come up here. She surely thinks Darren is Canada's Casanova, always stealing other men's sweethearts so casually," Elizabeth asserts with tense humour.

"That's exactly what Erica predicted when you didn't come up immediately," Darren blurts, relieved for not being obliged to go with Erica tonight. He also tries to imagine Mahroo's face and tenacity to simply wait and watch the skirmish between Jeff and Elizabeth. He giggles tensely.

"So why didn't you come down to rescue me, my hero?" Elizabeth asks Darren teasingly. "Was your fight with Erica more important or exciting?"

"I thought you guys were still talking private stuff. Besides, my intrusion might've provoked him into making another scene."

"You were right as usual! He was nasty. The caretaker finally threw him out of the building," Elizabeth says charmingly while watching Erica's irate reactions from the corner of her eye.

"Now Mahroo has come all the way here for you, too?" Erica asks tensely, resenting the rising difficulty of re-owning Darren.

"You see how popular I am? Jealous?" he says giddily before turning to Elizabeth, "What did Jeff say about his affair?".

"The same silly story without giving any evidence."

"What story?" Erica asks.

"He claims that his married boss doesn't want himself or his mistress dragged into this. His boss can't trust me with his secret in case my relationship with Jeff ends. I'm sick of his excuses!

8

Elizabeth's diplomatic indulgence of Darren embarrasses Erica in front of him. Even worse, her show of claim over him, while knowing Erica is still his wife, totally revolts and infuriates her. Still she maintains her composure.

"Are you sure you aren't making a big mistake?" Erica says. "Maybe Jeff is telling you the truth. Maybe you're punishing him because of your own guilty conscience. Besides, Darren isn't reliable for a long-term relationship."

"I'll take the risk," Elizabeth replies so casually Erica wants to run over and strangle her.

"Rest a little and then we'll go out to dinner without Darren."

"No, I'm tired. Just want to collapse in front of the TV."

"But you must talk to someone tonight," Erica insists. "You're building this rash hostility toward Jeff that could stress you out completely. Even if you want to leave him, you mustn't decide when you feel so vengeful."

Darren watches a master at work, speaking like the devil in a psychiatrist's chair. He sighs with distress for being, as recently as this afternoon, a victim of her manipulations himself, and yet incapable of learning any lesson even from this firsthand, fresh experience. His amazement triples when Elizabeth, who seems totally exhausted, finally breaks under Erica's pressure and agrees to go out with her for dinner in one hour.

Darren starts to work on the *Path to Heaven*, to complete the under-painting tonight at least. His repeated big sighs prompt the loud ladies to take their corny conversation to the bedroom. He nods with appreciation and turns on the music, which resembles a subconscious ritual now for drawing the Masters' attention. Not always asking for their help, he still welcomes their presence when the music resonates and the ideas fly fluently in his mind. His trust in them is no longer vague or half-hearted. His deep conviction in fact gives him a superb confidence and motivation beyond explanation, and right now, he feels particularly blessed to attempt something new. He paints the fields by superimposing horizontal lines of complementary colours and allowing them to mix on the canvas naturally. The results are astonishing and novel, which build his confidence to venture new ideas. His stress subsides as he dissolves into painting and music. He waves to Elizabeth and Erica, who are standing at the door on their way out for dinner and deliberation.

Darren turns the music up another notch and keeps painting, now confident that his experiments would not fail, as they will represent the Masters' hand at work. To paint the details of the foreground and fields in the near distance, he mixes a variety of harmonized shades for grass, takes a medium-size bristle brush, and attacks the canvas with big, bold strokes. In one hour, the near-distance fields emerge with stunning results, which appear acceptable as final for this part of the painting. The details of the middle-distance fields are completed with a smaller brush within twenty minutes. He leaves the painting alone to dry.

While relaxing on the sofa, he considers calling Reza to whine about his sneaky plan—using Mahroo as an excuse—to get the *Woman in the White Dress* for Erica. But quickly he changes his mind. He must save his energy for when either Erica or Elizabeth wins her claim over him. In either case, he will face many more controversies, as rivalry between the two old friends to own him will intensify, as if fighting over the ownership of a slave. They will compete more fiercely to manipulate him for their ultimate objectives. He is merely at their mercy while they pretend he is in charge. He will be only a trophy for the winner.

His helplessness, despite his seeming power over so many beautiful women, is annoying. He longs for the willpower to get rid of all of them and ignore the joy and convenience they afford him. All these hassles and humiliation merely for eluding the fear of loneliness is shameful. He strives to avoid these disruptive thoughts and restore the tranquility gained earlier during painting. *Why can't I stay in a no-thought zone and meditate like before?* his spirit asks his brain. He could master a no-thought state nicely until recently, even during depressing situations, like the time he had lived in Iran and dealt with the side-effects of the loneliness, war, and a career that seemed to be going nowhere. *My damn career!*

He remembers Nora's message this morning. The possibility of Jerry dumping him stirs his sense of insecurity, too. He doubts his status as an established artist without active sponsorship. Various depressing thoughts besiege him with agonizing pain. Every heartbeat spouts boiling blood through his veins aimlessly, barely sustaining him to suffer the thoughts of failing in both his career and relationships.

To raise his spirit, he calls T.J. and feels lonelier when nobody answers. T.J.'s regimen of working at home has spoiled Darren for a quick access to a wise, patient ear. Usually a second-best remedy would be to start a new painting, but today even that seems futile. He glances at the door with shame, hoping it opens momentarily and either one of those ladies returns to end his loneliness. Such a silly desire when he could hardly wait for them to go away two hours earlier—to leave him alone! Now suddenly he can hardly wait for *the winner* to come and claim her trophy. He does not even mind engaging in wasteful arguments with her, if that should be the ultimate price to pay. *So helpless, I believe, my psyche has become.* He considers calling Nora, but it feels too pathetic and a meaningless gesture. *What can I talk to Nora about? I already belittled myself enough this morning, by begging her to plead my case with Jerry, to no avail.*

He lingers in front of the open refrigerator to find some food. Nothing strikes his fancy, but the bottle of salsa makes him think of canned tuna. He makes a tuna sandwich spiced with lots of salsa, opens a bag of potato chips and tries to cheer himself up by sipping a beer. Amidst his fiesta, Elizabeth arrives, exasperated.

"What's wrong?" he asks with a giggle, sort of anticipating what must have happened.

"Erica's really a handful when she wants something. She thinks I don't see through her schemes to discourage me from leaving Jeff. She's just going nuts about the possibility of losing you to me. Winning this competition is now her strongest goal ever so suddenly."

"Where's she now? What'd you do to her?" he asks giddily.

"She left in distress."

"I don't understand her sudden interest in me. She's never made any serious attempt to reconcile since I've been back in Vancouver."

"Isn't it obvious to you?" Elizabeth asks.

"I'm not quite sure!"

"She believes you're on the verge of becoming a successful artist—a type of man she can respect and boast about. Now she doesn't mind being associated with you or succumbing to your needs occasionally. Besides, my interest in you has driven her crazy. And of course, she's getting old and lonely, too."

"True… She seems lonely," he says with an air of empathy, as if justifying Erica's behaviour.

"How about you? Are you considering to reconcile with her?"

"No… How about you and Jeff?"

"I'm totally exhausted and confused about this issue. Now suddenly a big dilemma is destroying my relatively quiet life. I thank God for causing all the coincidences that exposed the man I might've devoted my entire life to. Then again, maybe things would've stayed simple if we hadn't met, or at least not gone to Harrison Hot Springs. With both Erica and Jeff in the middle of our relationship, it's hard to decide about us with a clear mind. Anyway, I'd like to stay with you, until you get sick of me and ask me to leave."

"What do you think Jeff will do? His pride is hurt, because of me mostly. He would've reacted less drastically if you'd eloped with a stranger."

"True. Yet no one expects so much despair and rage from him."

"Perhaps he's really in love with you, or dependent on you."

"There's not much we can do about that, is there?"

"I don't know," Darren replies.

His ambiguous response annoys her, yet pursuing the matter feels useless. She is too tired to argue with anybody tonight. "Why don't we go out to dinner tomorrow night; my treat?"

9

The following week proves equally challenging for Darren. He strives to stay calm amidst Jeff's annoying calls and complete the paintings for Elixir. Meanwhile Elizabeth tries to adjust to her new life and lover. They pledge to stay together, with an implied commitment from Darren to terminate his other relationships. Yet, neither of them brings up Erica and what must be done about her. While struggling to stay optimistic, two fundamental questions boggle Darren's mind: First, why should a person like him, handsome and soft, with beautiful women usually chasing him everywhere, feel so lonely and anxious about the possibility of ever finding a meaningful relationship? And second, why should a person like him, talented and hardworking, feel insecure about his career and luck? On both accounts, he at last blames mostly the absurdity of social values. People like him, in pursuit of a simpler life, are outcasts in a world ruled by competition and materialism. He cannot create a marketable image of himself and he is simply incapable of indulging women.

Despite his melancholy, Darren devotes lots more time to painting, jogging, shopping, and household chores by getting up earlier every morning. He hopes to distract himself and his gloom by working harder. Meanwhile, Elizabeth's presence has brought him a somewhat sharper focus. He looks forward to her return from work every afternoon and planning their evenings together. The completed paintings are technically correct and beautiful, but they lack lustre and the vivacity he has been usually capable of blowing into a painting. He is unimpressed with the outcome of his new works, but does not dare touch them anymore, either, considering the risk of delaying the delivery dates. He calls Nora to arrange for the pickup of the paintings, but she says Jerry has decided not to store more of his paintings until the old ones are sold. In response to Darren's surprise, Nora makes only vague, frigid comments. She blames the market's sudden slump and clients' extra fussiness about investing in art at such high prices. She also hints about a job offer from a gallery in London, her upcoming travels to Europe for various exhibitions, and the possibility of settling in England permanently within six months. She sounds so cold and uncompromising he is tempted to dump her on the spot. All her warmth and presumed love for Darren seem to have evaporated over night.

He feels depressed, thinking he would soon be pressed for income, even for maintaining a simple life he has been craving all along. According to his agreement with Elixir, he can sell his paintings privately, but should still give Elixir some commission, though the main problem is finding buyers. His only consolation is that his mortgage-free apartment is worth a lot if he is forced to sell or mortgage it. His heart twinges with pain. He suspects Nora's schemes as a cunning bluff to test and raise Darren's level of commitment to her. So he might still have a chance to stop her if he desired, but he has no peace offering to tempt her with. Finally, he decides to do nothing. If he changes his mind about her later, he can always contact her in London.

Again, he feels stuck in a bizarre, agonizing stalemate similar to the one after his separation from Erica, four years earlier, just before going to Iran.

Chapter Ten
The Lion and Crocodiles

1

Immersed in financial planning and fretting, the phone chime startles Darren. Reza's voice agitates him swiftly as it triggers Erica's confession. The matter must be discussed with Reza soon to prove his duplicity and learn about his hidden agenda about the *Woman in the White Dress*. But he is too glum today to bring it up. Reza informs him of Mahroo's plan to return to Tehran in a week. She has hesitated to contact Darren because always other women have been around his apartment or answering the phone. Besides, he has not attempted to call on her recently. Yet, she likes to see him and say goodbye before leaving Vancouver. After Darren promises to call her right away, Reza continues, "But the main reason I called is to clarify another matter. I couldn't confess earlier due to my promise to Erica."

"What matter?"

"Erica told me yesterday about her arguments with you about the *Woman in the White Dress*. I don't know what she's told you, but I can imagine your frustration with me, if not disappointment about my integrity." After an awkward silence, Reza continues. "First of all, her intentions to buy the painting seemed sentimental rather than sinister to me, at least then, as a gesture of continued feelings for you. She stressed that a painting done in her memory was precious to her—emotionally, I assumed," Reza says.

"Maybe… She is really hard to understand," Darren replies.

"Maybe she'd also thought that a painting showing an artist's true suffering and emotions was bound to become precious sometime. It's hard for me now to judge her intentions. But then I was convinced she merely found this painting a memento of her memories with you, similar to your urges for painting it. I know I forced you to part with it under false pretences according to a plot invented by her based on her knowledge of Mahroo's misery. Although I took part in her scheme, while under her love spell, my plea to you about Mahroo's situation was true. Not only did I give the painting to her and she still owns it, but also I broke up with Erica when she kept pushing me to get the painting from Mahroo at any cost, like robbing a baby."

"Yes, at least you did the honourable thing at the cost of losing her love. That must've been a tough decision and sacrifice to choose between your love for Erica or your sister,"

"It was in a way," Reza says with a sigh.

"What now?" Darren asks.

"The whole matter has gotten out of hand, obviously, but if Mahroo ever returns the painting to me, I still feel somewhat obliged to give it to Erica. I hope you can forgive me, mostly for being a puppet in Erica's hands. All of us humans are trapped by love and greed, at times, and some continue to live that way all their lives. I've always tried to be conscious of such traps. But that incident with Erica was exceptional and it has already spoiled many years of my life. I'm looking for salvation, very much like you, mostly as a result of being her lover for a short time. I must keep my promise to her. But mostly, I should protect my business partnership with her as well. I can't afford to make her angry with me."

"I understand your dilemma," Darren says.

"She now tells me that you two are still married and may get back together."

"Hmm… I don't know…"

"I hope you know what you're doing! Just remember four years ago, all your problems and depression of separation."

"Unfortunately, I am weak. I forget bad experiences fast."

"We're both still at her mercy, aren't we?"

"I guess…"

"You're still married to her and I'm tied to her in business, plus my outstanding promise to give her the painting. Besides, I think we both feel sorry for her, too, for the kind of person she's turned out to be."

"Are you still in love with her, too?" Darren asks half-wittily.

"I honestly don't know. But are you in love with her yourself as well?"

"I don't know either… She must've done something to both of us, it seems…," Darren replies.

"At the very least, we can't help seeing her as an old friend and helping her when necessary. Anyway, I hope you'll forgive me."

"One of my problems is that I cannot hold grudges against people. I just cannot learn a lesson despite my conscious efforts to beware of my weakness around Erica at least."

After hanging up, Darren frets over the prospect of his most precious painting and Reza's plan to give it to Erica. He calls Mahroo and arranges to meet her on Monday afternoon, since the weekend belongs to Elizabeth. He then calls T.J., whom he had promised to call a week earlier. He might be able to help him put his growing problems in some perspective. *Poor T.J.,* Darren ponders and murmurs humorously, *always dragged into my muddy affairs and life conundrums. No wonder he ponders and prepares corny phrases to mock me while stating the truth about my affairs. Especially, I both liked and loathed his recent account: One must be prepared to pay a price...*

They agree to meet in one hour.

2

At Ambleside Park, Darren recounts the recent events to T.J., especially about Erica's schemes, Mahroo's and Nora's looming departures, the rivalry between Elizabeth and Erica to own him, and Jeff's daily contacts and intimidation to win Elizabeth back. He adds, "Jerry's swift about face regarding the commission work, my London exhibition, and representing me in general is annoying, too. I feel stuck like four years ago again."

"Just try to find another gallery and hopefully things will work out fine. But I'm most surprised about Erica," T.J. says.

"She wants me back probably because of the newspaper's flattering article about my works and her obsession to compete with Elizabeth over me."

"So she doesn't know about your fallout with the gallery?"

Darren burst into loud laughter. "Not yet... She'd probably change her mind about taking me back as soon as she finds out I'm no longer a famous painter all of a sudden..."

"Here we go, we solved one of your problems already," T.J. says with a chuckle.

"Yes, that's a good idea. I must find a way to let her realize I'm a nobody again!" Darren replies and they laugh.

"On the other hand, she didn't have to hold on to the divorce papers if she didn't care for you and wasn't hoping to get you back someday. What other motive could she have?"

"It's possible. But she's also a hoarder and calculating person. She keeps everything as long as it has a potential use for her and doesn't impede her immediate plans. Had she found a suitable man for her extravagant taste, she would've signed the papers without hesitation."

"You can probably judge her best!"

"Do you remember Reza's ambiguity about the *Woman in the White Dress* last Saturday?"

"Yes."

"Erica had manipulated him to get it for her at all costs, even lying to me about his real intention. Can you imagine that? Going through all that deception just for a painting! Reza still feels obliged to give it to her. He's a man of honour, I know. But it's mostly Erica's charm and spell over both of us that make us so helpless when she opens her mouth and forces her desires on us."

"Yes, we men are too weak," T.J. says with a sigh.

"Let's not go there again," Darren says with a chuckle.

"Okay… I agree… It's just useless reminding ourselves!"

"But I just can't get over my stupidity on Sunday, agreeing to go back home with her. Thank God, at least Elizabeth was strong enough for both of us to get rid of her. I guess I need Elizabeth's protection, for now at least, or else Erica will lure me in again."

"That's true. Elizabeth is good for you while you sort out all the new issues and get your divorce papers, too."

"But she pushes me in a different way herself."

"Worst of all, you get softened fast by any pretty woman!"

"Why are people so selfish and weird, T.J.?"

"Well, we live in our own peculiar worlds with our odd needs and somehow put many demands on others, too. We cannot avoid our wicked nature… All of us...," T.J. says.

"I feel out of place in this world. People seem to show it, too, with their stares, like facing an alien, someone not ambitious enough or haughty like them."

"Welcome to the club. I feel exactly the same way, especially the way neighbours talk behind my back," T.J. says with a sigh.

"Maybe we give people bad vibes somehow unconsciously as well. But I can't think and behave like the rest of the world, and this makes me both sad and happy."

"How?" T.J. asks with a chuckle.

"Well, I feel sad sometimes when people don't include me in their world or take me seriously. But I'm happy in my seclusion, because anytime I happen to visit their world, I get bored and anxious. I want to flee as fast as I can."

"Often I get the same feelings too," T.J. says with a giggle.

"Yet I feel privileged for not belonging to their world, because mine is more peaceful and meaningful for me as long as I'm not disturbed by the remnants of the commoners' lives."

"Like what?!"

"For example, I must behave in certain ways these days for Elizabeth's sake or I'll lose her, too. I do silly things just to avoid loneliness and despair. I compromise my integrity and lifestyle to keep at least a minimal contact with the commoners' world."

"Commoners' world!" T.J. says, laughing again.

"I had a strange dream last night!"

"What was it about this time?" T.J. asks with a smirk.

"I dreamt that an imaginary friend—no one I knew—invited me to a vast, beautiful resort. It looked like heaven, with colourful fields extending to eternity in all directions, the fragrance of flowers filling the air, the sound of water burbling in creeks, and birds singing soul-soothing songs. But all this majesty was empty of humans. Only animals roamed around, although many huts stood across the vast fields. I was the only human walking in this heaven, until I suddenly arrived at my friend's house. As soon as I got inside, two things happened: First, I didn't know why I'd accepted the invitation since I didn't know neither the host whom I'd imagined to be my friend, nor the big crowd ambling around the house aimlessly and ignoring me. Second, an ultimate notion of order and law besieged me. I didn't realize the severity of the problem until I visited the washroom to relieve myself. Behind the closed door, as I got ready to do my business, a huge lion rushed to bite my leg off. So I ran around the washroom and screamed while it chased me sluggishly. My friend opened the washroom door and stared at me blankly as if I were an idiot. 'That's the rule,' my alleged friend said. 'There's a lion in every house and everybody must do their business while avoiding it. You must be fast and learn to relieve yourself piecemeal. You can't sit there forever and enjoy yourself; it's not allowed!' He then left me alone again with the lion, which was sitting quietly, listening to my wise friend with similar surprise at my stupidity. As I approached the toilet, it began chasing me and threatening my leg with its huge, wide-open jaws. I ran around the washroom and relieved myself randomly before noticing a door that opened to the woods. I opened it to escape outside and perhaps find a less intimidating spot to shit in. As the light and fresh air poured in, the lion leaped toward me, I squatted swiftly, the big lion landed outside, and I closed the door behind it. Comforted slightly by the thought of defeating the lion, suddenly my friend appeared and yelled at my foolishness again. The lion roared behind the door ferociously, so he quickly opened the door and let it back in.

"My agitated friend advised me with some air of ultimatum that 'the windows in these houses are solely for peering through them to enjoy the wonders of nature from time to time, only if the affairs inside the houses give us a chance to do so. But nobody is allowed to open any door or window or go outside.' Frustrated about all these crazy rules and my helplessness, I got out of the washroom. Now I could witness how the whole house was in complete mess. Human feces were piled everywhere, indicating people's fear of the lion in the washroom. I tried to scream, but my friend's glare, forefinger on his lips, blowing a 'Shshshsh,' halted me in despair. For a few days, I tiptoed around the house fretfully and suffered from the odour, order, and oddities. My only joy was peering through the windows and listening to the dim sound of nature that penetrated the thick walls of the house. Often I planned to escape, but remained gutless, until one night when everybody was sleep and the coast seemed clear. I opened the window and scurried into the forest like a leopard. I was out of breath, running fast, not knowing where I was going in the dense darkness of the woods at night.

"After running a long distance in the horrifying dense woods, tripping and jumping back onto my feet, I reached a lake, but couldn't stop. I plunged into the cold water and still struggled to run, which only caused splashes around me and wakened the beasts. A sense of relief and cleanliness grabbed me after all the suffocation in that house and all the stinking filth sticking to me. Soon I heard a hissing sound and noted the water's gentle ripples around me, yet I couldn't see anything. At the last moment, my eyes detected several log-like objects floating on the surface of the lake, approaching me inconspicuously. By the time I realized the danger and began to swim in one direction, the jaws of the first crocodile tore my body apart, and then others joined in. I woke up shaking, wet with sweat, my heart thumping louder than a drum, but I was happy, anyway, about not living in that shitty house with a lion in the washroom."

"Your dream resembles life on our planet!" T.J. suggests.

"Maybe we'll analyze it over a few puffs of pot and explore it in more detail. It should be fun."

"Another excuse to smoke pot again, eh?"

"Why not? But the dream may have some special meaning for me personally."

"Like what?"

"Maybe it's emphasizing how shitty my life is. The fact that I had to become food for crocodiles after succeeding to escape from the madhouse is puzzling me the most. Why did I have to die even after earning my freedom?"

"It possibly symbolizes that you deserved a punishment for disobeying the order of society. On the other hand, it may also symbolize your salvation and ultimate freedom. Could it be a clue about the events and news around you these days?"

"Yes, it's possible."

They walk a long distance to the end of the Seawalk, from where they stroll to Marine Drive and find a coffee shop. Talking with T.J. and the brisk air drenched with ocean moisture and faint fishy odour help Darren recover his spirits.

"Why's Mahroo going back?" T.J. asks.

"She must go protect their properties before people, including the servants, put a claim on them because of owners' absence."

"How about her parents?"

"They'll stay awhile longer for their immigration papers, but they'll go back too, for a business emergency. They like Canada but now that the war is over, they'll visit Iran frequently."

"Can they manage in Vancouver without Mahroo?"

"Much better, I'd presume! She gives them more headaches with her arguments and disappearances than helping them. Reza is in Vancouver quite often, anyway."

At dusk, they split after agreeing to get together again before Reza returns to Iran.

3

The weekend is uneventful and unromantic between Darren and Elizabeth. Erica and Jeff continue to call and annoy them with their stories and demands, though everybody seems more used to the new arrangement. Darren tries to adjust to the newest crisis after Nora's depressing news. He sets the main painting projects aside and focuses solely on the self-portrait painting. He paints wet on wet, a rare attempt that requires a great deal of courage. A sense of submission and passivity about destiny's inevitability fuels his resolve for calm. Playing Brahms' and Faure's requiems non-stop ironically incite his craving for chivalry with their sombre moods. He spatters a lot of paint around, on his robe and sheets covering the floor and walls, so much so they could be sold as abstract paintings by themselves. Elizabeth is fed up, particularly with his music, but whines only once. Finally she decides to go shopping alone to take a break from his bizarre painting approach and murky music. The painting shows lucid originality and boldness, though. An old man strolls in the middle of the meadow, gazing intently at the horizon and sky. But the clouds aren't right and he still has no idea how other elements, including his father's face, should be added. He stops painting later in the afternoon, since the final touches are too important to handle casually or hastily; he should be exceptionally inspired again for all that.

4

Despite Darren's indisposed, withdrawn attitude, and the dismal music played the whole weekend, Elizabeth remains optimistic about their relationship when she leaves for work on Monday morning. Darren, on the other hand, feels weirdly depressed while snoozing in bed until eleven o'clock. The idea of meeting Mahroo perhaps for the last time disheartens him vaguely. She will probably return to visit her parents, he presumes, but even if she does not, why should he care when he has all along tried to deny his attraction to her? Yet, for the first time, his feeling for her is weirdly different. All of a sudden, he can relate to her long struggles and sufferings. *Why now; why am I so curiously and ludicrously inclined to discover her? Is this another one of my deranged sentiments, erupting at the wrong time about a wrong subject?* He tries to summon his emotions of ten days earlier in T.J.'s house, when he had flatly rejected the idea of teaching her painting, even though both Reza and T.J. had insisted it might inject an impetus into her depressed life. Now, he feels the opposite. He would be more than happy to teach her by holding her hand and moving it gently over the canvas for days, and even after she has learned how to draw and paint. Embarrassed by his seemingly endless childish infatuations, he tries to shake himself back into reality. Still the reality is manifesting in a bizarre light this morning.

As planned, he meets Mahroo in front of the building at two p.m. and they set out for coffee on Granville Island—apparently for the last time! She appears pale and tense like him, yet her eyes glitter vigorously with vivid signs of hope and determination. She is composed and quiet, with a mystical trace of resignation and peace. Still he detects deep passion in her sad face and solemn words, which now appear devout and justified—not at all a sign of her abnormality, contrary to his past perceptions. Now her love is wrapping and raising him smoothly to some startling divine spheres. When she holds his hand very casually, he trembles from excitement and grips hers tightly. Magical moments and musing drag as they ponder the meaning of such an enchanting experience; both reluctant to break the spell of their exhilarating sentiments; both unsure about the purpose of their unprecedented and unexplainable emotions. No words are exchanged as they stroll to the coffee shop, still hand in hand, and settle with their coffees in front of them.

"Why are you leaving so soon?" Darren asks finally.

"I hadn't planned to stay longer if you and I didn't hit it off, anyway. Also, I feel I must make a better use of my life."

"In what way?" he enquires.

"I don't have a clear idea yet, but I'm sure there're many things I could do in Iran now that the war is over and people need all sorts of financial and emotional assistance."

"Is this a new feeling or an old passion you're acting on?"

"I've often felt some sort of emptiness in my heart that might have even led to people's impression of my chronic depression. But recently I met some special people who encouraged me to look deeper inside myself. Now I must follow a different path for my salvation perhaps. It's a strange but satisfying feeling, even before knowing my mission in Tehran."

"I'm happy to find you so full of life. You seem determined and you'll surely succeed in your mission. I'll miss you though!"

"Maybe you come for a visit. Any chance of that?"

"I doubt it. I should work even harder to build my career. It appears the more I try, the less peace I find."

"How about your love life? Isn't that helping you?" she says with a smirk.

"No, not even my relationships help or make sense."

"No wonder! You're exhausting yourself teaching love all over town," she blurts with a chuckle.

"Maybe, but I don't mean to have a busy life or argue about love."

"Do you love anybody special?"

"Not since I tasted the bitterness of loving Erica."

"You shouldn't give up, though. Maybe someone can make you believe in love again."

"I doubt that," he says with a sigh.

"Have faith. Someone might change your mind again."

"Someone like you, eh?"

"Yes, maybe even a crazy girl like me!"

"I still don't know how you could've loved me when you knew so little about me?"

"Who said I love you?"

"Then what've we been arguing about the last few weeks?"

"I'm only attracted to you."

"That's an odd kind of attraction for three years!"

"I know that now. But then circumstances were different and I seemed to be under a spell. Besides, I believed you really loved me. You misled me in a big way with your painting and attitude."

"Everything is always my fault."

"Don't be so dramatic. Maybe you get a chance for salvation, too, after all," Mahroo says.

"Forget about me. And I suggest forget about love, too. It is such a flimsy matter anyway, like all other myths."

"Don't you feel the sensation of love sometimes?"

"Sometimes, but our quirks spoil it soon enough. Maybe two individuals find ways of sharing compassion and passion. But making it last long or a lifetime is unrealistic."

"How can you be so sure or pessimistic," she asks edgily.

"Well…, how do you think human love can be stronger or longer lasting than the effect of Nature or a masterpiece? We enjoy a piece of music, art, or scenery awhile. But soon our senses become immune to its power and splendour, however majestic, and then our love and joy diminish."

"Still, we cannot and shouldn't avoid love," she replies.

"But getting scarred over and over kills our spirits," he says.

"My love would never scar you if you simply stop being so cynical."

"Trusting love nowadays feels irrational to me, anyway."

"Logic and love never work together, as I said last time we talked. My feeling for you has no rationale, and I'd go crazier if I tried to analyze or justify it. Actually, the main proof of my feeling for you is that no logic or fact has weakened my passion, not even your erratic affairs with so many women."

"How do you know your feelings are real and not only some flimsy infatuation?"

"By being honest and realistic about it. I believe my mind is sharp in spite of my sentimentality and people's doubts about my sanity."

"But how can you be *realistic* if not by logic?"

"Just by giving my feelings and intuition a bit higher weight over all facts."

"You must have a special talent then!" he says with a grin.

"At least in our case, I have overcome all the facts that tried to ruin your image in my mind."

"Like what?"

"Well, the fact that you've rejected me hasn't discouraged me; the fact that now I have a serious commitment for a special mission hasn't altered my mind about you; the fact that your emotions are messed up around many women didn't change my mind about you; the fact that I've finally decided to leave hasn't ruined my love for you, and the fact that I don't need you also proves the purity of my passion. All these facts have pushed me away from you, but I didn't give up."

"Until today. Now you feel ready to forget all about me."

"I hope you're right! I'd like to move on as well. Factually, I should've given you up a long time ago. Yet I'm going to remember you and cherish my feelings for you. Sadly, we must pursue our missions separately now that we realize we can't belong together," Mahroo says.

"I wish we had time to learn more about each other and share our ideas about life," Darren says. She gazes at him in surprise and he continues, "I didn't expect such open-mindedness and analytical ability in you, not to mention your command of the English language."

"Well, we never got a chance to talk about important things. And thanks for your compliment. Maybe you knew that my sister and I were practically raised in Geneva."

"I didn't even know you had a sister."

"Mahtab returned to Iran only six months ago to marry Bijan, a man she dated while doing their Ph.D.s in Los Angeles."

"That's interesting! Is she younger than you?"

"One year younger, and a little prettier too," she replies with a sly grin.

"Maybe I'll see her someday and make a firsthand judgment myself!"

"Okay. That's a deal!"

"Let's hope we don't lose contact. Send me a postcard or a letter occasionally."

"Okay, let's hope we do that," she replies.

"It's a pity our fates didn't cross in the right circumstances and time zones," he says with distress. "I'm going to miss you and Nazi."

"Life is too cruel and tricky. Isn't it?"

"Exactly...," Darren says with a sigh. "We seem to be taking turns losing and finding ourselves and each other. Now that you're mastering your deep emotions and finding your niche, I'm facing a depression cycle. Your spirit is rising while mine is collapsing. Strangely enough, though, my sentiments seem to get sharper with the level of my suffering. Alas you must leave so suddenly."

"Are you having a change of heart about us?" Mahroo asks.

"I'm not sure about this new feeling. But I can't do anything about it now anyway, can I?"

"You can come to Iran with me and forget about everything here."

"I wish it were that easy."

"It is… Believe me…"

"No, I don't want to run away from my responsibilities all the time."

"Do you want me to postpone my return a few weeks or so?"

"No, I don't want to keep you here or get close to you at this time. I don't wish to hold you back," Darren says.

"I don't mind…," Mahroo says pensively.

"No, I have to solve my problems alone first."

"Anything I can do?"

"No. Mainly, I must get strong and focused before allowing myself to think about any serious relationship. I must have the proper mindset for it and be a real man when someone tries to know me, not the wreck I'm turning into these days. I'd better wait until I recover my soul, too, like you."

"I like what I hear, yet it's all promise and future."

"Because we must face reality."

"We'll do it together if you forget everything here and come to Tehran with me and Nazi. You don't even have to worry about your apartment, money, or anything else. Between us, we'll have everything to live comfortably. We can have a fancy life or go live in a village somewhere close to the Caspian Sea."

"I hear you clearly, my dear. I'm tempted to go with you, like last week when Erica asked me to go back to her and I agreed like a lamb. But I must know the meaning of my passion truly—as you suggested—before I change my routines and thoughts. I shouldn't do it just for the sake of escaping my troubles. Besides, some facts are inescapable, like the one I found out about only last week myself."

"What fact?" Mahroo asks.

"Erica and I are still married. She hasn't processed the divorce papers and she seems adamant to torture me on this matter for whatever reasons. Another fact is that I'm living with Elizabeth. Fate brought her to me and we must sort out our relationship somehow. I can't ignore my commitments. Still another major fact is that there is no guarantee we can get along and then I have nothing and no one to fall back on. These are serious facts I must face logically before putting my feelings somewhere else."

"We must trust our feelings sometimes, too."

"I agree and that's exactly why we're having this astonishing chitchat this afternoon," he says. "But we must also stay factual."

"On the other hand, only mythical beliefs bring relief to our fact-driven frantic lives and some temporary joy, like the ideas of afterlife, righteousness, love, wisdom, etc."

"You're right philosophically. But finding the right balance between facts and myths is tough, especially when love and logic clash," he says.

"All the facts in the world are shaky, anyway."

"How could you say that?"

"Because they're built around our crooked logic and habits. We can't even explain life and its purpose." She pauses and stares at his pensive face. "Even the fact that we must live brings us suffering and confusion all our lives, the same way the fact of 'death' scares us."

"Yet nobody can escape life, death, and reality. We must live and die as rationally as possible," he says. "We can't ignore all the sad facts, realities, deceits, and disappointments nowadays."

"Come on... Be brave. Let's forget our raw logic and focus only on love."

"I wish I had the courage I see in your eyes today. You've changed. I don't know whom you met and what you discussed, but your face glows with a mysterious divinity today."

"Something must've been in your food. Maybe the sun is bothering your eyes."

"No… Your mind and soul were already in my room this morning, and since then I have a strange feeling toward you," Darren says romantically, while dying to share his dream a week earlier about his meeting with the Masters on the ship. He wishes he could ask her if she had met the Masters and disembarked the ship just before he'd joined them. Had she been the woman in the white dress in his dreams while her family, including Reza, were looking for her fretfully. Luckily, he stops his big mouth from uttering such ridiculous hallucinations. He continues, "Yet, I still don't have enough courage to follow you now."

Mahroo nods. "Believe me, I understand your turmoil. That's exactly what happened to me three years ago unexpectedly. Only now I grasp its hidden wisdom perfectly. I also realize that some aspects of my infatuation hadn't been rational, either, especially the part of projecting myself onto a figure in the painting. But the effect of that painting was mystical, beyond logical explanation; as though my soul could survive only in that painting and only if I kept dreaming about you. Perhaps the whole episode made me look like a depressive maniac, but I think it saved my life. I might've committed suicide if my hopes hadn't been raised by the spirit of the woman in the white dress, as though she and I were sharing a particular spirit—the same soul. It feels silly in the hindsight even to me now that I've matured, but then 'love' was my only refuge to stay alive."

"I believe you...," Darren says while musing over Vincent's confession about borrowing someone's soul for enlivening the woman in the painting. "Love is the deepest type of hope."

"All the years I lived the life of the woman in the white dress…! We shared a life and a soul, but I believe it also brought us together here today, as a way of destiny playing its cards. How else do you think we might've realized that we may belong together? Both crazy and disheartened in our own ways, taking turns with depression! But perhaps we're suitable for each other, and perhaps that's the only way to overcome our depressions. So, fate—acting through that painting—and all other events were necessary, the same way you seem to have changed one morning —the morning before I leave you forever—to realize you have a special feeling for me, too, despite your stubborn pretences until yesterday. Now you think you do!"

"Yes…"

"What happened? Is this a symptom of true love regardless of where it may go or how long it may last? Perhaps the thought of losing me makes you breathless, the same way I felt and suffered for many years. Now you may realize that love can't be logical, except for the simple fact that one shouldn't expect it to stay fresh forever." She explains her own bizarre past experiences with love in great detail just to put his mind at ease about his sudden weird emotions. Then she tries some more to convince him to go to Tehran with her.

"I can't go with you to Tehran, but we must meet again before you leave. How busy is your schedule?" he asks.

"Maybe we can meet briefly on Thursday afternoon."

"I enjoyed our conversation today," he says after a long pause.

"Me too. It is nice having a long dialogue without arguing like usual, ha?"

"At least you didn't run away from me today."

"See…!? We can even communicate well and make a good team if you stop being negative and stubborn," she replies.

Three hours have passed, which feel more like three minutes to them. A unique, confusing afternoon for both of them. But their spirits are rejuvenated with glimmers of hope and their faces glow oddly, to the surprise of Elizabeth and Mahroo's parents when they return to their apartments. Elizabeth tries to get some details about his rendezvous with Mahroo, to no avail. Darren is rather edgy and withdrawn, even more than he had been over the weekend. To satisfy Elizabeth's curiosity, he blames his mood on his unresolved situation with Erica and the fact that Nora is going to London, forcing him to deal with Jerry or a new manager. Elizabeth anxiously buys both of his excuses and adds, privately, the possible effect of breaking up with Nora to his list of excuses.

She convinces herself that all these setbacks are transitory. The only thing she cannot grasp is the glow on his face when he had returned home. Nonetheless, she decides to forget the silly glow and instead console him to regain his confidence fast.

5

The next few days are dreadfully long and dreary for Darren. He believes accompanying Mahroo to Tehran is irrational under the circumstances, even if he knew things would work out for him in Iran. Most puzzling, however, is his sudden surge of love for a person he had considered a lunatic and the least viable candidate for romance. Soon his baffling romantic feeling for Mahroo actually rejuvenates his lingering doubts about his own sanity. Maybe his random and mysterious surges of passion are a clear sign of his looming madness. Only a lunatic loves a lunatic! His erratic deep passion towards different woman is probably another good clue about his mental collapse. So, the joy of love on the one hand, and the sorrow of his likely madness on the other hand, create another strong commotion inside him. They besiege him to the point he almost forgets his pressing issues with Nora, Erica, Jeff, and perhaps soon Elizabeth—if his mood does not improve —not to mention his finances. Then again, all these new feelings and possible lunacy may in fact help in lowering his tension and perhaps even becoming somewhat carefree for a while. *Maybe these bizarre sentiments just prove to be a blessing, after all. I surely need that!*

On Thursday, he meets Mahroo and they stroll along False Creek, then sit on a bench and hold hands. He avoids giving her any clue about their future despite his boiling emotions. It would be an imprudent, unfair gesture, not only because of all the facts hindering his ability to act or think straight about this issue, but also because of his newly emerging thoughts about the possibility of his recent stress and depression affecting his sanity. They stay mostly quiet, while pondering their immediate personal plans without the support of any love in their lives once they go their separate ways in a few minutes. Bidding farewell at last, he watches her walk toward the building. She turns and flings her arm in his direction. He beckons her. She wipes her tears and returns to him with hopeful eyes. He moves closer and dabs her new tears with his thumbs, his hands covering her cheeks. Then he leans and kisses her lips softly.

Chapter Eleven
Losers' Plot

1

Two weeks since Elizabeth has moved in with Darren. All the pleading and reasoning by Erica and Jeff to reconsider her position and leave Darren have failed. Oblivious of Darren's career setback and melancholy, they assume the naughty lovers are having the time of their lives at their expense, maybe even ridiculing them and laughing heartily every time the name Erica or Jeff comes up. Erica, especially, is quite maddened about her plan to reclaim Darren being sabotaged by her sleazy friend. 'Losing' would be a catastrophe in itself. However, losing to Elizabeth would be the end of the world—almost. Is Elizabeth so arrogant to assume she can just get away with her assault on Erica without any consequence, or simply too ignorant about the wrath of a sorely humiliated Erica?

Many restless nights in recent weeks, alone in her big house, Erica has tossed and turned in bed, pondering her needs and options obsessively. She is totally possessed with only one goal now—to win Darren back. She is, above all, haunted by the fact that she had already convinced him to return home and only Elizabeth's refusal to reconcile with Jeff had dented her plan. If only she had persuaded Darren not to wait for Elizabeth that fateful Sunday afternoon after they had made such wonderful love and he had been tempted by her promises, she would not have to waste so much time on this matter now. *What a smutty jerk this Elizabeth has turned out to be!* Erica murmurs to herself. Of course, Darren needs a lesson too. How dare he prefer Elizabeth to her, especially after Erica humiliating herself to earn his trust? He must learn who the boss is, and not confuse her keen affection with a sign of weakness. Horrific thoughts have chewed every fibre of her existence, to the point of losing track of her affairs. With huge success in business already, and having reached a certain age, the value of a reliable companion in her life now surpasses any business priority. Nonetheless, her distressed mind and sleepless, exhausted body are affecting her business responsibilities as well. Thus, she needs Darren in the background, so that she can refocus on SDI. *I'll be both mad and bankrupt soon if I can't reclaim Darren!*

Overall, the time for a more persuasive plan has arrived, since diplomacy has failed. After all, many years of fighting competitors, as the president of a major company, have taught her valuable lessons for inventing creative strategies, usually involving the use of other individuals, too. So why not analyze 'Darren case' the same way?—as a business target necessary for the survival of the company. And why not recruit others to assist in the most crucial goal of her life now?

Erica decides to exploit Jeff as an ally because of his deep involvement in the case. Darren himself can be a nifty ally, too, as a more penetrable piece of this puzzle than Elizabeth. He is a soft-hearted artist, not committed to a long-term relationship with Elizabeth. He would probably be even grateful if someone convinces Elizabeth to get out of his apartment and leave him alone. With these facts laid before her, Erica calls Jeff and shares her idea for ending this silliness. Her interest in joining forces intrigues Jeff, while suspecting her motive. They agree to meet at a Starbucks near her office to mull over their options.

2

Elizabeth and Darren try to cope with the rickety circumstances surrounding their relationship. She still attributes his sudden depletion of lust and lustre to his artistic temper and setback. Also, with little business activity, he may be bored or worried about money. Of course, she will be able to support him for a while, which would actually fortify their relationship. Thus, to her, everything would soon turn out for the better if Erica and Nora leave him alone, too, like smart Mahroo.

Darren, on the other hand, is struggling to redeem himself both emotionally and financially. Although his love affair with Elizabeth feels shaky after the sudden second thoughts about Mahroo, she is still his main ally if his income level does not improve. She has insisted on buying the groceries since she is not paying rent. So, all the coincidences leading to Elizabeth's moving in with him maybe viewed as another clue about destiny's mysterious way of helping him. If only his mind could focus on one woman, she could be the right one, despite the circumstantial tension between them. But thinking about Mahroo has now become a daily ritual. He recalls their last conversation and how he had been mesmerized in two hours by the woman he had deemed psychotic all along. Weirdly enough, he is now struggling personally with the same type of psychosis that Mahroo had portrayed until recently before her sudden enlightenment. So anybody can potentially lose his or her balance occasionally, due to life circumstances—not an extraordinary revelation or taboo! *She is okay now… and I'll be okay soon too!*

While pondering his erratic life and finances, he works on the self-portrait painting. But his efforts to illustrate his father in the painting remain futile. His mind is not sharp, although it is furtively nurturing the idea of traveling to Iran and selling his paintings there. He would probably make enough money to live comfortably for at least one year. The other option is to find a job in computer networking or something similar. But working as a technician with little prestige and pay feels depressing. Why should not he be able to make a living as an artist?

The paintings hanging on the walls, together with those at Elixir, would make a good collection for shipping to Tehran. Still a bigger motive for traveling to Iran would be to discover Mahroo and the meaning of his sudden emotions for her. And another advantage would be to test his feelings for Elizabeth, away from her. Lastly, eluding Erica and Jeff for a while would probably help him think straight and lift his spirit a little, too. So traveling to Iran appears more appealing every minute, while he also worries about the high likelihood of his dwindling mind pushing all these desperate solutions. *Is it still working?*

He calls Reza and asks him to explore the possibility of an exhibition in Tehran. Reza mentions Mahroo's high spirits and positive comments about her last meeting with Darren. Her change of mood has amazed Reza. Darren tries hard, in vain, to convince him that Mahroo has changed due to some mysterious revelation and he has had nothing to do with it. Still he does not hide his eagerness to see her soon, too. Reza also mentions Mahroo's earnest voluntary work in a new rehabilitation centre for the war veterans, helping mostly sad amputees. Her caring, positive attitude at the centre has incited lots of optimism for the veterans and her devotion has inspired the staff, too. She has become a Mother Teresa overnight in the art of compassion and caring, working many hours tirelessly every day, with an imperishable grin. Darren is thrilled hearing about Mahroo's incredible mental overhaul so swiftly, now suddenly becoming a symbol of hope after many years of depression and cynicism.

"Ask her not to kill herself," Darren asks Reza.

Reza feels grateful and equally amused at Darren's atypical attention. "I'll give her your message. And we'll look forward to seeing you in Tehran soon," Reza says. "I'll call you with the exhibition dates."

Quite rejuvenated, Darren sets out to finish *the Path to Heaven.* He starts Beethoven's Emperor Concerto and calls upon the Masters to inspire him. His mind synthesizes the main symbols of the painting to determine how its elements must be integrated. Soon he senses Vincent's presence and suddenly the plot becomes clear: All the remaining elements must be worked out subtly in the clouds. No wonder the sky and clouds had all along presented so much problems; their essential role had been ignored. He repaints the sky and includes two clumps of soft clouds side by side. He imagines Vincent holding his hand. In the smaller clump, on the left-hand side, he draws a soft outline of his own face looking up to the bigger clump, which shows his father's face with a subtle grin. The faces also look up into the sky, toward heaven. The father's head is slashed at the end, where it turns into a third face resembling either the Satan or a saint. This mysterious profile presents nicely, and symbolically, Darren's suspicion that either an angel or the devil controls his father's head nowadays.

"Is this Satan or a saint?" he asks Vincent.

"I can't say," Vincent replies.

"You sound like my father, avoiding straight answers but pretending to be holy and wise about God's plans."

"Whether your father is insane or blessed stays a mystery. But these are the right faces for completing this painting."

"Thanks for helping me so generously. This painting has a special value for me, like the *Woman in the White Dress.*"

"Be clear! The only benefit of summoning me is that it stirs your creative subconscious and helps you stay focused. Your romanticism is so deep you doubt your ability to manage it or express it artistically all by yourself."

"Romanticism? Don't make me laugh!"

"Don't you think you're a foolish romantic?" Vincent asks.

"Only four weeks ago, my heart fell for Elizabeth, and now it longs for Mahroo. These feelings aren't even sexual to write off as animalistic urges. I'm just dying to find a meaning for them. So, Mahroo is probably another clumsy infatuation, yet I'm going all the way to Iran just to court her—the very same woman I'd done everything to avoid when she'd come all the way here to court me. The way my mind and heart quarrel all the time worries me about a genetic defect, if not my sanity."

"Most people have similar doubts."

"How oddly my karma is unfolding! Will I ever get a break, you think?"

"Your break will come soon. I promise."

"Not soon enough… Can you imagine that the best years of my life consist of the time I lived in Tehran, under the constant fear of missile attack and bombardment?"

"How come?"

"I'd found peace in the middle of war. It'd forced me set my priorities straight. Nonchalant about financial and emotional issues, I faced life head on. But now I can't find a moment of peace again with all sorts of silly worries ruining my focus."

"Maybe this is another subconscious urge goading you to go back to Iran and maybe live there forever?" Vincent suggests.

"It's possible. But why has my life been always so hectic?"

"My life wasn't much fun either, so much so I ended it in spite of my strong passion for painting. Artists feel betrayed by destiny. But suffering and deprivation are the main features of mortal life, anyway. Some can pretend happiness better than others by concealing or ignoring their deprivations," Vincent concludes and fades away as the music stops.

Darren muses on his erratic mood and infatuations as well as Vincent's depressing comments. After Erica, he had tried not to let his relationships depress him. But now again, love, or a lack of it, is causing him too much melancholy. *Is love supposed to be this confusing? Or Mahroo has inflicted me with her kind of love disease?* More troubling is that nowadays his depression and suffering make him more susceptible to love; he feels romantic more often recently, whenever his mood plummets. This must have been exactly what Mahroo had felt. She had embraced 'love' as a defence mechanism to survive her despair, very much like how pondering Mahroo soothes his depression now. *Love, even an imaginary one, is at least a good potion and excuse to stay alive when existence becomes unbearable.*

3

As planned, Erica and Jeff meet at Starbucks to conspire.

"You look like crap, Jeff!" Erica blurts bluntly.

"You don't look so pretty yourself!" Jeff replies rapidly with irritation. Her rude remark has nipped his shattered nerves, as had been her exact intention. She had slyly planned to provoke Jeff's sense of self-pity, if any pride was still left in him to be marred. She intends to make a stronger ally out of him just by aggravating his anger toward the cause of his degrading health and distress. What she had not expected had been an equal blow from Jeff, though she knows Jeff is right. Her insomnia and mounting distress are affecting her looks, too, especially apparent in her dulling skin and the undue wrinkles around her eyes. Jeff's honest remark blows her guard, but also strengthens her resolve—the same effect she had meant and made on Jeff herself. So they are both ready and vengeful enough against their common enemies—Elizabeth and Darren.

"That's more reason for us to separate these two love birds," she says.

"I agree," Jeff replies. "But what's your interest in this case? Are you now jealous or offended?"

"A little of everything," she says in a softer tone.

"But why? What's at stake for you?" Jeff queries naively. "Oh… don't tell me you want to lure Darren back?"

"Yes. Are you happy now? I want Elizabeth out of his life."

"Wow… Okay… You're really serious!" He gasps a sigh of relief, realizing fast that Erica is as dismayed about Elizabeth's shacking up with Darren as he is, if not more.

"Of course, I am…"

"But what can we do about it?" Jeff asks.

"I don't know yet. But we must take action, the two of us."

"Absolutely! I hate thinking that your bastard ex-husband is screwing my beloved Elizabeth every night."

"But you must agree she is guiltier… Did she mention how she got involved with Darren?"

"No, she doesn't talk to me and that's driving me nuts. I wanna go strangle her sometimes, or push her off the balcony."

"Why don't you?" Erica says half-teasingly.

"You'd like that, huh?"

"It'd solve all the problems."

"Don't be silly… What's your real plan?"

"All I know is that she's too stubborn and a slut. I couldn't convince her with compassion, logic, or even insults."

"I can't either," Jeff says pitifully.

"She should be destroyed, like you just suggested."

"Stop talking nonsense… What're our real options?"

"Killing her is a real option, even if you don't want to do it yourself," she says. "Just think about her initial treason and now teasing you in Darren's arms."

"That bastard...," Jeff exclaims.

"You think you deserve to suffer for loving her and cry so much while she's screaming in ecstasy under your devious friend's sweaty body? I don't see any justice in that."

"I can't kill her, or anybody else. What're you thinking?"

Erica herself is aware of the absurdity of her words, but unable to resist raising the murder option either as a manner of provoking Jeff, or teasing him; or perhaps even as a serious solution? Or merely out of spite for Elizabeth and rage! She is so amazed and eager to know what is making her talk like the devil more than ever in her life. "Of course you can!" she says. "I like your idea of throwing her off the balcony. Even if they accuse you of murder, you claim insanity. But at least you'll get your revenge and regain your sanity. How much more do you want to hurt yourself and mourn her betrayal?"

"Erica, I thought you were kidding around, but you're crazy. What would killing Elizabeth bring me, other than the love of inmates in jail? What's the point of living without her if I kill her? I've already achieved that milestone! Besides, I'm sure I'll get over her sooner or later, if I realize she really loves Darren."

"In that case you shouldn't wait long. It looks they're falling more in love every day and pretty soon they'll marry."

"I don't think so!"

"Think so! That's exactly what she said in my face in fact."

"She did…? What did she say?"

"She said she loves Darren more than she'd ever loved you. She said it in front of me and Darren last week."

"Did she really say that?"

"Yes. Do you still think she deserves to live after pretending to love you last ten years and now saying such outrageous words so publicly after only a few weeks with Darren?"

"You're driving me nuts, Erica… Did she really say that?"

"Yes. You know Darren is weak if a woman as pretty and mischievous as Elizabeth sets her mind on marrying him."

"Still I can't kill her out of spite or jealousy. I still love her!"

"I know you do, idiot! Then why'd you cheat on her?"

"I didn't. Has she sent you to get a confession out of me?"

"No. No way! I'm on your side, remember?"

"It's hard to believe! Maybe you're pulling my leg. Maybe you're in cahoots with Elizabeth, ha?"

"No, I really care about Darren. I want him back."

"But why? What happened suddenly?"

"I've always loved him."

"Then why did you divorce him?"

"Listen… I was distracted by my business and another man for a while. Seeing his picture and the article about his success in the papers recently made me realize we're made for each other and how much I want him, after all. So, finding out that my sleazy friend has started an affair with him, especially at such a crucial time, is driving me nuts. I can't lose him to her. He's mine, and you must help me straighten out this mess."

"Elizabeth had mentioned your mentality! Now that he's becoming somebody, you want him back. And because you resent losing him to your best friend, you want him even more."

"I want him, period. Let's stop this nonsense."

"But you want him alive, don't you? Selfish woman!" Jeff blurts. Luckily, their loud words and allusions about murder are garbled amidst the general noise in the crowded Starbucks.

"Listen, are you in this with me or not? Instead of arguing, we should use our energy for our ultimate objective."

"I'm in. They should pay for this. We must separate them or kill both of them together," Jeff cries.

"All right… If we have to, we'll kill them together."

"So you agree and have the guts to kill both of them?"

"Yes, if it becomes really necessary," Erica replies.

"You're really pissed off, aren't you?" Jeff asks with pity and surprise.

"Yes, but first, let's spend some time to find an easier option and discuss everything tomorrow."

"Wow, you're really as crazy these days as I am, eh?"

"You'd better believe it. You'd better be careful, Jeff…!"

4

After extensive analysis, Darren decides to go to Tehran as soon as Reza confirms the dates for an exhibition in Iran. A big load seems to have come off his shoulders just by making this final decision. Eagerly, he begins organizing things and packing the large paintings. To minimize the shipping costs, he decides to dismount the canvasses off their supports to roll and carry with him, to be re-stretched for the show by gallery staff. He calls Nora to ask for his paintings but she is out of town. Instead, Jerry promises to return six of his unsold paintings and expresses willingness to cancel their contract if Darren desires. With mixed feelings, he agrees, hoping that perhaps later he can try other galleries, although the prospects are weak. At least he is now free to sell in other galleries. Nevertheless, the idea of going to Iran feels even more justified, although mostly by his subconscious urge to see Mahroo.

He finds it unwise to advise Elizabeth about his trip to Iran, yet. He does not want to give her the impression of abandoning her at such an emotional time. Besides, he abhors the idea of being lonely when he returns from Iran. Despite his mystical sentiments for Mahroo, he remains sceptical about finding his future in her arms. Therefore, Elizabeth still appears his best bet for a long-term relationship, unless a miracle unites him and Mahroo deeply. His newfound energy and chirpiness surprise Elizabeth, although she still worries about his mood swings. She is also puzzled by a bunch of his paintings returned and he dismantling them keenly, but decides not to pry. Shrewdly, she has resolved to make the best of the situation and use her energy to fight with Jeff, who seems more determined to win her back without proving his innocence or accepting guilt. In fact, he seems to have gained more confidence, too, although she can never imagine it were all due to his alliance with Erica.

5

Erica has some ideas to share with Jeff when they meet again after two days. Yet, she likes to test and tease him a little first.

"You look much better today. Maybe because you've found a solution?" Erica asks.

"No, I found nothing, except a freaking nightmare last night, exactly like the scenario you kept pressing on me yesterday."

"What scenario?"

"I went to Darren's suite and found them making passionate love. They laughed at me when I begged Elizabeth to come back to me. So I grabbed her and threw her over the railing in the balcony. It was horrible watching her body smash into pieces on the asphalt in front of the building."

"I wish I were there to see it," Erica says with a chuckle.

"Why do you put these vicious thoughts in my head and make me sicker than I already am?"

"Because we're desperate and you're good for nothing these days. What do you wanna do? You wanna let them get away with their arrogance and mocking us? You wanna just suffer because of your inability to win her back?"

"But you sounded like devil yesterday," Jeff says.

"Yesterday, I felt doing away with Elizabeth was an option simply because she's betrayed both of us and doesn't give a damn how we feel, either. It's still a solution, if we can't take care of the business any other way. But let's explore other options first."

"Like what? What can we do?" he asks with stress.

"You give up so fast. What's the matter with you?"

"I'm just realistic instead of proposing ridiculous solutions. You don't have any sensible option to suggest, either, but keep pushing and insulting me."

"Actually I do have a plan."

"Oh…? You do?"

"Yes, I do… Since we can't deal with Elizabeth, perhaps it's time to do something with Darren. We should go scare him a bit somehow. He feels comfortable with her, so we must make him realize that staying with her would cost him badly."

"It's another crazy idea. How can we scare a grown man?"

"I don't know yet. Why can't you think of something?"

"You're the brain. What if we elope to make them jealous?"

"Don't be silly. They know I have a better sense and taste."

"Let's prove them wrong. Let me move to your house and see how they react. We'll then invite them to dinner, too."

"You've really lost your mind… Can't you think straight these days? It's a pity you weren't man enough to scare him in the first place when he stole your woman. It would've been the easiest and most natural way, as your honour would've been your excuse for punishing him."

"Why don't *you* try to scare her off? You're a tough broad!"

"I tried, but she's too stubborn to be scared off easily."

"I agree. All broads are in fact too tough to intimidate."

"You're right," she says, trying to humour Jeff, who seems enough agitated by her insults. "So, let's focus on Darren. He's a soft and sensitive creature and can be easily intimidated."

For twenty minutes, they approach the matter from several angles and ponder other options besides scaring off Darren. All along, Erica keeps insulting Jeff to hide her own frustration and despair. It the end, they believe the only sensible option is still Erica's idea of bullying Darren somehow. At least theoretically, it sounds viable, though someone must find a way to implement it. Jeff feels exhausted and embarrassed with no clue for a plan. So he decides to get rid of Erica with a bluff. "If that's what you think we must do, just leave it to me to handle it."

Erica feels better despite Jeff's apparent bluff. Still, until she finds a better solution, his promise is the best offer on the table.

6

Despite the rather peaceful ending, Jeff is terribly pissed off with Erica. After a stop at his office, he charges to his favourite bar, where he usually has a few, but recently more, drinks.

The bartender pours his usual drink. "How're things today?"

"Not very good, Greg! Not good at all, I'm afraid."

"What's the matter now? You should really stop bitching all the time. She ain't worth it, believe me," Greg says with pity, getting sick of hearing Jeff's grievances about his ex-girlfriend.

"Well, if one broad isn't bugging you, it's another one."

"So now another woman's messing with you, too?"

"She's supposedly trying to help me get Elizabeth back, but she's driving me crazy with her arrogance," Jeff replies.

"Why's she interested in helping you?"

"She's this son-of-a-bitch's wife who's seduced Elizabeth. Now she wants her husband back after three years of separation. When her plots fail, she gets nasty. Today she got mad at me for not kicking her husband's ass or finding ideas to bully him," Jeff explains nervously. He takes a big gulp of his scotch, gasps, and then drinks up the rest.

Greg refreshes his drink. "What's she really thinking?"

"She just comes up with stupid ideas and orders me around. But when it comes to action, she's dead empty. I promised to take care of the business somehow, just to get rid of her…"

Swiftly Jeff feels distressed and disgusted, shaking his head and looking pensive. Finally, he blurts, "I believe she tricked me into promising something stupid. It must've been her plan from the beginning—all her insults and arrogance."

"How did she do that?" Greg asks.

"She just put me in a vulnerable position to commit myself voluntarily. She might've taken my words seriously and now expects me to actually go kick Darren's ass. Now I know why I've felt so anxious and miserable since I left her."

Greg watches him with empathy and refills his glass. Jeff keeps whining, "Now I feel for Darren, living with such a bossy bitch for so many years. Maybe I should let Elizabeth stay with him as a reward; he deserves a break after tolerating this piece of work, Erica."

"That's a great idea. If a woman leaves you for another man, she doesn't deserve a second chance. Forget her," Greg says.

"I can't. I feel lonely without her. I'm going nuts and want her back."

"So you want to go fight with this guy?"

"I don't know! I don't know how!" Jeff replies with fluster.

"Forget Elizabeth. But if you decide to do something, run your plan by me or let me find some professionals to do it for you. Don't get yourself messed up even more."

"You can help me with this?" Jeff asks with joyous surprise.

"I've seen you suffer enough. I might just know some guys who do these kinds of jobs, but I don't guarantee anything."

"That's fine. Set up a meeting for me, please," Jeff requests, excited about bragging to Erica for his quick action. So many problems will be solved if Greg can really help: His promise to Erica would be fulfilled, Elizabeth would return to him, Darren would be punished and, most importantly, he would not have to deal with Erica anymore. *Erica is a genius then for her idea!*

"Do you wanna meet them here tomorrow night?"

Jeff nods, listens to Greg's explanations of the details, and rushes home to call Erica.

7

"Just to show you my seriousness, I've arranged a meeting for tomorrow with some thugs to discuss Darren—to make him an offer he can't refuse!" Jeff boasts on the phone and giggles over the famous quote from *The Godfather*.

Erica listens keenly, quite impressed by Jeff's unexpected sign of life and wickedness. "Good show, Jeff… Who're these people? Tell me the details."

"Just some people… No details… We must pay them, of course, which we'll split two ways. Okay?"

"How much is it gonna cost?"

"Maybe five or six grand… maybe ten if necessary."

"Are you nuts? Let's stick to five, unless they have a certain plan, in which case I'll need the details and time to think."

"Fine… We must give them his picture, too."

"I've got no picture." Erica pauses. "Get a good camera and take a few pictures when he gets out of the building."

"Are you crazy?" Jeff says.

"What do they need a picture for? Can't they just go to his apartment and ask for him?"

"I was told to bring one. Don't you have any picture?"

"Mostly wedding and high school photos. He looks different now. I didn't recognize him when I saw him two weeks ago."

"Those wedding photos are probably fine."

"But if something goes wrong, it's easy to trace it to me."

"Nothing will go wrong. Why are you so paranoid?"

"Let me think and look for them. I'll call you later tonight."

Jeff strolls toward the fridge for a beer but the phone rings.

"I just remembered," Erica says proudly. "His picture was in the *Vancouver Sun* recently. "I'll find it and make a photocopy at the office tomorrow. Can you swing by and pick it up?"

"Yes. Leave it with your secretary if you're going out."

"Okay. Anything else?"

"We should tell'em how much to intimidate him; it makes a difference on the fee."

"Let's go for the maximum; breaking up this love affair may not be easy. Besides, we only have one shot. If it fails, it'd be more difficult and costly to do it again. Anything else?"

"No," says Jeff, bursting into tense laughter.

"What's funny?"

"The way we try to solve all problems with money."

"It's reality. Love is scarce, so we must scare our rivals for it and buy it if necessary. I have no problem with that. Do you?"

"No, I wouldn't dare contradict you," Jeff says.

"Well then! I'm impressed. Good luck tomorrow."

"Impressed enough to elope with me."

"I said I was impressed, not an imbecile," Erica blurts gaily.

8

Worrying about his upcoming encounter with the professional thugs keeps Jeff restless all night. How to explain the job, avoid being swindled, and bear the risks of getting himself involved with some criminals. A nightmare about the thugs torturing Darren and Elizabeth awakens him distraught, apprehensive about pursuing this heinous scheme. He feels better, though, when daylight breaks and he goes to work early in the morning. Later, he collects the article about Darren and a cheque from Erica's office and withdraws two grand from his bank account.

At the bar later in the evening, Greg directs Jeff to a dark, secluded corner and introduces him to two young Oriental men, Albert and Edgar, no last names or interest to shake hands with Jeff. The lampshade defuses the overhead light at the table that glows only below their necks at not more than the intensity of a candle. They appear tense and tough in the dim light, rather suspicious of Jeff, only monitoring him while he waits for a cue to sit. Albert finally nods to Jeff and Greg leaves. In silence, their minds run rampant to decide whether to trust each other. In his twenties, bulky, with beady eyes, long hair, and an obvious sign of temper and impatience.

Finally Albert addresses Jeff. "What's your problem?"

"Problem!?" Jeff asks with confusion. He tries to look calm and cool. "You see, this man has lured my fiancée into going to live with him. As much as I've pleaded with him to let her go, he's mocking me and luring her to fall in love with him."

"What do you want us to do?" Edgar asks, playing with his well-trimmed goatee. He is slim, has a crew cut, also young.

"Greg said you might be able to scare him a little."

"Just a little or you want a guarantee?"

"What kind of guarantee?" Jeff asks with surprise.

"It's gonna cost more, but we'll somehow convince this guy to let her go or else."

"Or else what?" Jeff asks with apprehension.

"Whatever it takes…! No guarantee, we don't follow up."

"How much?" Jeff asks, now more at ease with the job at hand and pleased with his skill in interviewing the outlaws.

"Seven grand and travel expenses if he lives out of town."

"He lives in Vancouver. How about five grand?"

"Seven. Give me the picture, address, and half the money."

"I have only two grand now…"

"Bring it tomorrow and also never mention us to anyone."

After explaining his meeting with the thugs to Erica, they argue about Jeff's consent to pay more than five grand against her instructions. Jeff insists he had had no choice and the extra money is worth getting a guarantee. Finally, she feels satisfied after he mentions that the thugs' guarantee includes an 'or else' ultimatum to Darren. Jeff is in such a great mood in fact—and full of himself—he decides to tease Erica a little.

"You should thank me properly or elope with me for doing such a great job," he tells Erica on the phone. "You won't believe the questions these guys asked me to set their fee…"

"Like what?" Erica asks.

"For example, let me repeat our discussion when I told them Darren was trying to make my girlfriend fall in love with him:

"'But she hasn't yet, right?' the guy asked me.

'*She hasn't* what?' I asked him with confusion.

'Fallen in love with this Darren?'

'Why?'

'Because if she has, it'll cost extra and take more time to break them,' he told me.

'No, she hasn't yet,' I lied, although you'd told that she had.

'Are you sure?' he asked with anger as if he knew I was lying.

'Yes, I'm sure' I lied again to avoid the extra cost, I hope."

"Are you messing with me, Jeff," Erica yells on the phone.

Jeff bursts into loud laughter. "I'm trying to make you laugh a little. This whole thing feels both too depressing and funny."

"I'm glad you still have some sense of humour even under this horrible circumstance," Erica replies while giggling.

"I'm glad I could make you laugh, after all. Would you now elope with me. Let's teach Darren and Elizabeth a lesson of our own," Jeff says with another long laughter.

"Keep your sense of humour. You may need it," Erica says before hanging up.

"Can we at least pretend to have an affair of our own to bug them a little perhaps?"

"No… They won't believe it and only laugh at you more."

The next evening, Jeff returns to the bar before the meeting time and interrogates Greg about the reliability of the thugs. Greg reassures him and Jeff meets with Edgar half an hour later. He hands him the package with money and information about Darren. He leaves pensively, sceptical about getting into such a crazy scheme, while still wondering and worrying about the meaning of the thugs' 'or else' ultimatum to Darren.

9

While Jeff waits anxiously the following days for Elizabeth to run back to him and beg for forgiveness, Darren keeps planning for his trip, which seems imminent now. Elizabeth is curious about his behaviour, especially the rather reckless dismantling of more painted canvases. He explains casually he might ship them to Tehran for sale. Reza calls to announce his success to arrange a two-week exhibition for him. He then encourages Darren to plan quickly and bring the paintings to Tehran to be re-stretched and framed. He also mentions that his parents' travel papers are ready and they are going to Tehran in two days for a visit. It would be helpful if he could arrange quickly to accompany them. Furthermore, he offers to put Darren up in his apartment while he is in Tehran.

Despite the risks and hassles of a quick decision, including the matter of dealing with Elizabeth, he jumps at Reza's idea. He calls Reza's parents right away, gets their flight information, and reserves a seat for himself before he doubts his intuition to go to Iran. Still a nagging anxiety bugs him about something he has overlooked. And from experience he knows these kinds of hunches often have some meaning and consequence. He paces the apartment aimlessly, hoping for a clue, but none comes. In the bedroom, he lies on the bed and gazes at the painting on the wall. He delves deep into the formation of lines and the colours of the fields, extending into the horizon. The clouds manifest the smiling face of his father attached to an exploded head and his own face in another clump. Suddenly it strikes him that his anxiety probably relates to his neglect to at least inform his dad about his trip. Quickly, he uses the arduous process of dialling, hanging up, and redialling—according to his dad's instructions —until his dad finally answers the phone.

"I knew it was you, Darren! I've been thinking it'd be better if you moved to Toronto and bought a suite close to mine."

"If you're always inspired about who's calling, why do you force me to jump through hoops to talk with you?"

"The problem with you and billions of godless people like you is that you want to challenge and ridicule men of higher vision. Darren, you'd better fix your head and faith," he asserts firmly, as if instructing his five-year-old boy.

"Who are these men of higher vision?" Darren asks, while resenting his urge to challenge his already distressed dad.

"The handful true believers granted a special place in His kingdom."

"Like yourself, for example?" Darren asks like an imbecile.

"Yes, like me, for example…" He pauses five seconds before continuing, "So, when're you gonna move to Toronto?"

"Dad… I'm going to Iran to sell some paintings. I called to see how you were and give you my phone number in Tehran."

"I feel great and I'm healthier than you are. Yesterday, I bought a fifteen-pound watermelon and carried it home for two blocks. Just tell me who can do that?"

"Not me!"

"But this piglet upstairs has made all my toes stick together with the narrow air he blows into my apartment. God will soon punish him. You wait and see!"

"Dad, you better see a doctor to give you tranquilizers."

"I keep saying I'm okay and you keep telling me the same nonsense. What's the matter with you? Why are you going to Iran to make a living, anyway? You're so desperate, really?"

"No, Dad, listen—"

"I can give you some money. But come to Toronto first. We'll go to my lawyers together next week to talk about the piglet. I'll teach them a lesson. Will you come?"

"I have obligations in Iran. Listen, Dad… Wasting your money, time, and nerves to fight with your neighbours won't solve anything. Please give it up, Dad! Dad…? Dad…?"

10

Darren breaks the news to Elizabeth as soon as she arrives.

"Why didn't you tell me you've had problems with the Elixir?" she asks with a sluggish air of surprise.

"You knew some of it. Besides, I didn't want you feel guilty for making me dump Nora," he replies cunningly with a smirk.

"Oh? Sorry…! Feel free to go after her if you wish…"

"Nah, don't worry."

"How long are you planning to stay in Iran?"

"Three to four weeks, maybe less if paintings sell quickly."

"And what do you expect me to do in the meantime?"

"Enjoy the peace and quiet after living with Jeff for so long. It'll be good for you."

"Maybe I'll realize I don't need any man to be happy."

"That's my girl. What're men good for, anyway?"

"You want me to go to Iran with you?"

"Thanks for the offer. But maybe a short break helps us, too. Don't you agree?"

"Are you sick of me already?" she asks irately.

"No, just for appreciating each other more!" *What a pathetic hypocrite I've become!* his conscience nags.

11

The next day, Darren runs around making final arrangements. He freights the paintings to Tehran, collects his plane ticket, buys travelers' cheques, and finds a couple of gifts for Reza and Mahroo. He gets home, exhausted, around six. While checking his mailbox in the lobby, Mrs. Stanley arrives with her spaniel.

"Here you are!" she says with a glee for finding Darren.

"Yes, here I am. What's up?"

"Two guys were looking for you this afternoon. They were waiting outside a long time and asked me when you'll come back."

"Did they give you a name or business card?"

"No. They had big sunglasses too."

"Are you sure they were looking for me?" he asks rather anxiously.

"They mentioned your name and showed me your picture in a newspaper clipping."

"Then maybe they wanted to check out my paintings. By the way, I'm going out of town awhile, but my girlfriend will stay in my apartment, in case you bump into her and wonder."

"Which one?" she asks, but Darren walks away with a grin without answering.

Entering the apartment, he is delighted by the sight of the dinner table, set tastefully with flowers and candles. Elizabeth has planned to surprise him, coming home early to make the night before his departure special. She is dressed up elegantly and put on makeup and perfume. She offers him a glass of wine as he sits on the sofa beside her and kisses her cheek. Her nice gesture and mood are too touching to ignore, so he postpones his final packing to the next day. An exquisite dinner and wine, music and passion, then a good night's sleep in each other's cuddle create a memorable experience to cherish for the next few weeks, at least.

12

Around eight a.m., Elizabeth kisses Darren goodbye with great passion and leaves for work. She sheds long tears in the elevator, missing him already, somewhat apprehensive about their future together. *The play of destiny is so wild and cruel sometimes,* she believes. *What if I never see him again?* If she were braver, she would run back home and hold onto him tightly and convince him to cancel his trip. *I'll buy all your paintings if you just stay,* she plans to tell him jokingly. But she knows he would not appreciate those kinds of mushy gestures at all. *Why are some men so hard to tame? And they think they're naive and manipulated by women! What nonsense!* She turns into her office parking lot and parks, then wipes away her tears.

13

Darren dozes off with the aim of waking up in thirty minutes to have a light breakfast and pack. Soon he starts flying so lightly in his dream. Initially, he is standing on the top of a high hill, overlooking a vast, colourful field that extends to the horizon. Softly he lifts his hands and floats immediately in midair like a seagull. He flies on, turning left or right by flapping his arms effortlessly. People stare at him enviously and point him out to one another in bewilderment. He goads them telepathically to fly, too, but they cannot lift off as much and hard as they try; Darren wonders why. He soars to odd places with staggering shapes and shadows resembling a mixed configuration of the Rocky Mountains and the Grand Canyon, yet unearthly, with exaggerated contrasts of lights and shades, colourful fields and forests, and finally a land of total darkness with twinkling stars. He arrives in a secluded spot where only flickers of broken lights penetrate the woods and the shrieks of owls break the silence. As he staggers in haze a few steps, his right toe strikes a bulging tree root and he trips. He stares at his bruised hands and suddenly wakes up in a panic from the telephone shriek. It is Elizabeth calling to say goodbye one more time, amazed to find him still in bed. She hastens him to go pack.

While taking a quick shower, he remembers T.J., whom he has planned to contact for the last two days. He calls him and explains everything hastily, while grabbing the clothes to be packed and throwing them on the bed. Then he runs out and takes the elevator to the basement storage to fetch two suitcases. He puts his shirts, pants and sport jackets in one suitcase and fills the other one with shoes, gifts, and small stuff. He calls the cab company and then rushes downstairs to help Reza's parents with their luggage. As the cab turns around the curb into Pacific Street, two guys with the descriptions given by Mrs. Stanley the day before approach his building. No time to go back and talk to them. So he turns his face and gazes at the road ahead.

Later that afternoon, settled in their seats in the airplane, he finds a chance to reflect on his dream that morning. It still feels like a magical experience, despite its bad timing causing so much agony, especially for packing in such a hurry. Similar dreams about flying had enthralled him in the past—quite often, actually—but not recently. Exhilarating is not only the ecstasy of the flying sensation, but also visiting all those exotic places, totally beyond worldly dimensions and perceptions. Gazing at the bubbly clouds dancing around the small window, he wishes he could really fly, but the thought of being swallowed by a jet engine gives him a sudden jolt. He then thinks about Elizabeth, who seems sincere and worthy of his love, and Mahroo, whom he has not been able to keep out of his mind, not even when resting calmly in Elizabeth's arms.

Chapter Twelve
Enlightenment in Evin

1

Near midnight, the pilot announces their approach to Tehran Airport and the nosy passengers scramble to get a glimpse of the glittering city lights before fastening their seatbelts. Nostalgia and joy besiege Reza's parents as they exchange timid smiles with Darren. He feels rather sentimental himself, but is drained after twenty-four hours of traveling. At least their plane is not chased out of Tehran's sky by Saddam's missile, like last time when they had to go to Tabriz instead. He is looking forward to a deep sleep on a comfortable bed in Reza's apartment soon.

The sheer number of arriving flights and passport officers' meticulous interviews have created a long queue, consuming the last grains of Darren's patience. Forty minutes later, at last Reza's parents complete the formalities and wait a few steps beyond the booth for him. Totally bushed, Darren still delivers a grin to the officer along with his passport.

The officer examines his passport against a list and then pulls out another folder from the desk drawer. He scrutinizes back and forth between the lists and the passport, verifies his findings, writes a note, and attaches it to the passport. He nods to a guard standing nearby, whispers a few words while passing the passport to him, then motions Darren to follow the guard. Darren stares at them alternately with bewilderment, and then glances at Reza's parents for any clues about the situation. They only shrug with surprise. He moves forward to object, but the officer makes a firm gesture at him with a frown to follow the guard. Helplessly, Darren approaches the guard and waits ten seconds for him to finish reading the note on the passport with great curiosity slowly. He then stares at Darren leisurely with pity, before cocking his head to follow him. Darren and Reza's parents chase the guard in long strides toward the luggage claim area. They murmur timidly while waiting for their luggage after asking the stern guard for an explanation, who remains dutifully defiant, only peering at them furtively.

After collecting their luggage, the guard states Darren must go with him for questioning, but that is all he knows. Reza's father pleads for more information, while the guard groans and urges Darren to gather his luggage and follow him. Darren gazes at Reza's parents fretfully and they shrug again timidly, leading him to believe the matter is serious. At last, he begins chasing the guard, who looks flustered by Darren's hesitation and useless questions. Just before turning into an adjoining corridor, Darren recognizes Reza and Mahroo in the crowd behind the glass door of the customs. He delivers a dry grin to them just as he turns and disappears down the corridor at the far end of the customs.

In a long corridor, they pass by several noisy offices before entering a large, quiet room. Two officers are working behind large, old-fashioned, metallic desks in a light green finish, with piles of papers stacked up on the desks and adjoining tables. A dozen tall filing cabinets are scattered around the room, some with open drawers and binders pulled out halfway. The guard announces his entrance with a loud stamping of his heels and an army salute. As the officers nod, he advances attentively and hands Darren's passport to one of them. The officer reads the attached note, appraises Darren with a cynical stare, strolls to one of the filing cabinets, pulls out a file, returns to his desk, and begins reviewing its contents. He frowns and scratches his scalp until he digests the information in the file. He then re-examines Darren's passport closely, turns the pages slowly, and compares the entry and exit stamps with the information in the file.

Finally, he closes the passport and drops it in the folder in front of Darren's amazed eyes. Then, he orders the guard to put Darren's luggage on the big table in the middle of the room and motions Darren to open them for inspection. Irate and impatient, still Darren decides to stay calm, imagining Reza showing up any second to release him from this humiliating situation.

The officer examines Darren's luggage, removes some items casually, and piles them up on the nearby table or in the corner of the suitcase. He pulls out one of Darren's sport jackets and feels its pockets from the outside. Something attracts his curiosity, so he gives it to Darren and asks him to empty its pockets. After checking the two outside pockets, Darren's hand freezes inside the breast pocket. A plastic bag triggers some bizarre familiarity and fear in his subconscious. The officer notices his hesitation and motions him to proceed. Anxiously, he empties the pocket, anticipating a disaster. Swiftly, under the keen eyes of the officer, he melts at the sight of the big marijuana bag he had been looking for recently. It has just decided to appear in the worst possible circumstance. His stupidity for not checking the contents of his jackets during the rushed packing enrages him. *The stupid flying dream...*

The officer sniffs the bag, shakes his head, and enquires about its contents. Darren considers lying, but then decides not to insult the officer's intelligence. The officer grimaces deeper and asks his colleague to join him in inspecting the contents of Darren's suitcases once more in detail. Finally, he returns to his desk and begins writing a report. The other officer motions Darren to go repack his belongings. A massive confusion besieges Darren in the dreadful silence that lingers, while the officer prepares his report. He asks Darren a few questions about the marijuana while jotting down some notes. He then tags the bag, puts it in a large envelope, seals, and attaches it to the folder containing Darren's passport.

The process of inspecting and booking Darren ends near two a.m. The officer makes a short call, sits back in his chair, drinks the tea he pours from a flask, and makes another call. He speaks softly and mysteriously on the phone for ten minutes. He then stares at Darren and nods his head, gesturing him to wait. The guard who had brought Darren to this office has long gone and the officers keep busy with papers. Darren waits with agitation for a decision, which he hopes would be an apology for the big mistake, despite the bag of marijuana discovered on him. He has heard about the Iranian government's tough stance toward drug dealers and often sentencing them to death. But some marijuana for personal use should not be a serious issue, he hopes. Besides, he was brought here prior to the discovery of the marijuana. So the cause of this interrogation should be something different—a misunderstanding that has probably been rectified already. It is only a matter of formality that he is still sitting there; he will be on his way to Reza's apartment shortly.

The room remains very quiet, except for the occasional sound of a page turned or a piece of paper crumpled and thrown into the wastebasket. One hour later, two men in some kind of military uniforms show up and exchange some papers with the officer. One of the men advises Darren that he must stay in custody until morning for interrogation by the Justice officials. The other man helps him with his luggage while the three of them march to the end of the corridor, then one flight down the stairs into an open area. A Mercedes without official decals is parked there with a driver snoozing behind the wheel. Darren sits in the back with one of the men and the car rushes away. Darren is too intimidated all along to resist the orders, although a few times he mumbles some words of objection that nobody seems to fathom, anyway. They only nod to him coldly as if bearing him only out of duty.

After twenty-five minutes of speedy driving through the empty streets of Tehran, they arrive at a large building, which Darren assumes to be the Justice Department. He follows the guards through long corridors with apprehension and exhaustion. His luggage is checked in at a desk, except for some personal items he is allowed to carry in a small plastic bag. Then two other guards guide him through a long, wide hallway to a checkpoint that opens to a large field resembling a military compound, with rows of large buildings on the east and west sides. One of the guards asks him casually whether he prefers a private or public accommodation for the night. Darren, delighted by the generous offer, requests a 'private' accommodation.

The guards chuckle and exchange derogatory remarks before directing him toward the east side building of the compound. They pass through several hallways and checkpoints before a new guard opens an iron gate leading to another long hallway. They stop, finally, in front of a small cell. Darren trembles at the sight of this so-called 'private' accommodation, but obediently obliges the motion to get in. The cell is less than forty square feet with hardly any room to walk about the small wooden bed. Still he is delighted to see an empty bed and a chance to sleep at nearly four a.m. The door slams abruptly and the cell is emptied of light, except for the tiny rays penetrating the small window of the door. The stench of the soiled mattress and humidity fill the creepy darkness, but he dozes off swiftly after plunging onto the bed undressed.

Sleep deprivation, jet lag, and the tension of being caught with pot, let alone the anxiety of not knowing the cause of his arrest, have wrecked his body and mind. Stuck in the twilight zone, he keeps kicking the air and the wall while wriggling his tightened, tired muscles. His brain is numb and he moans without even dreaming. He does not have time to dream, anyway. The guards' shrieks and inmates' commotion awaken him in panic, unable to remember his whereabouts. He shivers from a rush of adrenaline running through his body after recalling his pitiful situation. But his mind jumpstarts and reignites the rest of his energy to think straight and defend himself. The cell door opens and he rises at the sight of a guard's silhouette: "Out... Go wash your face."

Darren pulls his wrecked body out of the cell and notices a line of half-asleep, depressed inmates, staggering like zombies. Reluctantly, he joins and follows them to a big, smelly lavatory. Surrounded by a morbid crowd, foul odour, and water and urine on some parts of the floor, he stands confused and helpless. A guard yells at him, shaking him out of bewilderment, gesturing him to move. He reels to the big urinal at the end of the lavatory. After relieving himself with difficulty, still totally baffled about his situation, he returns to the front of the lavatory and stands in the line for using a hand basin. He washes his face and follows the crowd to a room where everybody is lining up again, this time in rows. For three minutes, he watches them lean and kneel and touch the floor with their foreheads—the Muslims' prayer ritual. Unable to decide, he notices the inmates leaving the room after their prayer. So he returns to his cell after some struggle to find it. Some inmates take a cup from a counter in the corner of the hallway, which he quickly reckons to have something to do with breakfast. He is thirsty, so he charges out, picks up an empty cup, and returns to his cell, somewhat surprised at his agility to adapt. He lies down on the bed again as he feels weak and dizzy. Before his mind relaxes, another round of commotion brings him back to a snoozing consciousness. A guard knocks on his door and shows him a big kettle. Assuming it must be water or coffee, Darren grabs his cup and extends it toward him. The guard pours hot tea in the cup, while another guard throws a large loaf of Barbari bread on the bed and closes the door.

He wolfs the bread and the cup of tea, amazed at his appetite under the circumstance. Slightly energized now, he tries to assess his situation and options. But the only rational thought crossing his mind is that if he is going to be interrogated today, he had better prepare himself for it by relaxing a little instead of tiring his brain with speculation and planning. Promptly he lies down and falls asleep. He is awakened five hours later for lunch: A loaf of Barbari and a bowl of bean soup. The sleep and the lunch revive him and he feels more capable of defending himself against whatever he may be accused of. He peers through the tiny cell window toward the big iron gate at the end of the hall. A guard passes by the small window of the gate and gapes inside the hall occasionally to ensure everything is in order. He notices Darren, too, and gazes at his pleading eyes behind the cell window, but simply ignores him and walks away.

2

Darren keeps pondering the possible cause of his detention. Its peculiarity resembles a nightmare, although it is so unlike any of his previous dreams or visions. He pinches and slaps himself, anyhow. The pain assures him he is not dreaming all this travesty and he must plan to get himself out of this place. He considers asking for a lawyer or a phone call to the Canadian Consulate in Tehran. However, such requests would probably only be laughed at, he assumes from his limited knowledge of the bureaucracy in Iran. Even asking for a telephone call is not ordinary under normal conditions; forget a case like his, which is apparently deemed a big crime, deserving such harsh treatment and arrest at the airport. "But what could I have done?" he asks his dull brain. No answer comes!

Many questions boggle his mind, though: Did not someone tell him he would be interrogated today? So what happened? Did the pot cause more complications? What is the cause of all this delay? Maybe they do not know how to apologize to him for their mistake? Well… some delay should be expected in any uncivilized country! Especially in Iran, with the kind of justice system he had heard enough about in the past, surely one could not depend on logic and a proper judicial process. But hopefully the authorities have now realized their mistake and the matter will be resolved soon, he concludes. Meanwhile, his biggest consolation is that Reza knows about his situation and is surely investigating the charge against him and the means of securing his speedy release. He imagines Mahroo pleading his innocence with the authorities, trying to convince them to let him go *because I love him so much.*

Two days pass without any interrogation, explanation, or a letter of apology from the authorities. He is losing both his faith and patience. The prison routines continue weakening his spirits, despite his efforts to cope with the rudeness of the guards and the excruciating condition of prison life. He has no book or magazine to amuse himself with, either, although reading in the dim light of the solitary would be impossible. He just lies in bed for hours, stares at the walls and the dusty, grey rays pouring through the tiny window. Sometimes he walks the full length of his cell—the narrow strip alongside the bed—in three steps—and then returns to the other side. Occasionally, he halts at the window to survey the gate at the end of the hallway and the guard patrolling it. One time, he recognizes the guard who had first brought him here. He notices Darren, too, and gazes at him intently, with some pity, before disappearing past the window. After two hours, however, his face startles Darren behind the window of his cell. The door opens and he asks Darren to come out. "When you... come first... jail... I ask you want... 'Private,' or room with more man. Remember?"

"Yes, I remember," replies Darren.

"Private good? No? You go... want... room in... more man?"

Darren understands he is offering him a second chance for a shared accommodation. He tries to explain that he wants to know about his status more than anything else, but the guard confirms he has no authority or knowledge of these matters. Darren finds it useless to grill him, yet going to a shared cell is probably preferable to living in this dungeon. He might get information about affairs around here, if they do not molest or kill him first. "Yes, I'd like to go to a cell with more men."

"Bring your bag," the guard orders and starts toward the gate.

They pass through several corridors toward the west wing. The guard talks to an officer, then takes Darren to an unusually large cell, containing five inmates. Darren looks around and nods to the group sitting around a samovar. The guard blabbers awhile in Persian, which Darren imagines is about him from the way the inmates stare at him sporadically and burst into laughter. After five minutes of chatting and sipping tea from a small glass cup, the guard pats him on the back and leaves.

"Sit, have a cup of tea with us," says the only beardless man in the group. All the guards and inmates have one. Darren's beard has grown long, too, soon to catch up with the norm of this lazy society. Darren drops his bag in a corner and joins the group.

The man tending the samovar pours tea into a small glass cup for Darren before addressing him, "The guard mentioned a story about the night you arrived."

"What did he say?" Darren asks.

"He said he gave you a choice for a 'private' or 'shared' accommodation, and apparently you assumed they were offering you a hotel room," the samovar man explains and everybody joins with him giggling again. Darren smiles diffidently. "He said he felt sorry later for teasing you, because solitary cells may be stressful and cause hallucinations. He thought you appeared like a decent man, deserving another chance to reconsider your choice. What're you here for?"

"I don't know. I was arrested at the airport when I arrived. I lived in Tehran from '85 to '87, but I can't recall doing anything to deserve this," he says nervously while pondering whether to explain the matter of the marijuana as well—just in case they can assess the severity of his situation. "Of course, they found some marijuana in my suitcase, too. Do you think that's an important matter?"

The group bursts into laughter before exchanging glances and arguing in Persian. At last, the beardless man addresses him. "We can't agree on the severity of your marijuana charge. Some of us think it could be serious if they wish to make an example of you for trafficking drugs. They show zero tolerance with smugglers. But some of us believe it won't be a major issue unless they wish to connect it to another charge, or like to harass you by making a big case out of marijuana. They'll probably use it against you one way or another. But don't worry about it now."

"Boy, you're so brave bringing weeds with you…" another guy says. "Good for you! Do you know anybody in Tehran?"

"I have some friends. I'm sure they're trying to free me. But I'm still here! Is it a bad sign?" he asks anxiously before musing: Perhaps Reza has not been trying hard enough? He agonizes awhile before realizing the silliness of this thought. But then if Reza has not succeeded so far, that is cause for more concern, he concludes. Maybe Reza himself is behind all this? Maybe he has filed a weird charge against him? *What a silly hallucination… I must be really losing my sanity…*

"It's hard to say what's going on outside," the samovar man says. "Many people are being arrested casually these days and finding the right channels and authorities to release you won't be easy. Stay positive." Everybody nods in agreement.

Yet he does not feel optimistic. Reza's failure to rescue him probably reflects the gravity of his crime. But at least he can talk with some humans now, instead of suffering in solitary. They speak good English and look like professionals educated abroad. So mingling with them might mitigate his depression.

Darren gathers his nerve and asks. "What're your charges?"

"We're mostly accused of expressing political opinions."

He surveys the four men sitting round the samovar to get an impression of political activists. He detects a special glee and courage in their eyes. As imaginable about devoted martyrs, they laugh around the samovar in the face of death that could grab them any minute. Their convictions and ideologies engulf every fibre of their existence and they look careless about their destiny. He turns his face toward the far corner of the room, where another cellmate has crumpled under a long brown cloak covering his entire body, with his head hidden between his knees and hands. Only the white turban on his head shows atop the cloak. Daren points him out to the group and whispers, "Why's he so miserable?"

"He's a mullah who'd been in charge of the religious affairs in a village," the samovar man whispers. "Apparently he's taken bribes and confiscated some properties in the name of Islam for his personal benefit. Some mullahs hear stories about authorities abusing their power and getting rich quickly, but don't know how to hide their tracks or somebody in high places to protect them when their corruption is revealed. In fact, the new regime looks for fools like him to punish, as a show of intolerance. They take him away and whip him every day. He's lost his dignity on top of the pain of all the whippings. We've tried to console him, but he prefers to stay in that corner and weep like a baby."

"Let me try to bring him around," says the beardless man.

"What makes you think you can do better than us?" the samovar man asks sarcastically.

"I just thought we should give it another try."

"Okay. Be my guest. Show us."

The beardless man tiptoes cautiously toward the mullah and touches his shoulder, which is shuddering under the robe from his private sobbing. The mullah is startled and cringes swiftly like an intimidated child. The beardless man slithers against the wall, sits next to him, and keeps whispering to him. The mullah is defiant, but the beardless guy persists. Darren rubs his fingers through his growing beard and turns to the samovar man. "How the system works around here? Why aren't they interrogating me?"

"There's no system," the samovar man replies. "Don't believe in what they tell you, either. Even when an authority finds the time and interest to review your file, it's only the start of a long process. He examines the evidence, interviews the witnesses and claimants, and collects the information needed to interrogate you for getting a confession out of you. Depending on your crime, he must still consult higher authorities about the outcome desired for your case before hearing your side of the story. So my advice is to just sit back and wait patiently. There's no sense working yourself up about something totally out of your control. Then again, the fact that you're still in this prison is encouraging."

"Why's that?"

"Because, if you noticed, this building is a part of the Justice Department, with many offices in the main building. These cells are for temporary detainment to decide whether to charge you or not. An interrogation in this building would be only a preliminary one before sending you to a real penitentiary or releasing you."

Darren remains sceptical despite the valuable information; he is still at the mercy of a chaotic system. Sunk in his thoughts, he is startled by the heavy steps of the beardless man and a swift draft from the mullah's robe when they both sit next to Darren. Hinting at the mullah's sudden change of mood and shy grin, the beardless man gloats about his victory. "I told this nice Mullah that we're all at the mercy of a bunch of ruthless hypocrites who may try, convict, and execute us fast, regardless of our guilt or type of crime. Many innocent people have been sent to their deaths this way before they even realized what hit them. Their families are simply called to come and collect their bodies. I—"

"Actually the family must pay a hefty fee for the bullets used before they can get the body," another inmate adds hastily.

"Yeah, I forgot that. Anyway, I told Mullah that, like the rest of us, he can either sit in a corner and sob uselessly, or try to hold his head high and laugh during the last hours of his life. They never pity us. So we must remain defiant, out of spite."

Amazed by the mullah's sudden revival, everybody shakes hands with him. His greed and corruption are most likely the symptoms of social circumstances, Darren thinks. He has perhaps felt humiliated more than us, as a disgraced greedy mullah, in particular amidst this bunch of atheists and poor revolutionaries.

Nevertheless, maybe he deserves a second chance, or at least an opportunity to taste a smidgen of compassion in the last hours of his life. The samovar man pours him tea and everybody tells jokes in Persian that throw them into bursts of laughter. They translate some of the easier jokes for Darren, who attempts to grin artificially. Even the superficial laughter is raising his spirit. He remembers his solitary cell and feels good about the apparent improvement in his situation and state of mind. *Every misery in life is relative still, of course.* He wonders, however, how these inmates sleep at night in the absence of beds. Other than the samovar and a dozen blankets, the room is empty. Naively again, he imagines the possibility of guards taking them to a sleeping quarter at night. However, his dream turns into feeble humour when he notices the inmates using the blankets to make their beds around the cell. So he follows their example and soon he is asleep despite the grimness of the bed—the rugged floor.

Early morning mayhem awakens Darren with panic again. He lines up for a quick wash, skips the prayer ritual, has tea and a loaf of bread, and gets ready for inspection and assignment of chores. The warden appears once or twice daily for inspection and choosing a few to perform various chores around the prison. On his second day in the new cell, Darren is assigned to clean the lavatory and mop its floor. His cellmates caution him about the guards' rudeness and obeying their orders regardless. Therefore, he swallows his pride and washes the stinking basins and walls of the lavatory with basic cleaning materials. The humiliation and rage is clogging his throat and nearly suffocating him, but he keeps his mouth shut. *What the heck I came to Iran for?*

3

On the sixth day of his arrest, two guards arrive to fetch him. He jumps with joy, hoping that his case is under scrutiny at least, if not dismissed altogether. He grabs his small bag and shakes hands with his new friends, including the mullah, who has just returned from his daily dose of whipping and is struggling not to weep. After walking a distance in long corridors, finally the guards bring him to the exit door leading to a large field on the east side of the building. The sunlight, despite its smog-laden low density, pierces his eyes after living like a bat in darkness or dim artificial lights for six days. He welcomes the chance to breathe Tehran's air, though he knows it can sicken or kill a frail person. Again, an old Mercedes awaits them, with its engine running and the driver observing their approach in the side mirror impatiently. Once everybody gets in, he drives off to the main gate, shows some papers to the guard at the gate, and exits the compound. He accelerates jerkily to mix with the wild traffic flow.

"Where're we going?" Darren asks the guard next to him.

"Evin!" the guard replies edgily without turning his face.

"Where?"

"Just wait," the guard replies after the driver glares at him in the rear mirror with warning.

In thirty minutes, they arrive at a new complex, and again the driver shows some papers to secure entry. Darren believes they are still in the centre of Tehran, with all the parks, boulevards, and high-rises visible at every corner. In fact, he remembers this affluent part of the city. Yet, the complex looks like a fortress with huge walls isolating it from the rest of the world. Inside, old and new buildings are scattered across a largely wooded setting. Underutilizing this vast landscape amidst such an exceedingly populated city feels weird to him. Initially, he thinks it is another branch of the Justice Department and he has been brought here for interrogation, at last. Soon, however, the sight of hanging and execution sites along their path alarms him. He wonders what kind of a place it is and why he is there. He tries to stay calm by thinking positive, like seeing Mahroo soon, and this time kissing her passionately. Fear appears to be stirring his need for love, the same way depression had raised it in their last meeting just before Mahroo's departure. Behind the sudden surge of love, however, a sense of resentment for being here, in Tehran, for love, besieges him. Still, he is unsure whether he should hate Mahroo too, or only himself.

When the driver parks in front of an old building, the idea of finally learning about the reason of his arrest and ending this silly charade soothes Darren. Not knowing the charge against him has been more torturous than the imprisonment itself. "Why? Why me? Why now?" have banged the walls of his skull long enough. In a different country, the officials responsible for this outrageous misunderstanding could be sued for millions of dollars, but here he will settle merely for an apology and immediate release. With regained confidence and energy, he strides firmly behind the guard. Inside the building, he is delivered to a different guard, who marches even faster, while watching Darren from the corner of his eye to ensure he stays with his pace. After passing through several hallways and going down a dozen worn-out steps, the guard stops before an iron gate, where Darren is accompanied by yet a different guard to his final destination. They halt in front of a cell; the guard opens the door and motions Darren to get in.

"What the heck is this? I must talk with somebody," he cries with angst, trembling, his hands and the small bag in the right one flinging in the air defiantly. The guard, startled by Darren's unexpected outburst, cocks his head in disbelief, pushes him inside the cell abruptly, slams the door behind him with rage, and walks away, mumbling some swearwords in Persian.

4

Totally humiliated and helpless, his brain blistering from fury and frustration, Darren bangs the concrete wall and swears forcefully from the bottom of his tangled guts. Then he leans against the wall desperately and slithers while clasping his face fiercely, as if hiding from the reality engulfing him. Howling quietly on the cold floor of the cell with his head drooped between his legs, he recalls the sobbing mullah in the previous jail and the beardless man whispering his words of wisdom.

"Bullshit," he cries. "What the heck is wrong with God?"

In the darkness, he imagines a shadow at the far end of the cell—a swift distraction. He halts howling but his mind screams: *Oh, God, why do You tease people who wish to become purer humans? Every time I beg for mercy, I get more misery out of the blue. Why? Yet, You give so much room to so many idiots who're exploiting and running the world? Why, God? Aren't Thou supposed to be fair?*

"Fairness is another naive invention of humans for making a moral society," says a familiar voice from the far end of the cell. "The idea is so divine we attribute it to God, too. But like goodness and wisdom, fairness is only a hazy mirage we can never grab."

The cell is a narrow, dark hole, about four feet wide and seven feet long. The rays penetrating the small window on the door are brighter than the dirty light bulb in the ceiling. Darren's eyes have not adjusted to the dim light after exposure to sunlight and the fluorescent lights in the corridors. He crawls cautiously toward the voice and gazes at the man greeting him.

"Dervish Ali?"

"Yes, it's me. How're you, Darren?"

Darren cannot believe Dervish Ali still remembers his name after seeing him only once, a long time ago. Even more amazing is his seeming psychic power. "How'd you read my mind?"

"That's why I'm here."

"To read my mind?" Darren asks.

Dervish Ali bursts into laughter. "Maybe that too… But I'm here because the new regime believes I'm a psychic with some followers."

"That's their reason for putting you in prison?"

"Yes."

"What kind of a charge is that?"

"They've accused me of spreading satanic words. Komiteh arrested me to teach everybody in the neighbourhood a lesson and reduce my influence over young people. Even my small power was too threatening to them."

"That's their reason?"

"Actually, an egomaniac mullah lives in my neighbourhood. I mentioned his corruption to my followers, and a spy reported it to him with added spice."

Darren's nerves settle a bit, suddenly feeling safer with the idea of Dervish Ali being around and in the same mess he is.

"So you felt and interpreted my frustration?" Darren asks.

"It wasn't hard to read your mind."

"Maybe I was screaming all my thoughts?"

"No, in special situations, like today, I feel the vibes in the room. I recognized you in the hallway light. Then I heard your words with the guard and God. Watching your desperation and mourning in that dark corner, your sense of God's unfairness was clear. The thought would've been in your subconscious, even if you hadn't run it in your head consciously."

"So you agree that God is unfair?" Darren asks with disbelief, considering Dervish Ali's rigid religious convictions.

"Who said God is fair? Like many other human fantasies, fairness is a figment of our imagination. In the unimaginable scope of God's plan for the universe, and the laws connecting all these fine elements, fairness is simply irrelevant. More complex fundamentals probably surpass any need for it."

"But if you believe in God's will and power to set our fates, He must be ultimately 'just', or else His will and our fates would be arbitrary and pointless."

"Again, we don't know what majestic logic or principles rule the universe. I admit that humans' inferior logic cannot reconcile the principles of fairness, fate, luck, and many other myths. On the surface, He appears *unfair*, maybe even cruel, considering the conflicting natures of so much misery and extravagance in the world. We witness them all the time—diseases, discriminations, starvations, natural catastrophes, and the distribution of health, wealth, and pleasure."

"Exactly… God is deliberately unfair. He intentionally teases us by bringing us face to face with all sorts of aggravating and sinister situations," Darren stresses anxiously as if out of spite for Dervish Ali.

"They're all part of a grander wisdom we'll never understand. But they're necessary for the existence of even a single cell."

"Still the bottom line is that the entire world and humanity are totally fucked up; everything I touch gets fucked up. I beg God for mercy and receive malice." Darren is crying again with rage and anguish.

"But what have I done to you?" Dervish Ali asks timidly.

"You still believe in God even after admitting his unfairness. What kind of God are you worshiping then? What kind of God should give a decent creature of His, someone like you, so much agony? You're a hypocrite like the rest of us," Darren shrieks with anger, while Dervish Ali smiles coolly.

"Well, if you don't believe in God, why do you make so much noise and fuss? Who're you angry at then, if you don't believe He may hear you?"

"I don't know," Darren whispers timidly. "I guess I'd been too hopeful about the break that Vincent had promised me."

"Who's Vincent?" Dervish Ali asks, pitying Darren's clear breakdown and sad appearance, possibly even hallucination.

"Van Gogh. He's my spiritual and artistic mentor. Sometimes we talk in a special way I can't explain. He'd promised I'd get a break from my gloomy life soon."

"Be patient, my son," Dervish Ali reiterates with pity, now more concerned about Darren's sanity.

"What's the purpose of this life, anyway?"

"In general? Or the purpose of human life?"

"Both," Darren replies.

"Nobody will ever know the meaning, scope, or purpose of the universe. We're too insignificant to grasp it. But I believe we should somehow be able to invent a rather meaningful purpose for human life eventually, when we finally get tired of so much greed, dogmatic philosophies, and prejudices. We either perish soon or find life's true purpose. It must be something simple… something instinctual… Finding happiness and life's purposes to redeem our souls seems to be programmed deep in our genes. Although finding happiness per se isn't the purpose of life."

"I don't quite understand your meaning."

"That's all right. I'll explain again later."

After a long pause, Darren murmurs, "I'm sick and tired of all this torture…"

"What're you charged with?"

"I don't know."

5

At night, when the light inside the tiny cell is switched off, the enormity of the sleeping arrangement turns into a vile, comical episode. Two normal bodies cannot lie side by side, even if they did not have to move and roll in their sleep. The task is even more gruelling considering Dervish Ali's rather large body and huge belly. They burst into laughter in disbelief. Their lives have been reduced and ridiculed to a point where they have no room to even stretch their legs in a universe of infinite space. Suddenly Darren feels claustrophobic too.

"This cell is even smaller than my solitary in the previous prison," Darren says.

"Evin is Tehran's main prison and must hold a large number of criminals and political activists."

"It seems we must sleep sitting up, leaning against the wall."

"Let's take turns lying on the floor," Dervish Ali suggests.

"But there'd be hardly enough room for the other person to sit," Darren objects.

"One person can stretch across the cell with his head in the other person's lap for two hours at a time."

"But it's torturous for the person sitting not to stretch his legs, while also bearing the weight of the other person's head."

"We have no other choice… Let's agree that the person sitting may stand up occasionally to stretch his legs… Okay?"

"Okay. Let's try it," Darren says. "Nobody would believe us if we tell them about this situation and how we slept in a cell."

"I agree. Nobody would believe any of your experiences in this or previous prison even if you wrote an official documentary and swore to God that they were absolute truth and not fiction," Dervish Ali says and they burst into laughter.

Strangely, they soon adapt and get some sleep.

Unlike the normal routine of waking up with the shrieks of guards and inmates, Darren is awakened at dawn by the sound of gunshots and then a few blasts at intervals of ten seconds. He gazes down at Dervish Ali lying on the floor and blinking rapidly with tension. When their eyes meet, Dervish Ali sits up and stares at Darren's inquisitive impression blankly.

"You heard the gunshots?" Darren asks.

"Yes. They executed seven by a firing squad."

"Seven? How do you know?"

"I counted seven relief shots, one for each victim."

"They execute this many regularly?" Darren asks fretfully.

"In fact, more inmates may be put before the firing squad later today and many convicts are hanged for drug, sexual assault or theft charges. A firing squad is usually for political traitors."

Darren remembers the samovar man's comment that once the authorities ascertain a criminal case, they transfer the accused to the main prison—Evin looks like a real one now! So his guilt has been established and it must be serious. He is in big trouble and his position is much gloomier than he had initially thought. He trembles at the idea of being executed or sentenced harshly without getting an opportunity to defend himself. *Maybe I'll be executed without even knowing what I'm accused of. What a mess!* he murmurs with frustration.

"So how you ended up here if you don't even know the charge against you?" Dervish Ali asks.

"I was arrested at the airport, then they found some marijuana in my suitcase. If the mysterious charge against me is political, then maybe I'll be both hung and executed by a firing squad," Darren pushes himself to sound witty.

Dervish Ali laughs and pats him on the back: "A drug-dealing political activist... Yeah! That's who you are!" And they laugh again, superficially. "Let's hope your charge isn't related to drug smuggling. But it's strange you haven't been informed of your case after so long. Are you sure you didn't do anything abnormal the last time you were in Tehran?"

"I can't think of anything."

The morning routine of the guards and inmates stirring a commotion breaks their conversation. After prayer and breakfast, they engage in chitchat again, mostly to forget their anguish.

"I recall Reza's words about your heavy schedule to see me a second time... Now we have nothing but time and we must talk to keep our sanity. Isn't this funny?" Darren says in a sarcastic tone.

"True! That's a big irony. We can't avoid each other now, but you must use this chance to contemplate and prepare yourself for the break Vincent has promised you."

"You think I'll get my break soon?" Darren asks.

"Only a hunch... Vincent's promise and the course of events bringing you to Tehran and this prison are strong clues about some big changes in your future," Dervish says to humour him.

"Yes, enough is enough." Darren sighs and continues, "I've suffered enough. But I'm afraid that even my 'break' would be weird and painful."

"Our suffering is still pale compared with the hardships of a large population on our disturbed planet. Only they've learned to face it better, when you and I cry and complain at the slightest inconvenience."

"But their simpler lives are probably less stressful. A rich and healthy individual may suffer more than a poor or sick person."

"Maybe... At least we're both lucky enough to be together here instead of sharing this tiny cell with a lunatic," Dervish says.

"Especially considering the sleeping arrangement… Still all this torture feels foolish!"

"Maybe God is testing you before making you an immortal artist," Dervish Ali suggests with humour.

"I doubt that very much…," Darren replies with self-pity.

"What is really bugging you, Darren, other than being here with me?" Dervish Ali asks, frustrated.

"Right now I'm just too sick of everything; I've lost my faith, mind, and urges. I wanna give up. I wanna die."

"That's your choice, of course," Dervish Ali says jokingly. "But what other worries you had before being arrested."

"It's hard to explain my mind and feelings when my spirit has died. I'm tired of analyzing and rationalizing things all the time."

"Try…, try anyway," Dervish insists. "Dig into your deepest feelings again and express your worries. Let's meditate."

"No, I don't even wanna try. I'm sick of it all," Darren yells.

"Then there's nothing left to say!" Dervish Ali blurts bluntly.

"There's nothing right to say, either!" Darren replies irately.

Intimidated by Dervish Ali's direct demand, Darren yawns and stares at him blankly. Subconsciously, however, he feels obliged to indulge Dervish Ali at least for his past kindness and advice. He wants to relieve his sense of indebtedness to him. He wants to break from the entire world without owing anybody anything. Indulging Dervish Ali would be the first step. One by one, he would abandon everybody, perhaps the same way his father had done. Was his father right, then, avoiding reality and people? Maybe this is the kind of 'break' Vincent had meant?

6

Two hours of pensive silence calm Darren's nerves eventually. He gasps a deep breath and ponders Dervish Ali's request more positively. Yet reaching his inner emotions feels absurd. All his supposedly well-crafted spiritual convictions and philosophy of life seem unnatural and rather comical under the circumstance.

How proud he had felt of himself and his vigour to take life in his stride! Not anymore. He has been reduced to such a debilitating self, not merely for all these recent setbacks, but also for failing all along at all levels, particularly in terms finding a career and a reliable companion. Another hour of silence, however, revives his basic urges and immediate worries partially. More startling, his fear of seclusion is resurfacing, which is an encouraging sign about his state of mind—a clue that he is not yet ready to preclude reality and people. He must gather enough strength to express himself, enough to engage Dervish Ali in some chitchat, enough to at least mitigate his own blasting urge to scream from despair and the suffocating silence.

"My efforts to find my 'self' are constantly ruined by trivia; I can't concentrate enough to meditate," Darren says with a mixed air of passion and pessimism. "I'm trying to grasp love and life, which, by the way, I believe are somehow connected. However, nothing in my life makes sense, nor can I find some peace."

"Because that's a very ambitious goal," Dervish Ali replies.

"Seeking basic peace isn't merely a selfish desire, but rather a first step for knowing and defining my 'self.' Alas, financial and emotional difficulties overwhelm my soul-searching efforts."

"My advice about your financial difficulties is to keep your life very simple. But what's your emotional problem?"

"After the long agony of leaving my wife, I mostly restored my identity and passion for painting during my last stay in Iran. Your views of 'love and relationships' also helped me understand the purpose of passion and relationships through self-awareness."

"Okay…"

"But recently, I've been getting confused about everything again. Sometimes my artistic urges and efforts feel flimsy and futile. Sometimes my erratic passion for women appears shallow again, like the time I was a teenager. Sometimes—"

"What's bothering you in particular these days, Darren?" Dervish Ali interjects, trying to get to the bottom of his problems faster, instead of letting him nag forever.

"Well… I'm suddenly attracted to a woman whose childish passion only made me laugh until recently. Now I'm behaving the same way myself, like a moron. I've traveled halfway around the world, brought myself to this dismal state, and am going crazy, all for an absurd infatuation. I can neither trust my sudden feelings toward her, nor grasp how I could've fallen in love with her without knowing her enough. She's actually shown signs of lunacy sometimes, to be more precise. Perhaps I deserve to rot in this prison for my shaky feelings and principles."

"Now I can see the root of your confusion. But you should decide soon," Dervish says, gazing at him like a guru gauging his keen pupil while communicating the clues to him telepathically.

Darren tucks a flock of loose hair out of his forehead and holds it in his right fist, droops, and closes his eyes in meditation. He stays in a trance for thirty minutes, then raises his head, and releases his crumpled hair out of his hand.

"I must first decide about the kind of man I am or like to be in order to find a mate and avoid loneliness," he says.

"What kinds are there?" Dervish asks.

"Well, a man can try to be mostly a competent companion, a compassionate lover, or a conventional womanizer."

"Which one have you been all these years?"

"Amazingly, I guess I've tried to be all three. We like to play all these roles erratically so arrogantly," Darren replies. "We do it due to our bad experiences, neediness, and self-gratifying urges."

"That's true. That's why we never build a strong identity and learn who we are on top of feeling lonely a lot."

"And that's also a reason we can't give an image of a reliable character to people around us, thus lose our credibility as well."

"We discussed love in our first meeting two years ago and you're still struggling with this matter. When're you gonna grow up, Darren, and forget about love?"

"I wonder myself and that's exactly what bothers me, too. I know all these facts, especially my stupidity. Still, I like to test my chance of learning to be a compassionate lover, realistically this time?"

"That's a risky ambition as you said it yourself."

"I know… That's why I still prefer your old advice to look for a good companion, instead of taking risk with love again!"

"Yet you sound unsure and confused!"

"True… Because I've also failed to find a good companion so far. I can't adapt to a lacklustre relationship, it seems."

"You still seem obsessed with love deep down. You're too romantic for your own good."

"You're right. But can I ever overcome my naïve nature?"

"Maybe…, if you really mature," Dervish Ali says.

"And that's still what you suggest?"

"It's only your decision. But I still think it's always safer to find a good companion without relying on 'love.'"

"Then I must return to Vancouver right away, if I'm released from this place… I know a woman waiting for me in Vancouver who can give me that if I try just a bit harder."

"It sounds wiser to me, too, but it's up to you to decide."

"You're right… It is time for me to grow up and forget about love forever…"

"Good…!" Dervish Ali says with a sigh of relief.

"But…," Darren pauses pensively with a great of deal of pain and confusion showing on his face, then continues. "But should I return without even trying to see if I can be a compassionate lover for this ultra romantic woman I've chased all the way to Tehran like a foolish teenager?"

"Your turmoil is quite cleat to me now," Dervish says. "But how do you think you can be a compassionate lover again?"

"By remaining realistic this time," Darren replies pensively.

"How?"

"By recognizing love's ordeals and flimsiness, but don't elude it in fear of getting hurt, or follow shallow relationships to replace real passion. I should treat love only as another kind of attraction that some people grow toward nature or even a tiny plant—a kind of spiritual wisdom for love, I presume."

"That's a big and odd conviction. You think you can do it?"

"Don't know… Maybe… Sometimes I think I must try it."

"You'd better be sure this time…," Dervish stresses.

"Yeah… It may be my last chance to get a life through love!"

"You may have good ideas about handling love with wisdom, but sharing them with your lover won't be easy."

"I know… I must also be ready to pay a price, since even real love often leads to disappointment and loneliness. I must know how to minimize my pain when it happens, perhaps by building some other sources of spirituality along the way."

"So, do you know where you stand now?"

"Close, but not quite… I just hope my break comes soon!"

"I'd say your break depends on you making the right choice."

"What do you mean?" Darren asks.

"Not everybody is lucky enough to find true love in his or her lifetime," Dervish says cautiously as if feeling obliged to qualify his harsh notion of love. "If you think this mystery woman in Tehran might be able to turn you into a happy compassionate lover, making a right choice is tough. You need a good reason for giving her up, despite love's high risks and disappointments."

"Are you saying that my break for a better life depends on making a right choice about love?"

"Yes, about your impression, interpretation, and application of love. You made a point earlier yourself about life and love being linked… Your present situation offers a good example of it."

"So, you agree they're linked?" Darren asks with surprise.

"Yes, although we have only basic clues about this link."

"What clues you have…?" Daren asks.

"Both human love and life erupt from nowhere by accident, we can't predict or control either, and they perish swiftly, often sooner than we're willing or ready to give them up. We can never grasp their meanings despite our great enthusiasm for doing so. Life feels empty without love, but love often ruins our spirit of living…," Dervish pauses awhile. "Like happiness, they're myths and enigmas that appear only after we doubt the meanings of facts and logic. But the problem is that without logic and facts, we're merely helpless creatures and perish fast."

"Are you saying that life and love are connected, but only as conflicting choices for humans beyond common logic?"

"Mostly, but it is a bit more complex than that. Love and life are often, but not always, contradictory. Yet, they are the main choices we face and we'd better know how to manage them in a delicate mix, if we crave love. Life without love is simpler and more manageable, but it needs more wisdom and self-reliance."

"You've made my job even harder now with more paranoia!"

"Also remember this linkage applies only to 'love' between two humans."

"I think I get your point. Other kinds of love grow within their own unique realms beyond these discussions, right?"

"Yes. Besides, our choices are personal once we recognize the nature of love and still feel ready to accept its inevitable agonies."

"Then again, maybe a joint heavenly wisdom for love and life exists beyond our grasp and control—maybe even beyond their likely conflicting roles for building our psyches," Darren adds.

"It's possible," Dervish Ali replies. "Our experiences, pains, deprivations, and thoughts about our spirits and the real meaning of the 'self' might have a surprising meaning within Godly logic, in line with the role of mysterious coincidences all our lives."

"So maybe our break comes when we stop fearing the loss of love or life!"

"Yes… Neither fearing nor trusting them."

"How about your break then? You've supposedly made the right choices to be free from the prison of life, but then are here, in a space the size of a grave, which you must share with me. Despite your relative mental freedom, you can't enjoy it without physical freedom? What're they going to do to you?" Darren poses a philosophical question, but is genuinely concerned about Dervish Ali's fate.

"Freedom is another myth, although the challenge to capture it keeps us busy in life. We try to find some degree of freedom with self-expression, but usually put ourselves in a bigger jam with our big mouths or even love affairs. Nevertheless, we must bear physical pains for even that relative mental freedom and for coping with social limitations forced on us."

"I'm worried for both of us," Darren says.

"I appreciate your concern; I'm probably facing the ultimate limitation of being—death. My chance of surviving this ordeal is small. They may not hang me or put me in front of a firing squad, but I may be left in this dungeon to rot or be murdered by a rude cellmate who doesn't like the idea of compromise and sitting up half the night, like you do, to let me get a little sleep."

"Yeah, that possibility would be horrible."

"Letting inmates murder each other is the cheapest type of execution and the least problematic. They wash their hands of any responsibility when one of their enemies is eliminated and they find a stronger excuse for executing the other inmate—the murderer. All they must do is to create the right environment—like this tiny cell—and watch us kill each other."

"Wow! You're right. We have been lucky to be sent to this particular cell together by such miraculous coincidence, instead of a cell with a crazy cellmate!"

"That's exactly what happens in our daily lives, too, outside prison," Dervish Ali says.

"What do you mean?"

"Well, our socioeconomic order is squeezing and shaping our brains by making us arrogant and competitive, and politicians make us believe there's not enough room for all of us to live peacefully on this vast planet within a simple life. Worst of all, our own stupidity and fanaticism is turning life into hell for us all. We fight and kill each other relentlessly in the name of religion, patriotism, passion, and other stuff, while narcissistic politicians presume they're the smartest breeds of human race," Dervish Ali asserts, as they're interrupted by the guards giving them a loaf of Barbari and a bowl of bean soup… again.

After eating their meals in silence, Dervish Ali lies on the floor leisurely, with his legs folded near the opposite wall. He closes his eyes, as if his brain were empty of any worries or wishes, unlike Darren who is still wrestling with deep thoughts and emotions. Leaning against the wall, Darren stares at the big mound of flesh stretched before him and wonders about the inner peace helping Dervish Ali be so carefree, so unlike him.

"Maybe they'll put more people in this cell?" he whispers wittily, hoping to feel carefree like Dervish Ali by throwing a funny comment.

"If you don't think fast about your life choices, God may squeeze you even more," Dervish Ali mumbles without opening his eyes. He is soon asleep and snoring like a happy giant. Darren wonders where Dervish's free spirit is at that moment while his physical existence is trapped here. Is at least his spirit free?

7

Darren ruminates on the sequence of crucial events in his life, especially the recent ones. All the experiences are disturbing or dull, except for his painting sessions, while conversing with the Masters, and the memories of Mahroo. Recalling his juvenile views and reactions during these periods, he feels embarrassed about his behaviour and pointless worries. His earlier rejection of Mahroo, based on rigid principles he had invented to protect his ego, seems particularly childish now. His worries about money and failing to establish his status as a painter in Vancouver, for the second time, also feel silly in the context of a divine vision gradually lifting his soul. Only painting the majesty of nature and embracing a true love matter to him now. He wonders where this new feeling and vision is coming from so suddenly, though it feels genuine and novel. This torturous imprisonment is starting to manifest as a divine revelation to grasp a majestic truth. With such a strong conviction nurturing his mind, he gasps a deep breath and falls asleep like a baby upright in his carriage.

Half an hour later, he opens his eyes and notices the rugged, pensive face of Dervish Ali, sitting at the other corner of the cell, lighted by the fluorescent rays speeding through the tiny window. With his black, penetrating, round eyes, curvy nose, long grey hair surrounding his red balding head, and bushy eyebrows and mustache, he resembles a regal bald eagle. As their eyes meet, they grin and gaze at each other awhile, then Dervish Ali speaks. "I see a divine glow in you. Maybe you've found your way?"

"Maybe! Although, it'll probably shatter again soon with another round of life dramas and doubts."

"That's why you must nurture your convictions every day," Dervish says. "Don't let life trivialities taint your inner faith and spirit. Don't let your soul sink again. Cherish it, even if it means dropping all your possessions, ego, and phony facts of life."

"It's difficult, but I'll persist and pray."

"Trust your judgment today in this cell. Remember today."

"Do you like to know my pledges?"

"Yes."

"I've decided to be a compassionate lover if the right person comes around and to push my passion for painting faithfully despite all the setbacks. Nothing else must matter to me or stand in the way of fulfilling my dreams. I believe this mindset would bring me peace better."

"What's the first step then?" Dervish Ali asks.

"To fulfil my mission that has brought me to this city and to learn the art of loving life despite all its chaos and cruelties."

"Now maybe your spirit gets a chance to soar," Dervish blurts with a sigh.

"Although I can't go anywhere myself," Darren says with a sardonic chuckle.

"You're showing scepticism already? Learn to feel free, even if you're tied with a thousand strings. But there's also another possibility you must consider," Dervish Ali says mysteriously.

"What is that?"

"Maybe God has had a purpose for bringing you here…!"

"I felt it a minute ago myself… But it's interesting that you also get such a premonition suddenly."

"Yes…, and until you fulfill that purpose, you'll stay here."

"You mean another purpose besides the divine realization that stirred my convictions?" Darren asks with surprise and distress.

"Yes… But now it's time again for us to meditate awhile," Dervish Ali says sombrely, closes his eyes, and droops.

8

Two more long days and torturous nights pass and Dervish Ali mostly keeps his silence, while goading Darren to grasp the depth of his convictions through meditation. Dervish takes out a pad and a pen and keeps writing many sheets in Farsi. Darren feels they are letters, since he folds every few pages neatly and writes something, apparently a name or address, on the blank page covering the written ones. He stops after six hours and puts them away in his little bag. Every time Darren attempts to begin a conversation, Dervish only offers thoughtful prompts and hints, goading him to find his own answers. At last, Darren is as calm and quiet as Dervish Ali, with their heads down and speechless like two monks, the air filled with peaceful energy.

On the fourth day of enduring Dervish Ali's peculiar attitude and forced meditation, finally Darren feels a relative tranquility in line with his earlier sense of awakening. He is also struck by a realization: Perhaps the second purpose of his imprisonment and encountering Dervish Ali in Evin has been to come clean about Mahroo. He ponders the matter and his options for hours before finally gathering his nerve and addressing Dervish Ali.

"Let me confess—my dear Dervish—about my feelings for Mahroo. I'd feared insulting or annoying you, but I must admit to my weird attraction to your late nephew's wife now…"

Darren pauses, as Dervish Ali closes his eyes, frowns, and turns pale in a state of convulsion. His swift anguish distorts his facial muscles, twitching and blinking, while struggling to press his eyelids shut. He looks like he is having a seizure, so Darren leaps to help and maybe call the guards. He approaches Dervish Ali and kneels next to him.

"Dervish Ali… Dervish Ali… What's wrong?"

Dervish Ali is panting, but once Darren touches his shoulder, he swings his fist and smacks Darren fiercely next to his Adam's apple. The impact throws Darren against the wall in shock. He holds his throat to alleviate the excruciating pain, still unable to talk or breathe properly. When he finally moans, Dervish Ali opens his eyes and glares at him with bloody eyes and rage. As Darren stares at him in bewilderment, expecting an explanation, Dervish Ali jumps him, clasps his throat and squeezes it with his enormous right hand, exerting the force of a crocodile's jaw. In total panic, Darren struggles under Dervish Ali's forceful thrust, thinking he has gone mad. He slithers toward the floor to mitigate the pressure on his throat and to free his legs, which are stuck to the opposite wall. But as he collapses on the floor, Dervish Ali tightens his grip by leaning on Darren's chest. He cannot believe an old man is capable of exerting so much power over him. He is twice his age, with no physique to match Darren's athletic body, but is about to crush Darren like a lamb in the grips of a ferocious lion. Darren is choking, unable to fight back. With his legs free at last, he kicks Dervish Ali, the walls, and the floor to free himself from his suffocating hold. But Dervish Ali jumps over him, puts his knee on Darren's groin and keeps pressing it relentlessly. Now, Darren is totally paralyzed, his eyes starting to roll up in the sockets, almost dying. Suddenly Dervish Ali releases him, leaps back to his corner, and keeps banging the wall with the soft end of his fists. He then droops and begins weeping with desperation, like Darren when he had arrived in this cell.

After twenty seconds, Darren catches his breath and sits up with pain and puzzlement. Now his mind is paralyzed, dying to know how Dervish Ali had gathered all that strength, why he had attacked him, and why he is now sobbing in that corner. He hides in his corner away from Dervish Ali, not even daring to ask him anything. Maybe Dervish has gone nuts after being in this cell for God knows how long. Ten minutes later, Dervish finally calms down and stares at Darren stealthily with angst.

"Darren, I'm very sorry about my outburst. I believe I lost my sanity...," Dervish Ali murmurs.

Darren remains silent, still in shock, unable to trust him anymore. After two minutes, when Dervish Ali finally raises his head and looks into Darren's eyes with a sign of remorse, Darren decides to measure Dervish Ali's state of mind and the risk of staying around him. Maybe he should call the guards and ask them to move him to another cell. But what if the situation with a new cellmate turns out even worse?

"What happened?" he mutters timidly. "Why'd you do that?"

"Please forgive me. I don't know what happened to me. But your confession triggered a sore memory…"

"About Mahroo?"

"About poor Zia… He was like the son I never had. My wife never bore me a child. So we raised him and his siblings like our own children. We were close until six years ago. But shortly after his marriage, he abandoned me… never came to see me, or to at least explain why he was so angry with me. That woman… that woman… Mahroo, possibly turned him against me, and then caused his death, too. It's been a terrible time for me… Zia and his brother, my dear sons, committing suicide within a month. And now, today, I learn you're 'the man,' the man Zia told me had seduced his beloved wife."

"He said I'd seduced Mahroo?" Darren asks.

"He said 'a man.' Too proud to say a name. How could you?"

"Dervish, you've been misinformed. When did you see Zia?"

"One night he came to my house unexpectedly, a desperate lover in ruin; a wreck. Seeing him after such a long time in that horrible state just shattered my heart. He cried his guts out for five hours about his failed marriage and his crushed feelings. Then he left to die the next day on his trip to Shiraz."

"I swear," Darren says. "No affection or affair existed despite Zia's imagination of my feelings for Mahroo or triggering her love for me. My stay in Zia's house for three days was Mahroo's and Reza's idea after I was released from hospital. Only a terrible misunderstanding existed all along with regard to the ownership and intention of the painting that Reza had innocently given to Mahroo under my name."

"But the way Zia grieved for five hours like a lunatic was so pitiful. He was sure Mahroo was in love with 'this man' and loathed Zia for being around her or alive. I know, Zia was desperately in love with her and believed she'd never care for him again. But I could never imagine he'd kill himself for a woman, regardless of the severity of his passion for her. Every day, since he passed away, I've suffered from the fact that I lost my chance of saving him when he came to me probably for some kind of support. I guess, I didn't grasp the intensity of his mental collapse; perhaps I could never imagine he'd be that weak. But every day since his death, I've cursed 'the man' who had caused his demise and brought me such a strong sense of guilt and grief. I can never forgive myself and I have all along built up hatred toward the man who's made me feel so awful about myself, let alone his sin for causing Zia's death and luring his wife away."

"So maybe it's been your curse haunting my spirit for so long and then bringing me here, too?"

"I hope so!" Dervish Ali says with distress. "Maybe God loves me and listens to me, after all!"

"I'm sorry if my presence in Mahroo's thoughts ruined Zia's life. I believe in my innocence, but still would like to receive your forgiveness," Darren pleads with a rasping voice and eyes wet from poignant emotion.

"I don't know… Even if I could forgive you, how can you and Mahroo forgive yourselves? How can you two forget all the catastrophes caused by your sinful love affair?"

"We've been paying for our unintentional sins, believe me."

"I hope so… I have cursed Mahroo too. Remember that…"

"I'm really sorry about everything. But I'm glad we had this talk and to learn about my possible guilt in causing your turmoil."

"I'm relieved a little, too, to at least see the devil who'd ruined my peace."

"I didn't mean it and I'm not too guilty," Darren says glumly. "I guess the wisdom of all the coincidences of coming to Iran, being arrested, and sent to this particular prison cell is clear now."

"It's starting to come clearer, though more revelations may still loom," Dervish says with an air of mystery or premonition.

"I hope things improve from now on… But most important of all, would you please forgive me."

"Swear you've told me the whole truth."

"I swear and beg for your pity from the bottom of my heart."

"I may forgive you, but I'll never forgive Mahroo."

"Please forgive her, too," Darren pleads.

"No… She's caused too much agony for many people. There is a divine justice, Darren, after all, I promise."

"I'm sure she's also remorseful, although she is not directly responsible for how she thinks and acts rather naturally."

"No, I can't forgive her… But mostly I wonder how you can ignore your principles about the person you've come all this way to love."

"Well, after all this turmoil and sacrifices, wouldn't it be an even higher sin to ignore our passion and the possibility of a true and worthy—perhaps divine—purpose for all these catastrophes and sufferings?"

"How can you think of Mahroo as a reliable companion?"

"This has been the real reason for my anxiety. I've had similar doubts and now I'm glad that at least you sense the cause of my turmoil when you condemned my blasphemies when I arrived."

"But now you're sure about loving her?" Dervish Ali asks.

"Yes, you told me to make a decision and that's my decision for better or worse. Now you're more responsible for my crazy decision than I am!"

"When did you feel love for Mahroo?" Dervish asks.

"Only recently, which is odd, as I said. Mahroo and I had some contacts and confrontations about a painting when she came to Vancouver. However, I'd dismissed the possibility of any relationship with her, mostly due to her mental instability. She appeared excessively emotional to the point one might've considered her psychotic. But one morning, a few days before her departure, I suddenly felt the purity of her sentiments along with a bizarre attraction toward her. When we met to say goodbye, my affection became clearer and I couldn't avoid showing it. I've known her for a long time, from a distance, but have never been intimate enough with her to understand her personality. Still, I believe she can restore my confidence in love. And for now that's all that matters to me. I'm no longer afraid of 'love.' I mustn't neglect Mahroo on account of not understanding the meaning of my love for her or even the fear of losing her someday. I simply want to know her better and I'll stay in Tehran for a while to gauge the meaning of our naive infatuation. Or at least establish its silliness for good. This trial would be my last test of love!"

"I sense the strength of your convictions, but make sure you don't lose your soul again…, now in a different way. Also, don't mention anything to anybody about our private discussion today, especially to Mahroo. Zia didn't want anybody know about his pitiful state of mind." Dervish Ali pauses and surveys Darren before continuing, "My guess is that you've now fulfilled your purpose of being here, so you'll be free soon, unless…"

"Unless what?" Darren asks anxiously.

"Unless Zia's curse brings you a deserved punishment."

"Punishment? What do you mean?" Darren asks with stress.

"They might convict and execute you quickly, despite your claim of innocence or simply by mistake!" Dervish Ali says with both humour and dread. "Let's hope they'll forgive you like me. Just let's hope Zia's spirit has not cursed you, too."

"I'm sure he has…Oh, my god…!" Darren exclaims.

"We'll see," Dervish Ali says, then opens his bag and pulls out the letters he had written two days earlier. "Ask Reza give these letters to my wife. This one is my will and testament, which I'd like you to witness by signing in this corner. Go with Reza to a notary to authenticate your signature. Can you do this for me?"

"Sure. But how do you know I'll be freed and you won't?"

"Only a hunch. I doubt you're charged with a political crime," Dervish Ali replies calmly, pointing to the line on his will for Darren to sign.

He gazes at Dervish Ali with concern about his fate, unable to imagine such a *normally* gentle, spiritual person—except today, of course—being accused of political crime and conspiracy, never mind facing a death sentence. This man has given him hope, the most precious commodity for him at his present dire condition. *He has not been a good example of gentleness in the last couple of hours, though! And his promise of speedy freedom isn't materializing, either. Then again, he's proven his holiness at least by forgiving me.*

9

Darren's faith in Dervish Ali's intuition—or his spiritual power—is collapsing more every minute he waits desperately for his exoneration order to arrive. What if, instead, Dervish Ali's hunch about Zia's curse comes through and they hang him by mistake? He blames his lack of faith for the delay sometimes, or his naïveté for taking Dervish Ali's premonition of his freedom too literally; maybe 'soon' means anytime during the following weeks or months. Yet he does not dare to ask Dervish Ali for clarification, for fear of offending him or receiving a lousy answer, like 'soon' means within six months. He is tired of the sleeping arrangement, the torture of sitting up half of the night, watching Dervish Ali's big head in his lap, and listening to his ear-piercing snores. At night, he can only amuse himself with the thought of seeing Mahroo and traveling to the Caspian Sea with her to enjoy nature and listen to the thunderous sound of titanic surfs crashing against the shores. *Will she go with me? Maybe I can paint her there, maybe even in nude!*

The next day he feels even more agitated. He tries to stay positive and calm by taking Dervish's promise of freedom less seriously. But prison life, precluding him from fulfilling his newly proclaimed convictions, tortures him: He craves to paint and to embrace Mahroo. But all he can cling to now is his long beard, which he has gotten the habit of playing with, as though measuring the severity of his predicament by its length. After lunch, he dozes off amidst Dervish Ali's strident snores and his own daydreams about freedom. However, before he loses total consciousness and real dreams emerge, the sound of the door clanking open alarms him. The guard tells him to get his bag, because he is free to go.

"Who? Me?"

How quickly the idea of 'freedom' triggers such jubilance! I'm not going to die. I'm going to paint again, and I'm going to embrace Mahroo.

"Yes, you. Darren. Hurry up," the guard cries impatiently.

Darren grabs his bag and awakens Dervish Ali with delight and gratitude. Dervish Ali smiles as if he had been expecting the exact moment of Darren's release. He shares the mixed emotions of joy and agony covering Darren's face and evident in his clumsy movements around the cell. He is trying to abide by the guard's order quickly, while hesitant to leave Dervish Ali behind.

"Dervish, can you forgive Mahroo, too, please?" he pleads pitifully again in hopes of Dervish Ali's possible last minute change of heart.

"No… I already told you!"

"But…"

"Go, my son. Ali's hand upon you," says Dervish Ali, as if sending off his soldier of faith to the battle of evil and ignorance. They hug and bid each other farewell in a hurry before Darren departs at last, contemplating on a positive note: *At least tonight Dervish Ali can get a good night's sleep alone in this grave.* But immediately a scary thought spoils his optimism: *What if they send a lunatic to his cell?*

Chapter Thirteen
A Broken Promise

1

On the good side of the Evin's gate, Darren sees Reza in the distance, waving and hurrying toward him. They hug cordially while another young man approaches and watches them keenly.

"I didn't recognize you with that yellow beard," Reza says. "But you look good after your mini vacation."

"Yeah… Vacation!" Darren shrieks, trying to hide his anger. "It was horrible."

"The important thing is that you're out, safe and sound. Let me introduce Bijan Bandari, my brother-in-law."

"Nice to meet you," Darren says, shaking Bijan's hand, but turns to Reza fast: "Do you know why I was arrested?"

"Bijan knows and will tell you later. He's succeeded in bailing you out for now."

"So there's still a case against me?" Darren asks nervously.

"Yes. For now you're released into Bijan's custody. You must consult him before going anywhere or meeting anybody," Reza announces quickly, as if discharging a duty Bijan had imposed upon him. He then glances at Bijan, who nods with a gentle grin for a job well done. Reza continues, "But now I'm sure you're exhausted and need to soak in a bathtub. Let's go to my place and we'll meet Bijan later in his house."

"We'll talk privately tonight, Darren." Bijan promises and leaves.

"Why am I in Bijan's custody?" Darren asks tensely as Reza merges with the traffic, driving jerkily toward his apartment.

"Your case is serious, apparently, but Bijan's trying to take care of it."

"You know anything?" Darren asks with stress.

"All I know is that the marijuana complicated the matter and Bijan had to work really hard to get you off the hook, for now. His father is very influential in the government, and still they had difficulty handling your situation. These days in Iran, a simple case can send a person to the verge of execution quickly without getting a chance to plead his innocence. You owe Bijan a lot."

"I'm sure… By the way, Dervish Ali was my cellmate in this prison."

"What? Oh dear…! What's he there for?" Reza asks in shock.

"Some kind of a political thing related to his psychic power, he said," Darren says with a mix of sarcasm and wit.

"He must've been arrested recently; I hadn't heard about it."

Darren recounts Dervish's seemingly severe circumstance and other stuff he knows by the time they reach Reza's apartment.

"Bijan must do something for him, too," Reza murmurs.

"Quickly, before it's too late…"

"Yes, yes. You feel at home and relax now."

"Thanks. When did you move here?"

"About three months ago. I'm closer to everybody here," Reza explains while opening the curtains to display the city view.

"Nice view too," says Darren, passing Dervish Ali's papers to Reza along with his instructions.

Reza shows him the guestroom and the bathroom. "These are clean towels. Put your laundry in that basket for the maid."

"Thanks. This is heaven after Evin, but I bet I smell like hell."

After a long relaxation in the tub and cleansing his body and soul, Darren feels fresh and hopes to write off the memories of the last eleven days, very much like shaving off his long beard. In the living room, Reza is talking on the phone in Persian. After chatting awhile, he passes the receiver to Darren. "It's Mahroo."

"Hi, Mahroo!" Darren says excitedly.

"Hi, Darren. I've been sick with worry. Thank God and Bijan for rescuing you," says Mahroo, bawling with joy.

"Halleluiah! It's been a nightmare, especially since I still don't know what I'm charged with. But at least I'm out. Perhaps now my big break comes after all this torture."

"I'm sure everything will be fantastic for you from now on."

"I hope you're right… But your certainty is most amazing!"

"Because I'll make sure it happens."

"How?"

"I'll tell you when I see you tonight."

"I look forward to it then… Where're you now?" he asks.

"At work. I've dug a bigger hole for myself than I'd intended. Many desperate veterans here depend on me now."

"Don't kill yourself. Take a holiday; let's go to the Caspian Sea."

"Caspian Sea? Oh, Darren… You forgot we're living in Iran? If they catch us together, we'll be punished severely and they'll force you to marry me, too."

"You'd like that, won't you?" Darren says with a chuckle.

"Not that way… But don't worry; we'll find ways to spend time together. I'll ask for some time off. I'll see you tonight…," she says as if in a rush suddenly, "Adieu."

Hearing Mahroo's voice in the safety of Reza's apartment brings Darren serenity. He plummets onto the soft, fluffy sofa, gasps a deep breath, and decides to build a wonderful image of the world now that he is free and blessed in so many ways. *Let's hope Mahroo's optimism and promise would materialize.* He wolfs the sandwich Reza has made, along with a cup of coffee.

"Have you collected my paintings from the customs?"

"Yes, Bijan and I delivered them to the gallery," Reza replies. "They postponed the exhibition opening to make sure you'll be available. If Mahroo hadn't driven Bijan crazy to follow your case every hour, your detainment might've lasted much longer."

"Is she enjoying her volunteer work?"

"Looks like it. She's making a big impression on patients, but also getting more confident herself. We're all happy for her, but I get worried sometimes about the way she's taking her mission so seriously. What can I do…!"

"It's like a miracle the way she's suddenly found her calling in life," Reza says.

"Good for her. Most of us never get a chance like this."

2

At seven p.m., Reza's car turns into the driveway of a mansion. After parking the car in a large, sheltered space designated for guests, Darren and Reza walk toward the gigantic building with a dark green marble facade. The striking entrance is surrounded by exquisite columns and statues in harmony with a big Roman fountain in the upper garden. Upon entry, Darren is stunned by the grandeur of the foyer, almost the size of a tennis court, with its beige marble floor ornamented by large, colourful Tabrizes and Isfahans in select areas. A ten-foot-wide, winding staircase soars majestically on the left-hand side of the foyer, twirling up toward the dome forty feet high. Half a dozen dainty crystal chandeliers highlight the splendour of the huge one in the middle of the foyer. Several doors open from the foyer, but a big French double door on the right leads to the large drawing room, where servants are trafficking in preparation for the big party.

A manservant greets them. Reza chats with him in Persian and then turns to Darren. "Bijan's waiting for us in his study." They stroll toward the end of the foyer, then to a corridor behind the stairway that takes them to a large, elegantly decorated study. The glass wall with a sliding door shows a view of an immense backyard with a variety of flowers and greenery deftly designed around a large pool, beyond which two large gazebos stand in the grassed area. Bijan invites them to sit down, but Reza excuses himself to go see Mahtab.

"You look brighter without the beard," Bijan asserts with a grin. "Do you like a drink?"

"Maybe a beer if you have one?"

Bijan orders drinks through the intercom, then looks up at Darren with some hesitation and discomfort. He seems to be searching for words, since the matter of the marijuana could by itself be embarrassing to discuss.

"How long are you going to stay in Tehran?" he asks finally.

"One or two months perhaps." Darren murmurs.

"Everybody will be glad to hear that. But once I explain your case, you'll realize we must observe some rules, to prevent more problems for you. In a sense, your freedom is restricted and you're supposedly in my custody until you leave. I'll tell you why in a second. However, in order to achieve even this level of leniency, I had to provide substantial guarantees and promise you'd abide by the restrictions."

"I'll do my best not to jeopardize your guarantees and honour. But maybe knowing the problem helps," Darren says nervously.

"Your case—" A subtle knock on the door interrupts Bijan. A manservant comes in with a tray and places it on the coffee table in front of Bijan and Darren. Bijan gives Darren the large glass of beer and clasps his own drink. The manservant puts a bowl of pistachios on the table and leaves. Bijan then lifts his drink. "Cheers."

"Cheers." Darren reciprocates and drinks a sip of the German beer, which tastes wonderful.

Bijan puts his drink on the table and leans back pensively to explain Darren's case. This time the phone shrieks and he goes behind the desk to answer it. Although speaking in Persian, his tone of voice and facial expression alarm Darren. He hangs up hastily and turns to Darren with agitation. "I'm sorry, Darren, I must go right away. We'll talk later. Wait until I come back... No, not here... come with me. Stay with the guests. You know some of them."

Bijan grabs Darren's arm and thrusts him toward the foyer. His swift, jerky motions remind Darren of Evin's rude guards and Tehrani drivers. Seeing Reza emerging from the drawing room, Bijan runs toward him, leaving Darren puzzled in the middle of the foyer. After whispering a few words to each other, they hurry outside the house, shouting some words to a manservant, who runs to the kitchen and returns with a woman ahead of him. She scurries to the portico, but returns immediately, apparently unable to catch Bijan. She finds Darren baffled and frozen right in the middle of the foyer like an ice statue. She strolls toward him with a grin and extends her hand.

"I'm Mahtab, Bijan's wife. You must be Darren!"

"Yes. Nice to meet you..." Darren is stunned by her charming resemblance to Mahroo.

"Do you know why Bijan and Reza rushed away like that?"

"No. I'm quite confused myself. Something serious must've happened. Bijan seemed upset."

"Don't worry. Let's mingle with guests. My parents are here, and Mahroo will come shortly, too. Don't be shy!"

He sits next to Mahroo's parents to make conversation, but his mind and soul appear misplaced. The loud Iranian music and teenage girls' passionate dancing are making him dizzy. Parents clap periodically while chatting ardently, words piercing Darren's ears. As the number of guests and group conversations increase, everybody yells louder to be heard in this chaotic war of words, music, and laughter. Servants keep serving appetizers and Mahtab mingles amidst the huge mayhem to ensure everybody is properly entertained. He feels a bit dizzy, so staggers to the foyer, where the noise and cigarette smoke are less irritating. He lingers by the grand piano, which is strategically placed near the drawing room. Holding the glass of beer, he moves about, touches the statues, and admires the piano aimlessly. *What is the meaning of this silly behaviour, appraising things like an idiot?* he thinks, trying to pretend to be amused like everybody else.

"Do you play piano?" a placid voice echoes behind him.

"No, just admiring it," he replies to Mahtab.

"I understand. You must be really bored in this noisy crowd?"

"I'm fine. Just a bit edgy because Bijan left me in suspense about my case. Don't worry about me."

"This isn't the best way to spend your first night of freedom. How was Evin?" Mahtab pauses. "Sorry, Darren, that was a dumb question."

"That's all right. It was a horrible experience," he murmurs, his voice diminishing gradually as his consciousness yields to the memory of the prison, especially the hellhole he had shared with Dervish Ali. His eyes move slowly around the expansive walls of the foyer and up to the high dome. He scrutinizes the dazzling colours of the chandelier crystals and feels a dizzy spell. Then, a subconscious comparison between the dungeon last night and this place tonight, with its sheer size and luminance, nauseates him. The prison experience has apparently made a deeper impact on him than he had realized.

"Don't you feel good? Do you wanna rest in a quiet place for a while?"

"I'm fine. Do you play piano?" He strives not to faint and be a more affable guest.

"Sometimes," she replies with a hint of worry about Darren's condition.

Darren gazes at her blankly, trying to find the right words to stop her fussing about him. Mahtab senses his struggle to appease her, so in return she feels a bigger motive to please him. "Perhaps I should play a bit, to change the atmosphere for you."

Darren nods with appreciation and a shy, charming grin.

"Then let me go turn off the stereo first. Some people are gonna get upset with me!"

"Then don't interrupt their fun, please," Darren says anxiously with guilt. "I'm sorry... I didn't realize."

"That's all right. Some of them would probably understand."

She rushes away and soon the music stops. The hoopla begins to subside a bit, too, as she returns to the foyer and sits behind the piano, preparing herself to amuse the guests. However, most guests appear baffled and unhappy about her decision to disrupt the Iranian music and dancing so abruptly just to show off her virtuosity. Only few seem to appreciate the kind of music she usually plays on that piano of hers. Mahtab waits at the piano in silence, ignoring the crowd's glares and those who persist in blabbering in loud voice. Darren stares at her face and glamorous hands ready to attack the keyboard if the guests quiet down a bit. When she raises her head and glances at him for a moment, he remembers Mahroo's eyes when they had kissed goodbye in Vancouver.

At last, Mahtab starts Chopin's Raindrop Prelude with great vigour and tempo. Soon the music replaces the guests' chatter. It resonates serenely in the spacious hall and calms Darren's ignited nerves. The stream of notes echoes smoothly from the walls, mixes in midair like a swirling tempest, hurls up to the dome layer after layer, then collapses like a moistening waterfall. His nausea mitigates a bit as his soul elevates and floats overhead freely. The placid moments are shattered sporadically, however, whenever his eyes meet Mahtab's and thunderous vibes splinter his spine and soul. *I'm a mentally sick man, for sure!*

After playing two short pieces, Bijan's abrupt arrival disrupts Mahtab's performance. He rushes toward her and whispers a few words in her ear with a horrified face despite his efforts to look calm. He then turns briskly and scurries toward and up the stairs without peering at anybody. Mahtab, agitated and puzzled by his bizarre behaviour, charges to the drawing room and returns with her parents, already pale at the sudden commotion. They follow Bijan.

Gradually the guests gather at the bottom of the stairs, looking up with anguish and curiosity. Other than some random whispers, they remain silent with anticipation. A few elderly moves forward and occupies the first few steps. Heavy thumps and loud screams from upstairs further alarm the audience downstairs. Like many spectators, Darren presumes a serious conflict has possibly risen between Bijan and Mahtab; maybe a case of infidelity. Maybe the chaos is related to his case, which is now getting out of control and affecting the lives of those who have tried to save him. *Still, how serious any of these scenarios could be to warrant such an urgent uproar right in the middle of the party?* Darren wonders with both horror and humour.

After twenty minutes of agonizing suspense, Bijan appears at the top of the stairs with a dismal face. He staggers down half the stairs lethargically, halts, gasps, and garbles a few words. The crowd seems not to hear or believe him, so they put their hands behind their ears or raise their arms in objection. Bijan speaks louder. A few guests scream, some run toward him in despair and disbelief, and a couple of women grab him and shake him like a tree. The rest freeze and shiver awhile before clustering closer to Bijan or sitting on the floor or stairs, howling and weeping. Promptly the foyer is a scene of mayhem and mourning, unlike anything Darren has ever experienced before in his life. About a hundred people suddenly embracing and shaking each other, screaming and crying as if the world is about to end this minute. Bijan remains motionless in the middle of the stairs with a pale face, probably feeling responsible and guilty for so much pain, as if devil had hired him for this particular occasion. He raises his head eventually and notices Darren, standing a little further from the crowd in absolute panic, stunned by the uproar. Bijan forces himself to regain his composure, descends the rest of the stairs, and approaches Darren with tension.

"Let's go out," Bijan commands, clutching his arm firm and pushing him toward the portico, again reminding Darren of the Evin's guards.

Darren is now sure this mayhem relates to his case and Bijan is taking him back to the prison that very instant. However, he feels helpless to resist since the initial shock from the scene has already numbed him. Outside, Bijan leads him toward the gazebo with fast strides, asks him to sit down, pauses awhile, and then at last murmurs swiftly, "Mahroo is dead."

"What…? What're you talking about?" cries Darren.

"There'd been an incident at the rehabilitation center and she got injured. She passed away in hospital."

"What incident? Poor girl! Oh, my God!" Darren feels dizzier and leans back in the chair to avoid collapsing. Everything is turning fast around him and human images hover in midair; most peculiarly, Vincent's.

"Listen, Darren… I understand your concern and feelings, but poor Mahroo is gone now and we must be strong for Reza and the rest of the family. I can't spend any time with you now. Let's find my driver to take you to Reza's apartment. Reza is still at the hospital. Sorry I couldn't explain your case tonight but I'll do it soon. Meanwhile, don't go out or contact anybody until we get a chance to talk. Okay?"

Darren finds it inappropriate to argue at such a horrific time. The catastrophe has shaken him too much to even think about his case at this moment, whatever it may be. So, he nods with sorrow and disappointment paralyzing him.

3

In Reza's apartment, Darren finds food and a half-empty bottle of wine. He pours some into a mug and plummets onto the couch, wondering how Mahroo could have vanished in a puff. Her poor family… How horrible they must be feeling now, losing such a wonderful woman so unexpectedly. *Even when we figure out our passion and life philosophies, and risk expressing them, destiny spoils our entire sense of enlightenment with another challenge. So, what's the point of all these struggles to refine our thoughts and feelings? Aren't we just thinking toys in the hand of God for His playful adventures?* He can hardly walk to bed after finishing the wine on top of the drinks he had consumed earlier at Bijan's house, and considering his exhausted body and mind after Evin.

4

The telephone shriek awakens Darren the next morning. With a pounding headache, he is disoriented for ten seconds until his mind processes the sequence of recent events gradually and he realizes he is not in Vancouver, prison, or Bijan's house, but in Reza's apartment… and Mahroo has died. He trembles after a big jolt. Recalling Bijan's order not to speak with anybody, he wonders whether he should answer the phone or not. It stops ringing and the answering machine turns on. "Pick it up, Darren. This is Reza."

He runs to the phone in the living room. "How are you?"

"You can imagine. I'm devastated like the whole family," Reza replies and begins howling.

"I'm so sorry… I know how you must be feeling."

"Thanks, Darren… Bijan and I are going to the Centre to find out what exactly had happened. Bijan's driver, Ahmad, will bring you hot meals regularly over the next few days while I'm with my family for mourning and the funeral. Things will be hectic for a few days; please excuse me for abandoning you."

"But I want to share your grief."

"It'll be boring for you to be here, with women chanting and chatting non-stop. Bijan and I will be busy, making funeral arrangements and investigating the incident."

"Am I under house arrest, then, or I can go out at least?"

"Bijan says somebody may harm you. That's all I know."

Darren takes two aspirins from the medicine cabinet. The idea of house arrest at the time he needs consolation feels awful. His condition has not improved much from Evin, despite the finer living condition and access to good meals and music. He could at least talk with his cellmates and Dervish Ali at Evin. Restless, he walks across the room with tension when a disturbing thought startles and halts him near the window: Could Dervish Ali's curse be blamed for Mahroo's untimely demise? Does some Supreme Authority or God listen to everybody's or some blessed people's curses and grant their demon wishes? "There's a divine justice, Darren, after all, I promise," spiteful Dervish Ali had prophesied.

Damn Dervish Ali! Damn, damn, damn!

Despite his dire despise toward Dervish for not forgiving Mahroo, he also misses him and wonders about his condition. Nobody would have time to help poor Dervish or follow his case now, until it is probably too late. *On the other hand, maybe he now deserves to die in Evin! He's done it to himself!* He then recalls his two plans he had mentioned to Dervish Ali: To love Mahroo and to paint—neither of them a viable option now. *Back to the drawing board. How Mahroo and her promise about his life becoming fantastic from now on were evaporated just in a few hours!*

Why did you break your promise, my darling saint? Darren whines and weeps.

5

The Director of the Centre invites Reza and Bijan to his office to explain the incident based on witnesses' corroboration.

"Apparently, Mahroo had had a telephone conversation that afternoon with her boyfriend or fiancée, who'd encouraged her to take time off from work. One of the patients, who had apparently been too keen about Mahroo, had overheard her talking with her colleagues about taking two weeks off to entertain a *special* man. Most war amputees are suicidal due to their traumas, but this guy had come with much greater emotional turmoil after losing his legs in the war. Mostly Mahroo's tenderness had calmed him, to the amazement of the staff. She had made a special impact on him, as some kind of refuge for curbing his suicidal tendency.

"The news about Mahroo's likely love affair and departure for good (or at least a long holiday) triggers his emotional imbalance and he slits his wrists with a box-cutter he'd stolen a few days earlier from the handyman. Another patient notices him, screams, and the staff rush to help. Mahroo gets too close to calm him. As she bends to grab his hand in one jerky motion, the guy flings his arm reactively and the box-cutter slashes deep through Mahroo's neck and aorta. She bleeds excessively by the time the ambulance arrives and takes her to the hospital. In the hospital, doctors try to revive her, but, despite some promising vital signs, she cannot be saved. The guy is in critical condition as well, but would most likely survive, now with more scars."

6

Early in the afternoon, Reza calls and gives Darren an account of the incident leading to Mahroo's dismal destiny.

'The guy had gone nuts after overhearing Mahroo's request for time off to entertain her boyfriend,' Reza had stressed in a rather heavy, sarcastic tone that had burned Darren's brain. *Was he sarcastic or I'm only imagining it?* Anyhow, now he is left with a gush of guilt for Mahroo's death on top of his seclusion.

Drinking a bottle of wine and sobbing loosen up the knot clogging his throat. But his guilty conscience hurts even deeper. He imagines a joyous Mahroo bragging to her colleagues about going away with her boyfriend right before collapsing with a slashed throat and waning eyes one moment later. An eerie image of the whole family glaring at him, cornered against the wall, gasping for air, haunts him.

Why did I ask her to take time off? Stupid! But how could I have known? I'm not responsible for this too, am I? Maybe the whole family is blaming me for it already, though Reza didn't say anything directly. Nobody will probably mention it. But they all know it and think about it. I know it myself for sure... I know what I've done. I finally killed Mahroo! First, I drove her crazy with my painting, then depressed her with my communication and attitude, and now finally she's dead, because I tried to be romantic at last. I can't even be sentimental anymore without killing people. Me and my big mouth!

He feels sick and hungry, but needs some fresh air more than anything else before suffocating. The apartment now feels even smaller than those dungeons in Evin. *This entire damn incident, including my new pains, probably relates to Dervish Ali's curse on both of us.*

Soon, Ahmad arrives with two pots of warm food and a big platter of vegetables and fruits.

"Take me to Bijan's house," he asks Ahmad after deciding to take the initiative of rescuing himself from the house arrest.

"No, I go... some place not... house of Mr. Bijan."

"Can't you take me before or after you finish your errands?"

"No," Ahmad exclaims somewhat rudely and scrams before Darren gets a chance to insist. His rough reaction indicates the severity of the instructions given him, but also the chance that even he had been apprised of Darren's guilt for Mahroo's demise. Even Ahmad hates him apparently.

The house arrest sounds serious. But he is tired of being cooped up for two weeks on planes, in prison, and now here. The thought of Mahroo is pounding his brain, too, despite the aspirins he has taken regularly all day.

Eating some food calms his growling stomach and gradually reduces his thumping headache and tension. He can think a little clearer now: Well, nobody has quite forbidden him to leave the apartment, although they had probably implied it. *Did they?* As far as he remembers, the instruction was "not to contact or talk to anybody." And that—how did they put it?—someone may harm him! But the walls are closing in on him, about to crush his brain.

He peers outside the window and the park near their building grabs his attention. As usual, the streets are filled with cars racing carelessly and pedestrians challenging them bravely as they cross the street, like a bunch of matadors eluding the angry, rushing bulls with similar agility and gestures. Considering the shock of losing Mahroo, a quick stroll without talking to people, while remaining vigilant, must be an acceptable compromise! *I can't sit here, not even another minute,* he shrieks. *I'll go for a short stroll and return before anybody misses me.*

Charging toward the door, the sight of small picture frames lined up on the television startles him. He picks up and peers closely at the two holding Mahroo's and Mahtab's pictures. Their resemblance is astonishing. Touching the photos punctures his nerves again and he shudders. The thought that one of those beautiful women no longer exists brings tears back into his eyes. He kisses Mahroo's picture and bids her farewell with love. Steaming emotions clench his face muscles and tears sluice down his cheek. He puts the pictures back with a weird, funny thought: *I hope I didn't kiss the wrong picture!* He flees the apartment with a sad sense of guilt, this time for disobeying Bijan's instructions. He locks the door carefully and drops the key in his pocket.

Drawing upon his experiences of living in Tehran, he crosses the street by zigzagging around the speeding cars with utmost diligence and bravery. He does not even look for a crosswalk, not from fearlessness or feeling suicidal, but because he knows it is hardly useful or even wise. In fact, intersections could be quite dangerous because not only drivers try to merge quickly or speed through a changing traffic light, but also they are not accustomed to pedestrians at crosswalks as their main means of crossing streets. *What kind of an idiot would cross the street right at a busy intersection?* Darren chuckles at his own untimely (or quite timely!) sense of humour.

More gloom engulfs him upon stepping into the park, though. The fallen and loosely hanging leaves, in the dying shades of orange to brown, depict autumn and death. The stinky air exudes the smell and taste of the fumes from the worn-out car mufflers. Still, he plans to make the best of his brief freedom before returning to the suite. He takes long strides and stretches his arms playfully to cover more space with his body, as if stealing more freedom by expanding physically. The thought of Mahroo's death is haunting him. So he decides to distract his brain awhile. The first thought that rolls in his head is Bijan's orders, which swiftly make him paranoid about an imminent danger.

He slows down to survey the park. The bird's-eye view from Reza's suite on the fifteenth floor had showed it surrounded by major streets, though he cannot see any of them from his present viewpoint. A large crowd lingers leisurely and a few people rush toward a street on another side of the park. Some rest on benches, some lean against a tree, and some lurch along a path. Besides furtive glances and glares, everybody seems locked in his or her own thoughts—a normal state of affairs. Except… Except for a young man leaning behind a tree in the far distance and peeping stealthily toward him, as if playing hide and seek with someone. Yet, the manner of ducking his head when Darren gazes in his direction hints that the subject of the game may be Darren. He ponders returning to the apartment, but this requires walking right up to the man and a possible encounter. So, he decides to hurry to the far end of the park and take a side street back to the suite. He wishes he had brought a sweater as it is getting windy, dark clouds amassing overhead and diminishing the daylight quickly.

He takes longer strides, halting every few paces to check his back. Every time, the man darts behind a tree. Darren rubs his eyes and gazes toward the tree to study *the image* teasing him. With people's constant mingling and tree branches wobbling in the mild wind, spooky shadows are scattered on the grass and paths and make any image in the distance look blurry. Maybe he is imagining things due to Bijan's warnings. Yet, losing his safe distance from the culprit feels unwise. So he keeps sprinting, panting, and checking behind him for ten horrific minutes. At last, he exits the park onto another jammed street with drivers honking their cars' horns and cursing each other. He has lost his sense of direction, uncertain to charge up or down the street. Time is running out fast and the image might be closing in on him. So he scurries aimlessly in one direction and then turns into a side street.

Darren halts to catch his breath and pinpoint the image amidst the sunset shadows sheathing the sidewalks and limiting his sight. Some cars' intense headlights are also starting to blur his vision and concealing the man chasing him in the growing mass of real and illusory figures. Hiding or running appears futile since the source or direction of the danger is unknown. Still his legs appear to have a mind of their own, sprinting illogically. He gasps a big breath and retries to discern his whereabouts and the path to the suite. Soon a light rain begins and pastes his shirt to his sweaty body. He craves the opportunity of returning to the house arrest status, instead of wandering aimlessly in the rain and wondering about his destination and dreadful destiny. Nonetheless, standing still or even slowing down feels risky. So far, he has inspected a few main and side streets and none of them resembles Reza's. He does not know its name to ask someone for help, either.

Without somebody's address or telephone number, an ID, or money, the situation appears hopeless. He curses himself for his shortsightedness, though he had merely intended to catch some fresh air and stroll only a short distance in the park. *What should I do now?* No idea emerges except for a crazy one: That the only person able to help him now is the man chasing him. What an irony! The enemy he has been eluding all this time is the only person who can recognize him and settle their conflict one way or another. Confrontation is the best option in this circumstance, despite Bijan's warnings. Only the enemy can rescue him. If he intends to harm Darren, at least he will find out why—an answer that Bijan has been unable to provide so far. Maybe Darren can convince him to accept compensation for the damage he might have caused him, and in return, appreciating Darren's goodwill to put things right, he would take him back to where they had begun this game. This man probably knows where the apartment is, most likely having shadowed Darren from the beginning. He is at the mercy of his stalker, and if he deserves a punishment for whatever he might have done, maybe it is more honourable and easier to accept his guilt gracefully rather than running from it forever. But it is just impossible to slow down; his legs remaining carelessly illogical. At a side street, as Darren turns to check the oncoming traffic, his right ankle twists and he hits the wet asphalt in the middle of the road like a dead bird.

An excruciating pain soars all over his body while his dignity sours immensely. He tries to rise and regain his pride in front of the pedestrians, some of whom have stopped to help, wondering if he is a homeless drunk. But as he puts his right foot down to carry some weight, he collapses in pain again—a hint that his ankle has twisted or broken. Grinning idiotically at the spectators, he leaps on his left foot in one jerky motion. With the right foot dangling in midair, he hops to the corner of the street, steps up on the sidewalk, and leans against a wall. Some people murmur around him in Persian, but soon they scatter.

He reattempts to put some weight on his toes or the heel of the right foot, to no avail; the pain is excruciating, just for touching the ground, let alone accepting any weight. Soon his left foot goes numb and aches from excess pressure. He considers finding a thick stick to help him limp, but realizes swiftly that not even a well-crafted cane can do the job. Only crutches might help. His wet shirt is covered with mud and his pants are torn around the knees, blood simmering from the bruised skin. His right shoe has stayed behind, near the corner he had collapsed, but he loathes to go fetch it. He leans against the wall, but soon his left foot falters and he slithers to the ground gradually. His leg, stretched partly across the sidewalk, obstructs people's movements. A few hit it accidentally and he screams in pain. So they stop and throw him money, assuming he is a lame beggar, either too helpless to move his leg out of the way or merely an arrogant showman. When he tries to object or explain by raising his hand and returning the money, they presume he is haggling for more—as all Persian beggars do. So they either throw him more money or just ignore or curse him.

Darren pulls his leg out of the way with difficulty and lays it near the wall. He is cold in his muddy shirt and ragged pants. He squeezes his arms over his chest and droops. His dismal stance near the wall and the money scattered in front of him, assures passers-by more pertinently that he is a beggar. So they contribute passionately to his loot. This much humiliation and anguish is uncalled for, and all for what? Mahroo's face appears in his tired mind, laughing about his misfortunes and the funny circumstance he has brought upon himself. Her image and laughter aggravates his distress, especially the pain of her death. He raises his hand and cries, "I came here for you; now see what has become of me without you. Laugh, my beloved; I'm glad I can entertain you on your way to heaven." Pedestrians assume he is complaining to God or cursing Him, which shows his level of misery and lunacy. So they throw him more money. *Is this really what you meant when you promised me my life would be fantastic now that I was here ready to love you?* Darren cannot stop thinking and whining about Mahroo's broken promise.

He looks in the direction the man had been chasing him, wishing God would send him over promptly, to hurt him or help him. Either way, it would be a better option and more honourable than sitting here in pain helplessly. Even if he hurts him, at least someone might take him to a hospital or morgue. Yet, there is no sign of the man Darren had been trying to elude with his crafty manoeuvres. His success has backfired miserably and he must now suffer the consequence. The man would probably not even recognize him in such a pathetic position if he comes around. He chuckles at the idea of having to call the guy himself, if he shows, and swear that this soaked, cripple beggar in such rugged outfit is in fact Darren.

Asking someone to take him to a police station would not help, either, even if somebody cared to listen to his plea. Without an ID, address, or telephone number, they will just send him to jail immediately. "No, no, please, no jail again," he cries to God. And people throw him more money.

The only information he remembers are Reza's and the gallery owner's names. Even if the police believed him, it would not be possible to locate Reza or anybody else quickly. The Iranian police surely have many higher priorities than looking for people at night or helping a foreign beggar even if they spoke English. The Canadian Consulate is probably closed at this hour, even if he accepted the humiliation of contacting them in such a pitiful stance. So, the best option is to rest awhile, to regain both his mental and physical energy, then try to move toward the apartment, even if he must crawl.

He rubs his sprained ankle gently despite the pain. He also tries to boost his spirit by thinking positively, reminding himself of the power of mind. He recalls the true story of a man who had gotten trapped under a big log in the woods somewhere in British Columbia, cut off his own foot with a small knife to free himself, and then crawled a long distance to the main road to be rescued. Darren's situation is not remotely as bad. Not showing similar resilience would be a big failure. After half an hour, he believes he has rested, meditated, and massaged his foot enough. It is time to put his plan into action and behave like a man. Leaning against the wall, he manages to stand up on his left foot, ready to put the right foot down. But the second it touches the ground, he realizes the absurdity of his plan and positive thinking. *Fuck positive thinking,* he swears!

Slithering down the wall again awkwardly, he realizes the grimness of his situation and the need for exploring a practical option. Hopping on the left foot all the way to the apartment might be an easier and more dignified option than crawling. But the apartment would be at least twenty minutes away at a fast pace, which means at least one hour of hopping, considering the need to rest every few minutes. That would not be too bad if he knew the direction of the apartment. However, hopping aimlessly in all directions, hoping to find the apartment eventually, would be too risky. He may end up going the wrong direction and facing weirdoes dying to mess with freaky foreigners. There must be better ways. "Mahroo, please help!" he pleads while holding his head and mediating.

Swiftly he cocks his head with delight as a plan crosses his mind: He will take a taxi and ask the driver to go around the park, which should be somewhere close by, very slowly, as many times as necessary, until he locates the building. It is adjacent to one side of the park, although he does not remember which side. Some minor details must be worked out, though. He already knows two kinds of taxis operate in Tehran: First, those carrying up to five random passengers at a time and running on specific routes along the main streets. So they cannot be used for a private excursion around the park. The second choice is to call a cab agency. But he neither knows his present location nor has access to a phone. No public phone is in sight and no shops or public places are in the vicinity to ask for a favour.

At last, he rationalizes the number of passengers taking the regular taxis will soon decline and he will be able to find an empty one and convince the driver to go around the park with the money people have thrown for him. In fact, waiting another hour to find an empty taxi will also assist in collecting more money. He is uncertain about the cost of going a few rounds around the park, considering the high rate of inflation in this country. He giggles at the thought of conceding to begging out of necessity. *Now I must really put my heart into it. The best way is to keep shouting at God and Mahroo and shaking my fist in the air.*

Despite his condition, he feels proud of his ingenuity to work out a plausible plan as well as his wittiness in such a humiliating condition! So he droops into meditation to gain more strength, spirit, and cash. Occasionally, he screams at God and Mahroo as a person approaches him. He ponders the details of his plan for finding his shoe and an empty cab to begin the search. Shivering and cursing his fortune, about to initiate his scheme, a familiar voice from the distance startles him: "Darren! Is that you?"

The sound of 'Darren' feels magical. Somebody out there knows him, someone who can take him home. He raises his head and recognizes Reza's car at the edge of the street. He is leaning toward the passenger seat and peering through the open window with absolute bafflement. Darren flings his hand, acknowledging Reza but also thanking God for sending a saviour. Reza gets out of the car and rushes toward him. "What's happened to you?"

Darren is speechless because of the cold, tension, and thrill of being rescued at last. Reza helps him rise carefully and notices his limping. He wraps Darren's arm over his shoulder to hop his way to the car.

"Take my shoe out of that ditch, please," he mutters, settling in the car.

Reza finds the shoe and the pile of money where he had been sitting. "Is this money yours too?" he shouts from the sidewalk.

"Yeah, it's mine. I've earned it!" Darren yells impatiently.

Reza shoves the money into the muddy shoe and drops it in the trunk.

"You drove us crazy with worry. We've been searching the neighbourhood for two hours; Ahmad and I have been checking the restaurants and the park."

"Sorry…"

"Are you badly hurt? Should we go to the hospital?"

"No, let's go home," Darren says. "Only my ankle is probably twisted."

"Did somebody do this to you?"

"No."

"You did it to yourself?"

"Yeah!"

"You did? Why…?" Reza pauses, startled by a thought, he continues, "Is this all because of Mahroo?"

"I guess!"

"Oh, poor Darren! I had no idea… We couldn't imagine the incident would affect you this much. I'm sorry for not including you in our mourning. But you must now get hold of yourself and be more rational. Nothing can bring Mahroo back. The accident has happened and she's sadly left us."

Darren is in pain and exhausted already, but the way Reza has interpreted his remark sounds like another mix-up, which revives bad memories in his pounding head. Reza is always the cause of misunderstandings, directly or indirectly, and now he has started a situation that may get out of control again. Naturally, Darren loved Mahroo in his own way, but he would never blame or hurt himself for her death, the way Reza had put it. All he had meant to imply in response to Reza's question, "Whether he'd hurt himself because of Mahroo," was that he has been enduring all these traumas because of his trip to Tehran to see Mahroo and test the meaning of their infatuation. However, he is too exhausted to explain his words or how he had gotten lost and twisted his ankle. Also, under the circumstances—the mourning and the mood of the family, especially Reza's—it would be rather rude to bargain about the depth of his love for Mahroo. Besides, he will be scolded for disregarding Bijan's implied prohibition to leave the suite if he cannot present a strong emotional reason or proof of temporary insanity. So, he shuts his mouth, hoping that it will be the end of that absurd conversation.

"You mustn't blame yourself too much, either," Reza says after witnessing enough of Darren's pensive silence.

He loathes Reza's remark—as if he should blame himself a little at least, anyway. Even worse, it seems the family is in fact blaming him! Maybe he blames himself slightly, but not enough to hurt himself. Still, he keeps his mouth shut.

Ahmad is waiting in front of the building, looking even madder at Darren—now for having to spend so much time looking for him on top of all his previous reasons. He and Reza carry the crippled, soaked, frozen Darren upstairs, help him take a shower, and put him in bed with his right foot elevated on two pillows. They then serve him hot soup and watch him eat it in gloomy silence. By now Ahmad looks absolutely pissed, while examining the money in Darren's lost shoe!

"What should I do with this shoe and the money inside it?" Ahmad asks in Persian.

"Leave the money on table and send the shoes for a polish." He then turns to Darren, "What's the story with the money?"

"People thought I was a beggar. You know, I've now learned a lot of tricks about panhandling. If you object to people or raise your hand and talk to God like a lunatic, they'll give you more money. So if I can't be a painter, at least I'm already good at panhandling."

"So you've been sitting in the rain and complaining to God all night? You poor man!" Reza asks even more earnestly.

Darren stares at him blankly in despair, speechless.

"I'd better call Bijan and tell him we've found you. He was really worried that something terrible might've happened to you," Reza says and leaves the room.

Darren sighs, bemused about the events manifesting around him and the remarks thrown at him rather sarcastically. He likes to object perhaps, but decides to stay cool. As he closes his eyes with despair, suddenly another crazy idea crosses his psychotic, witty mind in relation to the possibility of Dervish Ali's fatal curse on Mahroo. Is it now time to disclose Dervish's betrayal, just to set family's minds straight and exonerate himself in the process, too. *It's all Dervish's fault, not mine!* At last, he decides not to mention this ludicrous thought to Reza or anybody else, either, even at the cost of bearing all the blame himself. *Am I such a tactful gentleman or what?!* Yet, in a sickening way, this thought at least relieves some of his own sense of guilt about Mahroo's demise. Should he now only blame Dervish Ali forever? Has he been an agent to fulfil Dervish Ali's curse?

Reza talks on the phone a long time, apparently explaining Darren's condition and confession (about his messed up emotions and temporary insanity) when he was found. Walking restlessly all over the suite with his cordless phone, he pauses and stares intently and pitifully at Darren in bed whenever he passes by the guestroom.

"I just talked to Bijan," Reza says as he enters the room at last. "He'll send a maid and I'll buy a pair of crutches for you."

"Reza, I'm sorry for Mahroo and you, really," Darren says with tears gathering in his sad, tired eyes.

"I know. But nobody blames you, of course; remember that," Reza says. "I'm sorry if repeating the story of Mahroo's request for holiday to spend time with you gave you a guilty feeling."

"That's all right. I know you didn't mean to blame me too much, but I've caused a disaster indirectly, anyhow, and I realize it," Darren replies now tears actually rolling down his face.

"Let's stop fussing over the cause of Mahroo's death, Darren," Reza says. "Her death was just another kind of war casualty."

"Okay, I'll try...," Darren murmurs, glad for stopping his big mouth, again and again, from uttering his suspicion about the real cause of Mahroo's demise—Dervish Ali's curse.

But if the idea of cursing holds water, maybe Elizabeth, Erica, and Nora have put their curses on him, too, for ignoring their love pleas! These funny thoughts remind him that he has not called Elizabeth since leaving Vancouver. Strangely, she has not called him, either. He checks his watch and calculates Vancouver's time to be around ten a.m. and Elizabeth being at work. So he pledges to himself to call her later.

"I'll be busy in preparation for Mahroo's funeral, if the body is released and we get a death certificate, etc.," Reza says.

"Okay…"

"I'll come and get you for the ceremony. Now rest and put some of these depressing thoughts out of your mind for a few hours at least." He comes forward and kisses Darren's cheek. "You're a good man, Darren. You're a good man!" Reza says affectionately while struggling to hide his tears.

"You're a good friend…," Darren says.

"I've connected this telephone," pointing to the one on the night table. "Answer only after you recognize the voice on the answering machine. I'll see you soon."

All night, Darren wrestles with the pain of the twisted ankle while trying to keep it stable and elevated, yet he manages to sleep enough after learning to keep the damaged ankle steady even in sleep.

7

Darren wakes up late with the smell of coffee coming from the kitchen, swiftly reminding him of a similar experience a few weeks earlier with Elizabeth. The aroma is mixed with a strong fragrance of flowers, though. He decides to call Elizabeth before he forgets again. He dials the number, gazing at his watch and calculating the time to be ten p.m. in Vancouver.

"Hi, Elizabeth…"

"You promised to call when you got there… two weeks ago?"

"I was in prison."

"Oh, my dear… Why?"

"I don't know the charge yet, but I'm out on bail now!"

"What kind of prison?"

"How many kinds are there?"

"Well, I thought all along, when you didn't call, that maybe another woman has kidnapped or captivated you…"

"Don't be silly," Darren says with stress.

"So why would they put you in jail? Maybe you've actually been busy with something or somebody?"

"I'm not joking, Elizabeth. I'm telling you the truth."

"So why don't you know the charge? It sounds fishy to me."

"Listen, I really don't have much time and I'm not in the mood to argue with you or prove anything on the phone. I've been forced to feel guilty about many other stuff already."

"Guilty about what? What's going on, Darren," she asks.

"I'll tell you everything later. Any news in Vancouver?"

"Actually an Oriental guy with a beard knocked on our door last week. He asked when you'll return."

"Thank you. I'll talk to you later," Darren says, reluctant to add any sentimental expression before hanging up. Considering Mahroo's tragedy and prison experiences still torturing him, he is annoyed by Elizabeth's childish accusations. Expressing any kind of affection when he is not trusted feels unnatural. *Although I've not been the symbol of honesty, either!* He decides not to mention Mahroo's death at this time, either, in case Reza wishes to break the news to Erica and T.J. himself.

The maid knocks on the door. "Breakfast? Yes?"

"Yes, okay."

After delivering a large tray with eggs, toast, and coffee, she returns with a big flower basket and a pair of crutches. Darren opens the card attached to the flowers and reads the handwritten message:

> *Your affection for Mahroo is precious to me*
> *and my family at this trying time.*
> *Please take care of yourself, and we'll see*
> *you soon. With love! Mahtab.*

He is deeply touched by Mahtab's gracious gesture, and for being included in their grief, despite the possibility of family still blaming him for Mahroo's fatal request for time off. Reza's long explanation of his condition in the streets last night, apparently mourning Mahroo alone in his own way, must have caused this development. Eyes blurred from tears and throat clogged by the rushing flood of passion, he asks the maid to put the tray on the table and help him try the crutches. In the living room, he faces the greatest spectacle of his life: The apartment is filled with flowers for him, from Reza, Mahroo's parents, relatives, and even a small basket from Nazi. Awestricken, he lingers breathless and unsteady on the crutches, unable to recall so much affection in his life. *How can I ever respond?*

Having had hardly enough time to digest all this passion, a deeper parade of affection overwhelms him later in the afternoon when family shows up. Each one comes forward and kisses him as if sanctioning a belated wedding between Mahroo and him. *Great! Now I'm married to a corpse!* They stay two hours and recount many stories about Mahroo, especially her childhood and immeasurable sensitivity, mostly for his benefit it seems, as if bringing him up-to-date quickly, *for joining her soon with all the useful information apparently!*

Despite their gloomy mood, they keep recounting Darren's love ordeal in the streets. Reza recites an exaggerated account of the event and the shape he had found him in—his shoe lost in the ditch, Darren shivering from cold and pain, squeezing his body against the wall, and the money thrown at him when he flung his hand, complaining to God. In some instances, the family laugh their hearts out, imagining him with his torn-up pants and muddy shirt, lying in the rainy street. Although he does not comprehend Reza's energetic presentation in Persian, he laughs along with them, glad that the story of his misery in the streets is generating some relief for the family in this time of grief.

"Do you people wanna know what my only regret is besides Mahroo's demise?" Reza asks the crowd in English mostly to raise Darren's attention.

"Yes...," Mahtab and a few other relatives reply or nod.

"I wish I had a camera to take a few dozen pictures from him and the whole scene—the money, the shoe, and all the rest," Reza replies and the crowd bursts into laughter.

Before leaving, the family advise him about the funeral ritual. Reza tells him he should now behave like one of the men in the family. Darren wonders what the heck he exactly means, but then attributes his comment as merely another gesture of inclusion and gratitude for Darren's affection.

Chapter Fourteen
The Portraitist

1

The funeral procession is immense. A long queue of fancy automobiles solemnly follows the hearse and limousines carrying Mahroo and immediate family. In a black suit and tie borrowed from Reza, Darren rides in the second limousine. The caravan takes two hours to reach Behesht Zahra with the excruciating slow movement in the heavy traffic.

The burial grounds are deftly developed with symmetrical rows of tall poplars extending throughout in a serene garden—a delightful atmosphere for resting in peace. But as the cars stop, a chaos erupts with a big wave of howling, black clad mourners pursuing Mahroo's flesh wrapped in a white shroud and carried on a stretcher atop the relatives' shoulders. The scene reminds Darren of a similar picture in his dream—the dark clad Masters lifting the woman in the white dress, cheering, and helping her disembark their ship under the moonlight. The sound of passion today, however, is glum in the form of moaning, screaming, and chanting in the graveyard under the burning sun. It turns louder and gloomier with every few steps Mahroo's flesh approaches the grave, reaching its height when it is lowered slowly to the bottom of the pit. The shrouded body is put directly in the grave without a coffin, according to the Islamic law, the face exposed to dust: From dust to dust we come and go.

Some female relatives are clinging to the soil surrounding the grave, crying their hearts out. Peeling them off the ground is cumbersome, yet a job for men to tackle customarily nonetheless. Darren attempts to show his gratitude and courtesy by doing his share of moving Mahroo's mother and Mahtab away from the grave. His gesture, while facing the chance of toppling in the grave himself if his crutches crumble, looks bleakly funny. Yet he feels obliged to behave like all other busy men in the family, based on Reza's order. He wonders how much he or the crowd would care if he actually topples, or is pushed, into the grave next to Mahroo and they put all that soil on top of them, intentionally or without noticing his fall. Eventually, the caravan is on the move again toward Bijan's house, where a reception is held throughout the afternoon and well into the night. Early in the evening, when the situation with the mourners has settled down somewhat, Bijan fetches Darren to his study.

"I'm sorry our conversation was interrupted the other night," he says as Darren sits on the couch. "I must rush now to explain everything before another catastrophe stops me."

"Yes, please… I appreciate it."

"After Reza asked me to investigate your case, it took me three days just to find the right source and another two days for him to finally get a permission to explain the problem. And all of this became possible only because of my father's influence in this country; otherwise nobody could've helped you. I'm not saying this to brag or make you feel indebted to me. Only I would like to explain two things…"

"What?" Darren asks timidly.

"First of all, the people who've brought the case against you are as powerful as my father, and second, you're the only person who can verify the accuracy of the story they've told me."

"I'll tell you whatever I know."

"Do you know Sima Ibrahimi?"

"Yes, I remember her," Darren replies with agitation. "Why?"

"Apparently she lived with her parents in the same building you did."

"Yes, that's right."

"And you two started an affair."

"Just a casual one."

"Well, the meaning of 'casual' depends on person and culture. First of all, she was only seventeen years old—"

"But she looked older; she said twenty," he interrupts Bijan.

"And she was a virgin too. Right?"

"When I found out, I tried to terminate our relationship. But she insisted it didn't matter, even if our affair wasn't serious."

"And still you continued this relationship, anyway. Right?"

"She wouldn't leave me alone. She was jealous of my friends and kept bugging me any way she could."

"Okay, then what?" Bijan asks.

"We fought often. She dropped in as she pleased and expected me to entertain her. Gradually, she went nuts and got nastier."

"All because of your love, I presume?"

"More like a psychotic obsession. God knows how much I reasoned with her or rejected her, tactfully or harshly."

"But you still let this relationship continue?"

"I wouldn't call it a relationship. We met periodically, since no other strategy worked on her. Seeing her seemed to be the best way to keep her big mouth shut. She just wore me down and I wore her down. We both gave up and left ourselves to fate."

"And then you impregnated her?"

"What? What are you talking about?"

"So you didn't know you have a son?"

"I have a son?"

"Yes! But you're sure she didn't mention her pregnancy?"

"Yes, I'm sure."

"When did you two last have sex?"

"Let's see… Probably a month before I left Tehran."

"So she's probably telling the truth. He's really your son."

"I guess so."

"Anyway, she kept her pregnancy a secret until it was just too late to abort it and her parents found out about it. Her uncle is the influential man I told you about. He has a very high position in government affairs, especially for war-related matters. Sima's parents and uncle studied her options, one of which was to find you and make you marry her, but in the end, they decided to keep the matter confidential and hide her from the rest of the family until the baby was born two months ago. They then invented a story about the baby being adopted when his family had perished in a missile attack. The uncle had supposedly convinced Sima's parents to adopt him out of the goodness of their hearts in line with the government's plea to find homes for the war orphans." Bijan pauses, lights a cigarette, opens the patio door, and sits on the chair near the window to let the smoke out.

Amazed and amused by the news, Darren blurts, "Wow, it feels so weird, having a son. Just imagining it gives me a thrill."

"That's exactly where the problem begins," Bijan interjects.

"What? They want me to adopt my son, or marry Sima?"

"No. They want you out of here." Bijan stops for another puff. "The family had no idea whether you really knew about the baby or not, and couldn't guarantee that Sima wouldn't tell you if for any reason you happened to be in Tehran and met her again. Not only is the family getting attached to the baby and don't want any possible complications separate the baby from them, but also they don't want their secret to come out. So they don't want you near Sima or the baby under any circumstance. And to ensure all that, the uncle put your name on the list of suspected criminals who must be arrested at the airport. That was the only way to know about your arrival and keep you on a leash. They intended to punish you a little, too, before sending you back if you agreed to never return to Tehran—maybe even without telling you about your son in case you didn't know already. Discovering drugs on you gave them the added ammunition to build a strong case against you. They could also let you rot in prison, or find a silly, indirect way of getting rid of you. So, you're lucky you knew Reza, and with my father's influence, we've at least been able to learn the whole truth and get you out of the prison for now."

Darren says with frustration, "I won't cause any problem, but these people taking my son hostage upsets me a little."

"You're showing exactly the kind of reaction they expected from you if you knew or learned about your son. They had to cover up your big mess and make sure you wouldn't cause new problems. I'm sorry for talking so bluntly, but it seems, with such an emotional issue, everybody, including you, might take drastic actions that could cause irreparable damage."

"But you seem to be taking their side," Darren objects.

"No. That's not true. I'm on your side, but I must be frank to make you understand the severity of the problem we're facing here, and the kind of people you're dealing with. I should also stress that they can hurt you badly if you don't grasp the gravity of the situation, or get too emotional because of your pride or desire to see your son. There're many things you need to know."

"Like what?"

"First of all, my neck is on the line here, since I interfered in this case and have learned about their secret. They felt obliged to tell me everything in order to explain the case against you, but that was a big risk for them by itself—to tell me the truth. For sharing this secret and also letting you out of the prison, I had to promise to not only keep the secret to myself forever, but also make you understand that keeping the secret is the only way all of us can stay out of trouble. You've been placed in my custody since they want to make sure you won't bump into Sima or try to meet her or your son. If anything goes wrong, they'll make me pay for letting you out of my sight. So, I'm in a big bind. To be honest, if you don't like this deal, we can start all over and I'll wash my hands of it by giving you back to them. They'd probably keep you in prison until they find a solution for you. You decide."

Darren considers his dismal position and Bijan's dilemma. "For now, I guess it's logical for me to stay in your custody."

"This means you go out only when and where we agree."

"Fine. I'd better go home now. Do you agree?!" Darren asks half-jokingly.

"Yes, I agree...," Bijan replies with a giggle.

"May I borrow some books from you at least?" Darren asks, surveying the big collection of his books in the study.

"Yes. Choose whatever you like."

Darren rises on one foot to review the books on the shelves.

"Oh, another important matter," Bijan says fretfully. "Sit, please."

Darren plummets onto the couch and gazes at Bijan.

"I have received another piece of information in confidence."

"What's that?" Darren asks.

"Although Sima's parents and uncle have decided to choose a peaceful solution, her brother hasn't come to peace with you or his uncle's decision. I'm told he's quite angry and looking for you to avenge his sister's honour. He knows you're in town and it's hard to guess what he might do. He has his own power and influence, as he's in charge of a branch of the Revolutionary Guards. These people are dangerous, capable of doing anything they desire, and the law is behind them. I guess when it gets into someone's head that a case is a matter of family honour, he gets obsessed and crazy. That's another reason you shouldn't go out or answer the phone. Just be careful until we find a solution soon."

"I had no idea I was so popular! It gets weirder every minute."

"Yes. You're more important than you think," Bijan reiterates. "Now let's go find Ahmad to drive you home. With your twisted ankle, you won't feel too badly about the house arrest. Don't mention our secrets to anybody, not even Reza."

"Okay," Darren says, grabbing his crutches and getting ready to leave. Bijan carries the books Darren has chosen to borrow.

2

Ahmad takes Darren back to Reza's apartment and escorts him all the way inside, based on Bijan's instruction. He seems totally pissed with Darren now, as if finding all these extra services for him too humiliating besides his general loathing for Darren's varied well-established guilt. Slouched on the sofa glumly, Reza appears to have been crying. He grins at Darren, who takes the other corner of the sofa and watches him with compassion.

"Do you recall the moment you felt alive for the first time?" Reza mutters grimly.

"Actually I do. Ironically, it was the day I felt the notion of death deeply for the first time. I was four years old."

"How did it happen?"

"I was strolling down a shady street in spring with my mother and her friend. Near an old house, they slowed down, watched it anxiously, and whispered about a man who'd lived there and just died. I didn't even have to ask about the meaning of death. The tone of their conversation was so bleak I felt the finality of death on the spot. I also sensed my existence only after fearing death, as if shaken up into a 'being' in one instant."

"How did it feel?"

"Which one death or life?" Darren asks wondering about Reza's state of mind.

"Death mostly," Reza replies. "Life is indefinable, anyway."

"It was just a sad notion at that age, but it became more vivid and horrific when I got chickenpox and encountered both God and Azrael in my hallucinations. I was terrified and depressed for a week and asked a lot of silly questions from my parents. Later, my helplessness to find a reasonable logic for this looming reality of existence was quite excruciating. Finally, I guess life's endless enigmas and hassles must've helped me hide this dire eventuality in my subconscious, like everybody else, to find my courage to live; that's the way our ego deals with this harsh reality."

"Of course, our lives get even harder and sadder if we always remember and worry about death," Reza says. "But burying this awful fact in our subconscious makes us neglect our existence."

"Absolutely…," says Darren. "Unless we learn how to work it out within a positive life philosophy."

"Anyhow, Mahroo's death has shaken up both my daily life and beliefs. I'm wasting so much time and energy on business deals and social trivia. My brain is rotting while I'm focusing on work and wealth. Sadly, I've still not learned anything about real life, because I've been brainwashed like most people by norms and vanities so helplessly."

"True. We forget the value and purpose of life until it is too late and we face death."

"I've been confused enough in recent years, but Mahroo's demise has been a big wake-up call for me."

"I hope this sad occasion helps you at least…," Darren says.

3

Other than two meetings with the gallery owner under Ahmad's protection and attending Mahroo's memorial on the sixth day of her death, Darren spends one whole week inside Reza's suite. He tries to amuse himself with books, music, and the notion of being a helpless father. He curses his destiny: The woman he had fallen in love with mysteriously has vanished and the son he can never see has been born. He tries to control his emotions and nerves by drinking more gin, but still the persistent images of a gloomy Mahroo and a lonely boy calling his name make it impossible.

His exhibition opening is the only thing he looks forward to, tentatively. But the only good news about that boring evening is his ability to walk again without the crutches. The exhibition proves disastrous, since Bijan has not allowed publicity for the show in fear of Sima or her brother showing up. Only people on the gallery's private guest list are invited and only one of his paintings sells that night. As if expecting another defeat, he had drunk a great deal of gin in the apartment and remains relatively relaxed, anyhow. He is carefree but slightly withdrawn, which everybody attributes to the recent turmoil in his life, without even knowing about his sudden sullen sense of fatherhood.

After the gallery reception, Bijan invites him, Mahtab, and Reza to a new, fancy restaurant where Darren can taste a special Iranian cuisine. The fresh air and friendly conversation help him mitigate his depression from the dismal gallery reception and to focus on the pleasant company, instead. Bijan refills his glass with soda and makes a toast to him.

Darren grins, raises his glass, and blurts out of the blue: "I'd like to make a toast too… First, to the memory of dear Mahroo, who's probably watching us right now," staring at the ceiling and drinking a big gulp of his drink (so does the rest of the gang). "And second, to all three of you, especially Bijan, for saving me from prison, keeping me safe in house arrest, and showing all that friendly affection." Everybody raises his or her soda glasses.

Pondering a last toast to his son, he quickly realizes that Reza and Mahtab do not know anything about the matter. He controls his tongue in time, while the gang notices his hesitation and gloomy silence. They grin gently and assume his head is a little warm perhaps from drinking Reza's big supply of gin at home. Reza pats his shoulder and Mahtab interjects with a smile, "Now we realize how Mahroo's departure has saddened you. Forgive our ignorance about your affection for her. Not including you in our mourning at the beginning and leaving you alone caused you extra distress. So we owe you an apology in fact."

"Oh, not at all. I'll never forget your kindness. Especially, I owe Bijan a lot. Hopefully I'll pay you back somehow."

"Forget it, Darren. Though the time may come sooner than you think to do me a favour!" Bijan says with a smirk and subtle sarcasm. "Now let's drink again to the memory of dear Mahroo."

The gang raises their glasses and drinks some more soda.

"What do you want me to do for you?"

"Nothing to worry about now. The food is here; let's eat first and then we can talk about it over a shot of cognac when we go to our house. Let's enjoy the food!" Bijan commands.

The main course tastes particularly special to Darren despite his familiarity with Iranian food. Shish-kabob is barbequed in a novel fashion, somewhat like ribs, bones attached to big chunks of tenderloin meat on wide skewers and grilled on real charcoal for the traditional taste and juiciness. It is served with basmati rice flavoured by saffron and fresh butter. The stunning taste proves Bijan's point to focus on the food.

4

The full moon, navigating a deep starry sky, peeks through the windshield and windows as Bijan swerves his Jaguar around the corners toward his house. Everybody is silent, fascinated by the rare clear sky in Tehran and so many stars twinkling around the proud moon. The out-of-season rain and winds over the last few days have apparently cracked the stubborn smog that normally hangs over the city stubbornly. As if evoked by the majestic sight out there, they all seem lost in their private dreams, reminiscing in silence their personal memories of Mahroo and the possibility of she watching them.

"What a beautiful moon!" Bijan says when they arrive at the house. "Shall we gather in the solarium, Mahtab?"

"Sure," Mahtab replies solemnly.

"You and Reza go ahead and we'll join you shortly. I want to speak with Darren in the study first," Bijan says.

"I'd better go check on Mom and Dad," Reza says bleakly.

"Why don't you call them instead?" Mahtab asks.

"I wanna see them. Will someone give Darren a ride home?"

"Yes, don't worry about that," says Bijan.

Bijan and Darren stroll to the study, which now appears more like an interrogation room to Darren. He sits on the couch in his usual spot and monitors Bijan pacing the room, trying again to find the right words. "What're your plans now, Darren?"

"About what?"

"About everything! How long are you *now* planning to stay in Tehran?"

"I haven't really decided. Until I find out more about my paintings, I suppose," he replies with confusion.

"Your paintings shouldn't be of concern to you. I'm sure they'll be sold soon, and if not, we can oblige the gallery owner to keep them on display and publicize them until they're sold."

"You want me to leave Tehran soon?" he asks with irritation.

"Sorry for being blunt. But you'd better get out of Iran."

"Why? What's the rush?"

"Mostly I'm concerned about your safety. The longer you stay, the more everybody gets anxious and suspicious about your plans for your son—not to mention Sima's brother, who may really harm you if he catches you. I've also promised to get you out of Tehran in a timely manner. They asked about the purpose of your travel to Tehran and I told them it was for selling your paintings. They said the same thing I already told you."

"What's that?"

"Consider your paintings sold and we'll send you the money."

"So they really want me to leave?"

"Yes… Moreover, we want your promise to not do anything silly when you return to Canada, like pursuing ways of seeing, or getting the custody of, your son, or even mentioning the secret. I'm in a big bind and I must go back and provide an update about your plans. I'm concerned for both my father and myself. My promise to them is like my father's promise and I can't afford to jeopardize their trust in us. You see, your case could turn into a civil war in this country, if my father and Sima's uncle become enemies. Please understand me."

"I understand," Darren says with exasperation.

"Our family wants you to stay here longer—you're like a family member, especially now that everybody has realized the extent of your affection for Mahroo. But I don't want any harm coming to you or my father because of your long stay here or your attempt to follow up your son's case from Canada. Nobody must even hear about this secret; not even Reza or Mahtab. Can I have your promise on all these matters?"

Darren wants to stall as long as possible. He is reluctant to commit himself to something he may be unable to abide by. He has already realized and acknowledged that he owes Bijan in a major way. But the feeling of fatherhood, and being forbidden to ever contact his son, is new to him. What if he really craves meeting him? What if some unforeseen circumstance compels him to reveal the secret; for example, a case where the mother, Sima, tells the boy about his father? How can he deny the truth to his grown-up son for the sake of an honourable promise to Bijan today? He believes he should ponder this matter more freely now and in the future without defying Bijan at this point. "Is this the favour you wanted to ask me?"

"Yes, it's the major one," Bijan replies with a grin and tone of secrecy. "I guess Mahtab wants to ask you something, too."

"I'll leave if you want me to. But, I must assess unforeseeable possibilities in the future about keeping my son a secret forever. It's hard to imagine how emotional I'll feel about him later, let's say in a few or ten years."

"But you must decide soon and I must tell them what you think," Bijan murmurs. "Let's go join Mahtab."

Passing through the corridors on the south side of the house, they walk toward the west wing, then turn into a side passage, which brings them to a large, nicely decorated solarium. The lights are dim, subordinate to the moonlight that shimmers softly through the ceiling and large glass walls. A dozen flower baskets, hung around the solarium, add to the ambience, as their colourful shadows scatter softly throughout, too. The romantic mood is soothing despite everybody's worries and distress. Mahtab looks sad and reserved in particular, peering around blankly.

"Hi, dear. Are you all right?" Bijan asks her with concern.

"No, I think I'd better go to bed. Excuse me for leaving now, Darren, but I'm tired," Mahtab replies. "Can you come for dinner tomorrow night? I promise to be in a better shape."

Darren surveys Bijan, who nods. "Sure. Actually, I'm tired myself, and I'd better go home, too, *if you agree*, Bijan?"

"Yes, I agree and I'll walk you to the porch," Bijan replies with a smirk, both appreciating and resenting Darren's humour.

Bijan sends a maid for testy Ahmad who arrives groggy and grouchy with deep frowns upon seeing Darren.

On the porch, Bijan addresses Darren. "Please tell me your decision tomorrow night."

"Sure." Darren feels pressured, but realizes Bijan's concern.

5

The next day, Darren feels lonelier than usual while struggling with the dilemma Bijan has imposed on him. If he could at least talk with Reza or another friend, preferably someone who knew the feelings of fatherhood, he might have been able to make a rational decision. His own Father could be an excellent candidate, except he does not find it a possible option for a million reasons! Later in the day, he considers calling T.J., but it is quite late in Vancouver. Besides, how can they sort out such an emotional matter on the phone quickly, even if he dares to reveal the secret even to this presumed confidant of his?

He wonders what will happen if he refuses to promise Bijan anything, other than hurting his feelings, of course. Will officials possibly put him back in jail? Will Bijan's position and prestige be jeopardized? *Should he care about causing a civil war in Iran over this matter?* Maybe Bijan could just tell Sima's uncle that Darren has promised to keep their secret and would never cause any problem for the family? But Bijan would never lie for him, especially if he fears the possibility of Darren doing something stupid or revealing the secret someday.

Another problem is that poor Bijan, very much like Darren, cannot talk about this matter with any family member, either, not even Reza, to help him find a solution. So he will act decisively on this matter, to the best of his judgment, without the influence of Mahtab or Reza. He would support his father and their honour, not Darren or Reza. He feels guilty for already pondering cunning options that may hurt Bijan. Of course, keeping Bijan worried about Darren's possible mischief someday is also unfair. Thus, the more he contemplates, the more he is convinced to do the honourable thing and give Bijan the guarantee he wants.

Then again, the idea of never seeing his son shatters his heart every time this possibility crosses his mind. He even tries to think that the situation would not have been any different, in terms of meeting his son, if he had not heard about him at all. But now, simply disregarding his desire or right to see and hug his son someday feels silly and sad. He recalls the night a missile hit the building in Tehran adjacent to his. He projects his emotion for the dying boy in the ambulance as his own son, and imagines the feelings of that boy's father who was chasing the ambulance in such agony. He feels the guy's pain much better these days as a father himself. That desperate father never saw his son again and now it is his turn to face the same fate. That is a horrible feeling even for a father who has not yet seen his son and probably a torturous feeling for a son who would never see his father. Now, he can even step into his own father's shoes. He feels for him and guilty for neglecting him for years. *Has that poor old man felt so horrible and confused for years as I'm feeling these days?*

Before he can choose a viable option, it is seven p.m., testy Ahmad arrives, and in fifteen minutes they are at Bijan's house. In the foyer, Mahtab and Bijan, dressed quite elegantly, welcome Darren, who feels a bit out of place in his casual attire. Bijan leads the way to the lounge next to a dining room, where servants are busy setting the table. Darren is both surprised and relieved for being spared the agony of visiting the interrogation room first. Bijan seems to be in a good mood and extra courteous, serving drinks and amusing them with funny stories. Witnessing Bijan's unprecedented warm personality, or at least his effort to come across as such, feels surprisingly pleasant to Darren after all the grim, serious conversations he has had with him before. It feels as if Mahtab had issued a special decree about watching his mood! They relax on soft leather armchairs around a round, hand-carved mahogany table filled with appetizers, drink, and chat amiably, until a hint comes from the kitchen that dinner is served.

This time Mahtab directs them to the dining room, which is apparently used for small gatherings; only twelve chairs are around the table. Mahtab shows Darren his seat opposite hers, on two sides of Bijan's at the top of the table.

"Do you like pheasant?" Mahtab asks.

"Well, I've never tried it, but I've heard it's delicious."

As they take their places, hors d'oeuvres and the main dishes are served duly, including two broiled pheasants that smell and look scrumptious. They drink a variety of wines, chitchat about Iranian food and table manners, while more salads, cheeses and fruits are served in the end. Mahtab explains the soups and dishes in response to Darren's courteous appreciation and questions.

Then Bijan offers his opinion at last, as if bored to his teeth, "You might've guessed that we owe this lengthy dining process to Mahtab's particular knack for formality, which is completely contrary to the Iranian routine. One must be truly patient to go through this slow dining pace. I hope we haven't bored you?"

"No, I enjoyed everything," Darren replies with a grin.

"I personally prefer the Iranian custom to bring everything to the table at once and let people choose whatever they like, in any order, and eat as fast as they prefer without being considered rude or uncivilized. We usually attack and finish our meals in half an hour. I assume Canadians aren't used to this type of formality and too many long breaks between each course, either?"

"No. You're right. We have little patience for dining as well. We are also the 'attacking' type."

"This routine reminds me of school with both its classroom discipline and those agonizing breaks between classes when we wandered around the hallways and bugged one another hastily before the bell rang again. I wait anxiously, wonder about the next course, and decide how much *room* I should leave for it. We're expected to watch our consumption mathematically during each course. It's a gruesome task, although Mahtab usually gives our guests a hint in advance about the main course."

By now, Mahtab seems quite irritated by Bijan's gibberish. Bijan notices her grimace, too, and walks toward the window.

"Of course, Mahtab and I seldom have time to eat together," Bijan continues. "This slow, torturous routine mostly happens in some restaurants and when we have special company."

"You should've not gone through all this trouble," Darren says, hoping Bijan is not blaming him for the dinner routine, too.

"Listen, I'm only joking to amuse you for a change." Bijan tugs the curtain, surveys the sky, and continues, "Last night we missed the moonlight in the solarium. Such a starry sky with a full moon two nights in a row… Shall we go there now?"

Mahtab nods, and again Bijan guides them through a corridor to the solarium. "On starry nights, I like to listen to Bach in the solarium. Do you like his violin concertos?"

Darren nods and Bijan continues, "Ask him, Mahtab…"

"Oh, let the food go down his throat first before we start asking him for favours again," Mahtab says with humour, though she seems agitated again for Bijan's way of commanding her.

"That's okay. Ask me for anything," Darren says with a grin.

"Okay," she replies calmly, pauses, surveys Darren's curious reaction, then blurts, "We'd like you to paint Mahroo's portrait for us. It would be nice to have a significant memento to remind us, especially her daughter Nazi, of the kind of person she was. I suggested the idea and everybody loved it."

Darren notices her boiling emotions, despite her attempt to hide them by sitting straight and wiping the tears from the corners of her eyes as quickly as they emerge. He is touched by her deep sentimentality. After Mahroo's sudden demise, Mahtab wreaks a bizarre, but spiritual, resurrection of her in his mind—a perfect projection of Mahroo. She enlivens his limited memories of Mahroo and ignites soothing rays of hope in his lacklustre life. He would probably enjoy the challenge of painting Mahroo, too, but he is not a portraitist.

"Of course, I'd like to help in any way I can." He pauses to find the right words to present his feelings. A manservant comes to summon Bijan to the phone and Darren continues, "But I've never painted a portrait. You must ask an expert to do this."

"You're the best expert! I've seen your works!" Mahtab says.

"I know something about painting, but not portraits. I cannot accept the big task of bringing such a precious dream to life."

"The idea is not merely to do a portrait, but rather create a sentimental memento. An expert may do a pretty portrait, yet it'd have neither soul nor meaning. But your painting will have both; I'm sure you'll put your soul into it. We know her lover's passion has gone into it, which makes it ten times more significant than a soulless pretty painting done by a stranger. Besides, Mahroo's spirit would be delighted if you fulfilled this dream. Her soul would engulf us through that painting forever, during the painting and afterward. The portrait will become a sanctuary for all of us, for Mahroo, you, me, and the rest of the family to unite and communicate, regardless of the worlds we live in…"

"You believe in spirits?" Darren asks shyly.

"I believe if you did the portrait with the love you've shown for her, it'd become a refuge for our souls. Instead of trying to kill yourself for her, immortalize both of you in this painting and let us embrace this love. Just imagine building a shrine to be in touch with Mahroo permanently, almost as if she still lived with us."

"You're so passionate like her, with astounding resemblance. My senses are numb nowadays, especially when Mahroo seems to be resurrecting through you. I'm flattered, but I doubt I can do a good job, especially now."

"Didn't you say ask me for anything at the start of our chat?"

"Yes, I did… But…"

Bijan returns as Mahtab ponders Darren's words glumly.

"I must go out for half an hour. It's an emergency. Have more drinks and I'll rush back," Bijan says, and then turns to Darren. "Can I talk to you for a second outside?"

In the privacy of the porch, Bijan asks, "Guess who called?"

"Who?"

"Sima's uncle. He's going out of town and would like to see me to confirm our position. What should I tell him?"

Darren recalls the scenarios he has been contemplating all day, to no avail. But, at this moment, his time is up; he must commit himself one way or another. Despite Bijan's obvious hurry, Darren still tries to propose a mediocre, non-committal promise: "I can leave Tehran in two or three days. With respect to my son, what if I make a conditional promise; let's say, not to pursue this matter for five or ten years? Is that acceptable?"

"I doubt it. The longer they get attached to the boy, the harder it'll become to give him up, share him, or let the secret out. I don't care what you decide and what you want to promise or not. But I can't guarantee they'll like fooling around much longer."

"So you think they'd still harass me or put me in jail?"

"Most likely…"

"I'll go to the Canadian Consulate. How can they stop me?"

"I don't know how they'd react if I tell them you promise nothing or give them just a conditional one. But I don't advise you to take that route."

"Or I may renege on my promise later, after I leave Tehran."

"It's up to you. But don't tell me your intentions if they aren't honourable. When I see Sima's uncle, I must trust the integrity of the message I'm taking to him. I think you owe me this much?"

"Sure…"

"So stop asking me these hypothetical questions."

"But I must be more certain about my position, too!"

"We can't wait forever, Darren."

Darren remains silent under the anxious gaze of Bijan, who finally loses his patience: "What should I say? I must hurry."

Intimidated by Bijan's impatience, Darren decides to comply for now, without committing himself to never pursue the matter if necessary. As long as Bijan is off the hook, his conscience is clear, but Darren can always renege on his promise later, since he does not care what people think of his honour. He will assess the risks of dealing with these people later, away from Tehran.

"Okay, I promise on my honour neither to reveal their secret, nor try to contact, or claim the custody of, my son," he says with his fingers crossed in his pocket.

"Ok, I'll return soon," Bijan says and hurries toward his car.

6

In the foyer, Mahtab stops talking to servants to beckon Darren.

"Let me show you something," she says and starts toward the stairs. She turns back with a grin to ensure he is following her.

"Upstairs?" Darren asks.

"Yes, in the bedroom."

Darren trails her uncomfortably in silence, while the nosy, dazed servants watch them nervously. With the guest bedrooms in the detached building opposite the mansion, only immediate family ever goes upstairs, especially to the master bedroom—in particular during the master's absence. Mahtab enters the master bedroom and points to the wall opposite the humongous bed with a beige satin cover. "Voila!"

There it is, in front of Darren: The *Woman in the White Dress*.

"How'd this end up here?" Darren asks.

"It's a long story…"

"Its story has been quite long already!"

"Well…, it actually raised an odd sensation in me when I saw it in Mahroo's house. I asked her to give it to me for my wedding present, but she insisted it was a sentimental gift. Later I learned it was from you, although I had no idea you guys were in love, not until much later when she decided to travel to Vancouver. She even refused to trade it with any of our precious paintings you've seen around the house. But when she returned from Vancouver, she sent the painting over unexpectedly."

"She did?" he asks with surprise and a bit of disappointment. *The painting had apparently lost its meaning for her. Our last kiss in Vancouver hadn't convinced her of my possible reform, either!*

"Yes, she mentioned it no longer had its initial value for her, so I could have it. I thought your friendship had gone sour during her stay in Vancouver perhaps and she didn't want to have a reminder of you in her house. I'm completely confused, however, now that I see you two were still in love; what made her change her mind puzzles me."

"Does Reza know about this exchange?" he asks.

"No. Why?"

"Because he was the one who got it from me in the first place and started this mayhem."

"What mayhem?"

"First of all, he's meant all along to give it to another woman after lending it to Mahroo temporarily in hopes of warning her about her marital issues. But then she got attached to it along with a big emotional misunderstanding. Reza is still planning to give it the woman who had originally made him to buy it for her."

"Well, whatever the initial story, Mahroo believed she owned it and had a right to give to me. So, now it belongs to me and Reza cannot get it from me."

"The main issue is that this painting has caused only trouble from the start. I don't want to scare you, but it's probably cursed."

"Cursed…?" Mahtab shrieks with surprise.

"Well… It brings bad luck and feelings for people close to it. Get it out of this house, I suggest."

"No… I like watching it when I go to bed. Its soothing mood relaxes me to fall sleep with beautiful thoughts and dreams."

"Exactly my point! It already seems to have made its bizarre, soothing effect on you, too. But it'll eventually hurt your soul."

"I think you're exaggerating its power to scare me."

"I have no such intention, believe me."

"No, I don't believe you. If I were cynical, I'd say you were exaggerating the power of this painting just for your benefit."

"What benefit? I don't own it, anyway," he asks.

"But these mystical claims can influence people's impression of your works. You may get famous as the mystic painter of the modern era. Is that the reason?" she asks teasingly with a grin.

"No, I'm only stating the possibility of facing some emotional distress the same way Mahroo did. This painting is cursed."

"I like some excitement in my life, anyway," she says wittily.

Darren bursts into laughter. "It might be more headache than excitement."

"It's a rather hypnotic painting for sure. But I doubt it's demonic. The proof is that Mahroo got rid of it easily."

"But not until she gained the super power to break its spell over her. She suffered because of it for years, though. I know some things about this painting that actually sound unnatural."

"If they sound unnatural to you already, maybe they're only your imaginations. Don't you think?" she says.

Her scepticism and knack for debate are equally annoying like Mahroo's, while he feels helpless to explain his point further. *How can I tell Vincent's confession about borrowing someone's soul to make the* Woman in the White Dress *look alive?* It was even hard for him to accept Vincent's confession, but experience has proven that Vincent's claim may hold water. Since Mahroo has redeemed her soul—definitely after her death, if not when she gave the painting to Mahtab—Vincent might be seeking a different soul to keep it alive. Is not Mahtab's confession and attraction to the painting a good clue already about her soul being trapped? Did Vincent orchestrate the transfer of the painting between the sisters when Mahroo's soul became unavailable?

"What's the story behind it anyway?" she enquires playfully, since Darren's claim comes across to her at least fishy, if not a sleazy attempt to turn the painting into a mystical object.

"Which one? The mystical clues or the painting subject?"

"Both!"

"Let's forget the absurd mystical clues. But I did this painting during a severe depression after separating from my wife."

"So, is that woman your ex-wife and you're the man?"

"Yes."

"You probably had special motives for doing and interpreting this painting, which are interesting to know, but not now."

"Strange! You lost your interest already, thank goodness!"

"No, I'm still curious about your interpretations. But I'd like to enjoy my own impression for now!"

"Oh…?"

"Yes…! I adore the impressionists' and romantic paintings in museums and those we've bought for our house. But this one has mesmerized me differently. Maybe someday I'll explain it."

Her direct confession actually proves the effect of the damned painting. His nerves constrict at the idea of Vincent's cunning intervention in the destiny of this painting once more.

"I still suggest let me or Reza take this painting away," he asserts solemnly, realizing his ulterior motive and blaming the painting for it, too. *See how cunningly I'm trying to convince her to give it up even if it ends up in Erica's hands through Reza?* But he also feels guilty for painting it and exposing these women to Vincent's whims. Is Vincent finding the chance of teasing women from another world intriguing—maybe for taking revenge or just making up for his tough luck with women when alive?

"Never! I'm getting attached to it more every day."

"That's a bad sign, as I said…"

"One thing I specially like about this painting...," she says.

"What?"

"The boat on the horizon reminds me that 'everywhere I go nowadays, it's still not the place I want to be.' I've traveled most of my life, to so many places: Large cities, exotic resorts, safaris, and secluded villages. And I've met so many interesting people, but still can't find enough peace or happiness. Why?"

"Because happiness is just another myth regardless of where we live," Darren replies.

"Well, even worse, why do I feel emptier and sadder every day, despite all the excitements around me? I bet the woman in the white dress feels the same way about life and herself when she sees that boat disappearing on the horizon. I feel her anguish and sympathize with her. I wish I could jump into the painting and hug her for feeling exactly like me."

"Of course, that boat could have many meanings."

"Like what?" Mahtab asks.

"Maybe it symbolizes the fleeting life...," he replies.

"Maybe someday we share our interpretations and discuss the symbols hidden in this painting. All I want to say today is that you're a genius in my book for portraying so many subtle and sensitive clues in one painting."

"Thanks."

"You must've felt so much pain and then turned that passion into this artistic piece."

"Is my suffering that obvious?"

"Yes… In the way it depicts human feelings and misery…" she pauses to see Darren's reaction, but his silence goads her to continue. "And with all this talent, I just can't understand your resistance to paint Mahroo's portrait. The painting in front of us already proves my point. I believe you can make Mahroo look as lively as the women in the white dress."

"But landscape is all I paint. I draw humans metaphorically only if they add a profound meaning to the painting. I include a tiny figure to show the scale and the splendour of nature, and to show our pitiful and negligible role in the scope of the creation and the universe. Only twice have I had a mystifying urge to do this: This painting and the one showing me and my dad together."

"I like your cynicism about humans. We believe we are at the centre of the universe and that everything revolves around us to satisfy our selfish needs. Is that why you don't like painting humans?" she asks.

"And also because humans generally have nothing important to say, and when they do, it is radically intriguing and beautiful. Both of these moods are difficult to paint."

"Especially the former, I assume," Mahtab says with a giggle.

"Absolutely… Human stupidity is too deep to explain. Our wild egos hide our incredible helplessness until we face death or feel our naïveté."

"So you don't paint humans unless you have a divine urge?"

"I guess, you're right," he replies pensively. "There's no point painting humans unless the subject has a special message about his/her vulnerability, fears, or life's absurdities."

"That's very interesting… And exactly my point! Even going by this standard, you should paint Mahroo's portrait, because I'm sure it'll show the vulnerability of both life and love on top of our shared, torn feelings for this special subject," she asserts.

Darren stays quiet while staring at the painting pensively and thinking she actually has a very valid point.

"I like your analytical argument and running this long debate just to prove your point about the need to do this painting, ha?"

She chuckle. "Yes, you caught me… What do you say?"

"You're so tricky, like Mahroo… Let me think…," he says.

"Thanks, anyway, for talking with me so openly," she says graciously. "I'm sure you'll get a mysterious urge to paint Mahroo soon. Let's go back to the solarium and continue our conversation there." She starts toward the stairs and he follows her after a last glance at the *Woman in the White Dress*.

7

In the solarium, Darren refreshes their drinks as they enjoy the bright moonlight and its soft reflections around the colourful hanging pots in silence. Despite the romantic ambiance, they look anxious and sad like an estranged couple. Mahroo's portrait and the *Woman in the White Dress* have stirred up some tension and he feels guilty about his tenacity possibly alienating her.

"Did Mahroo mention the meaning of her name?" Mahtab asks at last to break the awkward silence.

"No…"

"Literally, Mahroo means 'Moon Face,' but romantically it means 'a face as pretty as the moon.' In Persian literature and culture, we glorify the moon as the symbol of beauty."

"Surely the right name for her. What does 'Mahtab' mean?"

"Moonlight. 'Mah' in Persian means moon."

"What? Ma?"

Mahtab spells it out: "M, a, h."

"Oh! Mah... Two Mahs. Two beautiful Persian moons!"

Despite his intention to soothe her tension with his tactful compliment, promptly Darren shivers in horror when the scene in the graveyard triggers in his mind: Moon Face's pretty cheek placed on the cold, moist soil, then covered with tons of dirt, and worms rushing in for fresh food.

"Alas we can't enjoy Moon Face anymore. She left us when we both needed her so badly," she says sombrely.

"Were you two close?"

"Very much. We spent every day of our lives together, except for the years I lived in Los Angeles, which made me appreciate her even more. We shared our feelings and hurts telepathically."

"I'm sure you miss her a lot. I understand!" he says.

"You're perhaps the only one who may feel my sorrow. My parents and Reza loved her a lot and I'm certain they miss her tremendously, but the way you and I felt her was unique, like a sacred love. We miss her intelligence and friendship and the way her existence complemented ours."

"That's true." Darren sighs. He is also amused by the way she speaks for him so liberally with confidence, as if she were privy to all his feelings for Mahroo! *She is right though, maybe based on Reza's story of my mourning Mahroo alone in the streets!*

"That's the kind of passion that can create the finest art and a lasting tribute to her. How can you pass up the opportunity to express this splendid passion of yours?"

"Your comment in fact confirms my reason for hesitation very nicely, better than I have been able to say it myself."

"What do you mean?"

"I'm afraid my expertise might not match my passion. In this particular case, anything less than a masterpiece wouldn't justify the cause and I won't be happy with the work and myself."

"Well, if you don't like the result, just destroy it. Nobody's depriving you of your right to judge and act in the end."

"But then I'd keep suffering for my failure…," Darren says.

"I see your dilemma… Sorry for not realizing it myself."

"Then again, fearing failure is appalling for a wise person!"

"I'm glad you feel and say this yourself," she says giddily.

"Of course, another hurdle is that it'd be difficult to do a good job when *the model* isn't present in front of me. I didn't want to express this awful reality, but then I'm obliged to show you that my resistance is not merely a thoughtless refusal."

"I wish she were able to sit for you personally, but perhaps her pictures can help your memories of her deep emotions?"

"I have a bad feeling about this project despite my desire to do something special for her memory. I also want to pay my debt to Bijan and you. Do you have any recent pictures of her?"

"No, they are four years old. Let me fetch them, anyway."

Soon she returns with Bijan. Darren asks him, "How'd it go?"

"I took care of things for now," Bijan states pensively. "You'll get your passport back at the airport on your way out."

"Thanks," Darren says with gloom.

"I see you've agreed to paint Mahroo's portrait?"

"Not really. Mahtab is just showing me some pictures to use as a model," replies Darren, picking up Mahroo's pictures from the coffee table and studying them carefully. "They don't look like her at all. These photo shops suck the soul out of the picture. She looks like a ghost with no distinguishable lines or character."

"That's another reason why nobody can do Mahroo justice but you. I'm sure you remember her face and feelings better than all of us, let alone strangers, no matter how expert they're in painting portraits. You must reconsider your decision," she insists with a direct tone but delicate charm.

"I'll be leaving soon, anyway and in Vancouver, I don't know how things will go, or whether I'll remember her face enough in a few weeks, even with all these pictures. In fact, the more I look at them, the more her image gets distorted in my mind," he says and drops the pictures on the table swiftly with annoyance.

"Have you asked him the other favour?" Mahtab asks Bijan.

Bijan hesitates pensively five seconds before replying, "Not yet." He looks rather tense. "I'm still not sure about bothering Darren with this particular request."

"Another one? Listen, why don't you send me back to prison? At least there I wasn't asked for so many promises and favours." Staring at Bijan and Mahtab, who look embarrassed behind their superficial grins, Darren bursts into laughter. "I'm just kidding. I like to fool around too, when I can. I'll do anything for you two."

The three of them laugh and Bijan explains rather reluctantly, "Mahtab, her parents, and Nazi are going to Barcelona for a while. Reza and I were wondering if you could escort them and stay in our villa a couple of days on your way to Vancouver. Reza and I are still busy and can't travel. Mahtab can manage on her own, but having you around a few days will help, considering the whole family's frailty and stress nowadays."

"When're you leaving?" Darren asks Mahtab, but turns fast and peers at Bijan.

"In two or three days. I'll book their flights tomorrow. If you agree, I'll get your ticket too," Bijan says, while Mahtab nods.

"I can stay a couple of days," Darren says, thinking a short holiday before returning to Vancouver may revive him. Visiting Spain while humouring Bijan sounds exciting. Subconsciously, though, he feels this plan somehow relates to Bijan's ulterior motive to get him out of Iran promptly. Nonetheless, leaving Tehran isn't a major issue, as long as his paintings are exhibited for sale in the gallery. In Vancouver, he will start fresh, perhaps with ideas for a new style of painting. He will survive financially for one year, while looking for opportunities to work with other galleries in Canada or the U.S.

"Maybe you can paint the portrait in Barcelona?" Mahtab asks.

"I'll think about it," Darren replies. "I'd better go now."

8

On the way to Reza's place and in bed, Darren ponders Mahtab's request. The idea appeals to him, but painting Mahroo as his first serious close-up portrait is risky. Her suggestion to destroy the painting if he does not like it makes sense to him, though.

But he is swiftly struck by an exactly opposite dilemma: What if it turns out to be a masterpiece? Who will own it? What if he gets attached to it himself, for not only the superb outcome of the painting itself, but also his deep emotions toward the subject? He should beware of the possibility of creating another emotional conundrum for himself by abandoning the new painting, like the *Woman in the White Dress*, and like the son he feels so close to without even having seen yet. Giving up Mahroo's portrait might become another source of torture. Why is he always forced to relinquish his precious creations? Luckily, he quickly realizes his silliness at torturing himself over a painting that has not even been created or considered. *What's the matter with me? Maybe I could paint her twice? One for Mahtab and one for myself. But this never works out in art. Besides, at the end, we'd both dislike one and want the other, even if I hide it from her! She'd know!*

9

In the morning, he finds a note from Reza to contact Mahtab.

"Hi, Darren. Did you sleep well?" she starts.

"No. I was thinking about Mahroo and your request a lot."

"Me too… Isn't that great?"

"Yes, it's wonderful…!"

"I hope you have good ideas too," she says with excitement.

"Oh! What good ideas have you cooked up now?"

"I thought maybe you can use me as a model along with her pictures and your own image of her to paint a perfect portrait."

"Hmm, it's a good idea in a way, and goofy in another way."

"What's goofy about it?"

"It'd probably be impossible for me to feel Mahroo and her unique soul when you're the live model, the breathing soul, near me, while we hope to contact Mahroo's spirit."

"Do you want me stop breathing then?"

"Sorry, I meant your distinct presence and personality, despite your great resemblance to Mahroo, will make the job difficult."

They both immerse in deep thoughts. Mahtab thinks she has already tried enough to soften Darren and maybe it is time to stop pushing him. Then suddenly a new thought jumps in her head and she decides to use it as her last attempt, "Didn't I play piano especially for you when you were feeling down the first night you came to our house?"

"Yes… Especially at the expense of annoying your guests for interrupting the Iranian music and dancing. That was a major risk and sacrifice by you… I realized and appreciated it."

"So now perhaps you should do the same thing for me and paint a portrait that can soothe my soul. I need a lively Mahroo!"

"Well… But another big issue occurred to me last night, too."

"What issue?" she asks.

"If I do this painting, I might get attached to it myself and be reluctant to let you have it. How about that?"

"But that's the favour I asked you to do for me. How can you keep it when you know I need it so badly?"

"How about me? I hate to nag, but what if I put my soul into it and create a lively painting with such effect we'd both love to have? Why should I always sacrifice my feelings?"

"What else have you sacrificed for me?"

"Not for you. But the painting in your bedroom was taken away from me, and…" He almost reveals the secret about having a son he is forbidden to see. He only sighs.

"It's wonderful that her portrait is presumed a masterpiece and we both long for it already. But don't you think it should be close to her family?"

"But every time I do a painting with emotional significance for me, a part of my soul gets trapped in it. While I own it, my spirit remains intact. It isn't possessiveness, believe me. It's a kind of passion similar to a mother's love for her baby. It merely becomes hard to give it up for adoption. For Mahroo's portrait, I must also put my soul into it. Actually this particular painting would perhaps be even more peculiar; it'd probably drain a great deal of my soul."

"I think I understand what you're saying. But explain why this painting is peculiar?" she asks.

"Because we must create a masterpiece merely from our imaginations and invest our souls—we're already doing it—and if everything goes well, Mahroo herself will also participate by bringing her soul into it. You said it yourself that it'd become a shrine for all of us for cherishing a lively Mahroo."

"You believe it can happen?"

"It's already happening. That's what scares me the most."

"The way you talk, I'm actually getting more anxious to do it at any cost. Please… We'll find a way to share it afterwards."

"I doubt it. Every line *we* draw will make it harder to decide about its destiny."

"I like the way you say 'we.' I'd like to be involved in this painting as much as possible. We shall create a masterpiece by mixing our souls on the canvas and hope Mahroo brings hers, too, in this incredible exercise of love, more amazing than all the love stories ever told in a book or on canvas. Darren, please tell me we'll do this. Mahroo's death is killing me."

"And painting her portrait may kill me, too. I can't bear the idea of losing another child," he says, mostly projecting, again, the fact of being forbidden to ever see his son. He realizes with amazement that the information about his son has made him many folds more sentimental than he had always been. Now, anticipating the lasting agony of not meeting his son ever, and keeping it a secret too, is torturous all by itself. "Not making this new baby may be wiser when we both feel so attached to it already. I'm wearing out emotionally."

Not knowing Darren's motives for talking rather bizarre, Mahtab is getting emotionally carried away with the idea of bearing a baby, too, although she realizes it's only a metaphor to express the depth of their tender feelings nowadays.

"I understand your agony of abandoning our baby, but you can always visit her in Tehran," Mahtab says.

"I'm forbidden to return to Tehran ever as a condition of my freedom."

"What was the charge?"

"A silly misunderstanding. But I'm only a helpless foreigner who can't change things or even object."

Mahtab's body aches with a deep gloom at the prospect of not seeing him again, and the way he appears to be treated unfairly. Her eyes glitter with tears for his suffering. But that is even more reason to raise his interest, to channel his pungent emotions into Mahroo's portrait. She abhors pushing him, realizing his anguish. Perhaps he will change his mind and paint Mahroo's portrait in Vancouver after regaining his confidence and overcoming his recent bad experiences. By then, however, he might forget her image and possibly his feelings toward her, which is the whole point of having the portrait done by him immediately. *No, he must do it right away and give it to me, too,* Mahtab thinks.

She knows she has reached a milestone as he has at least agreed to do it. The only hurdle is persuading him to surrender it to her. So she thinks tactically about the last item of negotiation. She finally throws in the towel. "Okay, Darren, you win. I'll give you the *Woman in the White Dress* instead."

Darren cannot believe his ears. It is a good omen to get this painting back before Reza finds a way to grab it from Mahtab somehow and give it to Erica. But deep down, he still feels that abandoning Mahroo's portrait might be more hurtful than the joy of getting the *Woman in the White Dress* back. The trade-off may be unfair, because the portrait will be like a newborn baby that not only brings lots of fresh joy and excitement, but also requires the attention and love of the mother more than an older child who can take care of herself. Besides, the portrait will be a reminder of a precious experience in his life—Mahroo's complex, tragic love —compared to the other painting, which is old news now about a woman who had hurt him so much. That old painting about Erica has been cursed, anyway, going by all the tragedies surrounding it, and his own animated claims when discussing it with Mahtab last night. On the other hand, the idea of spending some time with Mahtab, while painting the portrait of Mahroo is thrilling. So, in the end, he decides to stop badgering her.

"Okay. I will do it because you've proven how precious this portrait will be to you. I'll do it for you and Mahroo."

"Great. Let's go make our baby in Barcelona then," she cries with excitement.

"When're we leaving?" Darren asks with nostalgia for leaving Tehran rather empty-handed with so many gloomy memories and unresolved issues, including his son and his unsold paintings in the gallery.

"In two days," she replies.

"You think you'll finish Mahroo's portrait in Barcelona?"

"Yes, I will and it would be a great work."

"In that case, I'll get the *Woman in the White Dress* packed and shipped before we leave. You'll have it when you arrive in Vancouver. I will also ask our caretaker in Barcelona to buy a canvas for you. What size do you need?"

"Thirty by forty inches; the best quality he can find for oil painting, with heavy-duty frame. I prefer oil-primed linen, if he can find some. But I also need painting supplies?"

"I'll take you to an art store this afternoon after getting Bijan's permission."

Chapter Fifteen
Mad Cows

1

In his first-class seat on the plane to Barcelona, Darren Durant beholds the privileges and flamboyance of the rich while gauging his erratic social convictions and antipathy toward extravagance in a world full of misery. The family takes the four seats in row three and he sits leisurely alone in row four, content to be flying out of Iran intact and re-owning the *Woman in the White Dress*.

After two days of no contact, Mahtab seems reserved and cheerless this morning compared to the last time they had talked on the phone and gone to the art store together. They had chatted only briefly at the airport while saying goodbye to Bijan and Reza. He wonders about her mood and prays to God that she is not unstable, too, like Mahroo. *Maybe it's that freaky time of her period!* Or maybe she is struggling with the same thoughts and feelings vexing him, he imagines. They are facing a crucial and risky mission, venturing in uncharted territories. They are sensing many likely emotional challenges ahead, so now meditating in their corners very much like soldiers on a Hercules en route to foreign lands to fight unpredictable enemies. She is an artist like him and realizes the emotional burdens of creating a significant artistic work. The intensity of her sentiments was obvious from the phrase she had used to explain their project, "Let's go make our baby in Barcelona." Now he can rather justify her silence. He is overwhelmed by mixed emotions himself.

2

At the Barcelona Airport, Nader Dashti is waiting next a rental van, according to Mahtab's instruction. An Iranian refugee who had skipped military service during the war four years earlier, he lives in Barcelona by doing odd jobs, mainly as a caretaker for a few affluent families owning villas around the city. He loads the suitcases into the van and drives northeast toward the city centre, according to Mahtab's instruction again. She has decided to let everybody unwind by browsing awhile and having supper before going the rest of the way to the villa.

Nader parks the van close to Placa de Catalunya, the popular square in the heart of Barcelona, and they stroll amidst the flood of people pacing La Rambla Boulevard. The lively atmosphere along this long, cozy stretch, including the exotic street names, astounds Darren. The sidewalks and the broad, tree-lined middle section, around two narrow traffic lanes, are full of restaurants, cafés, ice-cream parlours, flower stalls, pavement musicians and artists, newsstands, art galleries, and an endless flow of people.

Darren browses leisurely with fascination, but soon Mahtab directs them to a restaurant since Nazi is hungry. She promises to bring him back another time to stroll in the lower part of La Rambla, adding proudly that it is considered the most famous street in Spain, always lively, day and night. They enjoy their spicy supper in a crowded restaurant amidst the animated hoopla, patrons laughing and chatting loudly. Then they meander toward the van among the cheerful pedestrians and noisy street vendors. Eventually, they drive toward the family villa near Badalona, at the top of the hills overlooking the Mediterranean Sea.

Mahtab leads Darren to the large guestroom just rearranged by Nader to serve as his painting studio as well. The bed is pushed closer to the wall, some furniture moved out of the way, and a few rugs are rolled up and leaned against the wall. A plastic cover is stretched in the corner designated for painting. The sight of the redecorated room startles Mahtab, though, although Nader has merely followed her instructions. She wonders how Darren would react to the idea of sleeping in this setting.

"Maybe paint in basement? But no window," Nader asks.

"No, this is perfect. But we should move the floor cover to the other side. I like the light from the right-hand side."

"No problemo," Nader replies, proud of his newly nurtured tongue.

"How's the canvas?" Mahtab asks.

Darren checks it and nods. "It's linen. Good job, Nader."

"Fine," replies Mahtab, baffled, "but we forgot easel."

"We'll improvise," he says, turning to Nader. "Do you have a folding chair or something that stands like an easel?"

Mahtab consults Nader in Persian before addressing Darren, "We have nothing like that. Nader can buy an easel tomorrow."

"It's not worth spending time and money on an easel for one painting. How about a small ladder?" Darren asks.

"Ladder, yes. One minute," Nader says and charges out of the room. Mahtab is annoyed by the idea of improvising. *Why's Darren so impatient? Is he going to put enough energy into this painting now that he must give it to me?*

Nader returns with a folding wooden ladder smudged with dried paint. He opens it in front of Darren under Mahtab's sore, sceptical eyes. Darren examines it closely and confirms eagerly, "This will do. Do you have long nails or big clips, Nader?"

"Yes, yes. Long nails," says Nader, getting equally carried away to make do with the existing supplies and avoiding a trip to town tomorrow to search for an easel. He runs out and returns with a dozen long nails and a hammer. Watching these two idiots at work agitates Mahtab. She just rolls her eyes and leaves.

Nader helps Darren measure the location of the nails and hammers them at the right angles for holding the canvas on the side of the ladder. Nader leaves happily and Darren sits on the couch and stares at the blank canvas on the make-do easel. He tries to fuse into the white surface and visualize the painting task ahead. Then he opens his small bag and pulls Mahroo's pictures and a sketchpad out. He studies her poses in the pictures and his own imagination to draw half a dozen sketches in different angles and moods, but none of them feels satisfactory. For ten minutes, he examines them closely before throwing them on the coffee table and charging toward the family room to find Mahtab.

She is chatting with her parents and Nazi is watching TV in another corner. They stop their conversation and Mahtab smirks at him.

"Did you make your masterpiece easel?" she asks wittily.

"Yes, it'll do the job," replies Darren with a grin.

"Come on in; have a seat," she says.

"No, I'm tired. I just came to look at you before turning in."

"You came just to look at me before going to bed?" she asks mockingly, yet amused by such a blunt, if not vulgar, proposal.

"Just don't mind me! I'm going to get a glass of water, too," he says, walking into the adjacent kitchen.

"There's fruit juice too," Mahtab yells from the sofa.

"No, thanks." He grabs a glass from the dish cabinet and finds a bottle of mineral water in the fridge. Then he goes to the family room and stands behind Mahtab's parents, sips the water slowly, and gazes at Mahtab intently, moving from side to side to survey her face, which is now flustered by his bizarre behaviour. After three minutes, he says goodnight and leaves.

"He's probably lost his mind because of Mahroo, or he's...," Mahtab says to her parents in Persian after he leaves, but pauses just in time before blurting the stupid thought in her mind.

In bed, Darren studies some images suitable for Mahroo's portrait. The main questions are whether she should be merry or melancholy, look at the viewer or outwardly in a pensive mood. How about showing her hand under her chin, like the gesture in one of her pictures? Mahtab's last image, imprinted in his mind a few minutes earlier downstairs, is still fresh and helpful for these analyses. Yet, this image is a distorted impression of Mahroo's personality, maybe due to Mahtab's uncharacteristic mood today! This thought switches his focus back to Mahtab's mood. She had left his room rather flabbergasted after Nader had brought the ladder. He wonders if he is responsible for whatever is disturbing her now. He is unable to think of any wrongdoing. Maybe she is sorry for giving up the *Woman in the White Dress*, even though she had made the offer without his influence. Has her soul lost its sanctuary now that the painting is shipped to Vancouver? He falls asleep without detecting the cause of Mahtab's seeming agitation or choosing a preferred image for Mahroo's portrait.

3

The crows cawing outside the window, most likely fighting over food, awaken Darren mid-morning. He checks his wristwatch and charges toward the shower. Afterwards, he hurries to the family room and finds everybody sitting in the same positions he had left them in last night, in different outfits. Mahtab directs him to the nook, serves his breakfast personally, then asks him about his plans and possible interest to go out with them.

"No, thanks. I'm ready to start painting right away."

"We'll return mid-afternoon. Can I get anything for you in town? An easel, maybe?" she asks wittily.

"No, thanks," he says and hurries to his room to sketch an idea occurring to him: Instead of painting a straight portrait, he would include a small window frame and a full moon that glitters a bluish hue over Mahroo's face. After all, it shall be a symbolic composition as the moon signifies Mahroo's name and beauty.

Also interesting is the way 'moonlight'—symbolizing Mahtab —glows on parts of Mahroo's face, to reflect Mahtab's sweeping love for Mahroo. The prevailing bluish hue of the moon on her face and throughout the painting would surely show some sense of melancholy, but that would be all right, too, for reflecting the agony they all, especially Mahroo, have endured.

He draws the outlines quickly. Mahroo's portrait will peer outwardly with a very subtle grin—perhaps as indiscernible as Mona Lisa's. A smooth shadow will cover half of her face. Her big eyes, especially, must be quite lively and filled with wisdom. The composition holds many symbols without jeopardizing its main emphasis—Mahroo. Suddenly he realizes he is the only one not included symbolically in the painting. He ponders several options, to no avail, so leaves the matter alone and starts copying the sketch onto the canvas. After completing the under-painting with a big round brush, he checks the outcome from a distance for composition and balance. It looks fine and he begins painting the window and the moon in some detail. Then he adds paints here and there on Mahroo's face without committing himself to any descriptive aspects of her face yet. He decides to tackle that part by asking Mahtab to model for him.

He lies back on the couch and assesses the outlines and colour combinations on the canvas. The progress so far convinces him the portrait will turn into another significant work. It would be lively despite all the blues he would use for creating the sad mood. Triumphant but tired, he decides to fetch himself a snack. In the kitchen, he makes a big sandwich with turkey slices and pastrami and grabs a can of soda. On the way back to his room, the cassette deck on the counter draws his attention. He borrows it along with a few classical music tapes.

Music playing loud, Darren reviews the painting with new energy and a semi-fresh perspective. It still looks flawless and promising. But then he recalls the idea of including himself in the painting in a symbolic form, too. Fifteen minutes of inconclusive musing only agitates him more, as his desire to be in the painting is rising. He recalls enduring a similar agony when painting the *Path to Heaven* before Vincent had come to his rescue.

Consumed by the problem at hand amidst the loud music, he cannot hear Mahtab's knocking on his door. "Hey, Vincent, send me a clue," he yells so loud Mahtab can hear him. He imagines Vincent's presence next to the painting-in-progress, surveying it keenly and nodding approvingly. "I'd like to include a subtle symbol of myself in this painting. Any suggestions?"

"What're you gonna show outside the window besides the moon?"

Darren approaches the painting, ponders, and understands Vincent's point. "Oh, yes. That's a great idea!" he shrieks with excitement. Mahtab, who has been waiting behind the door long enough, decides to leave. She is slightly intimidated by his refusal to open the door, while talking to himself so stridently. *All artists are weird somehow, I guess,* she ponders with mixed feelings. *I wonder if Mahroo's memory is still haunting him. Maybe he's yelling at her again for leaving him so unexpectedly?*

Another great idea, thanks to Vincent! He will show a horizon line outside the window with a tiny figure—symbolizing him—running toward the house. The idea of Mahroo peeping furtively into the horizon on and off to watch him run toward her excites Darren about the composition's portrayal of love on top of its resemblance to the *Woman in the White Dress*—now a woman watching a man in this new painting. That is another good omen at the start.

Quickly he places a teensy vertical line near the horizon to depict the man for now and calls it a day. He feels superb but lazy to clean the brushes. He will be using them the next day, anyway, and Mahtab has bought him so many brushes he can consider them 'disposable' if necessary. Descending the stairs with big satisfaction, he peers through the large window on the landing. A lot of daylight is left and the garden below, with a bench near a running fountain, is inviting.

In the garden, Nazi hurries to him with a cheer, gives him a kiss, and returns to playing with the water splashing from the fountain and her dolls apparently taking a bath. He lingers on the bench, inhales deep breaths, and reflects on today's progress. Mahtab yells from the kitchen window and waves at Darren and Nazi, who wave back. Soon she emerges and announces dinner will be ready in an hour.

"How was your day?" she asks.

"Fine. We can work together tomorrow if you have time."

"Sure. I knocked on your door earlier, but you didn't answer."

"Maybe the music was too loud. Sorry!"

"That's okay… Although I could swear I heard you yelling at someone!"

"Oh, yes…"

"Were you talking to Mahroo again?"

"No… Not this time… I was talking to Vincent Van Gogh."

"Oh…!"

"Sometimes I do that when I'm facing a problem or seeking ideas. I look for help from higher spirits when necessary."

"Does it work?"

"Often enough, when I ask it sincerely and it has a special value."

"Are you religious, Darren?"

"No. But I have my own beliefs and principles to guide me."

"Maybe you can explain them to me if they're not private."

"Maybe later, if we have time and know each other better."

Silence prevails, save for the sound of the fountain splash. He wonders if shrugging off her request has annoyed her.

"How about you? Are you religious?" he asks.

"No… In fact, I'm an atheist, kind of."

"Oh…? But I thought Bijan was very religious."

"Like his family, he's a fanatic Muslim. But that's his choice. He knew about my atheism before marrying me."

"He knew and still took the risk?" he asks with great surprise.

"I guess he loved me too much, at least then, even more than his religion, and in spite of the big risk of facing his parents' damnation," she replies with a charming, boastful grin.

"It's possible to live in harmony, I guess, if you don't waste your energies on convincing each other of your beliefs."

"Well… It often doesn't happen, however. Despite his liberal attitude and modernism, there're some deep differences between us that make life difficult for both of us sometimes. His parents have become extremely wealthy, solely because of their Islamic beliefs and ties with the government. He's an important official himself because of his ideologies, too; everything he does in his official capacity involves certain principles and prejudices way beyond my grasp. It's hard to understand how such an educated person can have such rigid and deplorable ideologies."

"But you're rigid too," Darren says, "denying the possibility of God in some form."

"Perhaps. But at least I'm not wasting my time and mind on ideas that have no scientific or logical explanation. Religion is built only on hearsay and emotional propaganda to fool people. It's just a way of taking advantage of people's gullibility."

"Forget about religions, but we can't deny the existence of the supernatural just because our flimsy logic cannot explain it to us. Besides, many people have experienced spirituality firsthand."

"Did you and Mahroo talk about this stuff?" she asks.

"No, we never discussed spirituality. Why do you ask?"

"These kinds of discussions bring intimacy between people, while they also learn about each other's vulnerabilities."

"Many other topics and arguments kept us busy already. We revealed our vulnerabilities enough, but enjoyed our arguments as well," he says.

"I can imagine how much fun it must've been. To be honest, I was slightly intimidated this afternoon when I heard you talking to yourself. But now I think it's cute that you ask higher spirits for help and actually believe they make it happen. I've never seen someone mystical, but sincere and intelligent at the same time. One usually associates supernatural with gullibility or treachery."

"People find myths and mysticism a waste of time."

"Do you think there is any truth behind all these myths?"

"Nobody knows. Though they bring us relief and inspiration. I recall Mahroo's persistence that only myths like 'love' bring us relief and tranquility, at least temporarily.

"I agree with her, of course," Mahtab says.

"Although most of us are sceptical about supernatural, we feel it instinctually. Our psyches connect us to a mystical world automatically. But we often doubt our instincts, and instead adopt the shallow reality that our poor logic pushes on us, including religious claims like hell and heaven. To me, this is odd, because we should've known by now that our knowledge and logic are too narrow to distinguish the reality."

"I agree...," she says.

"I think there's a reason for our psyches being so intuitively drawn to mystical ideas and spirituality. The only problem is that spirituality is often contaminated by religious frauds. We're just beginning to think about psyche scientifically. Perhaps, in a few centuries, we also learn more about soul and spirituality." Darren keeps explaining his beliefs for some time, until Mahtab's mom beckons them for supper.

"Let's continue this discussion tomorrow during the painting session," she suggests, intrigued by his simple beliefs.

"Not when I'm painting," he says half-seriously. "But music helps. By the way, I borrowed your cassette deck."

"Keep it for tomorrow if chitchat is not allowed. Is breathing okay during the session, master?" Again, this man is taunting her suggestion. *What's wrong with talking? What a weird artist! Maybe all geniuses are weird. Then this is another good sign. Still, he's too rude in the way he talks to me, although he tries not to be snobbish.*

4

Both Mahtab and Darren spend an anxious night pondering their next day adventure to create a masterpiece. Despite occasional arguments, they have come to respect and enjoy each other. For Darren, especially, it feels like resuming the old arguments and bargaining with Mahroo at exactly the same point they had left them in their last meeting. Mahtab wakes up early in the morning and makes omelette while the rest of the family and Darren come downstairs sluggishly. Everybody sniffs and admires the great smell of the breakfast, but still nags about all the racket she has been making. Darren imagines all that noise had been intentional just to start the day and painting as soon as possible. Like Elizabeth and most other women, Mahtab seems impatient and sneaky, too. *Good for her!* he muses amusingly.

Walking ahead of Darren on the way to his room, Mahtab blurts unexpectedly, "You were in my dreams last night."

He only grins and dashes into the room to hide the painting.

"I'm not allowed to see it?" she asks.

"Not yet. I'd like to get your first impression when it's done," he replies while pulling up a chair and deciding on a suitable spot for her. "Please sit there and relax completely. Loosen up your muscles, especially the ones in your face." He then looks for and chooses a cassette tape to play during the painting session.

She staggers toward the chair and slides onto it indolently. Her enthusiasm and composure appear to have vanished in a split second. He helps her sit comfortably at the desired angle, puts the canvas on the homemade easel, and peeps to check her posture. It has changed again. He returns and adjusts it. Back at the canvas four feet away, again she has changed her pose and looks edgy. After a few trials, at last he picks up the brush and begins loading it with the paint on the palette. With some effort, the outline of the face is affirmed in ten minutes, and he is ready to draw the eyes. But her pose is wrong and she appears too tense to let him paint a decent face, let alone one with a faint grin. She is simply a different person suddenly. *Oh, God!* Something on her mind seems to be disturbing her concentration. What has he done now? Maybe she is reacting to his indifference to her earlier comment about her dream. Maybe he should have asked her, "What was I doing in your dream?" But it was a silly question to ask then, and a sillier one now after all this time. So, he keeps his mouth shut. After two minutes, however, he loses his cool and snaps at her, "Why are you so tense? Is something wrong?"

"No," she replies without looking at him, subtly struggling to maintain her pose.

"It doesn't look like nothing," he says and drops the brush on the tray holding the painting supplies. "I don't wish to paint an angry Mona Lisa…"

She remains silent and he insists, "We can't work like this…"

Finally, she sits back in the chair, looks straight at him, and snarls, "Well, if you really want to know, it's the sight of this damn ladder in the middle of the room. I've gone through trouble to decorate this room and make my surroundings pleasant. But then you decide to put an ugly, dirty ladder before my eyes."

"Oh, my gosh…!" Darren utters with a sigh, stunned, peering at her with bewilderment.

She continues, "I suggested buying an easel and you refused. That's what's bothering me! I'd assumed you were sensitive about these types of details, being an artist and all."

"It's not the ladder. You just don't like to be contradicted, that's all!"

"No, it's the ladder. Just look at it, see how ugly it is."

"Sorry, I don't see it as an ugly or a horrible object when it's useful. Actually, I respect it for what it is and for helping me do an important task."

"So, you respect this dirty ladder more than you respect me and my wishes."

"It's not a matter of comparison!"

"That's how it sounds to me."

Maybe she is a lunatic like her sister, after all, he wonders.

"This poor ladder will be here only for a few days," he says calmly, attempting to reconcile with her. "Still, if I knew it would annoy you this much, I would've waited to buy an easel."

"I'm sorry. Perhaps I overreacted... But I feel you don't care about my wishes and perhaps even challenge me deliberately."

"Why would I do that?"

"I don't know exactly, but I can think of a few possibilities."

"Such as?"

"The saddest and strongest one is that maybe you really miss Mahroo and take it out on me subconsciously?"

"No, no... I'd never do that to you..."

"I'm sorry, anyway," she says.

"I'm sorry too. Let's make peace and continue. If you don't want this ladder here, I'll take it out right away."

"No; I guess I was upset about your insensitivity more than anything else. I'm okay now that you said you didn't mean it."

"Of course, I didn't mean it," he says, wondering about her brain again. "I didn't mean anything at all."

Darren glances at her and finds her posture dull. He moves forward and holds her head and cheeks gently to fix her pose again. But this time the smoothness of her hair and skin electrifies him with sensational pleasure. He retreats abruptly to hide behind the canvas with a blush. His mix of anger and attraction toward her at the same time feels bizarre to him, which again rekindles similar old feelings he used to have at times toward Mahroo. His jerky reaction also surprises and satisfies Mahtab. After regaining his composure, he peeps at her. She is posed properly, yet trying to find him from the corner of her eye.

"That's the right position. Hold it! Keep your eyes straight toward the window; I'm painting them right now."

Only the subtle sound of brushstrokes breaches the silence when the tape in the cassette deck ends. He is so wrapped up in the painting he is not aware the music has stopped. Gradually, she too feels relaxed, which improves her composure.

"Splendid! Show a very tiny grin on your face, please."

"Is this tiny enough?" Mahtab asks with a teasing charm.

"Yes. You look peaceful and pretty. What're you thinking?"

"It's hard to explain. It's a new experience: Something like flying with Mahroo and you, in a pleasant daydream, you might say," she says. "But didn't you say we weren't allowed to talk during the session?"

"I meant no serious discussion that requires thinking or might spoil the mood. I don't want to remember or explain my pathetic life while I'm painting. But small talks like this actually help. Tell me about your feelings if you wish," he says with satisfaction for his clever scheme to make her keep her gorgeous grin naturally in line with pleasant thoughts. The magical progress on the canvass is also raising his mood higher every second.

"I feel Mahroo's presence. I feel our souls—the three of us—floating around peacefully, exactly as we'd anticipated. Do you remember?"

"Yes. I feel it too. And the painting! I like what's shaping here, as if our souls were in fact flowing through the painting."

"Wonderful…," Mahtab cries with joy.

"Yes… It's actually looking so wonderful I might decide to keep it for myself, after all…," he says seriously and sombrely.

"No, you can't do that… You promised me…"

"I know, but I didn't expect it to become like this so lively and hypnotic. I can't give up this baby."

"I'll kill you if you do such a thing...," Mahtab screams and rises, looking at him with anger and angst.

"Okay, okay… I was only joking… Just sit down, please…"

"Oh, Darren, that was a horrible joke. Never do that again."

"Okay, I'm sorry… But sometimes I get a bit playful when I find a chance and I hope you forgive my childish jokes," he says.

"How much have you done?" she asks, after sitting down and shaking her head with a chuckle, happy about discovering this witty side of him as well.

"A lot… The main lines look fine. I'll let you go shortly, as soon as I finish a few small things here."

"It's okay. Actually, I'm enjoying myself despite the stiff neck and your silly jokes. I hope it doesn't look like me."

"Well, we can't help it. You two look very much alike, and a portrait never ends up exactly like the subject, either."

"Actually she was much prettier than me," she says.

Darren bursts into laughter.

"Was my comment funny?" she asks.

"Yes, in a way…"

"How?"

"Well, when Mahroo mentioned you in Vancouver, she said you were prettier than her, but she said a little prettier and you say not only the opposite, but also you think she was much prettier."

"I think I'm right and she was wrong. What do you think?"

Darren bursts into laughter again. "That's exactly what I was supposed to do when I happened to meet you. But now I can't."

"If you paint her properly she would be prettier," she insists.

"The main point is to show her soul in the painting somehow. Right?" Now suddenly he himself is uncertain about whom the portrait will finally resemble the most, Mahroo or Mahtab. This idea agitates him suddenly. He puts down the brush and rushes to the coffee table to look at Mahroo's pictures. Mahtab peeps at him with impatience, getting tired of sitting stiff, while he seems immersed in the pictures. "What happened, Darren?"

"I'm checking Mahroo's pictures. Take a break," he whispers, but then rushes to hide the painting.

"Let me see it? I can tell you whether it looks like her or not."

"Maybe tomorrow! Actually, you don't have to pose for me any more today. I'll work on other parts after a break."

"What other parts?"

"I've decided to add a background to help the composition and show Mahroo's character better, too."

"Explain it," she asks.

"A window will be in the background with the moon fully visible. The moonlight—Mahtab—illuminates Mahroo's face partially. Your names inspired me to symbolize your souls by showing the moon and letting its glimmer vitalize Mahroo's face, which also shows your desire to immortalize her in a painting. I'll always remember you two as Persian moons. In fact, let's name this painting *Persian Moons* as well."

"Okay… But I'm not comfortable with the background."

"Why?"

"Painting her in a room gives people a sense of entrapment."

Her philosophical observation startles him. He is happy she has found this major flaw, but sad about having missed it himself. *What're these Persian moons, then: lunatics or philosophers?*

"You're right!" He pauses. "But without a window, the idea of the moon as a main symbol of the painting won't be effective. I could show her sitting outdoors, on a beach perhaps. But that is not good either. Without any secondary objects in the painting, it would be dull even with the full moon. I need some vertical and horizontal lines." He ponders his new dilemma pensively, while peering at the bright blue sky through the window.

"How about using a solarium or gazebo in the background?"

"But she'd still be sitting in a confined surrounding."

"No… It wouldn't have any dull walls or a window. Narrow columns and railings could provide elegant lines and the hanging pots could enhance her surrounding. The moon glitters in the top corner and brightens the colourful flowers and the whole scene."

"Yes, yes… You're smart… You could be the assistant I've always dreamt about."

"An assistant only…? Thanks!"

"I'll make the gazebo look like a small garden. In fact, putting Mahroo in a divine surrounding would provide a sense of both serenity and security, which might be lost if we painted her in a dark room or on a beach. Thanks, Mahtab. You're a real genius." Excited by the improved image forming in his mind, he charges toward her and kisses her hand as a gesture of appreciation.

"Thanks." She blushes and pulls her hand softly out of his.

"But...," he says with a sigh.

"But what?"

"Well, there's another issue you might object to later, too."

"What is that?"

"The bluish moonlight is sort of gloomy and maybe even spooky," he says. "I like it myself since it reflects the melancholy we have all felt recently."

"That's fine. The melancholy gives it romance and warmth enough to offset the effect of spooky bluish rays. Don't worry."

"You're right again. Thanks... I'll make the changes before going for a walk. You can go now but we'll continue tomorrow."

"Fine," replies Mahtab, walking toward the door and thinking. "Would you like to go to the city and watch a bullfight?"

"Sure! But don't put yourself into any trouble."

"I'd like to go with you. We'll take Nazi with us too."

5

Darren's unexpected trip to Tehran and Barcelona has spoiled the plans of many people in Vancouver. Nora is an exception, as she has merely left a message on his answering machine about her departure to London, in case he misses her. But the interwoven plans of the trio—Elizabeth, Erica, and Jeff—as well as the thugs hired by Jeff are callously put on hold.

Having received only two calls from Darren all this time, Elizabeth is losing her patience with his selfish behaviour and erratic emotions. Is he really serious about their relationship, or just playing her with words worth less than the air carrying them? It took Jeff ten years to get somewhat presumptuous about their relationship, but only a few weeks for Darren to neglect her so casually. This is not a good indication, even if he is sincere about his feelings for her. Jeff seems by far more reliable, despite his possible affair with a bimbo. At least he has been demonstrating remorse and trying to win her back. Maybe he had been honest about helping his boss! Perhaps he would not have gotten into such a mess if they were married. These and similar thoughts have boggled Elizabeth's mind during the last four weeks amidst her suffocating solitude, Darren hardly calling her or showing any affection, and possibly lying about being in prison, too.

Erica, on the other hand, is becoming more obsessed every day with the idea of winning Darren back. She has always loved him despite their personality differences and his lack of ambition expected of a real man. He grasps her emotional needs better than any other man she has met. She has not dated many men to find an ideal one, anyway, since she is too timid about sex in a society revolving around it. She despises jumping into bed with men and feeling terrible the next morning. She cannot allow some wild characters in the 'love jungle' ambush her emotions and rip her heart and life apart. She wants a man capable of showing utter devotion—a desire too challenging nowadays. Therefore, Darren is her best bet while she can be proud of him as a real artist, too. *Oh, how stupidly I abused his love for me during our marriage!* She would like to stand beside him when his achievements are acknowledged internationally. So, the more she finds him out of her reach, somewhere in Iran, the more she wants him. She can hardly wait for him to return to Vancouver and her trap.

Jeff is extremely frustrated too, since the more time lapses, the harder separating Darren and Elizabeth appears to him. Her act of moving in with him and her rising apathy toward Jeff's pleas are the best proof of her growing attachment to Darren, even in his absence. He cannot do much but wait for Darren to return, so that the thugs can hopefully punch some sense into his silly head. He has not heard from the thugs, but assumes they are on the case, aware of Darren's travel timetable. He trusts them fully to bring Elizabeth back to him.

And the thugs keep contacting Elizabeth about Darren's likely date of return. They have borrowed money from a callous loan shark for another project that has gone sour. They are counting on the second payment from Jeff to relieve themselves of the mess with the loan shark. The interest and the chance of severe penalty for hiding are rising fast. They have not paid Greg's small fee for introducing Jeff yet and no other job is coming their way, either, since they cannot show their faces around for new business; their luck is depleting fast along with their patience.

6

Darren… if only he knew how many people's lives he has stalled with his sudden departure. He gazes at Mahroo's portrait after converting the background walls and window into a huge gazebo with narrow columns and colourful pots aptly placed in some corners. Still the background stays perfectly subdued to maintain Mahroo's prominence in the composition. She actually looks more vibrant and vivacious now. The new design is lively. "Thanks, Mahtab!" he exclaims with excitement. He puts patches of colour on the face by trying to remember Mahroo's distinct image from their last two meetings in Vancouver. He steps back and forth and squints to compare the portrait with the image in his mind. He believes her unique features have been captured at last. Overall, another successful workday ends and he leaves the wet painting with delight. He changes fast and hurries downstairs where Mahtab and Nazi are waiting for him. She drives to Placa de Braus Monumental, the bullfighting stadium.

"It's chilly....," Mahtab says as they settle in their seats. "I should've brought jackets for Nazi and myself. Aren't you cold?"

"No, I'm fine. I enjoy this breeze," he replies.

"This is such a special event, although some people detest its cruelty."

Darren smiles, reserving his opinion for later as the show gets underway. A group of junior matadors march into the stadium on foot and two on horses with their prods and swords, which they plunge into the bull's body.

"What's going on?" Darren whines with confusion.

"Be patient. Main matador will come later to fight the bull."

"But by then this bull will be dead or too weak to fight."

"These bulls are bred for fighting; they're very strong. These guys just make them a little tired and angry. If it were not ferocious enough the spectators would boo it out. Let me read the routine for you and Nazi from the guide." Mahtab takes out the guide to read, "First, a group of junior matadors, peons, test the bull and put it in the fighting mood. They may jump in to distract the bull, too, if the matador is in danger. Then the picador comes on a blindfolded horse that is protected by heavy padding on the sides against the rushing bull, yet gets wounded or killed sometimes.

"The picador plunges his lance into the bull's withers and then the peons return to tease the wounded, ferocious bull. After that, two banderilleros race toward the charging bull and shove a pair of colourful banderillas into its withers. Finally, the matador arrives and flings his red cape to lure the bull and bring the crowd to its feet by his fancy manoeuvres to defy the bull. At the end, when the bull is tired and useless, the matador places himself head on against the bull and inserts his sword directly into its neck, which kills it instantly."

"Big deal!" Darren says, making Mahtab burst into laughter.

The performance ends shortly after Mahtab's long laughter from his sarcastic jokes all along in line with her keen orientation. A team of dray horses drags out the carcass of the bull.

"Is that it?" Darren asks with another teasing gesture.

"No, the same routine will resume with two more bulls and matadors," Mahtab says after another long laughter.

After the show, she asks, "So, do you think it was it cruel?"

"Yes it is, but most importantly, I still think it is not a fair fight when the bull is attacked and wounded by an army in advance before that lousy matador comes for a show-off," Darren replies.

Mahtab bursts into still another cute laughter. "Oh boy, you're really funny and grumpy sometimes, too, like me."

"You're right, but today I have a valid case, I guess."

"So you think they should fight one-on-one from the start?"

"Absolutely… If it is necessary to have a fight to begin with."

"But bullfighting is part of these people's culture," she says.

"It's interesting how cultures clash. In India these bulls are holy and cared for, but here they're humiliated cruelly first and then killed ruthlessly. They worship the cows in one culture and waste them in another. We live in amazingly contrasting worlds on such a small planet connected by all symptoms of civilization, except for our minds."

"But these bulls aren't wasted," Mahtab says. "They end up in the butcher shop, according to the guide."

"That's even worse if they first make these cows angry and then feed their flesh to people or animals. I've heard that the meat of a deer killed after a chase is poisonous; why should it be any different for a cow that is not only tired, but also extremely mad when it's finally killed? Maybe a kind of 'mad cow' disease is already tainting the food supply and people's brains," he asserts. Mahroo's funny stare and grimace make him laugh. "I'm fooling around a bit, of course, you know! But maybe the world is going crazy from all the beef we eat."

She ignores his silly foresight or attempt for humour. "Let's go for a walk and dinner—maybe some madly juicy *beef*?"

"I'll have only seafood for the rest of my stay here."

They go to and stroll along La Rambla Boulevard again, then visit the Picasso Museum. They check the handicrafts offered by street vendors leisurely and Darren buys a souvenir for Elizabeth under Mahtab's inquisitive eyes. Once fully pooped, they choose a cozy restaurant that specializes in seafood and Spanish cuisine. During the fiesta, Mahtab confesses that, in her opinion, going to a nightclub to watch exotic Spanish dancing would not bother Mahroo's soul, but the family would frown upon such seeming disrespect. They agree to head back home after supper.

7

The anticipation of finishing the painting, for Darren, and seeing it for the first time, for Mahtab, brings them another restless night and early rise. Darren needs her to pose only for setting the mood and shadows on Mahroo's portrait. He adjusts her head toward left to let the light flow on her face and create a perfect ambience.

"I'm glad you pushed me to do this painting," he says.

"You like it now, ha?" she asks.

"Yes, but it was also a timely, soulful project for me. It helped me relax a bit and also learn to do portraits."

"So, are you feeling better these days?" she asks.

"Yes… We must somehow cope with all these sad realities."

"Like what happened to your plans with Mahroo?"

"Yes, and with all the wickedness and idiocy around us."

"I suppose your ordeals in Tehran, especially the prison, hurt you too much on top of Mahroo's death."

"Plus another issue I cannot even talk to anybody about!"

"Not even to me?" she asks with a charming smile.

"Unfortunately, not even to you…"

"Life is an endless and aimless struggle, isn't it?"

"It is. Anytime I believe I have my life figured out, something weird happens and ruins my peace."

"Even love is futile when our differences drive us apart."

"You seem to have everything necessary for happiness!"

"It only looks that way! I still feel like the woman in the white dress: Empty and desperate, as I said before…" she pauses with stress. "I shouldn't bore you with my confessions."

"No, don't worry! We all have concerns and insecurities."

"And they're hard to overcome, right? So what's the point of thinking about them and nagging, ha?"

"I guess… The bottom line is that we can't change anything or anybody," Darren replies.

"Happiness is a mirage, but what can we do to suffer less?"

"You're asking the wrong person."

"But how do you try to cope?"

"I just try to lose myself in some kind of passion. It keeps me amused and possibly fulfils my spirituality urges, too. The trick is to stop taking life too seriously or expect anything from it."

"But, not everybody finds the wisdom to feel and behave somewhat stoically just in hopes of finding relative peace."

"It happens naturally if we find our niche and passion."

"Isn't 'love' *a kind of passion*?" she asks wittily.

"It's supposedly the strongest kind."

"Yet it's usually the shakiest," she says with a sigh.

"Absolutely… That's why it is so rare and unreliable."

"I know… After returning to Iran and witnessing Bijan's mentality, life feels different."

"That happens in all relationships. It is natural."

"But not having someone to share our time and thoughts with is very stressful. He's careful not to upset me or force me to dress and behave according to the Islamic rules, but the environment is pushing us off the ledge and we're falling apart fast. I want to avoid conflicts, but I can't change myself or him. Sometimes, these days, I wish I were in Mahroo's place or with her. She was the only person who understood me and listened to my stories," she says, wiping away her tears.

"I couldn't imagine you were distressed this much!"

"I don't even have a career to keep myself busy."

"Why not?"

"Because I can't bring myself to dress according to someone else's rules, with all that Islamic hijab and no makeup."

"So you rather let all your education go to waste?"

"That's another reason I must go live in another country."

"Why'd you marry Bijan then?"

"I didn't know much about his Islamic beliefs and extremism until he started working with these fanatic people."

"At least you enjoy a rich life and he seems devoted to you."

"Our house and wealth belong to his father or are gifts from him. We've sold our souls in a way to enjoy an enviable lifestyle. Bijan must play their games, even if he were not so fanatical himself. Otherwise, we couldn't even afford to rent an apartment with the salaries we would make as regular citizens."

"Is Bijan happy himself?"

"He's enjoying his power like others, including merchants and businessmen who're abusing this chaotic situation."

"I see your dilemma! But I've also noticed you're a wise lady to salvage either your marriage or your soul if the situation gets unbearable. You not only look like Mahroo, but also have the same mentality and marital conflicts."

"Most people seem to have relationship problems nowadays. Her husband was mentally sick and mine is too obsessed with both his religious and political aspirations. But, you know, all women have problems with their husbands somehow."

"Poor husbands!"

"Yeah, poor men! Who's responsible for all this chaos then, if not men, especially in marriages?"

"I think the problem is that couples don't have a proper role model to build their relationships in this overly complex society. Phony values and rivalry have damaged the family foundation nowadays. That's why so many of them collapse or lead to sad situations where couples bear each other only out of desperation."

"Would these problems ever get solved?" she asks.

"I doubt it. We cannot solve such terribly tough, rooted issues easily. Just keep yourself busy with some worthy cause or hobby. Release the boiling energy I see in you before deepening your depression and damaging your marriage. I believe that's what Mahroo realized and did at the end, right?"

"Right. Actually I may volunteer at the same rehabilitation centre where she worked to find her soul."

"That's a risky thing to do though!"

"Why?"

"Well, I just wonder what the guy who killed Mahroo might feel if he happens to be still there. He'd freak out if he sees you, as if Mahroo had resurrected."

Mahtab bursts into laughter. "Yes, you're right."

"Maybe you should find another place to do volunteer work. You're a good pianist and maybe learn to paint, too. Maybe even do a portrait of Mahroo yourself."

"Are you looking for a student?" she asks with charm.

"I wish! I enjoy working with you. But we're reaching the end of our joint project. I must leave soon."

"Well, you don't have to if you don't want to!"

"It's time for me to face reality again. It was all a dream this last four weeks, with all the horrific and happy moments."

"It doesn't have to end yet. We can take the ferry to Majorca and stay for a few days—with the whole family. It'd be a good opportunity for you to relax awhile, without working or thinking so hard, before returning to your reality. It's a beautiful island full of topless girls sunbathing. You'd like the atmosphere."

"Your offer is tempting, but I'd rather not." Suddenly he feels sad, envisioning the future, his commitments, and having to bid farewell to her and other people he has now grown fond of. He is unable to think or paint any more today. The portrait looks good enough to set aside for the day, anyway. Any further brushwork today will ruin the perfect portrait he sees before him. "We're done for today. You wanna see it?"

"Oh dear, do I! I've been dying to see it for long enough!" she cries with excitement and hurries toward the painting. She stands speechless four feet away from the portrait, sunk in a deep trance, trying hard to control her emotion and tears. After a minute, she catches her breath and mutters, "Oh, God! My dearest Mahroo! I love you. Darren, she's really beautiful. You've outdone yourself painting such gorgeous eyes. And you thought you couldn't paint portraits! Really, everything is perfect. The gazebo and flowers are pretty and they show her vitality, too. Is it done?"

"Almost. I need very little modeling from you, if at all. I just have to tighten it up a little. Does it look like her?"

"I guess. Don't you think?"

"Yes, but it also looks like you. I've added special features and lines to show her unique charm, but I'm afraid of pushing it more."

"You can't help it, Darren. Everybody knows we look alike. Are you trying to deny that in your mind and the painting? It's just fine." She steps back two feet and gazes at the painting again keenly. "Hey, have you noticed anything strange about it?"

"Like what?"

"Come back here and look."

He stands next to her and surveys the painting carefully, squinting to detect *something strange.* "What's strange?"

"Look carefully," she says, tugging the curtain to let more light dance on the wet painting.

"Tell me before I go crazy," he protests.

"No. Now it's your turn to suffer," she says teasingly and starts to leave. At the door, she turns back and winks with a big grin, nodding in disappointment at his puzzled face.

Darren studies the painting, off and on, trying to figure out her innuendo, but nothing strange jumps out at him. Then, he goes downstairs to stroll in the garden. Nazi is playing by the pond, getting herself wet under the fountain sprinkles. Mahtab yells at her from inside the family room, worrying about her catching cold. Nazi, startled by her voice, retreats and glances at Darren timidly. But then soon she regains her composure and resumes splashing water with more vigour while monitoring the family room window, as if enjoying her defiance a lot. He smiles at her mischievous face approvingly and she returns a friendly smile to him. Her cute mischief will remain their secret. *Good for her!*

Later that evening, Mahtab teases Darren about his inability to find the *omen* in the painting—that is what she keeps calling the strange thing, which makes Darren even more curious. Later, they go to La Rambla again, the two of them, stroll for three hours, and drink coffee and cognac. They seem quite at ease and fearless about mocking each other. They laugh and joke, in particular about her comment about the omen. "You're lying, Mahtab, about this omen in the painting."

"I'll tell you what it is eventually and you'll be sorry for not detecting it yourself. But don't change anything on her face."

"Then you'd better tell me," Darren says.

"No, I'll take the risk. Do you need me again tomorrow?"

"No. If I need you, I'll come and get you."

They drive back and arrive at the villa close to two a.m.

"I'll find the omen in the painting tonight," he says.

"Dream on and happy dreams," she replies slyly with a grin.

He kisses her hand gently. "Thanks for everything."

She smiles at the door again, enjoying his friendship and the gentle kiss. Darren wonders about her liberal behaviour, going to the city with him and staying out until late, as though she were not married to such a fanatic Muslim. Her parents also seem used to these sorts of behaviour for two daughters raised mostly in Switzerland. *Nobody can ever tame these Persian moons!*

Mahtab wins: Darren falls asleep while squinting uselessly at the painting to find the omen.

8

At the top of a hill close to the villa, Darren finds himself strolling with Mahtab, who is still teasing him and chuckling. Picking juicy peaches from the trees and eating them ravenously, they look around for a fountain to wash their sticky hands. At last, they come across a house without walls on one side. A woman sweeping the floor with a broom notices them and points toward the back of the house, to a rushing stream. They wash their hands and return to the field atop the hill saturated with colourful wild flowers and crisp, refreshing air.

Nazi is playing on the side of the hill, peacefully approaching the end of the steep path where Mahtab and Darren watch her delightfully. With childish innocence and carefree spirit, she taps the rubbles on the path with the toe of her shoes. Mahtab yells at her to stop kicking the rubbles and hurry instead. Startled, Nazi leaps forward and backward, loses her balance, and plunges in a long fall directly into a big ditch that has suddenly opened up at the bottom of the hill. The horrifying hole resembles a deep cave or tunnel to the core of the earth with its opening full of heavy, mossy water of emerald colour. She plummets into the runny swamp in slow motion, but is gulped down the swirling funnel swiftly, so fast Darren realizes she is already out of reach in the depths of the earth, kilometres long.

He freezes after realizing that the chance of rescuing her is zero. She is gone, by all logical accounts, and jumping in to save her would be absolutely futile. It would be a stupid gesture, as he would surely be gulped down as fast as she was. A supernatural power lives in that swamp-covered cave. His demise would serve no purpose. As his initial shock mitigates and his brain recovers partially, he turns to Mahtab, who is standing in shock at the sight of the vanishing Nazi and his hesitance to jump in to save her. Unable to explain his position, watching her bewildered eyes is torturous, yet not as horrific as the sight of Nazi being sucked like a feather in a whirlpool. Despite his shame to look at Mahtab, he is suddenly keen to say, "Why don't you jump in yourself?"

9

Darren howls, opens his eyes wide, and sits up soaked in sweat, trembling. A dreadful fear about the nightmare's interpretation besieges him. He tries to ignore the corny idea of dreams' power of prophecy. Yet, he feels sad about at least two of the dream's main implications about him personally: First, he has shown no courage that prevalent social norms demand of *men only*. Despite the stupidity of jumping to his demise in hopes of saving a helpless child, even at a chance of one in a trillion, people still expect a man to do so, to show bravery regardless of the logic. Is he simply a coward then? Perhaps…! And second, he realizes, he had embraced life so dearly when the opportunity to face death had come up. So his occasional bluff of mocking death has just been baloney. He fears death like a mouse facing a hungry cat. How can he live with himself—such a coward, hypocrite man? *Aren't most people like me?* is the best excuse his brain can offer at five a.m. He tries to sleep again, yet Nazi's image would not let him. *Why was she in my dreams, especially in such a horrifying way? I've already killed both her mother and father! And that innocent child still hugs and kisses me any opportunity she gets. Oh, actually, maybe that was exactly what the dream was implying—maybe based on my guilt-ridden subconscious?!*

At first daylight, he goes downstairs with a sense of guilt and the thought of booking his flight to Vancouver. He takes only coffee and toast for breakfast and returns to his room to touch up the painting. After three hours, it appears complete. "That's it," he sighs with joy after plummeting onto the couch and gauging the painting from a distance. A deep sense of achievement and relief confirms the end of another chapter in his life and artistic endeavours. Indeed this painting qualifies as another one of his unique creations, in the way the subject matter has developed, the process, the outcome, and its sentimental value to him and others. He reckons only three of his paintings deserve such private status. His thoughts wander off and eventually stir conflicting emotions in him. They pull and push his nerves from all directions, as though a bunch of lost, desperate children, including his son and Nazi, were calling for help from the four corners of the room. He wishes he knew the name of his son at least.

Gradually the joy of creating such a masterpiece is tainted by a curiously strong nostalgia of unknown source. In spite of the painful experiences of the last few weeks leading to this riveting moment, he resents the idea of leaving these precious memories and people behind and returning to Vancouver empty-handed. The trip to Tehran and all the subsequent events have offered him an enlightening experience he will never come to grips with or forget. And going to Vancouver suddenly feels so unwise and unnatural. The last few days with Mahtab, especially, feel divine and dreamlike in his emotionally bankrupt, fatigued mind. But all he can do now is to stare at the painting blankly while his flimsy mind funnels the final fuels of consciousness.

In a fleeting moment, as he tilts his head slightly to shake off his melancholy, he sees what Mahtab has been referring to as an omen. He smiles with delight at his discovery while moving his head back and forth, and left to right, until he learns exactly how the effect works. He feels better, leans his head against the back of the couch, and gazes at the painting again with new admiration and joy, until he finally dozes off.

10

A sound awakens Darren with a startle similar to the one this morning after his nightmare. His heart thumps as that horrible dream about Nazi rolls in his head again. He remains numb for ten seconds until the knock at the door alerts him that somebody out there is anxious to see him.

"Come in," he yells, still dozy, trying to sit up on the couch.

The door opens and Mahtab steps in with a sombre look. She hesitates awhile, closes the door behind her slowly, and gazes at him for ten seconds. Then she walks fast forward with her hands stretched straight out toward him. "Hold my hands, Darren," she mutters from a distance while charging toward him in big strides.

Once near Darren, she lowers her hands so that he can reach them. He is caught completely off guard, numbly staring at her before grabbing her hands, pressing them gently, and then kissing them, one after the other. Maybe he is having another nightmare, or a ghastly one has terrified her. He does not know how to react, only pondering his nightmare and Nazi, uncertain whether to share it with her in hopes of preventing a bad accident. Yet, he decides it would only disturb the entire family without any reason to presume it would save Nazi's life, even if she happened to be in danger. What a selfish thought: Trying to save her now after letting her disappear inside that horrific sludge in his nightmare without moving a finger.

"Darren, we must think of something," she says firmly.

"Like what?"

"You and I. Something's happened. Don't you feel it? I'm not going to sit back idly. I must have a say in this matter!"

"What? What matter?" he enquires, still hazy.

"I say we must belong together," she states bravely.

His lower jaw hanging, his mouth wide open, she pulls her hands out of his and sits resolutely on the couch beside him, as if planning to hypnotize him with her sad, seductive eyes. Finally, he realizes the gravity of her request and responds with agitation. "How can we belong together when you're a married woman? Regardless of your new feelings about Bijan and his fanatic beliefs, I owe him a lot. What century are we living in, for god's sake? How long have I been sleep?"

"I've seen what Mahroo had seen in you, and I've found what she'd found in you. It's unfortunate you two lost each other, but should I lose you too, while we're both alive and healthy? Does it sound logical to you? I want to marry you if you're even half as attracted to me as you were to Mahroo. It's hard to find the kind of affection you showed for her in a man nowadays, let alone a man of your talents and sensitivity. I'm not crazy, unlike what you may think. Rather, I'm quite practical and perhaps a little selfish, in this instance, to force myself on you so candidly."

"Didn't I tell you that the painting Mahroo had given you was cursed," Darren exclaims. "It's certainly screwed your soul and mind, too, exactly like what it'd done to Mahroo."

"No, my attraction to you has nothing to do with a painting or its curse."

"It does… It does… I'm sure of it…," Darren exclaims.

"No, it doesn't… And I don't believe in these stuff," she says.

"But… B—" Darren stutters.

"But time is running out and we may never see each other again. I know Mahroo will be happy with this arrangement. She's been telling me this in my dreams and I felt the merger of our souls—the three of us—during the painting sessions. Love is a ridiculous thing; a myth, *but only myths can soothe our disturbed souls*—you said it yourself. Now it's time to stand by your words if you care for me. Take me as if I'm Mahroo. Get to know me the way you planned to know her. Mahroo and I are the same.

We've been destined to be your wife. Well… What say thou, as Shakespeare may put it—hey, my beloved?"

Her strong reasoning bewilders him. He is feeling fully numb hearing the truth—the crazy truth.

"Have you forgotten you're married?" he repeats with angst, unable to offer any other excuse for rejecting her bold demand.

"Do you forget we're at the end of the twentieth century?"

"But Bijan loves you—"

"But I can't love him anymore. I'll suffocate if I live like this for the rest of my life. I can't live in Iran anymore, anyway."

"But I owe him my life. I can't steal you from him as a token of my appreciation. Besides, have you forgotten his power? He can have us crushed in a flash if he wants to. I'm surprised you're not afraid like me."

"He loves me too much to hurt me. I may be able to convince him to spare you, too," she says half-teasingly with a smirk. "But, at the end, so what if he kills us? Aren't you willing to die for me if necessary? Ask your heart."

"Ask your brain!" he replies quickly with a chuckle. He is quite amused that such a beautiful woman is so witty or nuts, too —exactly like Mahroo. *This idiotic saga will never end!*

"Just tell me how much you like me." She decides to settle the matter before humiliating herself further.

"I've not given this matter any thought. I'd never imagined this kind of encounter in my wildest nightmares."

"Am I a nightmare? Have I scared you, my mushy man?" she says ardently, stroking his hair off his forehead.

He is dazed by her gesture, charm, and courage. "What have your parents fed you people? All three of you have some traces of lunacy in you, you know?" he asserts half-jokingly.

"Our ancestors are from the Bakhtiar tribes, known for their bravery, beauty, and sensitivity. We're brave, not lunatic."

"I see," Darren mutters desperately.

"So you don't like me? I can't fool around with you all day, arguing about something as delicate as love."

"I like you! I must confess! You sound and behave exactly like Mahroo, not to mention your total resemblance and lunacy. I never got a chance to know Mahroo as much as I've gotten to know you in the last little while. You're a wonderful woman, and I feel your sentiments as if Mahroo's soul is teasing me through you. She's avenging the heartache I gave her, I know! Oh, God, have mercy on me! But…" Darren pauses, as he cannot explain why he thinks they are on the wrong course.

"No buts! If you care for me enough, the rest will be easy. For now, we keep this conversation confidential until I sort out some of the details. I have to run now. My dad is feeling twitches in his heart and a doctor must check him. We have an appointment in an hour and I must rush; we'll talk some more later," she says and departs, sending him a kiss at the door.

She looks thrilled for fulfilling her urgent romantic mission rapidly just before rushing to attend to her other pressing, and possibly life-threatening, duty to her father! *Weird!! See how diligently she can handle two totally contrary, emotionally urgent issues!* Darren muses with surprise and admiration.

11

Darren is simply dumbfounded. A new height of eeriness has certainly been reached! Besides career and financial concerns, the anguish about his new-born son he may never see, the wrath of several high officials in Tehran conspiring to hurt him, the big load of sensitive, ominous secrets forced upon him, the threat of being mutilated by Sima's vengeful brother, being blamed for the deaths of Nazi's young parents—his own friends—so unfairly, infuriating Dervish Ali—his spiritual mentor—unwittingly, and worries about the sad state of his frail father, now suddenly Mahtab's marriage proposal is a new odd dilemma for him. As much as he strives to measure and mollify his emotional burdens, weirder dilemmas always emerge mysteriously out of nowhere to mess up his mind and life further. His dreams and daily dealings seem to be mixing up and manifesting in peculiar manners more every day. He can hardly distinguish his nightmares from reality nowadays whenever he muses over the oddity of his affairs. They all feel just too darn surreal.

He has made a firm commitment to court Elizabeth, who is anxiously waiting in his suite for his return from a long, horrific journey. He is still married to Erica, who has now realized she wants him back instead of a divorce, and now this: An implied consent to elope with a married woman—someone whom he has not even kissed as a sign of basic intimacy—all in a matter of ten minutes. He pinches himself to make sure he is alive and awake. It hurts. *Why is destiny playing these jokes on me? Have I finally lost my mind or I am merely a weak man?* He bursts into long, hysterical laughter.

His only thrill nowadays is the possibility of re-owning the *Woman in the White Dress* after four years of controversy over this seemingly cursed painting of his. Yet, even this revelation feels just like another one of his dreams finally coming true only through a bizarre miracle, yet possibly creating even more pains and catastrophes for him and others very soon. "Hey, Vincent, what're you doing to these women? And then turning them loose against me! Stop playing with our souls."

To his surprise, Vincent appears in the corner of the room and admires Mahroo's portrait, while listening to Darren's gibberish nagging. "I haven't done anything bad to anybody's soul."

"Yes, you have! First Mahroo loses her soul to the woman in the white dress and goes nuts. After she redeems it by giving the painting to Mahtab, you immediately borrow Mahtab's soul for the doomed painting again. She's gone insane now, asking me to marry her. What sane woman would give up her fortune in pursuit of a fantasy, especially with a poor, cynical, confused man like me? Why do they believe I can make them happy?"

"Perhaps they're content, free humans now, after lending their souls to the painting awhile! But you may be a good match for either of these women, anyway; *although Mahroo is dead now and you can join her only through heartiest love and courage.* As you saw in Mahroo's case, she repossessed the wandering part of her soul when she found a better cause to use it on. Then Mahtab gave up the painting, too. The painting does not steal their souls, but only helps them travel and live through a mythical sphere that keeps them safe awhile, like a cocoon protecting the flesh until it's ready to be born. Just gauge the merits of marrying Mahtab. Weren't you nostalgic this morning at the thought of losing her and returning home empty-handed?" Vincent disappears without giving Darren a chance to argue.

Then again, Darren ponders, if life is so erratic and chaotic, as it seems to be, why should he fight it relentlessly all the time with his demented logic and beliefs? Why not learn to take life in his stride? Why not let his soul and mind hover smoothly over all these common commotions, instead of clashing constantly with the jagged destiny? He recalls Mahroo's words in Vancouver when trying to convince him to go to Tehran with her. "Come on… Be brave. Let's forget our raw logic and facts, and instead focus only on our love."

But that's exactly what you've been doing hopelessly all your life, you fool, his conscience counter-argues immediately. He has seldom had any say about the relationships he has gotten into. Women—including Erica, Nora, and Elizabeth—have always forced him about making his relationship decisions immaturely, and now Mahtab is trying to do exactly the same thing, except more weirdly and forcefully. He remembers how, after one year of dating Erica, he had realized they were not compatible. He had reasoned, and even broken up, with her a few times, but Erica's charm had always drawn him back into the relationship. It was Erica who raised and forced the matter of marriage, like today's situation with Mahtab. Naively, he had assumed marriage might solve their differences, once they learned to work as a team. Alas, Erica never understood the meaning and means of teamwork! Then again, people, situations, and love vary according to their natures, too!

Despite the load of scepticism and his possible naivety again, he reckons Mahtab is a sensitive artist like him. She is willing to give up a life of luxury and the power and prestige of belonging to aristocracy—whatever it means in an Islamic society—all for the sake of his company and recapturing her basic life values! Is she real? Darren asks his brain. If she is true and sensitive, the way he has figured her out during the last few weeks, then maybe she is the soul mate he has been looking for. It would be a pity to lose her due to his own weird love principles. *Oh dear, how much I suddenly miss Mahroo! Why did she have to die so young? To solve the problem of Mahtab? Was that the reason?* he retorts, and suddenly the song from *The Sound of the Music* rings in his head: *How do you solve a problem like Maria…? How do you solve a problem like Mahtab…?*

After singing light-heartedly for a long while, his mind begins analyzing his situation again, still somewhat playfully. He admits that the strong personality and compassion he has witnessed in both Mahroo and Mahtab, during such short periods in both cases, resemble that of Maria's quite a bit. And Maria's love affair worked out so nicely in *The Sound of Music*. But honestly, stop being a clown, Darren. Maria was only a movie. Regarding Mahtab's problem, however, how potent is his information to use for committing to a relationship, especially one now requiring two difficult divorces. Curiously, he is not even sure, from his last encounter with Mahtab, whether he has already consented to her marriage proposal by his stunned submission to her desire—only by his silence perhaps. She had certainly taken it as his final consent, and even sealed the deal with a kiss from the distance, at the door. Nonetheless, he must just consider the ultimate risk: *I'm not asking her to divorce Bijan; that's only her choice. And I must divorce Erica somehow, anyway. The question is whether I like Mahtab enough to marry her eventually, if everything works out between us?* Affirmative, he concedes at last.

And of course, this is not just another emotional conclusion either, even considering his beleaguered state of mind after all the confusing events around him in recent months. He has arrived at this conclusion after long detailed analyses. A main goal is to find a reliable companion and stick with her before he goes totally cuckoo. He has compared Elizabeth with Mahtab in detail, and pondered the idea of returning to Erica, too. Oh, what a dreadful option, but still a strong possibility, knowing Erica's resolve. There is no way Erica could have changed enough to make their life together bearable; she still does not respect the concept of teamwork and sharing—not to mention her plot to own the *Woman in the White Dress* at any cost. She has always been too stubborn and selfish to soften, even after enduring many years of loneliness and lovelessness. So, he should somehow convince Erica to divorce him. *Gosh, is my obsession for so much analyses worth anything? Are they going to help me in the end?*

Deciding about Elizabeth has been a little harder, though. He had promised to be faithful to her, which he has been—mostly by accident perhaps. However, the bottom line is that he is not quite attracted to her since the day he had woken up in love with Mahroo. Somehow, the joy of courting her has diminished. He realizes Elizabeth is still one of the sexiest girls around, as much as Erica is perhaps. However, they do not have enough in common in terms of artistic passion. Of course, he admits his erratic mood has stopped him from learning about the poor girl. Nonetheless, he decides to confront her sincerely and express his inability to honour his commitment to stay with her.

12

Elizabeth answers the telephone ringing in Darren's apartment.

"Please don't hang up, Elizabeth!"

"Only if you don't make me angry… You understand?"

"Okay." Overzealous at the rare opportunity granted him, Jeff pauses to choose the right words. He is unprepared for such an unexpected fortune. His heart racing fast, nonetheless he should now offer fresh evidence and emotions to maintain her interest;

maybe even confess, true or false, if necessary, to keep her on the line. He is losing his nerve when an incredible idea jumps in his mind: "Can we go for dinner?" Daring such a blatant request is surely too risky, yet he hopes she would not hang up just for one question. On the positive side, however, a chance to meet will give him time to put his case together tightly. The risk of being screamed at will be minimal in a restaurant, too, while he can watch her face and stay on the right track while pleading his case.

"When?" Elizabeth asks.

Wow…! She seems to be softening, he reckons, but dying to know why. He is braver now and in control of the momentum.

"How about tonight? I can pick you up in twenty minutes…"

"Okay, I'll be ready," she says and hangs up abruptly.

Swell…! He muses, nervously proud of his progress so far. Apparently, a good chance to win her trust tonight is presenting itself, in spite of her rough attitude and pretence. Giddily, he puts on his leather jacket, sprays cologne on his face and clothes, and rushes out the door.

His confidence boosts further when Elizabeth appears in her elegant Chanel dress. That is another excellent sign, since she has taken the trouble of wearing one of her precious dresses and made herself so pretty for him. If she were not in the mood, she would have appeared in jeans without makeup. Yet, he decides to avoid overconfidence. For ten minutes, while driving tensely, he ponders his plan for winning her back. He has even invested six grand in it, preparing and praying for an occasion like this to arrive soon. In the restaurant, however, he is timid to implement a scheme that might backfire. She peers at him stealthily with mix feelings, hoping to hide her embarrassment for cooling down and meeting him after two months of ferocity. The dinner proceeds with corny conversations while they fear the possibility of ruining their chance to reconcile. *How weak and desperate I feel and look tonight,* both Elizabeth and Jeff think.

At last, Jeff decides to take a risk, hoping that perhaps a shock could break her unyielding resistance better than all his pleading and logic so far. At the very least, his offer would still reflect his sincere feelings, which may count for something in the end. He gasps, gathers courage, and grabs Elizabeth's hand resolutely.

"Please marry me? I promise to love you forever," says Jeff, reaching with his other hand into his pocket, taking out a small box, and opening it in front of her eyes. A one-carat diamond ring glitters brilliantly a few inches away from her bewildered eyes. As her first ever-received marriage proposal, his gesture feels like a big deal considering her recent state of mind due to loneliness and Darren's sudden apathy. Jeff senses a glimmer of hope, as she seems delightfully shocked, the way he had hoped. So, he squeezes her hand and pleads once more, "Please say yes!"

"No, this isn't going to solve anything. We still haven't sorted out your last goof-off, and your persistence in blaming your boss makes me angrier," she says, but in a much softer tone now.

"Just tell me what you want me to do for your forgiveness?"

Elizabeth knows that her guilty conscience has been the main cause of her resistance, all along playing the role of a betrayed lover and brainwashing herself as well! His infidelity still has not been proven, whereas she has already slept with Darren a million times and made up all sorts of lies to stay with him. But now that Darren seems unreliable, she might as well stop playing these juvenile games and return to reality. Besides, the ring looks quite gorgeous and the chance of living a quiet life with a professional man who loves her dearly is too good to pass up. She also thinks that pushing Jeff to confess to something he has or has not done would not solve anything. She might as well exploit this situation to build their future.

"The problem is that even making you confess won't solve anything, anyway," she mutters.

"Especially when there's nothing to confess...," Jeff says. "What should I do then?"

"I must believe you love me and will never cheat on me again... But how can I be sure?" she asks cleverly.

"Just look at my eyes. See if I'm telling you the truth."

Elizabeth stares at him with a seductive smile and bursts into laughter. "You've worn me down! I submit. But you must write a *promissory* note with all your promises tonight. This, I'll consider our peace treaty. God forbid if you break it!"

"Okay. But I want you to promise something, too." Jeff feels the need to stop her galloping for dominance before it gets out of hand. He has been gaining confidence and momentum, too, after noticing her vulnerability and subtle eagerness to make up. He is not a total fool, after all.

"What should I promise?" she asks, intrigued by his nerve.

"I want us to forget this incident. Stop mentioning it and don't get bossy because I've agreed with your demands tonight. Can you be a tender partner?"

Taken aback by his daring demand, she realizes the validity of his intention. She should stop playing the role of a tough broad forever, especially with the man she is supposed to love or at least share a life together. Deep down she wants to end this madness, too, to start a normal life and maybe even raise a few children. Therefore, it is time for reality check and reasonableness instead of bullshitting.

"It makes sense to forget the past and stop growling about it. I agree," she says, relieved that her immoral adventure has ended and she has no more use for Darren. Even better, now she does not even have to explain or confess her open, widely publicized, love affair with Darren! Then again, she ponders, Jeff's apathy to hear my confession is probably a proof of his deceit and affair. *He has fooled me, after all!* What a lot of deceitful human beings we have turned into!

"Thanks for understanding. Let's put this ring on your finger then. May I?" Jeff proposes while taking the ring out of the box. Elizabeth holds out her hand as he rolls the ring over her finger. He then leans over and kisses her on the lips. People around them deliver their seal of approval with their smiles and nods, and Jeff calls the waiter and orders a bottle of Dom Pérignon.

13

Mahtab had stayed alone in her bedroom last night after returning from the clinic with her father. She also appears lost in a cloud of melancholy this morning. Her timid grins look mysterious and sad to Darren. All her vibrancy and vigour yesterday to convince him to marry her have evaporated overnight as well. Now that he has accepted the merits of her proposal, she looks so cold. Now he is confused again, unable to interpret her erratic attitude or get her alone to seek clarification. At last, he reckons her decision to divorce Bijan has now sunk into her head and she is struggling with the matter of breaking the news to Bijan and her parents. It makes sense, as it is a major mission for her. So he decides to leave her alone to sort things out by herself and come to him for help only when necessary. After dinner, he takes an old copy of *Time* from the coffee table and returns to his room. Later in the evening, Mahtab knocks at the door and Darren lets her in.

"Sorry, Darren, is this a bad time to talk?" she asks with pain.

"No … What's bothering you?" he asks with passion.

"Us! It's not going to work!"

"Oh…!?"

"I was foolish and hasty yesterday...," Mahtab says.

"That's what I thought and said yesterday myself! But what made you change your mind today?"

"It's getting too complicated. I've just come to apologize for lighting the flares of a doomed romance," she replies timidly, turning slowly to leave.

"Well, that's fine… But you might like to know that I spent all afternoon yesterday to digest your weird marriage proposal and justify your sudden idiotic infatuation. And it took me a few hours to analyze your logic and believe in your dreams," he says with a tense chuckle and smirk, pauses, and stares at her with confusion. Mahtab droops with anguish and embarrassment.

Darren continues, "Your crazy proposal put a lot of extra strain on my already blemished emotions. But then I convinced myself you were right. Now, just one day later, you return and shatter, so casually, the foundation I'd built carefully yesterday after so much emotional and logical struggles?"

"Sorry, Darren…"

"What's going on in your head? Why have you two sisters and brother conspired to bring me down to the threshold of utter lunacy? What have I ever done to you people to deserve this?" he yells irately, but thanks God privately for clarifying the situation before things had gotten more out of control. It is a blessing to be rid of moody people who keep changing their minds about love every day. Swiftly, he reckons he has often done the same thing himself, most recently with Elizabeth. Had not he promised her to love her? How soon he has forgotten it. *What a hypocrite I am!*

"All right…," Mahtab murmurs. "I hate bothering you with details and rather confidential issues. But I don't want you to feel so badly about me, either. I'll explain."

"Yes… Explain… Please…"

"First of all, my feelings for you haven't changed. Don't ever insult and upset me by doubting my sincerity." Nonetheless, she is disturbed and speechless by the overwhelming emotions and the task of wiping her tears away. After a minute, she continues, "Yesterday when I took my father to the clinic for a check-up, it suddenly dawned on me to do a pregnancy test. My period is late often. But yesterday I got an urge to take a test. I'm…" she pauses and shakes her head with stress. "I'm pregnant…"

"Oh…! Congratulations…"

"This is usually a happy occasion for most women, but to me it felt like being thrown into an icy lake. It wouldn't be wise to abort it without Bijan's knowledge even if I were a deceitful wife. But I'm also against abortion in principle. I believe I'm responsible for this baby from now on. The matter of divorce would be too complicated, if possible at all, as soon as Bijan finds out he's a father. I can't give up my child and he won't divorce me easily, either."

"I understand...," Darren mutters.

"If all these hurdles weren't enough, the doctor confirmed yesterday that my father has a severe heart condition and should be kept completely away from further stress. I'm worried not only about the possibility of any news, like my divorce, prove catastrophic for him, but also about my mother's health in itself, and her worries about my dad. The situation is just getting too damn complicated, and at this time I can't accept responsibility for their demise, even though I should sacrifice myself and bear grave suffering of my own forever probably."

"You're right…," he whispers timidly.

"It's strange how destiny prevents us from pursuing our dreams despite our courage and convictions. We end up facing situations beyond our control that ruin our spirits and chances of fulfilling our emotional needs. They force us to compromise our values and ambitions and maybe even settle for a degrading life. Do you believe now that I'm trapped?"

"Sorry for doubting your sincerity and sanity! Forgive me," he says with guilt and subtle howling.

"That's alright. You've been under so much stress yourself these last few weeks. But I enjoyed your passionate lecture and disappointment for losing me, too. I loved your confession about our special bond and your desire to marry me, after all!"

"Still, I should've been more tactful. So much appears to be going on in your mind, and then I nag about my problems, too!"

"I'm sorry, Darren. I didn't mean to hurt you," she says.

"Don't worry about me. I'm used to disappointments. All my life has been like this: Fundamental setbacks and regrets."

For ten minutes, they sit quietly, gaze at each other, or stare awkwardly around the room and at the corners of the ceiling, as if a solution might fall off the sky. He thinks for a second about persuading her to reconsider their options more thoroughly rather than giving up outright. She could have been an ideal companion for him. Maybe there is a way they can still be together, perhaps sometime in the future. However, at last he admits the matter is too complex and reverts to being himself, not pushy or proactive.

Let it go, you romantic fool, he murmurs to himself. *Should I ask her to make love to me at least?* he ponders with wit and stress. *I'm a sick man or what? Just a funny sick devil!*

"I have nothing to do here then," he says, matter-of-factly.

She stares at him a long while hopelessly unable to challenge his conclusion. She nods and asks, "Is the painting complete?"

"Yes. I'll take a final look at it before I leave."

She looks for the painting but does not see it. "Where is it?"

"It's leaning against the corner of the desk," he replies.

Mahtab turns the painting over and examines it carefully from a distance, stepping to left and right. "Did you figure out the omen in it?" she asks passively. She is not in much of a mood to argue with him or tease him anymore, and Darren knows she will tell him about the omen right away without any fuss. Even more disheartening, he is not in a mood to play a game with her about this matter, either.

"Yes, her eyes...," he mutters.

"How is it possible?" she asks. "How can she suddenly turn her eyes toward me with a wider grin, only when I stand here?"

"It's pure magic. I couldn't have achieved such an effect if I'd planned it that way. Hide it again when you're done."

"A secret mystery about this one, too, already," she says.

"Just another divine mystery… Only for us to know, I hope."

"Thanks a lot, Darren. It'll be the shrine for our souls. The three of us will continue meeting there forever, I promise."

"That's how I feel as well. Can you please get a professional photographer make a large, clean picture of it and send it to me?"

"Sure. When will it be dry? I must go back right away, too. I'll feel homesick here without you!"

"In a week. A frame shop should wrap it properly, especially if you're traveling soon," he says lethargically with pain. He wishes a miracle would prevent this eventful trip and experience from ending. Mahroo's smiling image, however, is the only miracle manifesting in front of him for a few seconds while he watches Mahtab leave the room, without looking back.

Chapter Sixteen
Puccini's Ploy

1

Erica finally agrees to see Jeff at the Starbucks close to her office only after he swears the news will be exciting.

"What's the good news you dragged me here for?" she asks.

"Elizabeth and I are back together," Jeff replies.

"Really…? When did this happen?"

"Two nights ago. We're gonna marry in fact."

"That's wonderful! Congrats! Has she moved back in?"

"Not yet. She doesn't wanna dump Darren on the phone. But luckily, he's arriving tomorrow. She'll just pick him up from the airport, explain everything to him, and leave right away."

"Great! I'm happy for everybody."

"I've shown your stupid husband that I can beat his arrogant ass if I want something, especially if it was stolen from me in the first place."

"Right!" she says. "Get our money back from the thugs then."

"I've gone to the bar every night to cancel the contract, but there's no trace of them. The bartender is on holiday and nobody else knows these guys. I doubt we can get our money back, but maybe we can save the other half if I can convince them."

"Just don't pay them. They haven't done anything for us."

"Forget the money. I'm worried about something much more important."

"What?"

"Now that the matter has been solved peacefully, we'd better not be associated with these people."

"That's true."

"Especially if Darren finds out we've been conspiring to bully him, he'll be furious instead of intimidated."

"Why didn't you get a contact number from them?"

"I believed the bartender was a reliable contact. Besides, I'm sure they wouldn't just give away their address or number."

"What're you gonna do now?" Erica asks nervously.

"I'll keep looking for them at the bar. What else can I do?"

"I don't know…"

"Anyway, the main reason I wanted to meet you was to stress we must be prepared for the worst," Jeff says.

"What do you mean?" she asks impatiently.

"These guys have been contacting Elizabeth about Darren's return. So they probably know about his arrival tomorrow. I can't tell Elizabeth what we've done, either. She'll get angry and might even change her mind to leave Darren. So if I can't find these thugs in time, they may do their thing to him."

"It's silly to upset Darren now that Elizabeth is also leaving him, Damn!"

"That's exactly my sentiment," Jeff says.

 "So what're you suggesting?"

"I'm saying we'd better get ready to deny our involvement."

"I'm not sure it'll work," Erica says.

"We should take the risk. We'll mess up everything if we confess."

"Those guys will tell him they're working for you. Why are you so daft?"

"No, I've told them not to mention me to anybody, either, when they asked me the same thing. So, that's part of the deal."

"But Darren would guess you're behind this. Who else he'd think hires some thugs?"

"You, of course!" Jeff says with a smirk. "Darren knows you do anything to get what you want and hurt Elizabeth as well. So it's better we both deny and keep Darren confused and guessing forever."

"Jeff, you're really a jerk," Erica says and leaves with stress.

Angry about their plan backfiring, Erica plummets onto the sofa in her office. After pondering many scenarios extensively, she decides she must forewarn Darren of the situation in the least damaging way, unless Jeff agrees to go wait outside Darren's building for the thugs. Otherwise, Darren would definitely put two and two together and conclude that either Jeff or she has been behind it. He would alert Elizabeth about the mischievous criminal she is getting mixed up with just to win her back. So, Jeff's idea of leaving things alone and playing innocent is totally invalid. They should actually do the opposite and tell Darren directly as soon as possible.

She calls Jeff. "Your stupid plan is not going to work and I've just wasted two hours weighing our options."

"And?"

"We cannot leave the situation alone because Darren may win Elizabeth back all over again. Are you willing to take that risk?"

"No… So what do you suggest we do?"

"Try harder to find these guys. If you failed, guard Darren's building for a few days to catch them when they come around."

"Are you crazy? Is this what you've come up with after two hours of wasting your time?" Jeff shrieks.

"This is one of the options…," Erica yells back at him. "As I've said again and again, your brain just doesn't work…"

"How long you suggest I camp behind his building? Besides, they may come when I go buy a sandwich or to the washroom, or when I've dozed off. Or they may wait for him somewhere else."

"Then follow Darren everywhere until you find them."

"And then what? Confront them in front of Darren?"

"I don't know, damn it! You got us into this mess and you'd better fix it."

"Why don't you go wait for them if you think it's easy?"

"I'd do it if I knew them."

"I'll give you their descriptions. You won't miss them if you saw them."

"They won't listen to me to call off the contract, anyway."

"I can't go wait for them, anyhow. What's your other stupid option?"

"We must tell Darren everything then!" Erica replies.

"Are you out of your freaking mind? That's how you think your brain works better than mine?"

"No, I'm serious. And it shows that my brain works hundred times better than yours, by the way!"

"Think, Erica. He'll tell Elizabeth what we've done. That's even worse than the risk of Darren guessing who's behind it while we both play innocent."

"I doubt it. Darren will definitely consider you the most likely suspect."

"I'll deny it," Jeff says. "Darren and Elizabeth know who's sleazy enough to do such a thing—you."

"I'll tell them you came to me with the plot and I refused to participate. I'll give them enough evidence to believe me."

"I'll say the same thing and let them figure it out on their own," Jeff says. "At worst, I'll give them a copy of the cheque you gave me for paying these guys. I have a copy."

"Damn it, Jeff. Get serious before we screw up everything again. Let's give Darren a heads-up."

"But that's risky," he says with a sign of softening.

"It'll be riskier if we don't, and it's certainly a worse sin than the initial plot."

"Why?"

"Because then the plot had a purpose, and now it doesn't. We'll come across not only as devils but also cowards."

"How do you want to tell him?" Jeff asks, intimidated by her threats and conviction. *She's a real devil.*

"Are you sure you can't tell Elizabeth without upsetting her?"

"Yes… She'll go ballistic. I'm not sure she'll forgive me."

"She might think love was behind your plot. It'll show your assertiveness, too," Erica suggests dubiously.

"I doubt it. She'll only think about our conspiracy and feel sorry for Darren. She'll go back to him immediately."

"But if she forgives you, Darren's reaction when we warn him, or leave the matter alone, won't matter."

"That's too risky… Besides, you must be involved, too."

"Okay, then, just leave it to me. I think I can work this out. But let's agree I'll warn Darren promptly, and that you'll deny knowing anything about the plot if it ever comes out. Agreed?" Erica has already concluded these two conditions are essential for her plan.

"Fine by me!" Jeff is surprised. Erica's conditions sound like music to him, especially the second one, in which he is out of the picture totally and should deny everything. *How the hell is she going to pull this one off?*

2

On her way to the airport, Elizabeth rehearses the story she has made up to recite for Darren and convince him that her decision is not selfish, or contrary to the commitment she had insisted on so keenly herself. She feels even guiltier now for goading him to dump Nora. *You'd better go find Nora and get back together, for your career at least,* she plans to tell him. *You need her more than you need me!*

After a long delay on Granville Street, she finally crosses the Arthur Laing Bridge and drives tensely on the westbound lane of Grant McConachie Way, which will bring her to the airport in three minutes. With a busy mind messed up by rapid traffic signs, she turns off into the wrong lane and is forced to drive only forward after realizing her error. Cursing Darren while driving slowly over the speed bumps and at the crosswalks, she finally reaches the end of the lower level of the airport and returns to the eastbound lanes of Grant McConachie Way. She emerges into the westbound lane at last and starts her entrance slower this time, with keener attention to the signs, remembering now that Darren is on an international flight, not a domestic one.

On the sidewalk, Darren is waiting impatiently, checking his watch with a grimace. Yet, he smiles when she draws close to the curb after a twenty-minute delay. Despite his calm appearance and accepting her apology without fuss, she is quite agitated and indecisive. Is it still appropriate to break the bad news to him? But if not now, when? In return, Darren feels her gloom, guilty vibes, and tension dulling her face, which are most likely not related to tardiness, especially after her cold kiss on his cheek despite his desperate, warm approach. So, he tries to break the bizarre silence at least.

"So, how've you been?" he says tensely, loathing his naivety and fantasy during the long flight to Vancouver about Elizabeth greeting him with warm kisses and affection. He had hoped that returning to her embrace, at least for now, would remedy the agony of his emotional mayhem in Tehran and the peculiar love story in Barcelona. *I'm a hypocrite user too! Who am I? Dervish Ali was right when he ordered me in prison, 'Grow up, Darren!'*

"I'm fine," Elizabeth replies. "How was your trip?"

"It was an awful experience. I'm glad to be back home."

"Yeah…?" she mutters with cynicism.

"If I'd known what was awaiting me, I would've never left Vancouver. Other people's lives would've been in a better shape, too!" he says, wondering how he had found and lost two great candidates—which happened to be sisters too—for both love and maybe even marriage in a matter of four weeks.

"Did you find out why you went to jail?"

"Yes. But I'm not allowed to talk about it."

"Is anything about your trip not secret?" she asks with anger.

"Yeah. I can tell you lots of things, especially about Evin."

"Who is Evin?"

He burst into laughter. "It's the name of the prison I was in."

She takes his excuse for concealing the cause of his arrest as another clue about his hypocrisy or at least inadequate intimacy. One more reason for leaving him. Suddenly she gains more nerve to confront him with the bad news.

"I must say something important before I lose my focus."

"It sounds serious!" he says.

"Yes, I've decided to reconcile with Jeff. I know I'm breaking our commitment and going back to him may be a big mistake. But he seems genuinely in love with me and wants to marry me. I want to settle down, Darren, although I care for you a lot. You're still wandering in a dreamland in search of love while struggling with the scars of your marriage to Erica. I cannot wait for God knows how long for you to figure out your life. Jeff and I know each other, and that counts for something. He and I both made mistakes by taking our relationship for granted. But we have now realized we belong together, as companions at least." She pauses to catch her breath and take a glance at his sad, tired face. "I recall your comment the first day we met about not mixing up love and companionship. That's what I'm doing."

"Me and my big mouth!"

"Really! It's all your fault," she says teasingly.

"How about all your affections for me?"

"You'd better go back to Nora, for your career at least. You need her more than you need me!" she says smoothly and feels good about her delivery of such a corny advice after inventing and rehearsing it in her mind during the last few days. "You'd better go find her and make it up to her…!"

"I kind of anticipated this from your kiss. I wasn't a good candidate for you, anyway; perhaps not for anyone!"

"Sorry, Darren…"

"Maybe if I hadn't left Vancouver or was a little stronger now, I might've fought harder to keep you. I'll always remember you," he says with mixed feelings. He misses her, especially now that he feels so lonely and horny, but he is happy to have his suite back to himself and his commitment to her annulled. Seclusion will be more suitable for sorting out his many pressing issues.

"I knew you'd understand. It was nice knowing you, too. Jeff will probably have difficulty to stay friends with you, but I'm sure I'll see you around, maybe at your painting exhibitions."

"The third one…!" he murmurs unconsciously, as he recalls his thoughts a minute earlier about his bad luck with Mah sisters. *The third one I've found and lost in six weeks!*

"What?" Elizabeth enquires with surprise.

"Nothing… Any other important events in my absence?"

"Not really… Except for those guys who called a few more times, including last night. I told them you'll arrive today."

"Okay… I wonder who they are. They appear too persistent."

"Also, Erica called yesterday to congratulate me for getting back with Jeff. She sounded ecstatic about her chance of getting you back now that I'm out of the way. She's left you a message, anxious to see you right away."

"I'll call her later," he says.

"You're a gentle man and vulnerable to her charm under the present circumstances. Be careful not to make another mistake."

"It'll be your fault if I do..."

"Sorry, Darren… We had a good time, though!"

Darren smiles. "Anything else?"

"A customs' broker called about a package from Iran."

"Okay, thanks. So, when're you planning to move out?"

"We've moved my stuff and I'm going home after I drop you off," she says with a sigh of relief.

Even after all her depressing news about dumping him, he had still hoped and imagined spending at least one more night with her! He feels sad about being left alone tonight. However, quickly he ignores the murky thoughts and decides to make a plan with T.J. or Erica if he has any energy later.

Elizabeth drives away quickly after dropping Darren off in front of his building. She does not even offer to help with his big luggage, somewhat apprehensive about possible consequences upstairs. Clumsily, he drags his luggage to the elevator and his apartment, but is glad to be finally back in his own place, after all the bizarre adventures and most unusual sleeping places. The fragrance of a bouquet of yellow roses in the vase on the coffee table fills the apartment. Everything is clean and tidy, but all the signs of Elizabeth ever living there have disappeared.

3

Darren hears the telephone shriek as he finishes his shower. It stops by the time he grabs a towel and rushes out to answer it. He pours himself a cup of coffee, collapses onto the sofa, and turns on the TV. The telephone rings again.

"Welcome back," Erica says. "How're you?"

"Tired from all the traveling and time changes."

"I know but I must see you tonight. Have you had dinner?"

"No."

"Come to the Keg," Erica says, musing that the bad news must be broken to him over a juicy steak and wine.

"Okay. In one hour?"

They chitchat about his adventurous trip over a bottle of BC's famous Cabernet Sauvignon while waiting for their steaks.

"Reza told me about Mahroo's horrible accident," she says. "It must've ruined your time in Tehran, too."

"Yes. I didn't even see her in Tehran," he replies with gloom, recalling his last meeting with Mahroo—their brief romance in front of their building right before her departure to Tehran to die. *That sweet kiss at the very end!*

"I didn't like to ask Reza about the *Woman in the White Dress* now that Mahroo isn't around to enjoy it," Erica says, trying to explore his knowledge of it. Resisting her temptation to ask Reza has been tough enough and admirable, she believes, considering her concern about the painting going missing.

To Darren, however, the idea of Erica rushing to meet him only for exploring the situation with the painting is disgusting to the point of almost getting up and leaving this selfish bitch. But then he decides to wait around and see what she is really up to and perhaps tease her a little about the painting, too. He feels he should at least kill some time with her to negate his nostalgia of being back in Vancouver and feeling so lonely.

"He probably won't be able to give you an answer, anyway. He doesn't know anything about it," he replies.

"And you do?"

"In fact, I do."

"How do you know more about it than Reza?"

"Because I've got the painting," he says.

"You've got it?" she yells so loud a few patrons stare at her.

"Yep!" he replies triumphantly.

"It's in your apartment?" she asks sceptically. Maybe it is just promised to him or something like that. Yet, any information would be useful for pursuing the matter with Reza right away.

"No, it's not in my apartment yet," he says slyly.

"Aha! So who's promised it to you?" she groans.

"It's not a promise; I own it," he states with a smirk.

"You own it only when you have it."

"It's at the customs. I'll call them tomorrow to deliver it."

"I hate you… That's my painting. Reza promised it to me."

"He shouldn't have…"

"How'd you get it?"

"It's a long story, but Reza had nothing to do with it, and he still doesn't know anything about it, either. He lost control over it a long time ago. Mahroo gave it away and I bought it from the new owner; the end."

"Did you go all the way to Tehran just to steal this painting from me?"

"Are you nuts? I had more important business there."

"You're nasty, Darren… And just imagine me rushing here to protect you from danger."

"Danger?"

Now it is Darren's turn to fret. A gush of cold blood runs through his body as many scenarios cross his mind quickly. Maybe people chasing him in Iran—mainly Sima's brother—have tracked him here and are still trying to harm him. Or maybe Bijan has sent his people to punish him for having flirted with his wife and planning to elope with her. Maybe Mahtab has changed her mind again and asked Bijan for divorce, after all, because of her love for Darren. What chaos! And not knowing what Erica knows will be excruciating…, again. He reasons Erica could not have heard any of these secrets from a third party to use for speculation or manipulating him now. She could not have learned anything about his adventures, since not even Reza knew about the grudges against him by Sima's brother or uncle, Mahtab's marriage proposal, or Bijan's likely motive for harming him. So her information must be firsthand from a source in Vancouver. Maybe she knows about some people looking for him and has somehow learned they are planning to hurt him without knowing them or their reasons. Maybe they have been trying to find him through Erica. That is probably how she has learned about it. Thinking that she might know any of his secrets agitates him, as he is at her mercy again, especially if she intends to blackmail him now, at least to get the painting from him.

"I'll tell you everything if you give me the painting," she says.

Erica's blunt demand sort of proves his clever suspicions and 'rumination' power. In return, he decides to bluff and hopefully make her eager to talk. Besides, if someone is going to harm him, it is still hard for him to verify the information or prevent it.

"I'm not giving you the painting. Keep your secret… Why would anybody want to hurt me…? I haven't done anything."

"Oh yes, there is. Believe me," she insists, only thinking about Jeff's plot against him. If she knew anything about his recent struggles with all kinds of threats, she would have definitely used the information to exploit his vulnerability. But now, she agrees with him: Who in his sound mind wants to hurt a lamb like him? Nonetheless, she makes one final desperate comment: "I strongly suggest you reconsider before it is too late and you're dead."

Darren does not reply despite his growing fear and curiosity. She actually seems to know even about the severity of the danger he is in by her reference to death as a likely outcome! He pours wine for both of them and starts chopping up his steak. They exchange antagonistic glances in complete silence occasionally. Like two professional poker players, they have both bluffed coolly and now wait for the other to fold. The steaks are consumed and two bottles of wine are empty, yet she cannot see any sign of flexibility in him.

Although somewhat intimidated by Erica's blunt warning, Darren thinks that dying might not be a bad outcome, after all. What is the point of living the way life has turned up so far? Meanwhile, Erica believes that insisting on getting the painting would only complicate the matter at hand, especially since she should depend on some form of concession from him tonight, anyway. *Maybe I should focus on getting him back first, in which case the painting would come to me, too, automatically.*

They order coffee and Erica raises the main topic. "Okay, keep the damn painting. But if you still want me to give you my information, you must promise on your honour not to discuss it with anybody, not even your family or friends. No one else must know this vital secret. You should also forgive the guilty party, who's now totally sorry and ashamed of his actions."

"Here we go again!" he murmurs with a bitter smile, recalling Bijan's similar demands and the promises he had to make to him.

"What?" Erica asks.

"Nothing... I've been forced to give many promises these days and keep touchy secrets."

"What kind of promises. Have you promised somebody to marry her?" she asks with tension.

Darren bursts into laughter remembering that he had in fact done exactly that, too—promised to marry Mahtab—although she had luckily withdrawn her proposal in the last minute.

"No, forget it," he murmurs.

"So, are you going to promise to keep our conversations and some possible events secret?"

"Why should I promise, in case I need to defend myself somehow or punish the perpetrator?"

"Because he's repentant. And at the time he plotted against you, his actions seemed logical—stupid but justifiable under the circumstances. Besides, he doesn't want to let out his secret or incriminate himself without receiving some kind of indemnity."

"Is it useful information?"

"Very much."

"Is it related to people in Iran?"

"No, but it's very important."

Darren senses Erica's firmness about her conditional offer. He concludes that forgiving the repenting guilty party is better than not knowing the information or the culprit. Satisfying his boiling curiosity would also be another incentive. Since he has won the painting argument, accepting her offer would not be so terrible. "Okay, I promise on my honour."

"Put your hands on the table," she insists.

For a split second, he thinks she knows about him crossing his fingers when making his promises to Bijan. What a shrewd broad she is. She probably remembers his playful trickery and cheating at card games. So, he puts his hands flat on the table and repeats his word of honour.

"Remember, no tricks!" she says seriously. "You'll now take this secret to your grave."

"Okay. Tell me the damn secret already, woman!"

"Jeff was really desperate to get Elizabeth back. So he hired some guys who promised to scare you off. He's been trying to locate them to cancel the contract, but he can't. He's asked me to warn you. Just accept their request and send them away. He'll keep looking for them, but if he fails, he wants you to know he's sorry, although you're the one who stole Elizabeth from him in the first place. 'You started the whole thing,' is what he asked me to tell you."

"So that's who these guys are!"

"You know them?" she asks with surprise.

"Some guys have been asking my neighbours and Elizabeth about me. I guess Elizabeth doesn't know this?"

"No, she doesn't and she shouldn't. Remember our deal?"

"Jeff must've really gone crazy to come up with this idea. I'm glad Elizabeth took him back. They deserve each other."

"Yeah, they're both nuts but he loves her. Forgive him."

"He's done a stupid thing but it isn't a big deal. I'll accept their offer and send them away. Is that the end of it?"

"Jeff said they sometimes fire a blank bullet into the person's head and stress it'll be a real bullet next time. So, Jeff wanted you to be ready, again with his apologies. But he also insisted I keep telling you, 'You started the whole damn thing!'"

"He's an asshole, letting some hooligans shoot a bullet, even a blank one, into my head. Maybe I should stop Elizabeth from marrying this nutcase. She'll be sorry."

"No. No talking to anybody about this, remember? Besides, Jeff said he'd deny the whole thing if somebody finds out."

"But you can corroborate with me if I call the police, right?"

"No, I will deny our conversation, too."

"Are you also letting Elizabeth make a big mistake, on top of betraying me? What a friend you are, for her and for me!"

"She's quite snotty herself. She can handle him perfectly if necessary. But Jeff really loves her. He might hurt others or himself for her love, but he'd never harm her. Believe me. Don't interfere in their life."

"You all disgust me. What's your role in all this?"

"Jeff came to me because he was embarrassed and also too angry to face you personally. At least he had the decency to warn you. You stole his girlfriend of ten years! You started the whole thing, I must agree with him."

"I don't know… It all sounds too suspicious to me."

"I got mad myself and gave him hell, but then I knew I must warn you quickly."

"So, now what? Should I just wait for a jerk to fire a freaking fake bullet into my head? Perhaps I should teach them a lesson."

"No, just let it go. Just faint on the floor and they'll leave."

"I'll see… I'll have to think about it…"

"A better option is to move in with me tonight. They won't find you there… You stay with me until Jeff finds these guys."

"No… I'll take my chance with the thugs."

"You rather face these killers and get a bullet in your freaking head than staying with me a few days until this threat is over?"

"Yes, I'd rather get shot and die!" Darren says with a giggle.

"Sorry to hear that…"

"Just tell Jeff it was a stupid thing he did and I'm letting him off the hook too easy. Tell him to find these assholes and stop this nonsense." He pauses and yawns deeply. "I'm really tired and better go home."

"How about the painting, then?" she says, hoping to exploit his weakened spirit and apparent drowsiness. "Do you wanna sell it to me after everything I've been doing for you?"

"What's your obsession with this painting? I don't get it!"

"I don't know either! But who deserves to hold on to it more than me, anyway, if it's about me? Why don't you get it?"

"Get what?"

"That this painting is about me!"

"I'm keeping it myself." He proves not as weak or droopy as Erica had hoped.

"Can I see it at least? I've seen only its picture in the papers."

"Sure," Darren says as they separate outside the restaurant.

4

Just around the time Erica and Darren are wrangling over the *Woman in the White Dress*, the angry thugs are staring at its picture in the *Vancouver Sun* article Jeff had given them.

"She say he's famous painter," the bearded one, Edgar, tells the stocky one.

"Who say that?"

"This paper say his painting sell quickly."

"Lemme see!" Albert grabs the clipping, reads it, and gives it back to Edgar. "So maybe he better give us some painting for our troubles. He's been nasty customer… Stupid ass!"

"You think we should get something of him?"

"I think so… He make us wait so long for nothing."

They keep blabbering over the damages Darren's travel has caused them financially, professionally, and emotionally. They realize Darren knows nothing about them or his role in causing them so much anguish inadvertently. Still, he is, in their book, the core of their rising problems. He is their worst customer ever, not just a victim, which makes him responsible for their damages, according to the laws of criminals—not criminal laws.

"Okay, les get something of the asshole."

"You shoot a blank in his freaking head and we grab couple paintings. I put real bullets in my gun for running with paintings," Albert suggests nervously.

"Jeff may not pay if he find out we took fucking paintings."

"Fuck Jeff. He won't dare fuck with us, but who'll tell him?"

"Darren will tell him…"

"He'll think Darren's lying… when we say so."

"You sure?"

"Hey, man, his paintings is worth four times what fucking Jeff owe us, you know. Don't hassle me, man. Okay?"

"But we need cash quickly."

"Just grab his paintings, okay?"

"Yeah, okay."

"Lemme see that paper again." Albert grabs the article from Edgar again. "I wonder where this one is!" he says, pointing to the picture of the *Woman in the White Dress*. "She say this is his masterpiece. That's maybe forty grand, but she say it's in Iran."

"We get another ones from his apartment," Edgar replies.

5

Darren wonders why he is feeling so jubilant this morning. The travel exhaustion and jetlag symptoms have evaporated during the night after leaving Erica and driving home cautiously to avoid the police. He probably had more alcohol in his arteries than haemoglobin, forget the safe level for driving. He had started drinking on the plane after feeling quite homesick away from Persian moons and the *Persian Moons,* had a strong gin and tonic in his apartment, and then shared two bottles of wine with Erica. Feeling euphoric now, instead of hangover, is indeed weird.

It is a bright, cloudless morning, a rare event in Vancouver in this season. Yeah, everything feels perfect today and inhaling a dozen deep breaths out on the balcony, while watching the ocean and horizon, invigorates Darren. He feels fortunate to be alive and enjoy life so fully without fussing any more about anything or anybody. Except that all these exhilarating sensations revive the experience of six weeks earlier, when he had awakened deeply in love with Mahroo. Today's feelings are peculiarly quite similar. He has not dreamt or thought about her, but somehow senses her presence.

In fact, he feels so bubbly he forgives Jeff at once for his plot against him and laughs heartily about it. The plot seems childish and entertaining suddenly, which makes him wonder why he had reacted sharply toward Erica last night. He actually looks forward to meeting the bullies to laugh in their faces. He ponders a few options for encountering them, to make a complete fool of them and enjoy watching them sweat trying to convince him to give up Elizabeth. He can play it so cool or uncooperative they go nuts.

On the other hand, he can tell them Jeff has already confessed to him about the plot and the contract is off. If they do not believe him, they can call Jeff to confirm. It is hard to decide, though, as each option has its own merits and risks. To play it safe, of course, he must stop fooling around and instead comply with their instructions quickly or ask them to call Jeff. Though this option would not bring him any kind of fun that he is craving so much today. He has not had a chance to tease anybody in recent months and now a grand opportunity has just been dropped right at his feet.

Even more amazing, he feels so awakened and awkwardly joyous he calls Erica in the office and offers her the *Woman in the White Dress* free. He knows he could easily get some money for it from her, to help his upcoming financial distress. Yet right now, he does not care about money, either. He simply cares about nothing, period! And he is elated for being attached to nobody! He giggles at the tiny chance that his sudden urge to give the painting to Erica is a subconscious drive to test the curse of the painting. It might be fun to witness Vincent's messing about with Erica's soul now that Mahtab has given up the painting, too. It would be exciting to watch Erica going nuts in a different way and losing track of her business even more. Best of all, Vincent will be surely thrilled with Darren's effort to find him such a qualified new candidate to fool around with her soul. Keeping Vincent happy is a big incentive for Darren in itself, after all!

He had called the customs broker earlier in the morning and arranged for the delivery of the painting in the afternoon. So he tells Erica to come and pick it up around four p.m., before he changes his mind. He imagines the chance of having sex with her as well, to allay his burdens of sexless life in recent months. Erica is also eager to take the painting immediately, before *he* changes his mind. She is baffled and suspicious of his sudden change of attitude and generosity. *Maybe we could have sex, too, to make up for his generosity! Maybe he's ready now to come back into my life and love me passionately again!*

What else to do to create a perfect day on his first day back in Vancouver, in such a wonderful city, Darren ponders. "Painting! Of course! That's what I should do quickly, before losing my jubilation," he utters joyfully, charges to the storage closet, and chooses a 36 by 48 inch canvas. He hangs it on the wall, ready for painting. "But what to paint?" he consults his brain. *Tosca...* of course! The painting he had promised Giacomo when they had met on the boat—a scene from his opera. He contemplates and visualizes a composition from the last scene of the opera. That will look superb when done, he imagines.

He begins working fast without even preparing a sketch. The brush loaded with paint moves around fast and places incredibly delicate marks in remarkably meaningful designs. Listening to *Tosca* during this riveting painting exercise maintains the desired mood. His fast, expressive brushstrokes keep filling the large canvas. With such unprecedented vigour and speed, he might even finish the main features of the painting tonight. He pauses only briefly for lunch and to relax his arm and fingers. The soul of the painting is emerging: *The way it's evolving, it'll rekindle my fame and fortune in Vancouver.* What an experience! Energy and joy is lifting his soul beyond his normal self. *Maybe this is finally the 'break' that Vincent had promised to come my way?*

6

At 3:33 p.m., while the third act of *Tosca* is resonating for the third time today, the intercom buzzes and Darren lets the FedEx deliveryman in. He then opens the apartment door and watches him move the oversized box out of the elevator arduously and carry it to his apartment. He signs for the package and brings it in gently. When he turns to close the door, two Oriental guys with large dark glasses are standing at the threshold. Startled by their abrupt appearance and perturbing presence, he quickly guesses they must be the infamous thugs mentioned by Erica.

"What can I do for you guys?" he manages to say coolly.

They merely push him over, step inside, and close the door. Darren is undecided whether to confront them or play along calmly. Yet, his instincts tell him not to be brave, funny, or cool. Instead of teasing them, he should settle the matter quickly and get them out of his apartment to resume painting *Tosca*. So, he shuts his mouth and watches them survey him and the walls. The music is echoing loud with passionate arias and duets—the final promises of love and freedom.

Darren blurts finally, "I know who you are! Jeff told me he's hired you. But the deal is off. The woman has already gone back to him. He asked me to tell you the contract is cancelled."

The thugs' lifeless faces turn red as they lose their edge and wonder how to react now that their authority has been crushed by the alertness—the smartassness, actually—of the victim himself? Wasting time on their regular threats and intimidation routines is foolish if Jeff's demand is already fulfilled. Nothing is left to do, it appears. But they have spent so much time and the prospect of not even getting paid for the service, because the victim himself seems to have the authority to fire them, is ridiculous.

Albert gathers his thoughts finally and growls, "What the fuck are you talking about?"

"Jeff said to tell you—"

"Shut up, you sly son-of-a-bitch; Stop lying."

"No, believe me. Call Jeff if you want. Here is his number."

"Forget Jeff, asshole…"

"You can check the apartment. There's no sign of a woman living here—no clothes or even a strand of a woman's hair."

Albert withdraws his gun and points it at Darren nervously. "Shut your mouth, you bastard. Sit down there and be quiet," he shrieks while moving around with agitation. After so many years of successful planning and execution of much tougher missions, this is the first time he has faced such a weird and equally funny situation. But he is in no mood for laughing off the matter and going away empty-handed after all the snags chasing this haunted project all along and ruining their business and spirits.

Darren sits on the sofa obediently, enjoying himself slightly, too, while watching the thugs' desperate struggle to salvage their pride. He is not overjoyed, though, since the threat is not quite over yet; the guys do not seem convinced about letting him off the hook and they sure look crazy enough. *By the way, I'm not as brave as I'd planned to be today or often like to think!* he ponders in despair. *Just another proof after my recent dream about Nazi.*

With no finished painting visible in the living room, Edgar strolls to the bedroom and returns with the *Path to Heaven*. "This the only fucking painting here?"

"Yes."

"Too bad! Because now I have to kill you for lying; tell me where the rest of them are," Albert demands with anger.

"I took all my paintings to Iran and returned to Vancouver yesterday, as you already know! I'm just starting to paint again, as you see," he replies patiently, enjoying his cautious mocking attitude toward the pissed thugs a bit. "Maybe you wanna come back in a few weeks!"

"So you think you're funny, too?" Albert yells.

"What's in the big box?" Edgar asks, walking toward the box. They had actually slipped in behind the FedEx guy when Darren had opened the building door for him.

"It's not mine. Its owner will come to take it any minute," Darren says, hoping to hasten the guys out of his apartment.

Edgar opens the corner of the package and pulls the painting out. He stares at it for ten seconds before taking the newspaper clipping from his pocket. He grins triumphantly and exclaims, "Hey, this the painting in the article… *Woman* something…"

"It's our lucky day, after all!" Albert says joyfully.

"We'll take these paintings. Tell Jeff to bring our money or we'll come back and deal with both of you," Edgar commands.

"Leave them alone," Darren says, walking toward Edgar.

"Shut up or I'll kill you! Just go sit there," Albert cries, and then turns to Edgar. "Take the box; I'll bring this one. Les go."

Darren moves toward Albert to grab the *Path to Heaven*. "Stop fooling around, guys. Put them down, please!"

Albert thrusts him onto the sofa and yells, "You crazy? Stupid ass! You want me to blow your fucking head off?"

"Listen, I know your bullets are blank. Jeff told me also about your trick, so stop fooling around. If you don't get out now, I'll scream and alert the neighbours. Come on, put it down."

Albert charges toward him with fury and the gun shaking in his hand. "You know this bullet is blank? You think so, you motherfucker? Yeah? Yeah?" He keeps screaming, fully out of control, grabs a cushion from the corner of the sofa, puts it next to Darren's neck and fires. BANG! The sound of the muffled blast is mixed with the echo of gunfire from the big speakers near the end of the last scene in *Tosca*—Mario falls down to his death. Darren collapses too, onto the sofa and then to the floor. The whole world is revolving before his astonished eyes. The thugs pick up the paintings, leap swiftly out of the apartment, take the elevator, and run out of the lobby.

The arrival of two men at the entrance with a big, narrow box and a painting stops Erica Swanson from ringing the buzzer. Instead, she holds the door for them to move their big loads. The elevator is ready and she takes it, quite excited about seeing and owning the painting she has craved for three years. Before the elevator stops, however, the scene of the two guys carrying the big loads alarms her. *Could they have been the thugs?* Agitated, she charges toward Darren's suite as the elevator door opens. She knocks but turns the doorknob, too, and it gives. She shouts, 'Darren,' and enters, but neither a reply nor a sign of him comforts her. She reels forward, looks around nervously, and finds him sprawled unconscious on the floor. She drops her purse and rushes toward Darren, now certain that the guys she had so courteously held the door for had been the thugs.

"Darren, Darren! They're gone, my darling. Get up!" she yells and kneels next to him, thinking he has fainted. She lifts his head to help him sit up. But instantly, a thick liquid fills her palm.

She drops his head swiftly with terror and gazes at her bloody hand fretfully. She scurries to the balcony and sees the thugs in a side street, loading the big paintings into an old van. She gets furious, realizing the big box should have been the *Woman in the White Dress*. She begins screaming, "Come back, you thieves. Stop those killers."

The thugs hear her bitching from the balcony, but ignore her while attempting to load the paintings. Coolly they monitor the situation from the corners of their eyes. But, so far, her uproar seems incoherent to the bystanders standing under the balcony, wondering why she is yelling and what she is pointing to.

Erica loses her patience with the deaf and daft people in the street. Frantically she steps up onto the lower bar of the railing, bends over a little more, and yells at them more vigorously with her arms flinging in midair like a struggling swimmer amidst the ocean waves. "Stop those thieves, you idiots. That's my painting! That's my painting! Bring it back, you bastards."

But all this explosive energy breaks her balance on top of the round railing bar for a split second. She is airborne suddenly, at the exact moment Tosca throws herself over the parapet at Castel Saint' Angelo. Horrified and helpless, dazed by disbelief, Erica senses the stupidity of her life until this last moment when it is all over! SPLASH.

7

A fatal silence suddenly shrouds Darren's apartment after Erica's screams on the balcony end, the loud music of *Tosca* stops, and the noisy commotion of the last twenty minutes is gone with the dying daylight. Darren wishes they would all return immediately, back to normal. Sprawled listlessly on the floor, gazing at the corner of the ceiling fretfully, his heartbeat is slowing down fast with less blood to pump. A creeping darkness begins to crush him in the depth of the excruciating silence, his consciousness waning quickly and sending him into a deep coma. The faint sound of the telephone ring triggers an obscure notion of the rolling, monotonous existence, yet he has no urge or energy to answer it! On the fifth ring, the answering machine turns on and his father's rickety voice echoes, complaining about the piglet's new tyranny.

"Oh, Dad!" He gasps for a breath irately, cursing his failure to help his dad all these years. So frustrating his father's case has been all along, but mostly in recent years due to his rising senility and stubbornness! Past memories, both pleasant and petrifying, roll in his mind swiftly—about the times he had looked up to him as a reliable authority figure and then later when his father's lifestyle and worldviews had began faltering. What is going to happen to him now, Darren tries to envision: Just more agony. *Thank God, I won't be around to witness the misery you'll bring upon yourself.* "Goodbye, Dad," he whispers when the answering machine stops taping his dad's new account of the piglet's endless invasion of his privacy.

Next, from the corner of the ceiling, he observes his own flesh lying still near the sofa helplessly. Then the building caretaker and a police officer enter the room. They check his pulse and summon the paramedics attending to Erica's body in the street. Gasping for a breath, he swiftly flies at a horrendous speed into a dark, narrow, endless tunnel. He flies faster and faster in vain— there is more and more distance to fly in the darkness. "Still more struggles, even in death?" his fading consciousness nags at his flying spirit. Eventually he recognizes Vincent's voice echoing from the end of the tunnel, where a tiny light is flickering. "Come along, Darren! You can do it! This is the break I'd promised you, my friend. Just fly faster and you'll be with me soon. You can do it!"

Epilogue
Love or Life

1

T he eccentric ambience of the room looks familiar to Darren as he rests on a couch. An intense glow outside the half-open slit window in the far wall narrowly penetrates the dense plantations swarming its outer frame. A silky breeze also flows amidst the glitters and conveys the fragrance of flowers.

In the depth of the overwhelming calm, he can hear the birds chirping outside and a faint, rhythmic reverberation of the ocean surf washing the shores gently. A beckoning sensation picks his curiosity to go peep through the window, but he is sunk deeply in the new experience recomposing his identity. He lingers on the couch languidly to savour the exhilarating moments in the new habitat some more. It appears like a resort, a stopover sanctuary perhaps, an ancient mansion full of travelers' jolly memories of times they had spent in its soul-soothing serenity. In spite of the dark wallpaper and bulky, ancient furniture scattered throughout, the room is delightful by virtue of the pervasive glory emanating through the window. Its primitive calm ambience is majestically charming with no pretences of modernity—no wiring, electrical apparatuses, or any kind of communication devices. The wooden slit window, its two panels opening outside, has its own elegance despite the crooked edges and the peeling, light blue paint. Close to the slit window stands a small, square table decorated with a colourful embroidered cloth and fresh flowers in a tall vase at its centre. A narrow, wooden chair rests next to the table facing the window, indicating that habitants often sit there to enjoy the view out there.

After gauging his surroundings with awe and absorbing the novel ecstasy of the appeasing world welcoming him, Darren rises and strolls softly toward the window. Next to the chair, he stops and leans against it, puts his hands on its top bar, and peers through the window.

His viewpoint puts him in the upper floor of the manor, with a vast, colourful garden extending in three directions below his eye-level. Straight ahead, about seven hundred feet beyond the foot of the house, the garden connects to a white sandy beach. The emerald sea extends to the horizon and placid ripples swoosh the shore in soothing rhythms. In the far distance, a sailboat with glittering white sails moves leisurely on a tidy westerly course. Yet, he imagines it will soon cross past his viewpoint behind the tall trees on the right-hand corner. On the beach, a woman stands still, hypnotized by the slow motion of the ship, yet deeply worried about its imminent disappearance beyond her reach and sight. She is wearing a white, wide brim sunhat and a long satin dress, also in white, with a luxuriantly loose skirt.

Immersed in the splendour of the moment, Darren realizes swiftly why the room looks so familiar to him: He had in fact envisioned this exact scene for painting the *Woman in the White Dress*. He recalls Vincent's comment about helping him picture this composition. He then fuses deeper into the present instant as his spirit merges with the pervasive perspective.

He freezes in the precise moment and composition that the painting of the *Woman in the White Dress* had manifested.

He is definitely the man in the painting, peering through the window; it is established now for eternity! Yet, the identity of the woman in the white dress still remains enigmatic. Although he had created that woman—the one out there in the white dress— in the image of Erica, based on her melancholic behaviour, many events have since transpired and distorted the figure's identity. A few souls have been injected into and out of the painting all along, according to Vincent and his own experiences with the women who have owned or encountered the painting. Therefore, the soul representing the woman at this moment still remains a mystery while he watches her back. What is she doing out there, anyway, staring at the boat so solemnly?

Darren unfreezes at last when the woman in the white dress raises her arm and waves eagerly at the ship. It stops abruptly and turns around. Its scintillating sails swivel and the big boat slants to the right slightly, then it travels toward the shore. The closer it comes, the giddier she gets, as evident from her rapid flinging of her arms. Darren imagines she is responsible for good omens somehow despite her gloom. The boat looks bigger and busier as it approaches the shore, until it halts short of hitting the shallow waters. It is familiar to him, too, especially the sound of cheers and music echoing from a distance. Three dinghies are lowered from the boat. Two-dozen men board them and paddle the rest of the way to the shore.

The woman in the white dress dances with jubilation and splashes the waves with her bare feet. As the dinghies draw closer to the beach, she lurches in the shallow waters toward the men, with the bottom of her skirt floating musically over the slow ripples. Darren recognizes the Masters as they disembark the dinghies and hug the woman. The glowing whiteness of her dress vanishes amidst the big crowd surrounding her until, at last, they all follow her toward the garden. With the sun shimmering through her hair, gradually her face transpires as she steps out of the glistening sea. For just a moment, she resembles Erica. But soon he recalls those delicate lines mapping her face; his heart thumps, and his fingers move as if painting her again. Joyously, he mutters, "Mahroo…"

The crowd gathers at the far-left corner of the garden, near a huge gazebo shadowed by large, green leaves of tropical plants and tall banana trees. She chats with Vincent, glances toward the window, and points Darren out to him. She then peers at Darren with passion before beckoning him.

Ecstatic like the noisy crowd in the garden, promptly Darren finds the stairs and reaches Mahroo. They kiss passionately a long time in the shadows of a weeping willow tree, weaving and whirring woefully in the whispering wind. Vincent watches them from afar pensively and patiently. Yet, after their soothing, sweet kiss, Mahroo appears sad. Darren wraps his right arm around her waist as they walk up toward Vincent. Darren embraces him like an intimate friend.

"Good to see again, Vincent, and thanks," Darren says.

"What for?"

"For inspiring me and also protecting our broken souls in the painting for this blissful ending."

"What blissful ending?" Vincent asks edgily, stares at Mahroo stealthily as if sharing a sombre secret, and staggers away.

"For our reunion! Why are you so grouchy?" he shouts, then glances at Mahroo with bewilderment about Vincent's rudeness. *Oh, gosh, people are rude even here,* Darren ponders in despair and surprise.

"Come along, my darling, don't mind him," Mahroo whispers solemnly. "Let's take advantage of our short time together."

"Are you leaving me too?" he asks with confusion and angst.

"They've come for me and I must leave soon."

"How about me? You wanna leave me alone here?"

"You must return to your mortal life or stay in the mansion for now," she replies, reaching out to him and holding his hand.

"Why? What am I doing here then?"

"You're visiting! You're having a 'near-death experience.'"

"How do you know?"

"From the way you kissed and touched me?"

"Is that why Vincent left me, too?"

"Yes. But he'll still be your mentor. Don't worry."

"Why don't you go back with me?"

"I can't… My mortal life has ended. But you… I guess you still have a chance to return to life and make us proud."

He runs to Vincent, who is motioning Mahroo to prepare for departure. "Am I still not worthy to go with you?"

"You're not ready yet!" Vincent murmurs.

"But I'm here now. Can you help me go with you?"

Vincent thinks for a while before answering. "If you're really serious, I can get a special decree for you to choose between love and life."

"Good… Please do."

"Here we go…" Vincent pats Darren's head. "Now go ahead and choose."

"What happens when I choose love?" Darren asks.

"You'll die and enjoy Mahroo's eternal love. And together, you'll inspire desperate mortals who need help."

"And if I return to life? What would I do then?" he asks, as if trying to negotiate a deal with Vincent.

"Probably the same shit... You're so pesky, as usual," Vincent murmurs impatiently and staggers away.

"What? What'd you say?" Darren watches him disappear amidst the crowd. Running after him feels rude when he notices Mahroo's bewildered look, waiting anxiously for his choice and devotion. She is certainly wondering why he is so indecisive and behaving so bizarrely even under this circumstance. Why is he still so cynical even when he is facing the moment of truth and a chance to choose love or life?

Even in my 'near-death experience', I face dilemmas! What kind of a 'break' is this? The idea of letting her go away alone singes his heart. But the spirit of life is still engulfing him and stirring all kinds of justifications for leaving Mahroo and living. "One can't abandon one's spirit lightly. The body may break; the brain may stop; but the spirit goes on glowing, even creating this 'near-death experience' and all its frantic musing. Choosing life does not mean betraying Mahroo, *I hope*. I must return to finish my mission. Maybe this 'near-death experience' teaches me find my way of salvation. Escaping life is silly until I earn my right for immortality."

Mahroo approaches him, holds his cold hand, and leads him toward the manor. "Let's go, my lost lover. I'll walk you back to the House in Eternity. Go back upstairs and watch me sail away."

"You come inside, too," he insists, still gauging the notion of life being stronger than love contrary to common belief and what he often sees and enjoys in those mushy operas.

"I've lost the 'spirit of life' that's goading you to live. Maybe we could be together if you'd come for me sooner!" she says with a teasing tone as they reach the stairs in front of the manor, but maybe also a hint of sarcasm for his decision to abandon her.

"Sooner? Like when?" Darren asks.

"All the time you were begging in the streets of Tehran and teasing me, enjoying the bullfight in Barcelona, fretting about painting someone's portrait, or agreeing to marry Mahtab!"

"Oh…! Must you mock me even here?" Darren asks.

"Maybe if you'd jumped to save my daughter at least, when you had a chance to join me, now we could be together forever."

"Are you serious?" he asks, thinking she is making a good point. Her kind sarcasm reignites his memory and shame about his dream where Nazi, Mahroo's daughter, fell into the fast sinking whirling sludge at the bottom of the mountain. Then, he simply could not gather enough courage to jump in for one in a million chance to save her or survive himself. And now, jumping in to love the mother does not seem like a viable or useful option, either. *I really love my life and spirit, don't I? I didn't save the daughter and I'm not willing to oblige the mother, either!*

"No, I'm only teasing you for revenge," she replies giddily.

"Am I making the right decision?"

"Our decisions are personal and private. There are no right or wrong decisions as we're all different beings with weird minds."

"And we often make wrong choices and lose our chances."

"That's the wisdom to remember when you go back to live."

"Maybe I must return to make better choices now."

"Yeah! Farewell, Darren… Go now, my lost lover…"

Darren kisses her, steps onto the stairs, stands in the waiting room promptly, and peers at Mahroo through the window. She saunters along the garden path amidst the flowers and plants, picks a daisy and plays with its petals, turns and waves to him a few times, and finally steps onto the beach, toward a dinghy.

2

Darren watches Mahroo and the Masters board the ship and it sails away toward the horizon until it becomes a tiny dot, keeping him hypnotized… But swiftly the dot explodes into an immense light that blinds him briefly. As the luminous fog evaporates, two hypnotic black eyes appear, staring at him with passion, though everything else around him is a blur.

"Oh God, you're back, my darling." The soft voice of a pretty woman thumps his heart as blood rushes faster in his veins. He is disoriented but gaining consciousness quickly. The familiar face of the woman feels weirder than all the hefty hospital equipment around him. The woman peers at his inquisitive eyes. "I knew you'd come back," she yells and runs away. She returns fast with a nurse who checks his pulse before the doctor arrives. Darren is speechless with all the commotion around him, while wondering why the woman is weeping. The doctor keeps examining him and asking questions, and he nods or stammers incoherently.

His mind is fuzzy, though some blurry images of faces and incidents flash before his eyes sporadically and many questions roll in his head. Particularly, the woman resembles a lost spirit beyond his reach, for some unfair reasons he cannot recall. Yet, there she is, so pretty, ambling around with a charming mixture of joy, disbelief, and agony, her fingers covering her lips to hide her smooth howling. At last, the doctor says Darren must stay in the hospital a few more days for observation and tests.

Once everybody leaves, the woman walks to him and holds his hand. "You remember me?" she asks sceptically. He stares blankly. "Do you remember anything?" He does not reply, but seems to be contemplating her questions, which is a good sign, in her opinion. "You remember your name?" She is repeating the same questions the doctor had asked, but with more urgency and tension. He stares with more focus now. That is an excellent sign, she believes. He probably has not turned into a vegetable, after all, the way doctors had predicted, "...even if he comes to." Now she has even more reasons to be hopeful, relieved, and proud of her perseverance. His gazing at her and pondering her questions, especially the last one, is simply precious. However, the doctor's instructions ring in her head: "Let him recover and recall things gradually if he can." So, she stops probing Darren, although he appears ready, conscious of the questions asked and perhaps even recognizing her. She leans back in her chair next to his bed and plays with his fingers.

Darren tries to focus and contemplate, but his memory keeps eluding him. Yet, the answers seem obvious, wreaking a weird sensation within him. Anything to recall at all? Only the blurry images of the explosion and intense light before opening his eyes keep recurring with lesser distortion. He focuses on the glow that eventually zooms onto a boat emerging from the horizon. After a long time, as if the events rewinding in his mind, the boat returns closer and closer to the shore, Mahroo and the Masters get into dinghies and paddle the rest of the way to the sandy beach, then she saunters alone in the garden, plays with the petals of a daisy, then kisses him goodbye. "Farewell, Darren," she mutters. "Go now, my lost lover..."

"Darren...?" he murmurs.

"Yes, yes," she cries. "You remember anything else, Darren?"

Silence. He looks puzzled as ruminating halts. All day, she helps him stroll and feed himself clumsily. He stays quiet and she begins losing hope for his full recovery. Later in the evening, she says goodbye before leaving, "I'll come back in the morning." He wonders why but welcomes her promise. His spirit of life soars with the superb outlook for tomorrow when she will return. He senses her link to his past and future. So, he grins with his regained charm. And she feels ecstatic at his rosy reaction at the end—a positive sign to cherish overnight.

Darren falls asleep with the spirit of life bathing him in a magical stream of tranquility. His mind returns to the scene with that mysterious woman: "Farewell, Darren… Go now, my lost lover." Her face and the memories of painting it in Barcelona begin to resurrect in his mind. Mahtab is sitting on a chair with a subtle grin, modeling for him to paint the *Persian Moons*. His fingers begin moving as he keeps working on the portrait in his dream, telling Mahtab he will make the eyes gaze at them—only the two of them—privately, at a secret angle, even though the portrait peers pointedly toward left, and Mahtab nods happily. They promise to never share that secret with anybody else, ever.

Early in the morning, he awakens fully rested and refreshed, as if his identity and life were recomposed mentally during his nightlong dream and chat with Mahtab. He recalls the last event: A crazy thug shooting him in the neck; a fuzzy picture of Erica around him and screaming on the balcony; and then witnessing his own flesh from a corner of the ceiling. He also recalls his 'near-death experience' and the events in the glorious mansion— the house in eternity, the beach where he had painted the *Woman in the White Dress*, his odd encounters with murky Mahroo and testy Vincent, and how he was given an option to return to life or go away with her for love. Was it the right choice then to leave Mahroo behind? Even his mind is regaining its exhausting habits of questioning and analyzing everything. He is gradually gaining his normal form. *How shamelessly fast he'd accepted Mahroo's offer to abandon her and return to life. So 'life' is surely more important than 'love'? It must be! Yes, choosing life was the right decision. Where is she? What's she doing here in Vancouver?*

He shaves and takes a shower clumsily, eats breakfast, finds his watch and wears it, and lies in bed musing, mostly about her promise to return this morning. Briefly, he doubts his account of their long encounter yesterday and assumes the event had been a residue of his recurring dreams or hallucinations. *How could it be possible?* These days, with all the dreaming and his near-death experience, he might be confusing reality. *Was she really here yesterday? Did she promise to return today?* He paces the room and stands behind the window. He ponders, but quickly discards, the idea of asking the nurse regarding the woman who had been around the day before. *The nurse yesterday was a different one, anyway,* he thinks with relief.

He stares out the window and enjoys the white summits of the Lions in the far distance and the snowflakes dancing happily in midair. The scenery is stunning, but the thought of walking in the wet, slippery streets jolts him. Pedestrians are crammed under heavy winter clothes, gloves, and umbrellas, yet hurry towards their destinations to avoid the snow. Many commute around the hospital, but there is no sign of any woman resembling her. Discerning people's faces from such a distance is difficult, yet her elegant walk and posture would be hard to miss. He is going dizzy watching the swirling rhythms of snowflakes, turning and twisting and mixing, like performing a massive square dance. Focusing closer on the windowpane, he feels sad when some busy, ice particles hit the window, melt and slither in long, tiny patterns. They remind him of her subtle sobbing yesterday. He starts pacing the room again, checks his watch, and returns to bed when the nurse brings him snacks and juice.

Around 9:30, the aroma of her perfume finds its way to his room after the familiar sound of her footsteps halts. Ready to run out to confirm his hunch, the whispers outside the room convince him to wait. Soon she enters and brightens his life with her sweet smile and a bouquet of red roses.

"Good morning, Mahtab," he blurts with a jovial excitement.

"You remember!" Mahtab cries and runs to hug him, like a mother hearing her baby's first word.

"I remember everything, even the shooting," he says, also like a baby now expecting a reward or at least a kiss.

"That's wonderful," Mahtab says and kisses his cheek.

"What're you doing here?"

"I came to force you out of the coma. I read so many books and newspapers to you, hoping you'd wake up to at least fire me personally."

"The nurse said I'd been in comma for eleven weeks."

"That's right, but I came only five weeks ago."

"What about Bijan? How did he let you go?"

"It is a long, sad story…," she says.

"I'm sorry… What happened?"

"I was depressed after Barcelona and then hearing about your injury. I wanted to fly to Vancouver right away, but I had no courage or excuse for doing so. So, I usually sat in front of the *Persian Moons* and thought about Mahroo and you. I knew you two were together and tried to contact you through her portrait. It comforted me, and soon she began pushing me to do something for you. I didn't know what and how, and remained miserable. Then my father had a heart attack and passed away. Bijan and Reza were perplexed and unhappy with my gloom. Finally, a sad miracle happened. I had a miscarriage and lost the baby, perhaps due to my bad health and fatigue. After the baby was gone, no longer I had reasons to hide my feelings from Bijan. I told him straight I couldn't live in Iran or with his ideologies. We both knew he couldn't change his personality and wouldn't give up his flourishing political career to follow me in pursuit of some unknown adventures in foreign lands. He's agreed to separation for now… He gave me his permission, with rage of course, to leave Iran, supposedly for recuperating after the loss of our child. So, five weeks ago I came straight to Vancouver."

"It's so nice of you, but why? That's too much."

"We talked about us in Barcelona, but two other motives pushed me, too."

"What motives?"

"First, Mahroo's ghost blamed me for transferring the curse of the *Woman in the White Dress* to you by exchanging it with her portrait. The police have figured out that it was delivered only ten minutes before it was stolen and you were shot. I felt guilty and terrible for doubting your claim."

"We've all suffered because of this damn painting," he says. "Hopefully it's now the thieves' turn to face the curse. Sorry for interrupting you…"

"Second," she continues, "I felt I must make myself a bit more useful. Reza told me nobody was even visiting you. This was depressing enough, let alone pondering the possibility of you being still in danger. I believed I was the only one who could help you. And I had to prove to myself I was capable of engaging in a divine mission despite Reza's discouragements and protests, especially since he was the only one who knew about my hidden motive for travelling—mostly for helping you."

Indeed, Reza had felt angry and sorry for Mahtab, leaving her caring husband and comfortable life in Iran, to go waste her time and energy on a rotting vegetable. What had this man, Darren, done to his family: First driving Mahroo and Zia mad and dead, and now making Mahtab give up her enviable life and devoted husband just to nurse Darren? How many people should die and suffer just for the chance of Darren ever sorting out his love life?

"Where is Reza?" Darren asks.

"Tehran. He seldom comes to Vancouver these days."

"Why?"

"He doesn't get along with Cameron after Erica's death."

"Erica's death?"

"Oh, yes—you didn't know. Either the thieves threw her off your balcony or she jumped. The police haven't established which one, but they believe she jumped herself."

"You mean she committed suicide?"

"Maybe she really loved you and thought you were dead?"

"Oh, poor Erica... Still, I can't believe she committed suicide for me, like Floria! Probably the thugs did it."

"The thugs?"

"Yeah. The guys who shot me."

"You know them?"

"Erica told me about them the night before the accident. I was expecting them."

"So you may be able to help the police find them?"

"I may have some leads."

"Get ready to tell everything to the police. The nurse told me they'd asked the hospital to inform them if you came to."

"Especially after Erica's death, I must tell them everything Erica herself had made me promise to keep confidential forever. Some people may get into trouble but I don't care."

"Be careful. These people may return to hurt you, here or at your apartment. They surely don't want you to identify them."

"How about you? What're your plans?"

"My mission is now complete," she replies solemnly.

"Why are you suddenly a missionary like Mahroo?"

"Every mature person needs a worthwhile cause to amuse himself or herself with."

"Yet this much self-sacrifice appears unusual to most of us," he replies with gloom. "So you're leaving soon?"

"Unless you wanna hire me as your assistant?"

"You still recall my comment in Barcelona?" he asks giddily.

"I might consider taking the position if the salary is good. Maybe we could make a good team."

"That's a thought! But you should think about a real career more seriously now that you have a chance to do something more than missionary work.'

"I may try to get a teaching job or something. Or maybe I start an art gallery to run it together?" Mahtab says.

"That's another good idea... Maybe Jerry wants to sell Elixir and retire."

"Anything else?" she asks, grabbing and holding his hands.

"Maybe we can think more about us and other plans we'd discussed in Barcelona?"

"I hope so, too, if Bijan releases me from his grip."

"It would be hard, eh?" he asks anxiously.

"Yes, very… I'm afraid it could be almost impossible!"

"Especially if he finds out I am alive and you're my assistant now, eh?"

"Exactly… He'll go nuts if he finds out you're the reason for my stay in Vancouver," she says with gloom.

"Don't you think he's guessed that already?"

"He might've guessed, but maybe he's not sure, or has hoped you'll die soon. Reza knows for sure though…"

"Will you stay in Vancouver for a while at least?"

"I'll try, but things could get really nasty around us. You must know that Bijan is a vengeful and dangerous man. Reza is also mad at us."

"If you're afraid, maybe you'd better go away awhile , even if not back to him," Darren suggests.

"Do you want me to go? Are you scared of him, too?"

"I'm embarrassed more than scared, but mainly I don't want you get hurt."

"Let's wait awhile and see how ugly things get," she says.

"Bijan is not the only person wanting me dead. I have other enemies in Iran and here who are also chasing me."

"We're in a big jam, then aren't we?" she says with a sigh. "Maybe we should go hide in another country a few years?"

"Staying in coma would've made life easier for both of us."

"No, I'm glad you're back. I would've missed you a lot…"

"Then we must prepare ourselves for a big war."

"That's fine… I love you, Darren, for me and for Mahroo."

"And I love you two, too, my pretty Persian moons."

www.ingramcontent.com/pod-product-compliance
Lightning Source LLC
Chambersburg PA
CBHW020246030726
47499CB00001B/83